This Christmas

JANE GREEN
JENNIFER COBURN
LIZ IRELAND

ZEBRA BOOKS
KENSINGTON PUBLISHING CORP.
www.kensingtonbooks.com

ZEBRA BOOKS are published by

Kensington Publishing Corp.
119 West 40th Street
New York, NY 10018

ISBN-13: 978-1-4201-2564-1
ISBN-10: 1-4201-2564-8

First Printing: November 2005

10 9 8 7 6 5 4 3

Printed in the United States of America

CONTENTS

Vacation

JANE GREEN

Chapter One

Sometimes in life we get stuck. Sometimes in life we think we know exactly where we're headed, what we're looking for, how to get there, but once we reach it we don't know where else to go.

This is how it is for Sarah Evans. Sarah who appears to have everything in life she could possibly need: a husband who is a successful real-estate developer in Manhattan, a perfect 1960s colonial in a picture-book-perfect small town in upstate New York, and two beautiful dark-haired children—Maggie and Walker.

They have been married for eight years, but Sarah doesn't think about their wedding very often these days. Occasionally, when she dusts the enormous black-and-white picture sitting on the mantelpiece, she will pause as she gazes at her younger, happier self, and at the man she thought she was marrying. But her mind has emptied itself of the happy memories, the laughter they once shared, and looking at that picture she may as well be looking at two strangers.

Because this is Sarah's overwhelming feeling when Eddie, her husband, is at home.

A stranger. Estranged. Strange.

Her happiest times or, rather, the times when she most fully feels herself, are when Eddie's at work. Then she can operate as a normal person. She can vacuum the family room and drink gallons of coffee as she turns Z100 up to full blast and sings along to the Black Eyed Peas and Usher.

She can dance around the kitchen as the children sit at the kitchen table, wide-eyed with delight at how silly Mommy is, giggling as they play with the chicken nuggets and—in a bid to try to get some vegetables into them—corn salad, and if she's very lucky, peas.

Sarah can, and does, meet with her friends for impromptu coffee and conversation. She can put her feet up in front of the Cooking Channel and scribble down delicious-sounding recipes, vowing one day to actually make them.

She can sit at the desk in the kitchen, sifting through the ever-mounting piles, making phone calls, organizing household bills, getting on with the work of being a wife, mother, and household manager.

Occasionally Sarah will still try to delegate an odd job to Eddie, each time praying that he will actually do it, that somehow if he manages to fulfill her wish it will mean that their marriage will get back on track, that she, or they, will find happiness again, but each time Eddie forgets, and with a sigh of irritation Sarah finds herself adding another job to the next day's "to-do" list.

None of her friends realize quite how unhappy Sarah is. It isn't as if she sits around weeping, but this sense of dissatisfaction, of unease, of knowing that her life wasn't supposed to turn out like this, follows her around twenty-four hours a day, climbs out of bed with her in the mornings, scrubs her back in the shower, and keeps her company as she goes about her day until they both climb into bed at the end of the day, exhausted and preparing for more of the same the next day.

She did used to be happy. She knows that at some time in her life she used to be happy, but it was such a long time ago, and she's become so used to feeling the way she feels now, to this feeling of being stuck, that the memory of actually *being* happy has almost entirely faded away.

But today, as she dusts the mantelpiece, she stops as she wipes the cloth over the glass covering her wedding picture, she takes the picture over to the sofa and sits down, staring beyond the glass to nine years ago, when she was twenty-seven, the features editor of *Poise!*—a young women's magazine—living on Manhattan's Upper West Side and loving every minute of it.

She'd been dating a series of unsuitable men, had just finished a heartbreaking affair with a journalist at *GQ*, and had sworn off men completely.

"No," she kept insisting to her colleagues, "this time I mean it."

And of course doesn't it always happen when you least expect it, when you're adamant that this time you really don't want it. That was exactly when Sarah met Eddie. When she thought a relationship was the very last thing in life she needed.

On their very first date it had been, Sarah used to say, a true meeting of the minds, never mind the overwhelming physical attraction she felt to this dark, slim, confident man. From the minute she saw him she loved his brown eyes, his floppy hair, his slow smile, although she didn't let on until their first actual date.

In those early days every time Eddie showed up at her apartment to pick her up, or they met in restaurants for dinner, Sarah would feel her heart skip a beat when she saw him, a heady mixture of excitement and anticipation.

She thought she was going to marry him but she didn't *know* she was going to marry him for sure until the first time they slept together. Sarah had never had so much fun in her life. She wasn't performing, wasn't worrying, and she knew then that she never wanted to be with another man ever again.

They married less than a year later—a stylish and intimate wedding at the Cosmopolitan club, and the first three years were a whirlwind of fun city living, seen through the rose-tinted eyes of a couple in love.

Sarah loved the city, loved everything about the city, but when she became pregnant they started driving out to the suburbs on the weekends—just for a look around—and there was something about a white clapboard colonial with a picket fence and roses growing up an arbor that Sarah started to find increasingly appealing. Before long her fantasies were less about fitting into her favorite Ralph Lauren shift, and more about creating a proper home for her new family.

She gave up her job three months before Walker was born and attempted to settle into the house of their dreams before the big day.

In those early days it was much like playing a giant game. Sarah used to feel that she was playing house; pretending to be a grown-up, pretending to be her mother. She would study cookbooks and come up with recipes, even though prior to that Sarah had never cooked anything other than scrambled eggs—even that was rare—but once they moved into the suburbs Sarah was determined to do what every good suburban housewife should do: have delicious, nutritious meals prepared for Eddie when he got home.

Eddie would walk in the house, delighted at how well Sarah was adapting to the suburbs, thrilled at how she was cooking and making a home for them, and they would sit at the dining room table talking about their day, and saying over and over again what a great decision this was, how happy they were to be out of the city, away from the noise and the pace and the stress.

Sarah would never have admitted it but even then she wasn't completely honest with herself. She did love her new house—loved the space, and the large kitchen, and stairs—*stairs!* But she missed walking everywhere. She missed the convenience of the city; running out of their apartment whenever they needed something, and always being able to find it within a couple of blocks, any time of the day or night.

She missed the noise of the city, missed the noise of their clanking air-conditioning unit so much that Eddie came home one day with a white-noise machine, and they've been sleeping to a background of loud crackle ever since.

And she missed her friends, even though once Walker was born she realized that they were living in different worlds, that although she enjoyed living vicariously through her old friends—mostly colleagues on the magazine, all of whom were still single—once they'd caught up on one another's lives there wasn't that much in common anymore, and none of them were particularly interested in her life as a new mother.

They rarely made it out to see her, and Lord knows she didn't have time to get on a train and go and see them, not with a baby in tow, so filled with animosity she reluctantly joined a "mommy and me" group and much to her surprise started to meet women whom she liked, some of whom actually became friends.

By the time Maggie was born, Sarah and Eddie were definitely out of the honeymoon period. Those gourmet meals that Sarah used to cook were long gone, replaced by hot dogs, chicken fingers, and take-out pizza. Eddie gets home far too late for Sarah to cook and then wait for him, so she usually eats with the kids at around six, and Eddie now grabs something either in the office or on the way home.

Eddie has become more and more successful in

his job since they married. His hours are longer, the accompanying stress is almost unimaginable, and the last thing he needs at the end of the day is to be confronted by a miserable, nagging wife or children screaming and fighting for his attention, which is why, when he gets home, he relaxes by watching a sports game on TV with a few beers. God knows he works hard enough; isn't he entitled to some downtime?

And Sarah, poor Sarah who feels that she does absolutely everything around here, watches him resting his beer on his large, rounded belly and feels a wave of disgust wash over her. She has learned to ride these waves. They occur so frequently now she doesn't bother telling him he ought to lose weight, or quit drinking, or spend some time with the children. Every time she used to say that it would erupt in a huge row, and these days she simply doesn't have the energy.

Take a look at them tonight. Walker, already bathed and in pajamas, is playing with his Spiderman web shooter that came free in a packet of cereal.

"Look, Dad!" he says excitedly, dancing around Eddie, who is slumped on the sofa. "Look! Look! It shoots real spiderwebs!" He attempts a demonstration on the ceiling as Eddie smiles vaguely and moves Walker out of the way.

"Daddy!" Walker pleads. "You're not looking."

Before Walker can react Maggie comes in and snatches the web shooter out of Walker's hands, running off into the kitchen with it. Walker starts screaming, Maggie hides behind Sarah's legs, and Eddie explodes.

"Can't a man get any peace and quiet around here!" he shouts. "Sarah, for God's sake, tell them to keep it down."

"Why don't *you* tell them to keep it down?" Sarah snaps, picking up Maggie, who's now crying because Walker is trying to prise the web shooter out of her little hands. "Walker! Leave her alone!" Walker wails louder now at the unfairness of always being blamed just because he's the oldest.

"It's my web shooter, Mommy! Maggie took it!" Maggie smirks and holds the web shooter triumphantly above her head as Walker screams.

"Upstairs, both of you!" Sarah shouts, putting down Maggie, who instantly starts wailing, while Walker successfully manages to rip the web shooter away and run upstairs.

"Goddamnit!" Sarah hisses to Eddie, pausing to take in the fact that he's sitting back, his feet up, ignoring the screams from upstairs.

Sarah shakes her head. *Get off your fat ass you lazy pig and help me,* she thinks. Then, *that's it, fat boy,* as he cracks open another beer. *You just sit there like a slob while I do all the work,* but of course she doesn't say any of it. Once it's out there it can never be taken back, and even though Sarah's antipathy toward her husband is slowly turning into hate, there are some places she just won't go.

* * *

Later that night Sarah climbs into bed with her book and pretends to be engrossed as Eddie comes to bed. He's always slept naked, and in the early days she used to love how free he was about his body, how he used to tease her about always wearing a long T-shirt, but now she just tries to avoid looking at him, tries to lose herself in her book to stop thinking about how they became quite so unhappy.

Eddie clambers into bed and reaches out to turn off his overhead light. "Night," he mumbles, as he turns his back to a grateful Sarah.

"Night," she says disinterestedly. Long after he turns off the light and is gently snoring Sarah lies with her guilty thoughts. She thinks of something terrible happening to Eddie, something tragic and terrible that would take the decision out of her hands.

Not death, not necessarily, but maybe he would leave, fall in love with his secretary, announce it was over. She looks over at the back of his head with resignation. This is a man who can barely muster the energy to change television channels, let alone leave her. He's never going to leave.

Sarah lets out a long, dissatisfied sigh and lays her book down. Maybe it will all feel better in the morning.

Chapter Two

"But you said you'd be home tonight by six," Sarah sighs. "It's book club tonight and I'm hosting. How am I supposed to get the kids fed and into bed, and get book club ready?"

"What can I do?" Eddie snaps. "It's work. I didn't plan a five o'clock meeting but I can't turn it down. I don't want to go over this again, Sarah. What do you want me to do? Leave? You want me to leave? You want me to get a job locally? Sure, I could get some lousy-paying job in a local firm and we'd have to move to a much smaller house but I don't care. If that's what you want, say so."

Sarah grits her teeth and squeezes the phone, frustration rendering her speechless. "Forget it," she says. "Fine."

"I'll grab something to eat in the city," Eddie continues. "Seeing as you've got book club. I'll see you later."

Sarah nods silently and puts down the phone.

* * *

Before they had children Sarah and Eddie were not big believers in television. Before they had children Sarah and Eddie had many different beliefs about child rearing and parenting, beliefs that would make them, unequivocally, the best parents in the whole history of parenting. Ever.

They would never use the television as a baby-sitter, Sarah remembers saying, when Walker was only two years old and she had come back from a harassed play date where the mother had put the television on for everyone to get some peace and quiet toward the end of the day.

Sarah had been horrified. "We'd gone there to play!" she'd said in horror to Caroline. "Not to watch television. I had to take Walker home."

So Sarah and Eddie had vowed never to use television as a baby-sitter. They'd looked at one another firmly and said they would never use sugar to calm a child down, would never raise their voices to their children, and would treat their children with kindness and respect.

At 5:30 Sarah runs into the family room to find Walker screaming as Maggie disappears behind the sofa with an evil grin on her face. Sarah's heart plummets. How can this three-year-old who looks so angelic be such an unbelievable handful? Walker is her mama's boy. Sweet, gentle, and sensitive, he's always been a good boy, always done exactly what he's been told, and if he has any fault at all it's that he's too sensitive, that he has a tendency to collapse, like now, in tears, at the slightest thing.

Walker never had the terrible twos, a fact she and Eddie put down privately, and horribly smugly, as the result of being such amazing parents. They have had to reconsider with Maggie; Maggie who displayed such extraordinary stubbornness and willfulness since the day she was born.

Even when she was a baby, when Maggie decided she wanted something, she would exert what Eddie called the death grip until whoever was holding it—usually Walker—had to let go.

"My girl's a winner." Eddie would smile proudly, and Sarah would shake her head as she comforted a crying Walker, wondering whether all girls were inherently more evil, or whether it was just her daughter.

Sarah pulls Maggie out from behind the sofa, a wriggling monkey who tries to writhe out of Sarah's grip.

"Maggie, what have you got?" Sarah says sternly. She then turns to Walker and shouts, "Be quiet, Walker! Stop crying."

"Nothing," Maggie says, little fingers clutched tightly around something.

"No!" Walker wails, before dissolving in hysteria.

"Walker! Be quiet or you'll go upstairs to your room. Maggie, give it back to him or you will get a smack." Maggie keeps her fingers tightly closed until Sarah manages to pry them open, to find Walker's favorite Power Ranger there.

"Here you are, Walker." She gives it back to him, then says, "Oh, for God's sake, will you now stop crying? Maggie, do not take Walker's toys!" she berates, but even as she says those words she knows they're having no effect.

For Maggie has no fear. Has never had any fear. Threats of time-outs turn into real time-outs, and whereas Walker will sit in his room during a time-out in floods of tears, Maggie will sit quietly singing to herself, or playing with her fingers, or somehow keeping herself amused, and Sarah knows that the punishment doesn't bother her in the slightest.

Sarah now threatens smacking, in the hope that that will frighten her daughter into behaving well, but Sarah knows she would never actually be able to go through with it, and the threat sounds empty even to her ears, much less to Maggie's.

"I want M&M's," Maggie suddenly calls out from the pantry. "I want M&M's."

"Oh, me too!" Walker says eagerly, Power Ranger fiasco forgotten. "I want M&M's too."

"Neither of you gets M&M's until after dinner," Sarah says, looking at her watch.

"Oh, please!" Walker starts whining.

"I want M&M's," Maggie repeats as her face starts to crumple, hand reaching up for the shelf where the M&M's are hidden.

"I'll make dinner now," Sarah sighs. "How about some television?"

Walker's eyes light up. "I want to watch Spiderman!"

"No!" Maggie comes running into the kitchen. "I watch the Wiggles."

"No," Walker wails. "Spiderman."

"Wiggles!" Maggie says firmly, raising a hand, about to hit Walker.

"No, Maggie!" Sarah scoops her up and drops her on the sofa in the family room. "I get to pick tonight and we're going to watch *The Lion King.*

"Twenty minutes," she says to the children, "and then the TV goes off and we're having dinner."

There's no reply—they're already absorbed in Simba's world.

An hour and a half later Sarah has made a fruit platter, laid the cakes and magic bars out on the table, and got the coffee cups and wineglasses out, the wine already chilling in the fridge. She has tidied the kitchen, put on the laundry, had a super-quick shower, put on clean clothes and a dab of old lipstick, and shoved her hair back into its usual neat ponytail.

"Mom!" Walker shouts out from the family room. "It's finished."

"Damn," Sarah mutters to herself as she shakes slices of frozen pizza bagels out of the box and onto a grill pan. "Right," she says, in an upbeat tone. "Who wants delicious pizza bagels for dinner?"

"Me! Me! Me!" the kids shout, and they come into the kitchen and sit at the counter, where Sarah keeps them quiet with Goldfish until the pizzas are ready.

"As a special treat tonight," she says, looking at her watch, "it's a no-bath night."

"Yay!" Walker whoops with joy, and Maggie copies him, even though she adores bath time.

"First one into pj's gets M&M's," Sarah says, collecting the dishes to wash up as the kids run upstairs shrieking and giggling. "And then"—she walks to the bottom of the stairs and calls up after them—"the mommy monster's coming to get you." Shrieks of delight waft down the stairs as Sarah smiles. How can she love them so much when they're so difficult?

"How can I love them so much when they're so difficult?" she says to Caroline, the first to walk through the door for book club.

"I know." Caroline smiles. "Clare woke Maisie up at five o'clock this morning, and by four o'clock this afternoon they were both *melting*. It's been horrific at my house."

"Not much better here," Sarah says, handing Caroline a glass of wine. "Cheers."

"Good Lord I need this." Caroline takes a mouthful of wine. "Now please tell me you read the book because I couldn't get through it and we can't keep meeting for book club with none of us ever reading the damn things."

Sarah winces. "I didn't. I was hoping *you* had." The swoop of a car's headlights shines through the kitchen window as the others arrive. "Let's hope someone has or it will be another night of moaning about our husbands."

"Wasn't the last book club kind of racy? If I remember rightly weren't we all horribly revealing about sex?" Caroline grins. "Although it was at my house and I was very drunk."

"I was pretty drunk too." Sarah smiles. "But, yes,

I do remember it being pretty racy. Do you remember what Lisa was telling . . . Lisa! How are you? Come in, come and have some wine! I was just saying that the last time we spoke you were saying you would definitely read the book this time."

Lisa grimaces and shrugs in apology. "Wine?" Sarah and Caroline laugh as they all toast one another and sit at the kitchen counter to wait for the others.

Book club has been going on for two years and is the highlight of Sarah's month. She's never dreamt of telling her friends in the city that she's part of a book club—the very words *book club* conjure up such parochial, suburban images, and yet she has come to value these meetings, the friendships she has with these women and, in particular, the dynamic they have when they all come together for book club, above all else.

There are now five women. Sarah; Caroline, an English girl whom Sarah met when Walker was in the two's program with Clare at the local preschool; Lisa; Nicole; and Cindy.

The women met through a series of coincidences. They don't socialize together when not in book club, other than Sarah and Caroline, who have become the closest of friends, but they have found a freedom and support in book club that they have not found elsewhere, a trust that whatever they say when at the meetings will stay there. All the women agree they have a unique bond.

Once upon a time they did all read the books.

They would meet and talk earnestly about what they thought, attempt to analyze in a way none of them had done since school, relate the topics to their own lives, but as they got to know one another more, as they grew more comfortable with one another, they started to share their lives, and now it is rare the books are even read, and the discussion that ensues is usually cursory, an attempt to validate the meeting before moving on to the real topics—life, love, children, friendships, husbands.

In a relatively short period of time these women have come to know one another intimately; such is the nature of their sharing at the monthly meetings.

They know that Caroline and her husband, Louis, once separated for two years, before they had children. They know that Lisa is married to a recovering alcoholic who has been in AA for six years. They know that Nicole had four miscarriages before finally accepting she could not have children and adopting instead, and they know that Cindy hates the East Coast and spends every night dreaming of going back to California, where she says the sun always shines and it doesn't snow, although in truth Cindy only feels this way in winter. In summer she's quite happy.

And they know that some of them are happy with their husbands, their marriages, their lives, and some of them are not, but none of them know quite how unhappy Sarah is with hers.

The unhappiness, when it emerges, emerges in the form of jokes. They will laugh about their husbands. Roll their eyes as they share the same stories of the husbands thinking they do nothing all day, wondering what the husbands would do if the five of them took off for a weekend, left them with the kids and the house. Then they'd know, they laugh, knowing the husbands wouldn't be able to handle it.

Tonight is one of those nights. No one, it transpires, has read the book, and tonight is a night when the women each bring their frustrations to the table and vent them in a safe environment.

"Here's what kills me," offers Nicole. "I've been with the kids all day, they're exhausted, I finally get them into bed, and then Dan gets home from work and goes in to see them and gets them all excited again and then they're wide awake. I can't stand it. I keep telling him not to but he doesn't understand what it's like for me, how hard it is to get them into bed. I thought I was going to kill him last night."

"At least he comes home and wants to see the kids," Sarah says, now on her third glass of wine. "Eddie doesn't care. All he wants to do when he gets home is slob out in front of the television with his beer. God forbid the children should get in the way of a beloved sports game." Sarah studies the wine in her glass as she sighs. "He's become this disgusting slob who doesn't care about himself, doesn't care about us, doesn't care about anything. I wish he'd just leave but he's too goddamned lazy." She finishes her wine, unaware that there is now a shocked silence, that nobody knows what to say, that nobody knew it was quite this bad.

"Well," Cindy says brightly, "nothing quite like a bit of soul baring at book club. I'm going to get some cheesecake. Can I bring anyone some?" She rises out of her chair, as do the others, all murmuring about getting more coffee, or cake, or another of those delicious brownies.

Only Caroline stays behind, sitting next to Sarah on the sofa, and when Sarah puts down her wineglass, Caroline takes her hand.

"I didn't know it was that bad," she whispers. "You should have said so."

Sarah looks at her as it finally registers that she has confessed out loud. "Oh, my God," she gasps. "I just did, didn't I. Tell me I didn't say that out loud."

Caroline winces.

"Oh, shit," Sarah mutters. "I guess I'd better have another glass of wine."

Chapter Three

Caroline was the last to leave. She wanted to make sure Sarah was okay, wanted to see if there was anything she could do, offer a shoulder to cry on if that's what was needed.

"Are you sure you're okay?" she says, eyeing Sarah warily as Sarah washes up the coffee cups. "That was pretty momentous, what you said in there."

"Caroline, be honest with me. Was it really that momentous? Don't you sometimes wish that Louis would leave? Don't you just hate him at times?"

Caroline nods, and it's true, she does sometimes feel that way, but only if they've had a really big row, and only once in a blue moon, and only for a very short period of time, never enough to mention it to anyone, to even dwell on it at all.

"See?" Sarah attempts a light laugh, which comes out sounding ever so slightly strangled. "I'm just having a bad day." She dries her hands on a paper towel, then reaches behind to tuck her hair back into her ponytail, using the stainless steel on the microwave to check that it's all in.

"Do you ever wonder what happened to yourself?" Sarah says absently as she fiddles with her hair.

"What do you mean?" Caroline smiles. "You mean, what happened to that cool chick who men used to whistle at in the street?"

"Kind of. Yes. What happened to the woman who wore great clothes and makeup, and cared about what she looked like?"

Caroline grins as she gestures down at herself. "You mean instead of Gap sweats and Merrills, even if they are the most comfortable thing in the world?"

"I know. Look." Sarah lifts a foot to show off her own ugly but practical shoes. "I just wondered what happened to me. I was looking at my wedding picture earlier today and thinking about the early days, and it's not even that I feel it was such a long time ago; it's that I feel it happened to another person, in another lifetime.

"I get up in the morning and I see this middle-aged woman . . . ," she continues.

Caroline interrupts. "Middle-aged? You're thirty-six; that's hardly middle-aged!"

"But I *feel* middle-aged," Sarah insists. "I see a woman with bags under her eyes and gray in her hair because I haven't the time nor the inclination to get to a hairdresser. A woman who used to have a wardrobe of beautiful clothes, who used to read *Vogue* every month, who worked at *Poise!* for God's sake, and now look at me. I just want to know how I got here. Where I lost myself. What happened."

"You got married and had kids," says Caroline gently. "It happened to all of us. But aren't you happier now? I sometimes think the same thing but then I look at my girls, and at my husband, and I know I have a great life and I wouldn't change anything."

Sarah looks at Caroline for a few moments, then shrugs. What would Sarah change?

Pretty much everything.

They both jump as the side door closes and Eddie walks into the kitchen.

"Hi, Caroline!" he says. He's always liked Caroline, likes how sensible she is, how down-to-earth and practical.

"Hey, Eddie." She smiles at him and waves.

"Hi, honey," Eddie says, walking over to Sarah and leaning down to kiss her cheek, something they are both doing for show, because there is someone there.

"How was your day?" Sarah asks in a dull monotone, feeling like a parody of herself.

"I'd better go." Caroline picks up her purse. "Thanks for a great evening, sweetie. I'll call you tomorrow." And with a final wave she's gone.

Sarah's reading *People* magazine in bed when Eddie comes in.

"How was book club?" he says, as he starts undressing.

"Fine," she says. "Good."

"You seem like you've had a bit to drink." Eddie grins, thinking that maybe tonight he might get lucky.

Sarah lays the magazine down, with a sigh of exasperation. "Do I ever say anything to you about the number of beers you drink every night when you get home?" she says slowly, trying to control the anger in her voice. "What difference does it make to you if I've had a drink? So what? Anything else you'd like to criticize while you're at it?"

Eddie throws his hands up in the air and shakes his head. "Forget it," he spits. "Just forget it."

Five minutes later Sarah looks up at him. "Did you call the contractor today about the wall?"

There's a silence while Eddie tries to look for a way out. He's been meaning to call the contractor for weeks. Sarah keeps nagging him to call, wants the wall between the kitchen and family room taken down as soon as possible, but for some reason he keeps forgetting.

He could lie, he figures. It would be so much easier to say he left a message, but in the time he's trying to figure out the lie, Sarah knows.

Eddie shuffles his feet, feeling like a guilty child, feeling like he's been caught doing something he shouldn't have. He hates this feeling, hates not living up to her expectations, and yet somehow he just doesn't seem to be able to.

He sees the way she looks at him when he walks around the bedroom naked. He knows what she's saying when she asks him if he's been to the gym recently. Does Sarah think he hasn't noticed himself, how much weight he's put on? His pants are all straining at the seams, his stomach resting over the top as he hoists them up all day long. When he shaves in the bathroom in the morning he no longer looks at his entire face but focuses on the razor, or looks into his eyes, so as not to see the increasing chins.

He resolves, on a daily basis, to get back in shape again, to be fit, stop the beer, go back to the gym. He even bought a new pair of trainers, but work is so busy, and so stressful, and now there seems to be even more stress at home, and the only thing that makes him feel better, comforts him, and helps him step out of his life is beer. And food.

He comes home later and later because the atmosphere is so unbearable. He comes home later and later to try to avoid yet another fight. He has become a barfly—joining colleagues after work in one of the neighborhood bars, just a few beers before heading home.

He sees how unhappy Sarah is, and were he more enlightened, he would realize how unhappy he is, but Eddie merely drowns his feelings out and wishes that somehow, magically, things would go back to being the way they used to be.

And, no. He still didn't call the contractor. He shakes his head.

"There's a surprise," she says sarcastically, as she pretends to read. "You forgot again."

Eddie snaps. "Do you have any idea how busy I am at work?" he says, his voice rising into a shout. "You're always nagging me to do this, do that, but you have no idea what kind of a day I have at work, how there just isn't time to do these things. Why don't *you* call the contractor for Christ's sake? It's not like you have a job. You're at home all the time; you could call him."

"Oh, I see"—Sarah puts the book down—"I'm at home all the time, doing what? Reading? Meeting the girls for lunch? Sunbathing in the backyard? You tell me how busy you are but what about what I do? I'm with the kids all day and when I'm not I'm damn well cleaning up this house and doing your laundry and making sure your life runs smoothly. I barely ask you to do anything, and the one thing I ask you to do you can't even manage because you're too goddamned lazy."

"Don't call me lazy!" Eddie yells. "How dare you call . . ." And they stop as they hear a cry from the corridor.

"Oh, shit," mutters Sarah. "Great. Now you've woken Walker." And then as she walks past him, under her breath, "Asshole."

"What's the matter sweetheart?" She sits on the bed and cradles Walker. "Did you have a bad dream?" she asks hopefully.

"No. You and Daddy were shouting," Walker says, tears streaming down his face. "Why were you shouting?"

"Sometimes grown-ups shout at one another," Sarah says. "Sometimes we get angry at each other just like you and Maggie get angry. But it doesn't mean anything. Sometimes you have to shout to make everything better. Remember when you and

Tyler had that fight and you didn't speak for a while and now you're best friends again?" Walker nods. "Daddy and I had a little fight; that's all."

"So are you friends again?" Walker says, eyes huge and scared.

"Of course we are." Sarah hugs him.

"No." Walker pulls away. "That's too quick. You have to not be friends for a while and then you can be friends again."

Sounds like a plan to me, thinks Sarah, but she just squeezes Walker tight. "We are friends."

Sarah tucks him in, tells him she loves him, and gives him a kiss good night. As she softly closes the bedroom door, Walker calls out, "Mommy? Do you still love Daddy?"

"Of course I do," she says, and the words sound hollow, even to her.

"I don't," Walker says suddenly, and Sarah comes back into his bedroom.

"Yes, you do," she says. "Sometimes you might not feel that you love him, or you might be angry with him, but you do love him, and he loves you."

"No, he doesn't," Walker says calmly. "But that's okay, Mommy, because we love each other, don't we? You're my best friend in the whole world."

"And you're my best friend in the whole world." She blinks the tears away from her eyes as Walker snuggles up with his Power Ranger. "Now go to sleep."

When Sarah gets back to her room Eddie is asleep, but she can't fall asleep for ages. Should she tell him what Walker just said? Surely that would hurt him too much, and he probably wouldn't believe it anyway, would think Sarah was just using it as ammunition to hurt him, but didn't he have a right to know the effects of his not spending any time with his children? Shouldn't he know the damage he's causing?

But Sarah hasn't got the energy for another fight. She's only just got the energy to get through each day intact. She now knows what single parents must go through, how hard it must be, and yet in some ways she thinks she has it harder because she has this added extra burden.

Wouldn't they all be so much better without him?

Sarah imagines herself telling him to leave. Telling Eddie they're leaving him. Imagines him drowning his sorrows in a sea of Sam Adams and Taco Bell burritos.

Something in her won't let her have that conversation—not yet. But something in her knows it's just a matter of time, that when she reaches rock bottom she will have no other choice.

It's just a matter of time.

Chapter Four

"There's something I need to talk to you about."

Sarah pauses, shrimp halfway to her mouth, as she looks at Eddie in alarm. Is this it? Is this how it's going to happen? She finds herself waiting for him to tell her he's having an affair, he's leaving, half aware that it's only wishful thinking, that it's not actually going to happen like this, only in fact happens like this in the movies.

The waiter comes over and asks if everything is okay, and Sarah forces an impatient smile as she nods. It's not often they go out these days, and she was surprised when Eddie had suggested they go to their favorite fish restaurant this Friday, surprised because it was so rare these days that the two of them go to dinner for no reason at all.

She had arranged a baby-sitter, had met Eddie at the train station, and now here they were, halfway through their shrimp cocktails, and Eddie looking like he's about to drop a bombshell.

Sarah puts the shrimp back on the plate and raises an eyebrow in anticipation, waiting for him to go on.

Eddie takes a deep breath. *Good Lord,* Sarah thinks. *Maybe I am right. Maybe he is leaving.* And relief washes over her.

"You know that building we're buying in Chicago?"

Sarah nods, although she doesn't. They don't tend to talk about work anymore. About anything anymore.

"Well, it's become complicated. The lawyer in the Chicago office just left and they need someone who's there to take things over, and they want me to go." Eddie looks at Sarah expectantly.

"Right." She nods, waiting for him to continue.

"So, I haven't really got a choice," he says. "They want me to take his position in Chicago, and obviously it's not really commutable, so . . ." he trails off.

"So you're moving to Chicago?"

"Well, that's what we have to talk about," Eddie says, unable to read what Sarah's thinking. "I know you love this town," he says, "but Chicago's a great city, and one of my colleagues offered to send me information about the schools there, and the thing is it may even be temporary. They want to see how things work out with this deal, but I think you would really like Chicago—"

"Whoa"—Sarah raises a hand—"let me just take this in. They want you to go to Chicago and you want us to come with you?"

Eddie looks wounded. "Of course I want you to come with me. You're my family."

Sarah looks at him in amazement. Is he really that obtuse? Is he not, surely, as unhappy as she? Why would he want them to come with him? This is it, she realizes. It's now or never. God has presented this opportunity to her on a platter and how can she not take it and run with it.

She takes a deep breath, wondering how to say it, how it could be so hard to say when she has rehearsed this moment for weeks, months, when she thought she knew exactly which words to say, and how to say them.

She would be kind, but firm, she had decided, all those long, lonely nights lying in bed and planning for her single future. She would tell him it was best for the children, and even though he might not be able to see it now, he would eventually realize that it was best for all of them. He deserved more happiness, she would say. They both deserved more happiness.

"Eddie," she starts, all her preparation having flown out the window, "do you really think it would be a good idea if we come?"

Eddie looks confused for a moment. What is she trying to say? "Well, I guess I could work something out, maybe three days a week in Chicago and home for weekends—"

"Eddie—" Sarah stops him by placing a hand on his. Now this feels familiar. Now this scenario is turning into the one she had thought about, the one she had planned for. "Eddie," she says again, "stop. Do you have any idea how unhappy I am?"

The blood drains from Eddie's face. Now he knows where this is going.

"Eddie," she says softly, "do you remember what it was like when we were first married? Do you remember how happy we were? How we used to make each other laugh, and how we always used to say how lucky we were that we were each married to our best friend?

"When was the last time we laughed, Eddie? When was the last time we had any fun together? Or even talked, for Christ's sake, without it ending in a huge row, in us screaming at one another?"

"Yeah," Eddie says finally. "But all couples go through bad times, Sarah. This is just a patch. It will get better."

"This is a patch that's lasted for three years," Sarah says, not unkindly. "Eddie, it's not going to get better; it's only going to get worse. Listen, you are a great guy, but I think we're just not the right match anymore. We've grown apart and, frankly, I want what's best for the children, and they hardly see you anymore; they hardly know you."

Eddie is silent. He can see Sarah has made up her mind. What is there left to say?

"I think this is God's way of telling us we should have a trial separation," Sarah says quietly. "This has happened for a reason. I'm not saying it's necessarily over, but face it, neither of us can carry on the way it's been going. You going to Chicago will give us both time to think about what we really want."

Eddie sits in shock. Of course he knew things were bad, but how did they ever get *this* bad? His parents had fought about the same amount as he and Sarah, and he didn't remember ever seeing any open affection between them, but they never thought about a trial separation. They stayed married until his mother died of ovarian cancer at seventy-nine, after which time his father started referring to her in Godlike tones: the most wonderful woman in the world; the love of his life.

"It's for the best," Sarah says gently, thrown slightly by the shock on Eddie's face—didn't he *know?* Didn't he guess it was all going to end this way? And a trial separation is really a way for Sarah to soften the blow—everyone knows a trial separation means it's over, but Sarah can't quite kill all his hope in one blow—what would be the point?

"We'll tell the children in the morning," she says, as the waiter comes over to collect their half-eaten plates. "We'll have to make sure they know we still love them and it's nothing to do with them."

Eddie watches her mouth move in a daze.

How does a marriage end so quickly? So quietly? So conveniently? How did they ever get here?

The first time Eddie saw Sarah was at a Halloween party in their neighborhood bar. Ninety percent of the women had gone as sexy nurses, sexy witches, sexy devils. If Eddie had a dollar for every pair of fishnet stockings he saw that night, he had joked to his friend Todd, he would be a rich man.

And then Sarah had turned around, and Eddie and Todd had cracked up laughing.

"She must be new here," Todd had said, slapping his friend on the back with mirth.

"Or maybe no one explained to her how the women here dress on Halloween."

It wasn't true that Sarah had misunderstood the unspoken rules of Halloween; it was that she was fed up with following them. She knew that all of her friends tried to look as sexy as possible, and up until this year she had done the same thing, but some Machiavellian impulse had stopped her from donning her red patent platform boots and satin devil's tail tonight.

Tonight Sarah had come as a corpse or, to be more specific, as she had explained to her horrified doorman who had turned from waving goodbye to a group of gorgeous witches and Queen Malificents, she was one of the evil dead.

"Uh huh," had said the doorman, who wasn't even sure who this horror was until she spoke. God, he had thought when he realized it was the girl from apartment 26. Such a pretty girl, why did she choose to look like this on Halloween?

Sarah had blacked out half her teeth, had turned her skin to a deathly shade of gray, complete with sunken eye sockets and hollow cheeks. She was wearing filthy, ragged clothes, and to cap it off her hair was hanging in greasy tendrils.

The truth was that Sarah had decided she was sick of New York's dating scene. She was sick of the men, sick of the scene, and was absolutely determined to stay single for a while. This was her statement, she had decided. This was her way of absolutely, positively ensuring she didn't get drunk and do anything stupid on Halloween, for who in his right mind would look at her like this? She was going to meet her girlfriends, have a few drinks, and have a great time.

"A hundred bucks if you get her phone number," Todd had nudged Eddie, indulging in their ongoing game that had started when they were frat boys in school together.

"Oh, no way," Eddie had groaned, his eye already on a luscious redhead on the other side of the room. But once the gauntlet had been thrown down the rule was it had to be picked up. Goddamnit.

Eddie had walked up to Sarah and said, "Nice costume."

"Go screw yourself." She had smiled pleasantly at him and turned away as her girlfriends giggled.

"What?" Eddie, resplendent in his Superman costume, was not used to being turned down, and particularly not when he could have done so much better. Hell, he was only doing this for a dare.

"Go screw yourself." Sarah had turned and smiled a toothless smile, and Eddie had jumped in front of her, his cape billowing, and had raised a hand in Superman's salute.

"Young lady," he had said in a deep, powerful voice, "if this was Clark Kent talking to you, you would have every right to tell him to go screw himself, but it is Superman, the most powerful superhero in America, and"—he had pulled a green plastic crystal out of his belt, brandishing it high—"by the laws of kryptonite I command you to have a drink with me."

The room had erupted in applause, including Sarah's friends, and although she rolled her eyes, she had to admit she was impressed.

Half an hour later Sarah and her girlfriends left to go to another party, and Eddie had walked back to Todd, triumphant, phone number in hand.

He hadn't meant to phone her. Hadn't thought he would ever think of her again, but she had been funny during the half hour they had chatted together over their dirty martinis garnished with a plastic spider. She had been sarcastic, clever, and opinionated.

Oh, what the hell, he thought, one night when his date canceled him at the last minute, leaving him with a reservation at Bouley. *I'm sure she won't be able to come.*

But she had been able to come, and when she walked in, this time in tight black pants, high-heeled boots, and a plunging white shirt, her hair a deep chestnut brown, swinging at her shoulders, her skin as clear as the day, Eddie had almost fallen off his chair in shock. And delight.

And that was how it had started. So how in the hell did it ever come to this? How did that clever, funny, sophisticated woman turn into this nagging, miserable, constantly tired wife?

How did the two of them, who had once been such a sought-after couple, sociable and fun, become two ships that pass in the night, only coming together for collisions and fights?

Is there any way for him to make it better? Is there any way for Eddie to stop his marriage from disintegrating before his eyes? He looks at Sarah, sitting there so firm, so resolute in her decision-making, and he vows to make this work. He knew, almost from the start, that Sarah was the one for him, and even though they've both been blown off course, he will put it right. He may not be able to do it immediately, but he won't let go this easily, despite what she thinks.

"You're right," he finds himself saying, knowing that doing anything other than agreeing with her will result in more confrontation, and that isn't what he wants. "I think a trial separation is the right thing to do."

Sarah now looks shocked that Eddie has conceded so easily. Her words of sympathy and comfort no longer needed. "I'll start looking for a place in Chicago immediately."

Sarah nods, and Eddie plans. He needs time to think. Time to get a plan of action into place.

Chapter Five

"I'm coming over." Caroline puts down the phone, leaving Sarah sitting quite still, listening to the dial tone.

Caroline calls back ten seconds later. "Can I call an emergency book club meeting or do you not want me to tell anyone?"

"You can call the meeting," Sarah sighs. "Right now I could do with the support, never mind the company."

"Gotcha. See you within the hour."

From time to time the girls will call an emergency book club meeting, or an EBC, which occurs when, naturally, an emergency comes up. The last time an EBC was called was when Lisa's son was beaten up on the school bus by a kid known as a bully and all-around general bad kid. They all agreed long ago to drop everything and come over should an EBC be needed. Within the hour, all of them, except Nicole, who is on vacation, are once again sitting around Sarah's kitchen table, looking at her with soulful, sympathetic eyes as she explains how unhappy she and Eddie have been, how it is better that he has finally gone.

"How terrible for you," they murmur.

"We never realized."

"You're so strong."

"But I'm not strong," Sarah sighs. "I'm scared. I know I've fantasized about this for months, but I didn't really think it would happen, and certainly not this quickly. I mean, one minute he was here, albeit barely"—she rolls her eyes—"and the next minute he's gone."

"Does it feel lonely?" Caroline ventures.

"Well, that's the odd thing. I would have thought no, because I'm so used to being on my own, yet it kind of does. It just feels surreal. Every now and then it kind of hits me, but only for a short while, and then it carries on feeling like it didn't really happen, that he's going to walk in this evening and sit in front of the set drinking beer."

Lisa leans forward and looks into Sarah's eyes earnestly. "Have you ever thought he may have a problem with alcohol?" she says slowly.

Sarah shakes her head. "I think he may have a bigger problem with pizza." She manages a grin. "Do you think there's a support group called Pizzaholics Anonymous?"

"You may laugh," Lisa says sternly, "but you do always say he drinks a lot, and I'm just wondering whether he may need some help."

"I know you're trying to help"—Sarah puts her hand on Lisa's—"and I know how much you know about it given Max's situation, but I would tell you if I thought there was a problem. Seriously, I would."

Lisa sits back and shrugs. "Okay. I was just trying to help."

"So how do you *feel?*" Cindy, in true Californian style, asks.

"Comfortably numb?" Sarah offers hopefully.

"Have you thought about what's going to happen?" Caroline reaches for a brownie from the plate in the middle of the table, giving the others license to follow suit. "What you're going to do? Whether you're going to stay in the house?"

"Of course I'm going to stay in the house. This is my home. But I have been thinking that maybe I could get a job."

"A job!" The rest of the women eye her suspiciously, all of them having been successful career women who gave up their careers in the blink of an eye once they gave birth.

Cindy is the only one who is truly happy as a stay-at-home mom. Caroline has started working part-time as a grant writer at the local arts center now that her kids are in school, and Lisa, when not at Al-Anon meetings, is heavily involved in the Junior League and chairing various charitable events, which she claims to be doing for solely altruistic reasons, although she can't help but secretly love the fact that she's climbing the social ladder while doing so.

Nicole, once the CEO of a large advertising

agency in the city, now "CEOs" her kids with just as much enthusiasm and drive. Whatever ambitions she once had were left behind on the birthing table, and now that her children are in elementary school she is pushing little Nicky into baseball, soccer, and the Suzuki school of music (the baseball he loves, the rest he would happily leave), and little Tori into ballet, art class, and theater (the ballet's a win, the others, a disaster) with just as much determination as she once used to win some of the biggest ad campaigns in the business.

Aside from Caroline—Caroline who is itching for her kids to be old enough for her to go back into the workplace on a more permanent basis, who knows she needs to be defined by something other than her kids—the members of this book club are proud, occasionally smug, in their decision to be "stay-at-home moms."

"Why would you want a job?" Cindy is furrowing her brow, truly perplexed.

Lisa touches on the subject all of them are thinking, none of them daring to say. "Are you having financial concerns?" Her voice becomes earnest again. "Because you know if Eddie does have a problem with alcohol, it wouldn't be unusual for him to have a problem with spending too. It's called cross-addiction, and it's—"

"Lisa," Sarah stops her, "I promise you, Eddie is neither an alcoholic nor a compulsive spender. No, there is not a problem with money, but in the couple of days since this happened I've done a lot of thinking, and part of that thinking has been if this is permanent, what am I going to do with the rest of my life?

"And, Cindy, while I think you are the greatest mother in the world, and I know how much you love being with the kids all day, I'm starting to feel that I need to do something else. Clichéd as it may sound, I want to give something back, and find some purpose in life other than just living for my children."

"Good job," Caroline almost cheers, as Cindy sits perplexed, wondering how on earth anyone could not think that being a mother was the most fulfilling job in the world, and Lisa wracks her brain trying to think of what it would take to organize an intervention and how she could get Sarah to come with her to an Al-Anon meeting.

"So what are you going to do?" Cindy finally asks.

Sarah shrugs. "I used to be a features editor, so it makes sense to stay in journalism."

"Could you do some freelancing for your old magazine?"

"I thought about it but I'm not young and single anymore. I'm exactly the demographic that terrifies them, and, to be honest, I'm not that interested in writing anymore. Also, I know this sounds ridiculous, but I find it very scary, going back into the workplace. I feel as if my brain shrunk to about a quarter of its size once I had Maggie. I could never do some high-powered job. I'm just looking for something small that keeps me busy."

"If it makes you feel better," Caroline says, "I

have no memory anymore, and I manage my job. Just . . ."

Cindy laughs.

"No, I'm serious," Caroline says. "This morning I opened the door to the fridge in the butler's pantry three times before I remembered why I was doing it. I kept opening it, looking blankly inside with no memory of why I was there or what I was looking for. Then I'd go back to the kitchen, remember what it was I wanted, go back to the butler's pantry and whoosh, there I'd be, staring blankly into the goddamned fridge again with no idea why I was there. Three times that happened. Can you believe it? *Three times!*"

They all start laughing. "I went to the mall last week," Cindy admits, "and had no idea where I parked the car. It took me an hour and twenty minutes to find the car—can you believe that? I just parked, got out without looking which floor I was on, or which bay, or anything. Just merrily went off shopping and didn't even think about it until I was in the elevator and they asked me which level and I had no clue."

"You know what you should do?" Caroline, ever the sensible Caroline, says. "You should get a car that's a crazy color. Like bright pink or green. That way you'd never lose it."

"Or a Hummer," Lisa says. "You'd always find a Hummer."

"Especially if it was banana yellow like that woman's at my gym."

"Oh, my God, I hate those cars," Sarah says.

"You can't get one of those cars, not unless you have a tiny penis and a huge superiority complex."

"The last time I looked I had neither." Cindy grins. "And don't worry, I won't be getting a Hummer. I'm quite happy with my minivan."

"I think I may get a Porsche," Sarah says suddenly.

"No!" Their voices, a combination of shock and envy, echo round the kitchen.

"Oh, I'm just kidding," she says. "But isn't that what you're supposed to do when you're suddenly single? Get a fast car, lose loads of weight, and get a whole new wardrobe? Mind you, the losing weight thing I could cope with." She gestures to the spare tire around her middle. "Maybe I should join a gym."

"You'd better not change too much or we won't be able to be friends with you anymore," Lisa jokes, although there is a hint of seriousness in her voice—after all, she feels safe with these women, is not threatened by any of them, but what could be more threatening than a newly single, newly skinny glamorous divorcée in their midst?

"Never gonna happen," Sarah sighs. "I haven't got the energy."

"So bring the local paper over," Caroline says. "Let's have a look through and see if there are any jobs that sound interesting. Hell, why don't we even help you get your resume together."

Sarah's face brightens. "You'd do that for me? You wouldn't mind?"

"Of course not. That's what friends are for."

* * *

By the time the women leave, at the untraditionally late hour of 11:30 that night, there are four sealed envelopes sitting on the kitchen counter, waiting to be mailed.

Each contains a letter that was written by Caroline and Lisa and edited by Sarah, and an updated resume, which made Sarah's life, or at least the last five years of it, sound infinitely more interesting than it actually was.

The resume had her organizing various school events (trueish—she had provided the cookies for the annual bake sale), co-chairing charitable committees (she had attended as a guest), and being household manager of a busy household (true, but only because Eddie had never done anything that had been asked of him).

Even Sarah had to admit it was fairly impressive. Unfortunately, there hadn't been many jobs that she was suited for. She had ended up applying for a retail job in a clothes store, an administrative manager position in a realtor's office, and a job as a personal assistant to an accountant.

Now it's just a question of time.

By the time Sarah goes upstairs and checks on the kids, she's far too excited to sleep. She runs a hot bath—a treat she rarely makes time for anymore—pours in almost half a bottle of Crabtree & Evelyn bath foam, and lies back in the steaming water, thinking about Eddie, wondering what he's doing, how he's getting on.

* * *

Eddie has been wanting to call Sarah all evening. He just wants to hear her voice, find out how the kids are, how she's doing, whether she might have changed her mind. Several times he's picked up the phone and started dialing, but each time he placed the phone gently back in the cradle, knowing that he can't chase Sarah, can't phone her or pursue her until he's figured out exactly how to win her back; exactly how to make his marriage work again.

He's staying in a hotel in the city for now. His office has already found a serviced apartment in Chicago for him, and he's planning on going out there after the weekend. He's going back to see the kids, and then flying out on Sunday night.

The last couple of nights he had initially accepted invitations to go out and hit the bars with his younger, single colleagues. They had tried to encourage him to let loose a little, but the truth was that now that there was nothing for him to get back to, now that there was no home waiting for him, even if it was a nagging, unhappy home, the prospect of drinking all night and ending the evening with a pizza in front of the game just wasn't that appealing right now.

In any event he had stayed for one drink, then had gone back to his hotel room. He'd thought about a few beers but realized he didn't really want them. The evening had stretched out ahead of him, so he'd put on some sweat pants and a T-shirt that barely covered his expanding girth and had headed upstairs to the hotel gym.

What the hell, he thought, as he breathlessly pounded the treadmill, sweat dripping off the end of his nose. *What else am I supposed to do to kill a couple of hours?*

Eddie woke the next morning with calves that were cramping in agony. "Shit!" he muttered as he sat up in bed and massaged the cramps away, stretching his legs in almost-forgotten exercises. But he had to admit, despite everything that had happened, it felt pretty good to have exercised last night.

Sitting on the edge of the bed in the darkened hotel room, Eddie decided that step one of his resolution to make his marriage work was to work on himself. *I'm going to get myself in shape, even if it kills me.*

And that morning Eddie went to work with a bounce in his step that he hadn't felt in a very long time.

Chapter Six

Eddie can't wait to see Sarah. It's his turn to take the kids this weekend, and even though a hotel in midtown isn't exactly the perfect spot, he's off to Chicago next week, and the kids will probably enjoy it. The hotel staff have already set up two cots in the adjoining room, and sitting on top are teddy bears and a selection of games—compliments of the hotel.

He's been working out the last few nights, and he checks himself one last time in the mirror before he leaves. Pulling in his stomach as far as it will go, Eddie gives himself the once-over. Not bad, he has to admit, or certainly not as bad as it has been. Of course he doesn't really look any different, but he's starting to feel better, now that he's replaced the beer and TV with the treadmill and water.

He and Sarah have had the odd, tense conversation since he left. They've tried to sort out arrangements with the kids, or Sarah has phoned to query yet another letter or bill that Eddie was supposed to sort out but hadn't had time, and usually the conversations end in a fight, or, at best, exasperated sighs from Sarah.

He's determined to play things differently today. Even if Sarah starts a fight, Eddie's going to back down. He's going to apologize. It's too early for him to come clean about wanting to try again, but he's going to take the first steps to smoothing the path.

Because Eddie misses Sarah. He misses the kids. Hell, he misses his life. He's lonely in this hotel room, lonely in the gym with the other business travelers who will be returning to their wives and children any day now. Eddie has nothing to return to except a tiny hotel room, a room-service meal, and more of the same tomorrow.

"Daddy!" Walker and Maggie cry out in unison as they thunder down the hallway, arms outstretched as Eddie scoops them up, burying his face in their hair, feeling as if his heart is going to break. God, he missed them. He didn't realize until this moment quite how much he's missed them.

"Daddy! Come play with my tea party." Maggie takes his hand and gestures toward her room, where she's set up a tea party for her eight favorite dolls, all of whom, rather bizarrely, are named Gracie Abigail, Abigail Gracie, Gracie, or Abigail.

"No!" Walker jumps up and down. "Come see my new Spiderman web shooters, Dad! They're so cool!" Walker starts dragging Eddie down to his room to show off his new acquisitions, a direct result of Sarah's guilt over Eddie's leaving.

"Hang on, guys," Eddie says. "Where's Mom?"

"Hi, Eddie." Eddie hears Caroline's voice at the end of the hallway, and he turns to her, a wave of disappointment washing over him.

"Hey, Caroline. Where's Sarah?"

"She had to run out to do some errands. She asked me to come over and watch the kids." Caroline can barely look him in the eye as she says this, she and Eddie both knowing that Sarah doesn't want to see Eddie, that of course this is just an excuse.

"Right." Eddie turns away and scoops Maggie up in his arms. "Come on, Maggie," he says quickly, in a bid to hide his pain. "Let's go get your bag and you, I, and Walker will take the train into the city."

"Yay! The city!" Walker shouts, running down the hallway into his room. "Can we go to the museum with the dinosaurs?"

"Yup," Eddie says. "We can do whatever you want."

"Can we go to American Girl Place?" Maggie asks deviously, even though Sarah has said she is not to get another American Girl doll until her next birthday, many months away.

"Absolutely," Eddie says. "We're going to have the greatest weekend ever." He turns to Caroline, who is leaning in the doorway watching them. "Tell Sarah I'll have them back Sunday by five."

* * *

"What do you mean he looked good? He's not supposed to look good."

Caroline shrugs. "I'm sorry, but you said you wanted to know the truth. But on the plus side he looked devastated when he realized you weren't here."

"He did?"

"Yes, and how come you like hearing that? You're having second thoughts aren't you? It's not too late, you know. My impression was that Eddie really misses you all; he'd come back in a heartbeat."

Sarah shakes her head. "I know you're probably right, but I don't think I can do that. Of course I miss him, but I don't miss the Eddie of today; I miss the Eddie I married." She sighs. "I wouldn't take back the Eddie of today."

"He can't have changed that much," Caroline says. "He's still the same person, surely."

Sarah shakes her head. "I don't think he is, and if I thought there was any chance at all of him becoming the person he was, I wouldn't be doing this; I'd be working through it."

"And what about you?" Caroline asks quietly. "Do you think you've changed? Are you still the same person Eddie married?"

Sarah snorts. "I barely know who I am when I look in the mirror anymore, let alone who I was when I got married. Seriously. Like I said the other night, I look in the mirror and wonder who in the hell that is looking back at me. And I hear myself screaming at the kids and I hate myself for it and wonder what happened to the happy, easygoing, fun-loving person I used to be."

There's a pause before Caroline offers gently, "Do you think it's possible that Eddie feels the same way?"

But Sarah shakes her head. "If he had spent any more time with us he might have noticed. But he was hardly ever here. I really don't think he cared."

Eddie would never admit this to anyone, but he was dreading this weekend. He'd missed his kids enormously, but the truth was he'd never spent any real time with them. Occasionally he would take Walker out somewhere, but it was rare for him to take the two of them out—he'd always thought of that, he realized painfully, as Sarah's job.

He was terrified of spending an entire two days with them, without any help, but he wound up having one of the greatest weekends of his life. They took the train into Grand Central—an adventure in and of itself—jumped in a cab and went to the Central Park Zoo. Hot dogs from a street stand for lunch, then Toys R Us in Times Square complete with Ferris wheel, The Natural History Museum, and American Girl Place.

The kids, as expected, loved the whole experience of staying in the hotel. They loved that they had picnic room-service dinners on the floor in front of *The Lion King 2,* they loved that they both slept in cots in the same room, and mostly they loved that they had never spent so much time with their daddy by themselves.

They were in heaven.

On Sunday they went to the playground in Central Park, then to see the Concorde at the U.S.S. *Intrepid*, then to the movies. The only hard part was saying good-bye.

Eddie takes them back home and hugs them hard, trying not to cry. Chicago suddenly seems a very long way away, and for the first time he realizes how much he is going to miss them.

"I love you," he says as he clings on tight, squeezing Walker until he complains. "Look after your sister and your mom for me until I get back."

"Okay, Dad," Walker says. "Will you come back tonight?"

"No, Walk, I can't come back tonight, but I'll come back just as soon as I can. And, hey, maybe you guys will come and see me? You could fly over on an airplane. How would you like that?"

"Cool!" Walker says, flying his toy Concorde high in the air. "Hey, Mom!" Sarah opens the front door, knowing she has to face Eddie. She catches his eye and Eddie forces himself not to look away.

"Hi, Sarah." His voice is cool, far more cool than he would have expected given his churning emotions. "The kids had a great time. Thank you for letting me take them. Maggie spilt some ketchup on her pajamas, which I tried to wash out but couldn't, hope that's okay."

"Oh, sure." Sarah is surprised to have been thanked. This wasn't what she was expecting. "No problem. What did you do? Did you have fun, kids?" She leans down to give them hugs and kisses.

"Look, Mom! Concorde! It's the fastest plane in the world and we went to see it!"

"And look, Mom!" Maggie runs up to Sarah holding out a doll. "Daddy did get me this from American Girl Place."

"Oh, isn't she lovely." Sarah thinks about reprimanding Eddie, but he wasn't to know, she thinks with a sigh, and so what if the children get a little spoiled while their parents separate. The spoiling won't go on forever, and it's nice for them to have something nice. "What's her name?" Sarah asks, stroking the doll's long dark hair, hair just like Maggie's.

"Abigail Gracie," Maggie announces seriously, and Sarah and Eddie catch one another's eye and laugh. It's been a long time since they've laughed together, and both of them are surprised at how nice it feels. But it won't last, Sarah thinks. It never does.

"Call me when you get to Chicago," Sarah says as Eddie prepares to leave.

"I will," Eddie says, and he turns to look at her, wondering whether to kiss her good-bye, just a peck on the cheek perhaps, a purely platonic kiss. But Sarah turns to go inside and the moment has gone.

"Bye." Eddie raises a hand and his shoulders sink as he makes his way back down the garden path.

"I got a job!" Sarah tells Caroline three weeks later.

"Great! That's unbelievable! Which one?"

"Well, that's the problem." Sarah winces. "There was nothing going on at the local paper, even though they said they'd consider freelance features, and none of the others got back to me. I was at the playground yesterday and I ran into Jennifer Lucas."

"Don't tell me! You're going to be working at the spa!"

"Only part-time, but I told her I was thinking about doing something and she said she could really do with some help now that the holiday season is starting. She said it's her busiest time."

"God, I love that spa. They have the greatest treatments, not to mention the gym. Please tell me you get discounts."

Sarah laughs. "I have no clue, but I'm really excited. I thought I'd end up doing something completely different, not working in a spa, but now I think that this is probably a great way to ease myself back into the workplace. I'm really looking forward to it."

"I think it's just great!" Caroline enthuses, giving Sarah just the support she needs, because the truth is Sarah isn't sure. She felt it was ridiculous, a mother of two, an ex-journalist not putting to use any of her journalistic skills. But maybe this would better suit her life right now: a job that doesn't require any research, doesn't require any out-of-office hours, merely turning up, sitting at the front desk, being helpful and friendly, and going home at the end of the day without having to think about work again until the next time.

"The only advice I have to give you," Caroline says, "is make sure you go to bed early. You won't believe how exhausted you're going to be, working again, even if it is just sitting at the front desk all day."

"Well, here's the greatest thing. I explained my situation with school, and she just wants help in the morning, so I'll be done by two, and I can pick the kids up and spend the afternoons with them. I swear to you, this couldn't be any more perfect."

"Have you told Eddie?"

"No. Should I? I don't know what he'd think, and he's also not living here. Now that we're separated I don't know what I'm supposed to tell him anymore. I don't know whether he is a part of our lives or whether he's not. I feel like I'm in limbo. I never knew how strange this would feel."

"But you're still married," Caroline says. "And he's still the father of your children. Think about it. If he were making any major life changes, wouldn't you want to know?"

Sarah nods. "You're right. I'll mention it to him the next time he phones."

"Does he phone you a lot?"

"Mostly to speak to the kids, but maybe I'll call him instead." Caroline raises an eyebrow at her and Sarah shrugs. "Okay, okay. I'll call him. Just not tonight. Let me work out what I'm going to say first."

Chapter Seven

A week later Sarah sits cross-legged on the bed and flattens the piece of paper out in front of her as she reviews the topics of conversation she is planning to talk about with Eddie.

It still feels surreal to her. She hasn't had to write down a conversation list since she was a teenager, and she's not sure why she feels nervous. He is her husband, and there are things they need to discuss, although Sarah's not yet ready for the big stuff, the serious stuff, the word that begins with *D.*

Walker's basketball camp
Maggie wants a kitten
Contractor coming to quote for the wall
How is Chicago
My job (!!!)

Sarah started work two days ago, and already she feels as if the whole town has come in to see whether the rumors are really true. One by one other mothers she knows from preschool, women she has seen at various events, friends of friends have come into the spa expressing surprise at seeing her there.

A few, she knew, were genuinely surprised. A few definitely didn't know she was working there, but others were *too* surprised, too false in their joy at seeing her, too casually inquisitive about how her life was.

A couple even had the temerity to ask, in deeply concerned tones, whether she was okay, whether they could do anything, could they perhaps bring round a dish for the kids.

"I'm absolutely fine," Sarah had trilled, given that the women in question were renowned for passing on town gossip.

"How is Eddie liking Chicago?" one had inquired, praying that Sarah would give her the full story.

"He's very busy," Sarah had said, although in truth she hadn't known, hence the phone call now. "Excuse me," she had said as Jennifer had caught her eye. "I think I'm wanted in the office. But good to see you." She had smiled widely to hide her exasperation. "Have a great day and thanks for stopping by."

Is it possible to feel so rejuvenated, so energized after just two days of work? Already Sarah is starting to feel like herself again. True, she still doesn't recognize the woman in the mirror, but the very fact that she's doing something for *her,* something that doesn't involve the children, something that allows her to be surrounded by grown-ups, is making her feel like a real human being again.

And while there are undoubtedly some of her peers who look down at the fact she is working in a mere spa, Sarah is thrilled to rediscover how much she likes people. How much she likes seeing the different faces that come in, how much pleasure she gets in reconnecting with the real world.

It was, she remembers, one of the things she liked most about being a journalist. Back in the early days when she started as a feature writer, she loved being out there and meeting people, going to parties, premieres, events.

In her twenties Sarah had been intensely sociable, and she had thought that she had naturally changed as she grew older, that marriage and children had exhausted her to the point where she didn't have the time, the energy, or the inclination to meet new people.

And yet here she is, meeting new people all day, and loving every minute of it.

"You're a natural," Jennifer had said with a smile at her at the end of her first day. "I'm just worried you're going to be bored."

"That's the last thing you have to worry about," Sarah had said with a laugh. "I've spent the last few years being bus monitor, on the PTA, being room mother. Trust me, this is the most interesting thing I've done in years."

* * *

Sarah takes a deep breath and picks up the phone. Eddie's secretary had e-mailed his new details, and she dials the unfamiliar number, hoping that his answering machine will pick up, that she will be able to say something along the lines of: Hi, how are you? Sorry I missed you but just wanted to let you know that the kids are great and we wanted to wish you luck and by the way I've got a new job, which isn't much but it's something, and that's about it, talk to you soon, bye.

But of course Eddie picks up.

"Hi, it's Sarah," Sarah says, the thought crossing her mind as she does that who else would be phoning Eddie late at night. What other woman could it possibly be?

Which sets off a whole new chain of thoughts: Would she mind? How would it feel to think of Eddie with someone else? As she starts to imagine she almost snorts with laughter. She can see Eddie now, lying on the sofa, his sock-clad feet on the coffee table, belching as he finishes off his third or fourth beer, reaching out for the last slice of large white pizza on the table.

"Hey," Eddie says, genuine warmth in his voice. "Nice to hear from you."

Sarah is slightly taken aback. "So, what's up?" she says.

"Nothing much. I'm just cooking dinner."

There's a pause. "You're cooking?" Sarah lets out a short bark of a laugh. "Let me guess, you're putting a frozen pizza in the oven?"

"Good guess, but no. I'm actually sautéing some onions and garlic for a puttanesca sauce."

"A what?" Sarah is incredulous. "How do you even know what sautéing means, never mind what a puttanesca sauce is? You can't cook!"

"I realized that pizza and burgers probably aren't that good for me so I went to the bookstore and asked for a cookbook that was entirely idiot-proof. Let me tell you, I've cooked every night this week and the meals have been delicious."

There are a few moments of shocked silence. "I don't believe you. What have you cooked?"

"Roasted cod in miso sauce," Eddie says. "Rosemary and garlic chicken with wild rice . . ."

"Oh, my God," Sarah gasps. "You have got to be kidding me! Is this some kind of sick joke where we split up and you suddenly become the perfect man? I suppose you've been working out too." Sarah is joking and laughs until she realizes there is silence on the other end of the phone.

"Just some running in the mornings," Eddie says, "although I'm thinking of getting a personal trainer."

"Am I living in *bizarro* world?" Sarah frowns. "Is this Eddie Evans I'm talking to? I think I have the wrong number. I'm really sorry to have troubled you. Good-bye." And she puts the phone down to try to get her head round what she just heard. The phone rings less than fifteen seconds later.

"You're nuts," Eddie says, but he's smiling. This is the Sarah he fell in love with. The Sarah who had character. Strength. Balls. The Sarah he thought had disappeared.

"I'm not nuts," Sarah says. "You're the one who's gone crazy. Tell me, seriously, were you kidnapped by aliens sometime in the night? Because you are not my husband. My husband's cooking skills are limited to heating up McDonald's in the microwave, plus my husband is severely allergic to exercise."

Eddie sucks in his breath at the sound of the words *my husband.* Sarah doesn't seem to have noticed but the hope those two words give him is immeasurable—she still thinks of him as her husband! She hasn't given up on him entirely! Eddie never would have thought such simple words could open up his world so much, but they do. He feels a great cloud lift, as he stands in his tiny kitchen opening a can of tomato sauce.

"Obviously you were a terrible influence on me," Eddie jokes.

"Thanks a lot," Sarah's voice is hard again.

"I'm kidding, I'm kidding. Relax. It's just there isn't much else to do with my time here. I don't know anyone in Chicago other than my colleagues, and I don't have my family here." Eddie puts the can of tomatoes down and goes into his living room, where he stares out the window at the tops of the buildings as he leans his head against the glass and cradles the phone into his shoulder. "I miss you, Sarah," he says gently. "This is really hard, you know."

"I know," she says softly. "It's hard for me too."

"Can we talk about it? Could you maybe come up with the kids this weekend?"

Sarah shakes her head. "It's too soon," she says.

"I'm still confused, and I still think we both need some space. I just need to sort my head out, to get some clarity about what our future holds."

"Okay," says Eddie sadly. "I understand. So tell me about the kids. How are they? I can't believe how much I miss them."

But you were hardly ever with them, Sarah wants to say. Except she doesn't. No point in saying that now.

"They miss you too," is all she says, before she takes a deep breath. "And there's something else I wanted to tell you."

Oh, shit, thinks Eddie. Here it comes. He knew it. He knew it. Marriages don't just dissolve into nothingness because of unhappiness. Marriages only ever end when there's someone else, and here it comes. . . .

This is the part where Sarah tells him she's fallen in love with someone else. Someone else is going to be sleeping on his side of the bed. Someone else is going to be waking up with his kids. Someone else will probably be a better father than he has ever been, for do not make the mistake of thinking Eddie is unaware of his failings. Eddie is becoming more and more aware of who he is and what he may have done wrong. He's just praying it's not too late to fix it, but as he hears those ominous words the cloud that lifted earlier comes back with a vengeance, bigger and blacker than ever before.

Sarah takes a deep breath. "I got a job."

And Eddie wants to cry with relief. "Is that it?"

he says. "You got a job? There's nothing else you want to tell me?"

"Like what?" Sarah is flummoxed. This was not the reaction she expected.

"I don't know," Eddie lies.

"No, that's it. But that's pretty big for me."

"So what's the job? No, let me guess. You're working on the local paper? You're starting a new magazine? Editing a book?"

"Well, no, actually. I mean, I know I'm a journalist by trade, but I just wanted to start small, just to ease myself back into the workplace, to give me something to do while the kids are in school, and Jennifer Lucas needed some help at the spa, so I'm just helping out at the front desk there."

"That's great!" Eddie says. "Honestly, I think that's great. How's it going? Are you enjoying it?"

"Actually I love it. I'd kind of forgotten how nice it is to be out of the house and to be surrounded by people. And you know what, if I ever did want to write a book there's some great material—I've already heard some amazing stories."

"Like what?"

"Okay, I shouldn't gossip but seeing as you're in Chicago, you know that uptight Lynn Gorson?"

"The realtor? The one who always pretends she doesn't know who we are?"

"Exactly! Can you believe that she was caught having sex with the massage therapist in the sauna?!"

"No!"

"I know!" Sarah giggles. "Isn't that awful?"

"Sounds hot and steamy to me," Eddie says,

"and I don't mean in a good way. Ugh. Sex in a sauna. Not a good idea. Speaking of good ideas, though, maybe you could offer to help Jennifer with some of her PR. I think the job is great, but it would be even better if you could utilize some of your skills, and I'll bet she could do with some PR."

"That's a great idea!" Sarah says, particularly as it is something that occurred to her as well. "I probably shouldn't say this," she says, "but I was really scared about telling you I had a job. I thought you'd belittle it."

Eddie is bewildered. "But why would I do that? I've thought for years that you'd be happier doing something that gets you out of the house. I knew how isolated you were, how difficult it's been for you sometimes."

"You did? So why didn't you say something?"

Eddie shrugs. "I'm saying it now."

And as he says it he prays it's not too late.

Sarah sits in silence, flustered. This is not the conversation she expected to have. Eddie is not reacting in the way she expected him to react.

"I have to go now," she says eventually, to Eddie's disappointment, but her voice is gentle, and after Eddie puts down the phone he finds himself smiling. The light at the end of the tunnel now seems just a little bit brighter than it did before.

As for Sarah, Sarah is confused. Her world suddenly feels far less stable now than it did when Eddie first left. Sarah doesn't like not knowing where she stands; doesn't like her life not being cut-and-dried. First she was married; then she was separated. Soon she had planned on being divorced. So why aren't she and Eddie screaming at one another the way they had been for months? Years. Why did she enjoy their conversation? Why did her heart thump ever so slightly harder as Eddie picked up the phone?

Sarah takes a deep breath and goes down to the kitchen. When all else fails, she can always rely on Ben & Jerry to make everything feel just fine.

Chapter Eight

"I love this!" Jennifer stands by the front desk, waving a press release that Sarah had drafted the other day and placed in Jennifer's cubby with a note saying that it was just an idea, but if Jennifer wanted some help with PR Sarah would be happy to do it.

"You do?" Sarah looks up from the computer and grins.

"You're a genius. I loved the idea of starting Girls' Night-In! And then this press release makes it sound even more amazing than it's going to be. We're going to have to talk about more PR." Jennifer perches on the desk, smiling. "I'm always too busy to even think about the PR and marketing, but since you're so talented, we have to use you."

Sarah sits up straighter. "Great!"

"Can you come into my office in about"—Jennifer checks her watch—"twenty minutes and we can talk more about other projects? I'd love to have a brainstorming session with you."

"Absolutely." Sarah nods efficiently, hugging herself on the inside. She can't wait to tell Eddie.

The first Girls' Night In is a huge success. Sarah's press release had been printed, almost verbatim, in the upcoming events page of the local paper; it had been announced in the spa's newsletter; and hot-pink flyers, designed and overseen by Sarah, had been dropped off at hairdressers, nail salons, and preschools all over town.

Not to mention the word-of-mouth network. All the women in book club were coming, plus various friends and acquaintances, and the evening was a sellout.

There was a makeup artist giving free makeovers, a clothes consultant who freelanced for *The Today Show* giving consultations on updating your wardrobe and adding five key pieces for a modern look without breaking the bank, and various beauticians from the spa giving massages and manicures.

There were sushi, hors d'oeuvres, and cosmopolitans. The women start off huddling nervously together, clutching their drinks, smiling tight smiles at one another until the alcohol starts to flow through their veins, and as they loosen up they start laughing, all captured by a reporter and photographer from the local paper.

Jennifer and Sarah stand in the doorway as Caroline comes over and gives Sarah a hug.

"What a great idea!" She turns to Jennifer. "I love that you pulled all these women together, and it's such a treat to get out and feel spoiled. I just had the most amazing massage and I'm waiting for them to call my name for the clothes consultation, although I don't really know why I'm bothering. I'm not sure my preschoolers would appreciate bootleg pants with a bouclé jacket."

Sarah starts laughing at her usually fashion-challenged friend. "Since when do you even know what *bouclé* is?"

Caroline raises an eyebrow and smiles. "I happen to not only know what bouclé is, but also that fur shrugs are very in this season. Not, I might add, that I shall be buying one, whatever that *Today Show* clothes consultant might say."

"I'm impressed." Jennifer smiles.

"I'm in shock," Sarah says.

"Okay, okay. I confess. I was at my ob/gyn yesterday and they kept me waiting nearly an hour, and the only thing they had to read was *Vogue.* Happy now?"

Sarah laughs. "I knew it! There had to be an explanation."

"But if you were to ask me about the benefits of a down vest versus man-made fiber, that I could tell you about." Caroline smiles. "So how about you, my friend?" She looks at Sarah. "I hope you're going to get something delicious done tonight."

Jennifer turns to Sarah. "Absolutely," she concurs. "You're not working. You *should* do something." And before Sarah can protest Jennifer spies someone leaving the makeup artist's table, and the next thing Sarah knows she's sitting in front of the mirror looking at the bags under her eyes and the gray streaks in her hair as Jennifer, Caroline, and the makeup artist stand behind her examining her.

"Well, you did say you didn't recognize the woman who's been looking back at you in the mirror." Caroline shrugs with a grin. "Maybe we can turn you back into the woman you once were."

"Great!" Sarah turns to her. "So I'll be seeing a plastic surgeon tonight as well?"

"Oh, ha ha." Caroline gives her a friendly shove and turns to the makeup artist. "We will now leave you to make my friend even more beautiful than she already is."

"Not a problem," says the makeup artist, with a smile, and Caroline and Jennifer walk off giggling, as Sarah tries not to look at her tired reflection in the mirror.

Twenty-five minutes later the makeup artist stands back to survey her work.

"You look awesome." She smiles. "Ready to see?"

"Go for it," Sarah tells her, as she swivels her chair around so Sarah can see her new face in the mirror.

Caroline is busy talking to Lisa and Nicole when she feels a tap on her shoulder and they all turn around.

There's a silence as they all look blankly at the woman standing behind them, and then, in unison, all three of them gasp.

"Oh—my—God!" Caroline's hands fly up to her mouth.

"Sarah?" Lisa whispers.

"Is that you?" Nicole's mouth drops open, and then she leaves, muttering something about finding the makeup artist.

"Oh, great." Sarah rolls her eyes. "You're making me feel like I normally look like Quasimodo."

"No! But you just look so different," Caroline says. "I wouldn't have recognized you."

"I see that."

"You look amazing." Lisa laughs. "Seriously. I can't believe what you look like. What do you think? Do you like it?"

"Are you kidding me? I love it. Even though it feels as if I'm wearing about a ton of makeup."

"But what did she do with your hair?" Caroline frowns.

"You mean, where's the gray?"

Caroline nods reluctantly.

"She had some colored mousse. Apparently it will come out when I wash my hair, but it temporarily covers the gray."

"Okay. I'm your best friend," Caroline says, "so I think I'm allowed to say this." She takes a deep breath. "You look about ten years younger."

"That's it!" Lisa exclaims triumphantly. "I was trying to figure out why you look so completely different but that's exactly it! You look like a schoolkid!"

"I'm not sure that's the look I was going for."

"Okay, so I'm exaggerating a bit, but you look so much younger. Eddie's going to freak out when he sees you!" And then the three of them fall into an embarrassed silence. Lisa didn't mean to say it, had completely forgotten that Eddie wouldn't be seeing it tonight, nor any other night.

"I'm sorry." Lisa is mortified. "I really didn't mean to say that. I'm so sorry."

"That's okay." Sarah puts a hand on her arm to soothe her. "It's fine, and anyway, you're right. Eddie would freak out if he saw me." And as she walks off on the pretext of getting everyone more drinks, her shoulders sink. What is the point of doing all this, making all this effort when there's no one around to appreciate it? Sure, her girlfriends approve, but for the first time since Eddie has gone, it hits Sarah that she is now on her own, and excusing herself from the party she goes into the office, where she allows the loneliness and fear to overcome her, and she lays her head down on the table and weeps quietly before slipping out the back door and going home.

The makeup may have been washed off by the next morning, but Sarah still gets a shock when she looks in the mirror and sees her rich, chestnut-colored hair.

She pulls open an old makeup drawer and rummages around until she finds some eyeshadow, mascara, blusher. Trying to think about how the makeup artist did it last night, she plays around a little, painting the eyeliner on slowly, smudging it like the makeup artist did, sweeping the blusher over the apples of her cheeks.

Not bad. She looks at herself in the mirror. Not, admittedly, nearly as stunning as last night, but with the gray gone in her hair and some makeup on, she has to admit she looks a hell of a lot better.

"Mommy!" Walker and Maggie come running into the bathroom and stop still, staring at her. "Mommy? You look beautiful!" Walker sighs.

"Really?" Sarah's heart melts. Walker has never said this before in his life, and she gathers him in her arms and kisses him.

"Yes, Mommy," Maggie says, not wanting to be left out. "You a pretty lady, Mommy."

"Oh, thank you, darling," Sarah says, kissing her.

"I put on lipstick too." Maggie grabs the blusher and puts it on her lips as Sarah laughs.

The doorbell rings and Sarah frowns, pulling her robe tighter around herself. Damn. She hates going to the door when she's not dressed, but it's her own fault, she thinks, for messing around with her hair and makeup instead of showering and dressing as she usually does.

"Come on." She lifts up Maggie and gestures for Walker to run in front of them. "Let's go and see who's at the door."

"Hello?" a man's voice calls back. "Mrs. Evans? It's Joe." Pause. "The contractor? I'm here to look at your wall?"

"Oh, right. Sure." She'd completely forgotten, and she opens the door to find herself staring into a pair of bright green eyes, and a large dimpled smile.

"Oh," she says, instantly feeling vulnerable in

her robe in the presence of not just any man, but someone who's actually cute. And then composing herself, she extends her hand and says in her most businesslike tone, "Hi, I'm Sarah Evans. Nice to meet you. Please come in. Will you excuse me just a second while I get dressed?"

"Absolutely," he says. "Hi!" he says to Maggie, who smiles shyly and buries her head in Sarah's robe. "You're a cutie, aren't you. What's your name?"

"Maggie?" Sarah says. "Can you say hello?" There's a shake of her head and Sarah shrugs an apology as Walker comes dashing back into the hall in a Darth Vader mask wielding a light saber.

"Whoa!" says Joe the contractor. "I didn't know Darth Vader lived here. That's pretty scary."

"I'm gonna chop you with my light saber!" Walker says, and Sarah reprimands him.

"Walker, that's not nice. Say sorry."

"Don't worry." Joe smiles. "How old is he? Five?" Sarah nods. "I have a five-year-old as well. I'm well versed in *Star Wars.* I'll watch them if you want."

Sarah thinks for a second, but he looks normal, and he's a recommendation from another mother at school who had used him to redo her kitchen, so he must be okay. She smiles gratefully. "That would be great." She shows him into the kitchen and runs upstairs to get changed. *Oh, shit,* she thinks, catching sight of herself in the bathroom mirror. *What must he have thought of me, opening the door in full makeup and a bathrobe?*

She pulls on her track pants and a sweatshirt and then pauses by the bedroom door. Not that there's anything wrong with her track pants, and not, absolutely not, that she's trying to impress the cute contractor downstairs, who by the way, has a son and is therefore almost certainly married (not that she's looking), but didn't the *Today Show* woman talk about showing off your assets rather than hiding them, and doesn't this make her look rather middle-aged and dull?

Sarah strips them off and puts on some cargo pants with a tight, long-sleeved T-shirt. Thank God for Gap, she offers a silent prayer as she gives herself a cursory glance in the mirror and goes back downstairs.

All the cushions are off the sofa in the family room and Walker, Maggie, and Joe the contractor are huddled under the table.

"What's going on?" Sarah asks uncertainly, unused to seeing strange men crouching under tables in her family room with her children.

"Mom! Mom! Joe made us a fort!" Walker shouts delightedly. "And look! It has a doorway too. You can come in too!" The pillows from the sofa have been propped up in such a way as to create a doorway, Joe's jacket draped over the top.

"I don't think so." Sarah smiles, ever the grown-up. "And it's not Joe; it's Mr. Davito to you."

"I'm fine with Joe." He smiles at her from under the table.

"Are you sure?"

"Yes," he says. "They're great kids."

"Thank you. They are. You said you had a son. Any other kids?"

"No, just the one. But I'd love a daughter someday."

"Daughters are great." Sarah smiles at Maggie, who's now crawled out from under the table and has wandered into the corner to "make some lunch," even though it's nine o'clock in the morning.

"Mom!" Walker whines. "Come under here. Look, there's space."

"No, darling," Sarah says. "Mommy has to talk to Mr. Davito about the wall."

"I'm sorry, buddy," Joe says, as he crawls out from under the table. "Your mom's right. We have to talk about the wall, but how about if you make a huge pirate ship for us to sail in when we're done?"

"Yeah! Cool!" Walker leaps up and down in excitement as he starts to rearrange the pillows, and Sarah leads Joe into the other room, thinking with a pang that Eddie never played with the kids like this.

"You're a natural with kids," she says, as they walk into the family room.

"I think it's because I miss my son," Joe says. "He lives with his mother and I only get to see him on weekends."

"Oh," Sarah says, as a million thoughts go through her head. *So he's single. Or is he? Why is he telling me this? Does he want me to know he's single? God, he's cute. No. Don't be ridiculous. You're a middle-*

aged mother of two and he's totally cute and wouldn't be interested in you even if you were available. Which you're not.

But damn. I wish he'd stop smiling at me like that.

"So"—Sarah, flustered, marches over to the wall—"so this is the wall I was telling you I want knocked down."

Chapter Nine

Something happened to Eddie today that hasn't happened for as long as he can remember.

There he was, dripping with sweat as he pounded on the treadmill at the Reebok Club, when he felt someone looking at him.

Glancing up in the mirror in front of him, he caught the eye of a curvaceous, pretty brunette on the elliptical machine just a few machines away. She held his glance for a few seconds, until Eddie looked away. But Eddie remembered that look. Remembered exactly what that glance, held for just that tiny bit longer than was absolutely necessary, meant. That was the glance he used to give, back in the days when he was young and single. And free.

He looked again to check, because nobody has given Eddie a look like that in a very long time, and, yes, she was still looking. And this time she smiled. Eddie smiled back.

Not that she was his type. And even if she were,

Eddie's not looking. Eddie's priority these days is work, and filling up the hours he should be with his family by working out and thinking about how he can best get back to being with his family.

Nevertheless, Eddie is not a man immune to the charms of a woman who finds him attractive, and he found himself pulling in the little that's left of his protruding stomach, and running just that little bit harder, little bit faster until he'd finished his five miles.

"Hi. That looked like a big run." The brunette was now climbing off the elliptical as he passed.

"Yup." He smiled, having forgotten quite what to do in the face of flirtatious friendliness, but she extended a hand.

"I'm Jeanette."

"Oh, hi, Jeanette. I'm Eddie." And as he shook her hand he saw her look quickly down to the third finger on his left hand, where he still wears his wedding band. He is, after all, still married.

Jeanette saw that he saw her looking, and she gave him an apologetic shrug. "You have to try," she said, as she walked off with a smile.

Eddie walked home on a cloud. No one had flirted with him in years. No one had wanted to try *anything* for as far back as he could remember. He's flattered and excited by the attention, but despite his colleagues' invitations to singles nights and singles bars, Eddie isn't the least bit excited at the prospect of being single.

He doesn't want to go on dates. Doesn't want to start asking women to tell him how someone as beautiful/cute/special as they are could still be single. Doesn't want to share his history, his stories, what school he went to with anyone other than Sarah.

He doesn't want to struggle through a relationship with all the ups and downs until he gets comfortable enough to belch in front of a woman, or she gets comfortable enough to use the bathroom while he's shaving. He only wants that intimacy with Sarah, and with his kids.

And, God, how he misses his kids. He calls them every day, which he suspects is more painful for all of them, but now that they're gone he misses them far more than he would have thought possible. His office is scattered with photos of them, he happily tells his secretary all the cute and funny things they do and say, and most of all he wants to make up for all the lost opportunities.

For the first time, Eddie sees he could have done things differently. He lies in bed at night and thinks of all the times the kids pulled on his sleeves, danced in front of him begging him to play basketball, or have tea parties, or just hang out with them upstairs.

And all those times he'd say, "In a minute," or "Not now, Daddy has to work," or "Daddy's had a long day at work; Daddy needs to rest." He wishes he could turn the clock back and redo everything, be there when they needed him, spend all that quality time with them that he missed, but given that's not possible he's praying for a second chance.

It's almost as if he's come out of the trance he's been in for years. Cutting out the alcohol, the coffee, and the sugar, taking care of his body and himself for the first time since he's been married, Eddie feels as if he can see clearly again.

Not that he's happy, but he knows he could be happy if he were home. He knows, has never doubted, that Sarah is the one for him. All he's done is blame her for nagging and whining, for being a miserable wife, and yet now he sees his part in the equation. He sees how difficult it must have been with him gone at work for the best part of the day, sees how much it must have hurt for him never to want to spend time with any of them, his relaxation being the television and beer.

Eddie is determined that he will get that second chance. All he's doing now is biding his time, working out his strategy. Christmas is coming and Eddie's getting ready. As far as he's concerned, this, this separation, isn't permanent. It's a vacation is how Eddie is choosing to think about it. A chance for all of them to recharge their batteries, ready to start their lives, their real lives, fully refreshed again, and Eddie has decided that Christmas is when the vacation will end.

"Where's this place again?" Lisa's on the phone as Sarah's getting ready for book club.

"It's that new Mexican place on Water Street. Right behind Main Street. Where Pier One used to be."

"Okay, great. And you're dressing up?"

Sarah laughs. "You'd better believe it!"

* * *

For book club tonight they have read, or attempted to read, or are halfway through *Daughter of Fortune* by Isabel Allende. It's Caroline's turn to host, but she's having her house repainted so Sarah offered to switch, and because she now has more energy than she knows what to do with, because she has started wearing makeup every day, coloring her hair, actually living again, Sarah has decided to do something different for this book club.

Instead of being in someone's family room with dessert and coffee, they are going to a Mexican restaurant, and each has been instructed to come in bright, festive colors with flowers in her hair.

Sarah walks into Villa del Sol, squinting through the darkened restaurant to try to find her friends. She sees Caroline waving at her from a table downstairs in the corner of the room and makes her way down as a couple of waiters bow and grin at her with approval.

"Wow! This place is great!" Sarah gives Caroline a quick hug.

"I know!" Caroline squeezes her friend. "I asked them to move us over here because it's away from the speakers. The music's so loud in the front."

Sarah laughs. "I love salsa music, but it makes me feel so old to admit that I can't stand loud music in restaurants. But I can't!"

"We're not old; we're just interesting, and interested in actually hearing what one another has to say."

"Speaking of one another, where *are* the others?" As Sarah speaks, Lisa and Cindy appear, both with the requisite flowers, closely followed by Nicole.

"I love this!" Cindy says. "Why didn't we decide to go to restaurants before? This is a great idea, Sarah!"

"Thank you. And may I say you girls all look gorgeous."

"As do you." Lisa smiles. "I love your gardenia."

Sarah shrugs. "Fake. But the best I could do in early December."

Cocktails are brought; menus are studied; food is ordered. There is the usual, cursory pretense of them having come together for some intelligent, intellectual discourse about the book, and then Cindy and Caroline break off to talk about the First Selectman's latest comments about the educational system at the town meeting two days prior, and soon they have all abandoned the book.

"Poor Isabel Allende," Sarah says. "I hope she forgives us."

"Okay, I'm going to be honest," Cindy says. "I did read the book this time"—the others applaud as Cindy does a mock bow—"and I loved it, but there's nothing I need to say about it. Was it beautifully written? Yes. Did I sympathize with Eliza? Yes. Was it engrossing? Of course. But the bottom line for me is I come to book club every month to see you guys, not to talk about the book. I come because I get more friendship and support from all of you than anywhere else, and because you keep me sane, and reading a book is just an excuse to come together and talk about real life."

Caroline makes a face. "Does that mean book club is coming to an end?"

"Cindy is right, though," Nicole says. "I never have time to read the book and I come because of you. Maybe we should rename it dinner club."

"Or we could have a poker night instead," Lisa offers. "Actually, no. Gambling probably isn't a good idea."

"Given that we usually end up grumbling about our husbands we could be Wives Anonymous," Caroline jokes.

"Except of course for me," Sarah adds wryly. "Given that I no longer have one."

A silence falls upon the table.

"What do you mean, you no longer have one? Are you getting"—Lisa's voice drops to a hushed whisper—"divorced?"

The shock shows on Sarah's face as she adamantly shakes her head, and soon she is pouring out her confusion to the women.

"So give it another go," they all say. "If you feel that confused and you're that lonely, try again."

"But I can't," Sarah moans. "I can't put the kids through this again, let alone myself. I can't let him come back if it's going to continue the same way, only to have to split up again, next time permanently. I'm only going to damage them and myself even more."

"You could always put yourself out there and try dating. Just dip a toe in the water to see if you could face it."

"Are you nuts?" Nicole looks at Cindy as if Cindy

is completely mad. "How is that relevant? And, anyway, Sarah's loneliness isn't going to be solved by dating."

Sarah shrugs sadly. "First of all I absolutely, positively do not want to date anyone at all, not to mention that I am a middle-aged mother of two living in the suburban heartland where ninety-nine percent of the people are married and there really aren't any decent men to date over the age of twenty-four."

"So?" Cindy shrugs. "Demi Moore isn't complaining."

Sarah lets out a bark of laughter. "I'm hardly Demi Moore."

"I don't know." Caroline looks at her appraisingly. "With your new dark locks and plum lipstick . . ."

"Oh, be quiet!" Sarah says.

"Meanwhile," Caroline says, "what about Joe, the sexy contractor?"

"Who?" "Who?" "Who?" There's an echo of excited voices around the table, and Sarah actually blushes.

"Oh, God." She gives Caroline a stern look. "Why did you have to bring him up?"

"Who is Joe the sexy contractor?" Lisa's eyes are wide with excitement. "And why haven't you mentioned this before?"

"There's nothing to mention." Sarah shrugs. "He's just the contractor who's taking down the wall and he's cute—"

"And single, and interested in Sarah!" Caroline finishes off the sentence triumphantly.

"I'm sure he's not," Sarah says.

"Oh, come on." Caroline turns to the rest of the table and tells of how she went to Sarah's house a couple of days previously to find Joe the sexy contractor sitting at the kitchen table, drinking a soda, and talking animatedly to Sarah.

"We were talking about the wall," Sarah says helplessly.

"I'm telling you, he was staring at you. That man is attracted to you. You've just forgotten what signs to look for."

Sarah shrugs. "It doesn't matter even if he is. I'm not interested." But despite herself she turns to Caroline again. "But seriously. Do you really think he's attracted to me?"

"I don't think so—I know so." Caroline grins. "And you, Miss flick your hair girlishly and smile up at him through your long, dark eyelashes, were attracted to him too. Don't try to deny it."

Sarah laughs as she shakes her head. "Girls, I'm a married woman," she says. "Leave me alone." But Caroline's right. The second time Joe came over the attraction was even stronger than the first. Not that she's planning on doing anything about it. . . .

Several margaritas later, a live salsa band comes on and soon half the restaurant is up and dancing.

Sarah leads her table to the floor, whooping and laughing as they go, none of them caring when, an hour later, they are dripping wet, more than a little drunk, and rather flustered by the sudden appearance of dozens of men, far better versed in salsa dancing than they, who twirl the women around like dervishes.

None of them had had this much fun in years.

Chapter Ten

Sarah gets home from work to find her machine blinking furiously. Caroline, Lisa, Nicole, and Cindy have all left messages, sheepishly admitting to hangovers but all saying they had the best time, and thanking Sarah for breaking the routine of the usual staid book club meetings.

And despite her own slight hangover, Sarah feels energized in a way she hasn't in years. She feels younger, sexier, more sparkling. She looks in the mirror now and actually likes what she sees. She loves that both Maggie and Walker now tell her she looks pretty. She loves that she's taking the time to put makeup on, that she read an article in a fashion magazine that was lying around at work that advised women to buy only what they completely love and what makes them feel beautiful, and to discard everything else.

Sarah came straight home after work, resolving to throw out anything she hadn't worn in a year, anything that didn't flatter, that didn't suit. Walker was sent to Caroline's for a play date and Maggie laughed delightedly as she played dress up in Sarah's discarded pile.

The Prada jacket she used to wear all those years ago when she worked at the magazine but had never been able to get rid of because it was so expensive, now helplessly out of date, heads the pile. The fleeces and velour sweat suits, the stretch Gap pants that never flattered but were always comfortable, the chunky cotton cable sweaters that had long ago lost their shape but were easy to pull on first thing in the morning—all of them make their way into the discarded pile.

When Sarah finishes there isn't an awful lot hanging in the wardrobe. The cargo pants she keeps, and a selection of T-shirts. A few sweaters, two classic white shirts, and three skirts.

The shoes are a disaster. The boiled wool clogs go, as do the Merrills, and even the Birkenstocks. *What was I thinking?* she mutters to herself as she buries them under the pile.

And her precious designer clothes that she had saved all these years from when she worked at the magazine are now so clearly outdated. She loved those Miu Miu shoes way back when, but sadly she realizes she can't wear them now.

She checks her watch. An hour and a half to go before picking Walker up from Caroline's. "Come on, Maggie," she says, scooping her up and sweeping downstairs with her to wrap them both up in scarves and hats—the December weather has just started to bite. "We're going shopping."

* * *

No Talbots for Sarah today. No Gap. No Ann Taylor. She heads straight for the one designer store in town, a store she would once have felt so comfortable in, but hadn't been inside for years, too intimidated by the perfect sales assistants, the overpriced clothes, the air of expensive glamour.

Sarah doesn't remember the last time she went shopping for the sheer fun of it. She's been used to buying clothes when she needs them, not because she wants them. And most of what used to hang in her wardrobe was from catalogs. Too busy to send anything back, if it didn't quite fit right, or didn't quite suit, she wore it anyway.

Now she's buying because she wants to be beautiful. She's buying because finally she's able to pay for it with her own money. She's buying to empower herself a little, to bring her exterior, her appearance, more in line with her changing interior.

An hour later she walks out of the store smiling to herself, her arms laden with bags, feeling much like the Julia Roberts character in *Pretty Woman*.

She bought sweaters in soft angora wool that make her feel like she's wrapped in a blanket; slim-fitting bootleg pants that make her legs look endless; a chocolate brown quilted jacket with a fur collar that is both glamorous and practical; a black chiffon dress for the holidays; flat suede ballet slippers for every day; high-heeled pointed boots for going out.

Sarah hasn't just spent this week's salary; she's spent the future month's salary as well, but it's been worth it. She feels beautiful in every item of clothing, and as she drives to Caroline's house she finds herself wishing that Eddie could see her now.

Eddie walks home from the gym and smiles at the department store windows. He loves Christmas. Has always loved Christmas. When he was a little boy he used to wake up on Christmas morning at 4:00, and wake up his sister, who was always allowed to have a sleepover in his room on Christmas Eve, and they would both hurry downstairs to where the Christmas tree was blazing to rip open their presents.

The magic and possibility of Christmas have never left him. He loves putting the lights on the big white pine in their front yard, loves having the kids help him put the tinsel on the tree, loves going up to the attic to get the Christmas ornaments that belonged to his parents when he was small.

Now is about the time when he'd be taking the children out to the Christmas tree farm to pick the biggest tree that could fit in their hallway. Now is about the time Sarah would start shopping for their stockings, showing him the cute little presents she had bought, the Christmas-themed candies.

A heaviness weighs upon his heart as he looks through the window. He's not sure he can face Christmas here in Chicago on his own. He can't think of anything worse than a little tree in the tiny, cold apartment he could never think of as home.

I should be with my family, Eddie thinks, as he looks through the window. *I* need *to be with my family.* And as he stands there missing Sarah, Walker, and Maggie, he realizes how insane it is that he has let so much slip away. Not just by being in Chicago, but by refusing to pin Sarah down to talk about their future, and by all the missed opportunities: by not being the husband and father he could have been.

Now it's time, he realizes. Time to win them back. Time to show his family how much they mean to him. The vacation is finally coming to an end, and he pulls out his cell phone and dials a number.

"Can you tell me the availability of flights from Chicago to New York, December twenty-fourth?" And as he speaks the words he feels the cloud that has weighed so heavily upon him finally start to disperse.

"I totally forgot you were coming!" Sarah is shepherding Walker and Maggie into the car as a pickup truck pulls into the driveway.

"Oh, great," Joe laughs as he gets out of the truck. "Nice to know I make a good impression."

"I'm sorry. Life's just been so crazy. Are you starting today?" Sarah watches as Joe starts unloading dust sheets from the car.

"Absolutely." He grins. "I told you this would be the week."

"The door's open," she says. "Will you be okay by yourself?"

"Sure." He smiles and then winks. "I'm trustworthy. You don't have to worry about a thing."

Jennifer catches Sarah just before she leaves work. Sarah's anxious to get home to see how the wall looks, and if she's honest, to see whether Caroline was right, whether Joe might be attracted to her. Not that she's interested. Absolutely not. But how flattering. What a pick-me-up.

"Wow! Look at *you!*"

Sarah grins. "I went shopping."

"Clearly! I love it. Listen, I want to talk to you about a more permanent position in marketing and PR. You've been doing so much for us in that field recently and our membership is increasing as a result, and I know that you could do so much more. Can we meet tomorrow to talk about it?"

"That would be great." Sarah resists the urge to throw her arms around Jennifer and hug her, and as she gathers her things and walks to her car, a huge grin spreads on her face.

"I'm back," she says, as she climbs into her car. "Oh, baby, am I back!"

A cloud of dust greets her as Sarah opens the front door.

"Careful," Joe shouts out as she steps gingerly over the threshold into the kitchen, where there is no longer a wall, and she gasps as she looks straight into her family room.

"Oh, my gosh, it's amazing! I can't believe the wall is gone! Look how huge it looks!"

Joe appears from behind the little bit of wall that is left, and Sarah immediately flushes. He's shirtless. Gorgeous. And shirtless.

Good Lord, she thinks. *There is a half-naked man standing in my kitchen.* And then: *A half-naked gorgeous man.* And then: *Shee-it. Look at that body!*

But she can't. She's too flustered. She pretends to look for something in her bag as she starts backing out of the room. "I'm just going to make some calls in the office," she says, praying for the flush to disappear. "Just call me if you need anything."

"Wait." Joe walks over and stops her by placing a hand on her arm. Sarah looks up into his eyes, which seem to be laughing at her. "I need you to show me where to Sheetrock, how much of the wall you want out here." He gestures to the left side.

"Oh, um, whatever you think," Sarah says, unable to stop focusing on the fact that there's a half-naked man whom she's incredibly attracted to standing inches away from her, and he has a six-pack—Jesus, who her age has a six-pack anymore?—and he has his hand on her arm and all she can think about is what it would be like to feel his chest, to run her fingers lightly over his muscles.

There is a brief silence and then Joe says quietly, "You know, I probably shouldn't say this, but you look incredibly sexy today."

And Sarah gasps. Shit. It's all well and good having a fantasy, but fantasies are fun precisely because they *are* fantasies. She may think about schtupping George Clooney, but if he ever actually turned up on her doorstep she'd run a mile.

And she may be standing here thinking about running her fingers lightly over Joe's muscles, but that's not actually supposed to happen.

Oh, shit. Now what?

Sarah opens and closes her mouth at Joe in her best goldfish impersonation, and then she does something she knows she may regret for the rest of her life, but she can't help herself.

She turns and runs.

"He what?" Caroline splutters, as she puts her cup down and gapes at Sarah over the kitchen table.

"I know!" Sarah says. "You were right!"

"I can't believe he was that obvious! So what did you do?"

"I turned and ran." And Sarah flushes again at the memory.

Caroline bursts into laughter.

"So where is he now?"

"Probably still figuring out where to put the Sheetrock up. Oh, God"—Sarah buries her face in her hands and groans—"I'm so embarrassed. I can't believe I just ran away. He is so gorgeous but this is ridiculous. I'm not going to start an affair with the contractor for heaven's sake. I'm married! I don't do this kind of thing. He probably does this with all the lonely housewives in town."

Caroline nods. "I hate to agree but I think you're probably right."

Sarah looks at her with a frown. "You're not supposed to say that. You're supposed to say I'm special and different, and evidently he feels something very strong for me."

"Evidently he *does* feel something very strong for you, but, honey, he's way too confident for this to be a one-off."

"I know. I think that's what freaked me out. If he'd had a bit more humility, hell, I might have gone for it."

"Really?" Caroline's eyes are wide.

Sarah shrugs. "No. Probably not. But he seemed so sure that I was just going to sigh and fall into his arms. I know you're right; he must do this with everyone." There's a silence, and then Sarah says quietly, "But am I still allowed to feel flattered?"

"Are you kidding? Of course! The man's gorgeous, even if he is a sleaze, although you're looking pretty gorgeous yourself these days."

"You really think so?" Sarah's eyes light up.

"Oh, come on. You're like a different person. Eddie wouldn't recognize you if he saw you now. Speaking of which," Caroline continues in a more gentle tone, "I know you've been putting it off, but it's nearly Christmas. Have you thought about what you're going to do? Is he going to spend Christmas with the kids? At the very least, don't you think it's time you got together with him and talked?"

"You're right." Sarah nods slowly. "It's time. I was so scared of being on my own, but you know what? I can do this. I've been happier these last couple of months than for the last six years. I feel stronger, more contented, just better. I'd be lying if I said I didn't miss Eddie, but the truth is I miss having *someone,* although life on my own isn't nearly as lonely as I thought it would be."

Caroline's eyes widen. "Wow. So this is it? I thought you were going to say you'd try again."

"I can't," Sarah sighs. "Eddie isn't who I want him to be, and I know how naïve it would be to expect him to change for me. You can't change anyone—even I know that. I didn't ever think I'd be getting divorced, but then I never knew how unhappy I was until I experienced the alternative. I guess I just kept hoping it was a phase and would pass. Well," she attempts a bright smile, "the good news is it finally has."

"Are you going to see a lawyer?"

"Just as soon as the holidays are over."

"And what about Eddie and the children over the holidays?"

"We spoke yesterday. He said he wants to spend Christmas with them but he's going to stay at the inn, not at home. I don't want to spoil their Christmas. We'll wait until after the holidays to tell them, and as hard as it's going to be, we'll put on a united front until then for the kids' sake. It's the right thing to do."

Chapter Eleven

"No, Walker, honey. I know you want that giant tree but Mommy can't manage it by herself. We have to get something smaller."

"But Daddy always gets the biggest one," Walker whines, dragging his feet next to Maggie as they walk through the farm, Walker constantly pulling Maggie over to the giant trees while Sarah tries to direct them both to something far more manageable.

Sarah grits her teeth. "I know Daddy always gets the big ones, but small trees are way cooler." Oh, God, Sarah shakes her head. How ridiculous that she's speaking like a teenager in a bid to bond with her five-year-old. "You know why they're cooler?"

"No. Why?" Walker asks reluctantly. He doesn't buy it.

"Because you can reach the top and put the star on yourself."

"But, Mom!" He doesn't buy it. "Daddy always gets the ladder."

"Walker, I'm running out of patience," Sarah snaps. "We're getting a small Christmas tree this year and that's that."

And Walker bursts into tears, followed by Maggie.

"Shhh, Shhh!" Sarah hisses, praying for them to stop, as people start giving them concerned looks. "Please, will you stop crying. Please. Walker, here, do you want a lollipop?" Sarah fumbles around in her bag for the sugar bribes she has taken to carrying.

"No!" Walker wails. "I want my daddy."

Oh, God, Sarah thinks. Great. And the guilt starts kicking in.

"Okay, Walker," she says. "Daddy will be here in a few days so, okay, we'll get a big tree. Okay?" Walker's wails turn into sniffles. "Okay?"

"Really big?" Walker says, as Maggie also stops crying.

Sarah sighs. "Whatever." And Walker whoops with joy and runs off to the eight-foot-and-higher section.

They end up with a nine-foot tree. The men at the farm drag it out to the car and secure it onto the roof for them, and Sarah drives home listening to Walker and Maggie talking about Daddy decorating the tree when he gets home.

"Walker, sweetie," Sarah says finally, "Daddy's coming home on Christmas Eve, which is in a few days, and wouldn't it be nice if he came home to a tree decorated by all of us? That would make him so happy. Why don't we decorate the tree ourselves?"

"But Daddy loves decorating the tree," Walker says. "He would be sad if we did it without him."

Sarah thinks about Christmases past. And Walker's right. Eddie does seem to come alive at Christmas, does love the traditions, does actually get off of the sofa and choose the tree, help decorate it, help stuff the stockings.

But that was then and this is now. As much as she's determined not to ruin the holidays for the kids, Sarah also knows that they have to accept that some things have changed forever, and this is one of them.

"You remember when you spoke to Daddy yesterday?"

"Yes!" Maggie shouts out. "I love my daddy!"

"Yes, darling, I know. Well Daddy told me that he wanted us to decorate the tree because he said you were so good last year, Walk, that he wanted to see how you did it all by yourself."

Walker's eyes light up. "So all by myself? No grown-ups helping?"

"Well, no. He just meant you would be in charge."

"Yay!" Walker shouts with a grin. "I'm gonna make an *awesome* tree for Daddy."

Twenty minutes later Sarah phones Caroline.

"I feel really stupid but I need to borrow your husband."

"Sure," Caroline says. "Just as long as you don't

want to have sex with him. Actually, on second thought do have sex with him. It might take the pressure off me."

"Thanks, but no thanks. I'm standing outside my house feeling pathetic and hopeless but I've got a nine-foot Christmas tree on the roof of my car and I haven't got a clue how to get the damn thing inside."

"See? I told you men were good for something." Caroline chuckles. "I'll send him over right away."

By the time Louis has come over and enlisted the help of Sarah plus three neighbors to get the tree off the car and in the house, Sarah is exhausted, not to mention the kids.

"Who wants to make hot chocolate?" Sarah asks as everyone leaves.

"Me! Me!" A chorus of two little voices.

Walker breaks the chocolate into the pot, Maggie stirs as Sarah holds her, careful not to burn them, and both of them drop the marshmallows into the cups.

"Mommy?" Maggie sidles up to her and rubs her cheek on Sarah's leg as Sarah places the three mugs on the table.

"Yes, sweetie?" Sarah reaches down and strokes Maggie's hair.

"You the best mommy," Maggie says, as she flings her arms around Sarah's leg. "And I a mommy's girl."

"No." Walker jumps off the stool and comes

over, trying to shove Maggie out of the way. "I'm a mama's boy; you're not a mommy's girl."

"I am," Maggie starts to wail, as Sarah crouches down and takes them both in her arms, squeezing them hard. "You're both my best boy and girl and I love you. Do you know how much I love you?"

"Yes," Walker says and nods. "To infinity and beyond."

"Exactly," she says. "To infinity and beyond. And that's about as much as anyone can ever love anyone else."

"Mommy?" Walker says, after a few sips of hot chocolate. "After this can we go see Santa at the mall?"

Sarah thinks about everything she has to do today. About how she was planning to stick the kids in front of a movie while she vacuumed the house and did some laundry. And it's nearly Christmas. And it's Saturday. The mall will be a zoo. She looks at her children's faces and sees them looking expectantly at her.

"Okay," she says. "When we've finished we can go see Santa at the mall."

Maggie sits back in her chair and pushes her full mug of hot chocolate away. "I'm all done, Mom," she says, as she climbs off her chair.

There's a forty-five-minute wait to see Santa.

"Good Lord, I hope this is worth it," Sarah mutters to the woman who joined the end of the line just in front of her.

"If it keeps them happy and quiet then it's worth it." The woman gives her a smile and they both laugh.

"I hope it's good this year," Sarah says, again, as always, impressed at the huge tree trunk flanked by two elves and a sleigh. Twinkling lights surround the arched entrance into the tree, and Sarah knows from past experience there will be storybook dioramas on the way to see Santa, actors and actresses playing the characters. Last year it was *Beauty and the Beast,* which was magical, but the year before was a very disappointing *Cinderella.*

"I heard it's *Peter Pan,*" the woman says.

"Tinkerbell!" Maggie pipes up, hearing Peter Pan.

"Wouldn't that be fun?" Sarah says to Maggie, scooping her up and giving her a kiss.

"Just as long as the Captain Hook isn't scary." The woman's husband turns. "When our son watched the movie he didn't sleep for about six months."

"I did too!" An indignant six-year-old glares at his dad. "I wasn't scared."

For a split second Sarah watches the family standing in line in front of her and feels a pang. She misses being part of a family. Misses having a husband to come with, to help out. But even when she had a husband he never did this. Sure he loved Christmas, but he was never around to take the kids to see Santa. Sure, he was willing to look at the gifts she bought, but he was never available to actually come shopping with her and choose them with her.

Stop it, she tells herself. *I'm missing something I never had. Something I could never have had with Eddie. It's time to move on. Stop thinking about a past that never was.*

"Did you see Tinkerbell?" Santa says to Maggie as she perches on his knee with wide eyes and a shy smile. Maggie nods.

"Isn't she beautiful?"

Maggie nods again.

"And what did you think of Peter Pan?" Santa turns to Walker, perched on his other knee. "Did you see him fly?"

Walker nods. His five-year-old confidence has completely disappeared in the face of the real-life Santa Claus.

"But are you sure he's the real one?" Walker had whispered earlier as they rounded a corner and saw a glimpse of Santa sitting behind a sparkly curtain.

"Absolutely." Sarah had nodded seriously. "There's only one Santa and this is it."

"But what about the one at the grocery store?" Walker had said after a moment's thought.

Sarah had frowned. The one at the grocery store had been rubbish. A cheap polyester suit and a very fake beard. When they'd got up close Sarah had discovered that Santa at the grocery store also happened to be a cross-dresser, which was disappointing, to say the least.

"Mom?" Walker had asked as they left. "Is Santa a lady?"

"Not usually," Sarah had said. "But that's not the real Santa. That's just someone pretending."

"Ho, Ho, Ho." Santa—today's more realistic Santa—beams. "So, Walker and Maggie, have you been good this year?"

They nod.

"I heard you had been. My elves told me you deserved really good gifts this year. What would you most like for Christmas?"

In the silence that follows Sarah has a jolt of realization. *Oh, God,* she thinks. *I know this is going to turn into a Lifetime movie. Please don't say it,* she prays. *Please don't say I want my daddy home.*

She holds her breath as Walker struggles to think of what he most wants before turning to Santa.

"I want . . ." Another pause. "I want the really cool robots from the movie that really walk and talk and do stuff like this." And he gives an impromptu demonstration, which seems to give Maggie the confidence she has been missing.

"And I want a Barbie jeep," Maggie announces.

"And can I have a jeep as well?" Walker says. "But a cool army one, not a Barbie one because Barbie is for girls, but my sister can have a pink one."

"Ho, Ho, Ho," Santa says. "You only get one gift for Christmas but I'll see what I can do."

"Santa," Walker pauses and looks at Santa seriously, "actually what I'd really like is a light saber."

"Okay," Santa says. "Thanks for telling me." And he looks at Sarah and winks. Sarah gathers up the children and whispers a thank you to Santa. "And thank God for good old American consumerism," she mutters to herself on the way out.

"I am acting like a teenager," Sarah says to Caroline on the phone.

"Not for the first time recently." Caroline laughs. "Not that I'm going to be the one to remind you of how you blushed and ran away when Joe the sexy contractor made a pass at you."

"He did not make a pass at me." Sarah groans. "And anyway, we're not supposed to talk about that anymore."

"I know, I'm sorry. I just couldn't resist."

Joe hadn't shown up again. He was not used to being rejected by the lonely housewives he so often worked for and ended up in bed with, and had not come back to finish the job. Sarah was part furious and part relieved. She was mortified at her behavior, relieved she hadn't paid him, and even more relieved to find she had been put off completely by his overt advance and hadn't spent any more time fantasizing about his six-pack stomach. Nope. She'd been put off entirely and now was simply irritated that she had to find someone else to finish the job.

In the end it had been done by a handyman, and although the sheetrock wasn't as smooth as it could have been, at least her kitchen didn't resemble a construction site, and at least the handyman in question had been in his early sixties, and not the slightest bit interested in Sarah.

"But I am regressing," Sarah insists. "I can't believe I'm pretending to have a party tonight so when Eddie arrives he can see me all dressed up. I feel so bitchy, I just want to show him what he's missing."

"Well, it is kind of bitchy but also normal human behavior. It's that I may not want you but I still want you to want me thing. And anyway, look how awesome you look; of course you want him to see."

"So you're sure Louis won't think I'm weird coming over to your house for dinner wearing a black cocktail dress?"

"Weird? He'll think it's his lucky night."

Chapter Twelve

The best-laid plans of mice and men . . .

Naturally Sarah is in the middle of blowing out her hair when the doorbell rings. She sighs and gathers her robe around her as she goes to the top of the stairs and sees Walker and Maggie running to the door. They know they're not allowed to open it for strangers, but as they peer through the glass they start shrieking and leaping up and down with excitement.

"Daddy! Daddy! Daddy!"

And then Walker opens the door and both of them fling themselves into Eddie's arms. Eddie crouches down and squeezes them, as his eyes fill up with tears. He never wants to let them go. He never wants this moment to end. Oh, God, how he missed them.

"Daddy? Why are you crying?" Maggie breaks away and looks into his face curiously.

"Because I'm so happy to see you two." Eddie laughs through his tears. "I've missed you so much."

Walker doesn't say anything; he just leans his head on Eddie's shoulder with a beatific smile on his face, and Sarah swallows the lump that is now in her throat.

And once she has successfully swallowed the lump in her throat she takes a second look at Eddie.

"Eddie?"

"Hi, Sarah." Eddie disengages from the children and walks over to where Sarah is standing, halfway up the stairs, and he leans over to give her an awkward kiss on the cheek, and Sarah's mouth drops open in shock. She completely forgets her fantasy of wafting down the stairs in a stunning dress and just stares.

"You look amazing," she says, before she even has a chance to think about what she's saying. "What have you done?"

Eddie grins. "Just working out. I guess I've lost some weight."

"Show me your muscles, Daddy." Walker dances around him, unable to stop touching him, unable to believe his dad is finally here.

"Okay." Eddie flexes. "Feel that."

"Wow!" Walker gingerly prods his bicep. "Whoa, that's big. Cool!"

And Sarah comes back to the present, remembering that this isn't how he's supposed to see her, and flustered she starts backing up the stairway.

"Look, I hope this is okay but I have a cocktail

party at work. It won't be long but I promised I'd make an appearance. Do you mind looking after the kids for an hour or so?"

"Are you kidding? I don't mind at all." Eddie works hard to cover up his disappointment. He was looking forward to spending the evening with all three of them, but he's not going to show Sarah. He's going to be cool Eddie, play just a little bit hard to get, not show her how much he's missed her. At least, not yet.

But, God, it's good to be home, back where he belongs. He runs a hand lovingly along the chair rail, smiles as he sees the spot on the stairs where Walker spilt some grape juice last summer. He takes the kids into the kitchen and instantly feels remorse when he sees the missing wall. For a moment he feels like a stranger—how odd that something so big should have happened when he was away—but it passes quickly.

And Walker and Maggie have changed so much. In just a few months it seems they have grown louder, more confident. Both of them are crawling all over him, talking talking talking, each of them having so much to say, their excitement making their words spill and stumble together as Eddie laughs. In the old days he would have sent them off to watch television, and now he just wants to be with them.

In the family room the television stays off. Eddie sits on the floor and roughhouses as the kids shriek with laughter and hang off his neck.

"Daddy?" Walker says after a while. "Are you home now forever? Are you staying?"

Eddie takes a deep breath. "I don't know, Walk. My work is still in Chicago but we'll have to see what happens."

Maggie starts to tear up. "Please don't go, Daddy," she says, and Eddie scoops both of them up and hangs them upside down.

"Who wants to go to the diner for supper?" he says, as they giggle hysterically, not used to their father playing with them like this.

"Yay! Me!" the kids shout.

"And who's going to leave milk and cookies out for Santa tonight?" Eddie shouts, as he places them gently on the floor.

"We are!" They dance around him again.

"Dad?" Walker says eagerly. "You know what Santa's bringing me this year?"

"Hmmm." Eddie pretends to think hard. "A Barbie jeep?"

"No! That's for me!" Maggie shouts.

"Oh, okay. A pair of socks?"

"Ew! No! He's bringing me a light saber and an army jeep and a cool robot thing from the movie."

"I don't think Santa will be able to carry all those things, Walk, but I'm sure he'll manage one of them. Maybe even two."

"Oh. Okay," Walker says. "I hope it's the army jeep and the light saber."

Eddie thinks about the enormous robot sitting in his suitcase. "Are you crazy? The robots are the coolest thing in the world. If I were you I'd want the robot."

"Oh, yeah, Dad. I do. I want the robot."

"We just have to remember to leave the milk and cookies."

Twenty minutes later Sarah comes downstairs, feeling beautiful and confident in her black cocktail dress and heels. She debated putting her hair up but remembered how much Eddie always loved it down, so she left it softly curling on her shoulders.

"Mommy, you look beautiful!" Walker says, as Sarah enters the family room, and Eddie's heart skips a beat as he lets out a soft wolf whistle. Damn. He didn't want to be so obvious but she looks more beautiful than he's seen her look in years.

"Obviously I'm not the only one who's changed." He smiles. "You look beautiful, Sarah."

"Thank you," she says. "I made meatloaf for dinner, which is in the fridge. You just have to heat it up for about a minute in the microwave, and then the kids can have I-C-E-C-R-E-A-M. . . ."

"Ice cream!" Walker leaps up and down. "I want ice cream for dinner."

"Actually," Eddie says, "I thought I'd take the kids to the diner for dinner. If that's okay with you."

"Oh," Sarah says. "Sure." Of course it's okay, but Eddie has never offered to do anything with the kids before. In fact, she doesn't remember him ever having taken them anywhere by himself just for the sheer fun of it.

"So have fun at your party," Eddie says, forcing himself to turn away from Sarah. "See you later."

"Great. Sure. Have a good time."

* * *

"But he looks ten years younger!" Sarah sits at Caroline's kitchen table while Caroline pours her a glass of white wine. "God. He looks like the old Eddie."

Caroline raises an eyebrow. "Are you trying to say you fancy him again?"

"No!" Sarah says, a little too quickly. "Don't be ridiculous. Just because he's changed on the outside doesn't mean he's changed on the inside."

"And what if he has?"

"I'm sure he hasn't."

"But if he has?"

Sarah shrugs, thinking about the young, energetic Eddie she said good-bye to half an hour ago, and she leans her head on the table and groans. "Oh, God. Now I'm all confused again. This morning I was ready to sit down and tell him I wanted a divorce. Now I don't know." And suddenly she stands up. "I'm going to go to the diner. Damn it. The only way I'm going to know is to be around him, see if he really has changed. Do you mind?"

"Don't be ridiculous. I was going to say the same thing myself." Caroline gives her a big hug. "Good luck."

"Mommy!" Maggie sees her first and bounces up and down in her seat, holding her arms out for Sarah to give her a hug and a kiss.

"Hi, guys," Sarah says, feeling suddenly rather sheepish, not to mention overdressed, for the diner.

"That was quick." Eddie looks at his watch. "What happened?"

"Oh, you know. The party was filled with too many people drinking too much. And I thought that I should really be with my kids on Christmas Eve."

"I know how that feels," Eddie says, as he slides a menu over to her.

"So what's everybody having?"

"Pancakes and French fries!" Walker says.

"French fries and French fries!" Maggie says.

Eddie shrugs, an apologetic smile on his face. Actually, he hasn't been able to stop smiling since Sarah walked in. He knew it was a ruse. Of course it was a ruse. Did she think he hadn't got to know her at all in the years they'd been married? *If she turns up at the diner then this marriage will work again,* he had told himself. *If she turns up at the diner then I know there's hope.*

Sarah thinks about saying something, insisting on something healthier.

"It is Christmas Eve." Eddie shrugs, by way of explanation.

"Fine," she says. "I guess I'll have the French toast then."

Sarah and Eddie don't talk much over dinner. Most of the talking is done by the children, their attention focused on Eddie, and Sarah is surprised to find how comfortable she is.

She hadn't expected this. Hadn't expected to be sitting here with Eddie and the children, hadn't expected Eddie to be so interested in the children, and hadn't expected any of this to feel so . . . normal.

It isn't that it feels wonderful. Or special. Or unique. It just feels as if they are a family again, which in itself is something Sarah had forgotten. It is a feeling of contentment that surfaces, and she hadn't realized how much she missed it. Not just during the weeks that Eddie has been gone, but during the last few years. This, she realizes, sitting at the table, is the kind of father she'd always hoped Eddie would be. This is the kind of family she'd always hoped to have. Is it possible that she could finally have it at last?

By eight o'clock the children are in bed. Walker insists he's going to stay up to see Santa come down the fireplace, but when Sarah checks on him ten minutes later, he's fallen asleep in his bed, sitting up, with books scattered all over the comforter, clutching onto his favorite stuffed monkey.

Eddie appears behind her and walks over to Walker, gently removing the books, laying him down, and placing a kiss on his forehead. "I love you," he whispers, as he turns off the bedside lamp, and Sarah has to blink away the tears.

She lets Eddie check on Maggie as she goes downstairs and starts clearing up the mess the kids made as they baked chocolate chip cookies for Santa.

She had fully expected Eddie to do his usual disappearing act, but he had sat at the kitchen table with the children and helped them roll out the dough, cutting out the cookies with reindeer-shaped cookie cutters, then had insisted on taking them upstairs and giving them a bath himself.

Sarah had started to feel almost redundant. It was like a role reversal. There was her husband, her husband who had been so useless with the children, suddenly being Mr. Mom while she was left sitting on the sidelines, and of course the children were only interested in Daddy, which was to be expected. But still. She couldn't help feeling left out.

While Eddie had been bathing the kids Sarah had snuck into her office and phoned Caroline.

"This is getting more confusing," she had said. "I just don't know what to make of him."

"Just enjoy it," Caroline had advised. "And if I were you I'd pour myself a stiff drink."

And so she had.

Sarah finishes cleaning up the mess as Eddie walks downstairs, and as soon as he enters the room she feels the tension. Now that the kids are asleep it is uncomfortable. This, at least, is what she was expecting.

"The wall looks great. Or, rather, lack of it," Eddie says.

"Oh, yes. Thanks."

Eddie sighs. "I'm sorry I never got around to getting that done."

Sarah shrugs. "It's done now."

"Do you mind if I join you in a glass of wine?"

"No. Sure. The bottle's on the table."

Eddie helps himself to a glass and pours himself the wine.

"Sarah," he says eventually, and she knows he's going to ask to sit down and talk, and suddenly she doesn't want him to. Suddenly she wants to put it off, because what seemed so certain this morning suddenly seems so up in the air.

"Eddie," she interrupts him. "We have to do the talcum powder thing and get all the gifts together."

Eddie grins, relieved at putting the talk off, not sure yet quite what he's going to say. "Okay," he says. "You get the powder, and I'll go out and bring my gifts in from the car."

Sarah sprinkles the powder from the fireplace to the Christmas tree, and sits back as Eddie treads big footprints through the powder, creating the effect of Santa walking through a sprinkling of snow.

"Sarah," Eddie says, as he refills both their glasses once they've finished laying the gifts at the base of the tree, "please don't take this personally, but the tree looks terrible."

Sarah, slightly buzzed from the wine, snorts with laughter. "I know I shouldn't be passing blame onto a five-year-old, but Walker did it all by himself."

"God bless him." Eddie laughs. "I kind of figured as much given that the decorations don't reach any higher than his head. I can't deal with it. Please say we can redo it. We can tell him Santa did it."

"Thank goodness!" Sarah laughs. "I didn't have the heart to redo it myself."

"Do we have popcorn?"

"Naturally."

"Okay!" Eddie rubs his hands together with glee. "Let's get this show on the road, and while we're at it, do you mind if I build a fire?"

Sarah hesitates. Red wine. A blazing fire. Popcorn. It's beginning to feel strangely like a date.

Eddie forces a laugh. "Relax, Sarah. I'm not trying to seduce you. It's cold in here; that's all."

"Oh, sure." Sarah shrugs. "I didn't think you were . . . oh, never mind. Absolutely. Let's build a fire."

When the tree has been decorated the two of them sit down on the sofa and smile at one another. Tonight has been fun. They haven't talked about any of the serious stuff. They haven't talked about themselves. They've talked about the kids, Sarah filling Eddie in on all the funny things that have happened since he's been away, and they've talked about their jobs, their lives independent of one another.

"You've really changed." Eddie is the first one to say it, as he sits on the sofa opposite her.

"I have?" Sarah attempts a mysterious smile from over the rim of her wineglass. "How?"

"You seem . . . happy." Eddie realizes, with a pang, that it's true. Sarah does seem happy, and it never occurred to him that she could be this happy with him gone. Nor does it occur to him that she may be this happy because he's back.

But it occurs to Sarah. For the first time in years it occurs to Sarah.

"I am happy." Sarah nods. "This job has been incredibly fulfilling. I feel as if I've found myself again. Do you know what I mean?"

Eddie looks quietly at her. "I do. I'm not going to lie to you and tell you I'm happy, but I've found respect for myself again. I've got more energy than I've had in years and I feel like a young man again. Before . . . I felt middle-aged. I felt like my life was over, and now I feel that it's beginning again."

Oh, God. Sarah feels a jolt. Maybe he's met someone new. Maybe he has a girlfriend. The thought had never occurred to her before now, but then again the Eddie she remembered wouldn't have had the energy to go out and find himself a girlfriend, much less have the ability to attract one.

But this Eddie? This is the Eddie that chatted her up at that Halloween party all those years ago. This Eddie would have no problem attracting women. And, hell, even Sarah knows how big the singles scene is in Chicago. She's just never thought that anyone would be interested in Eddie.

"Have you . . . ?" She has to ask. She swallows hard. "Have you met anyone?"

Eddie widens his eyes in disbelief. Is she kidding? He spends every night missing Sarah, figuring out how to get her back. But maybe she's asking because she has? It's the one scenario he hadn't pictured, hadn't prepared to deal with.

He shakes his head and Sarah feels relief flood over her. "You?" he says, trying to sound as casual as possible.

Sarah thinks about her brief flirtation with Joe the contractor and smiles. "No."

And now it's Eddie's turn to feel relieved.

There's a long silence as both of their eyes meet until Sarah smiles and looks away, her heart pounding. This is the last thing she expected to happen. This is a date. It feels just like a date. She feels excited, and nervous, and scared. She's sitting opposite her husband of eight years, ever so slightly drunk, and she's wondering whether he might be thinking of kissing her.

And as she imagines him bending down to kiss her she feels a shiver of excitement and she flushes.

"Are you okay?" Eddie asks.

"Fine," she whispers, attempting a seductive smile, which comes out rather crookedly, thanks to the alcohol.

Eddie stands up. Here it comes, she thinks. Here he comes. Back home where he belongs. And her heart stops.

Eddie stretches, then checks his watch. "I'd better go," he says. "I've got to be at the Inn."

Sarah takes a deep breath. "Do you want to stay the night?"

There's a long silence. Too long. Eddie's trying to figure out what she means, trying to figure out whether his heart should be leaping with joy or whether he's misinterpreting what she's asking, and Sarah feels sick.

"I didn't mean *that,*" she says suddenly, blushing, even though that's exactly what she meant. "I meant in the spare room. Just so you could be with the kids in the morning. It just seems silly for you to go to the inn now. It's so late . . . this makes more sense."

"Oh, sure," Eddie says, disappointed. "Okay. Great. I'll just go and get my stuff. Oh, and Sarah?"

"Yes?"

"Thank you for such a special evening. For letting me be with the kids. For being so great about everything."

"Oh. You're welcome." Sarah forces a smile. Damn. This isn't the way she wanted it to go. "I'll go and make up the bed in the spare room. Sleep well."

"Sarah?" Eddie's voice is soft as Sarah turns expectantly from the doorway. "Merry Christmas," he whispers, and she smiles at him uncertainly and wobbles upstairs on unsteady feet to make up the bed in the guest room.

Walker and Maggie sleep in, given that it's Christmas Day. At 5:45 A.M. they get up and scramble downstairs to the Christmas tree. Maggie knows instantly that the huge box contains her Barbie jeep, and Walker is delighted that Santa heard him and gave him the robot *and* the light saber. They are both even more delighted that Santa clearly enjoyed his cookies and milk.

"Mommy! Look! Santa got me web shooters!" Walker bursts into Sarah's room, already in full Spiderman costume, Maggie following closely at his heels as Walker climbs on the bed.

Eddie rolls over with a smile. "Shhh!" he says, getting out of bed and leading the children into the hallway as he gestures to Sarah, sleeping soundly on the other side of the bed. "Mommy and Daddy had a very late night. Let's go and make breakfast for Mommy, okay?"

"Okay, Daddy." Walker and Maggie each take a hand as Eddie leads them out of the master bedroom and downstairs, and lying in bed Sarah smiles. She may not have known what she wanted for Christmas, but Santa certainly did.

Please turn the page for an exciting sneak peek of
Jane Green's
THE OTHER WOMAN,
now available in hardcover from Viking, and in
trade paperback from Plume.

Pulling a sickie is not something I'm prone to do. And, while I'd like to say I feel sick, I don't. Not unless prewedding nerves, last-minute jitters, and horrific amounts of stress count.

But nevertheless this morning I decided I deserved a day off—hell, possibly even two—so I phoned in first thing, knowing that as bad a liar as I am, it would be far easier to lie to Penny, the receptionist, than to my boss.

"Oh, poor you." Penny's voice was full of sympathy. "But it's not surprising, given the wedding. Must be all the stress. You should just go to bed in a darkened room."

"I will," I said huskily, swiftly catching myself in the lie—migraine symptoms not including sore throats or fake sneezes—and getting off the phone as quickly as possible.

I did think vaguely about doing something delicious for myself today, something I'd never normally do. Manicures, pedicures, facials, things like that. But of course guilt has managed to prevail, and even though I live nowhere near my office in trendy Soho, I still know, beyond a shadow of a doubt, that should I venture outside on the one day I'm pretending to be sick, someone from work will just happen to be at the end of my street.

So here I am. Watching dreadful daytime television on a cold January morning (although I did just manage to catch an item on "updos for weddings," which may turn out to be incredibly useful), eating my way through a packet of custard creams (my last chance before the wedding diet goes into full acceleration), and wondering whether there would be any chance of finding a masseuse—a proper one—to come to the house at the last minute to soothe the knots of tension away.

I manage to waste forty-five minutes flicking through the small ads in the local magazines, but somehow I don't think any of those masseuses are what I'm looking for: "guaranteed discretion," "sensual and intimate." And then I reach the personal ads at the back.

I smile to myself reading through. Of course I'm reading through. I may be about to get married but I'm still interested in seeing what's out there, not that, I have to admit, I've ever actually gone down the personal-ad route. But I know a friend who has. Honestly.

And a wave of warmth, and yes, I'll admit it, smugness, comes over me. I don't ever have to tell anyone that I have a good sense of humor or that I look a bit like Renée Zellweger—but only if I pout and squint my eyes up very, very small—or that I love the requisite walks in the country and curling up by a log fire.

Not that any of that's not true, but how lovely, how lucky am I, that I don't have to explain myself, or describe myself, or pretend to be someone other than myself ever again.

Thank God for Dan. Thank you, God, for Dan. I slide my feet into huge fluffy slippers, scrape my hair back into a ponytail, and wrap Dan's huge, voluminous toweling robe around me as I skate my way down the hallway to the kitchen.

Dan and Ellie. Ellie and Dan. Mrs. Dan Cooper. Mrs. Ellie Cooper. Ellie Cooper. I trill the words out, thrilling at how unfamiliar they sound, how they will be true in just over a month, how I got to have a fairy-tale ending after all.

And, despite the cloudy sky, the drizzle that seems to be omnipresent throughout this winter, I feel myself light up, as if the sun suddenly appeared at the living-room window specifically to shine its warmth upon me.

The problem with feeling guilty about pulling sickies, as I now discover, is that you end up too terrified to leave the house, and therefore waste the entire day. And of course the less you do, the less you want to do, so by two o'clock I'm bored, listless, and sleepy. Rather than taking the easy option and going back to bed, I decide to wake myself up with strong coffee, have a shower, and finally get dressed.

The cappuccino machine—an early wedding present from my chief executive—shouts a shiny hello from its corner on the kitchen worktop, by far the most glamorous and high-tech object in the kitchen, if not the entire flat. Were it not for Dan, I'd never use the bloody thing, and that's despite a passion for strong, milky cappuccinos. Technology and I have never got on particularly well. The only technological area in which I excel is computers, but even then, now that all my junior colleagues are messing around with iPods and MPEGs and God knows what else, I'm beginning to be left behind there too.

My basic problem is not so much technology as paper: instruction manuals, to be specific. I just haven't got the patience to read through them, and almost everything in my flat works eventually if I push a few buttons and hope for the best. Admittedly, my video recorder has never actually recorded anything, but I only ever bought the machine to play rented videos on, not to record, so as far as I'm concerned it has fulfilled its purpose admirably.

Actually, come to think of it, not quite everything has worked that perfectly: The freezer has spent the last year filled with ice and icicles, although I think that somewhere behind the ice may be a year-old carton of Ben & Jerry's. And my Hoover still has the same dust bag it's had since I bought it three years ago because I haven't quite figured out how to change it—I cut a hole in it when it was full one time and hand-pulled all the dust out, then sealed it back up with tape and that seems to do the job wonderfully. If anything, just think how much money I've saved myself on Hoover bags.

Ah yes, there is also the superswish and super-expensive CD player that can take four hundred discs at a time, but has in fact only ever held one at a time.

So things may not work the way they're supposed to, or in the way the manufacturers intended, but they work for me, and now I have Dan, Dan who will not lay a finger on any new purchase until he has read the instruction manual cover to cover, until he has ingested even the smallest of the small print, until he can recite the manual from memory alone.

And so Dan—bless him—now reads the manuals, and gives me demonstrations on how things like Hoovers, tumble dryers, and cappuccino machines work. The only saving grace to this, other than now being able to work the cappuccino machine, is that Dan has learned to fine-tune his demonstrations so they last no longer than one minute, by which time I'll have completely tuned out and will be thinking either about new presentations at work, or possibly dreaming about floating on a desert island during our honeymoon.

But the cappuccino machine, I have to say, is brilliant, and God, am I happy I actually paid attention when Dan was showing me how it worked. It arrived three days ago, and thus far I've used it nine times. Two cups in the morning before leaving for work, one cup when I get home, and one, or two, in the evening after dinner, although after 8:00 P.M. we both switch to decaf.

And as I'm tapping the coffee grains into the spoon to start making the coffee, I find myself thinking about spending the rest of my life with only one person.

I should feel scared. Apprehensive at the very least. But all I feel is pure, unadulterated joy.

Any doubts I may have about this wedding, about getting married, about spending the rest of my life with Dan have nothing whatsoever to do with Dan.

And everything to do with his mother.

The Second Wife of Reilly

Jennifer Coburn

Chapter One

Maybe it was the holiday spirit. Maybe it was pity. All right, if I'm being entirely honest, my motives were driven primarily by self-interest. But if my plan worked, everyone would get a happy ending. Reilly and me. Prudence and whomever.

It's not as if I was plotting the downfall of my new husband's ex-wife. I didn't want her dead—or even injured. I simply wanted her remarried and off the market. More specifically, I hoped that if she had a new man in her life, it would eliminate any crazy ideas she might have about reconciling with Reilly.

My friend Gwen proposed the idea as a joke when we spoke earlier in the evening. But the more I thought about it, the more it made sense. Finding a new husband for Prudence seemed like a perfect way to get her out of my life.

To be fair, it wasn't as though Prudence was stalking Reilly. In fact, I hadn't even seen her since my wedding to Reilly six months ago. She came to the ceremony with her friend Jennifer, a six-foot tall African American woman with a penchant for dressing in costumes from Broadway shows. Thankfully, Jennifer stuck to a simple cobalt blue slip dress at my parents' beach house reception. Just last year at her own wedding, she wore the Kristin Chenoweth's cast-off from her role as Glinda the Good Witch of the North in *Wicked.*

Anyway, back to Prudence. It was my idea to invite her to the wedding so we could establish some sort of neutrality. We weren't going to be best friends and form the Wives of Reilly Lunch Club, but I did want to make a gesture to let her know I didn't consider her the enemy either. After all, it was she who was indirectly responsible for Reilly and I meeting.

Last winter I took a class called Cooking without Recipes at the 92nd Street Y, and Prudence was there with some friends. She seemed nice enough, and I felt sorry for her because the teacher kept shouting at her to release her plan. No one knew what the woman was talking about, least of all Prudence, who later got a pretty serious cut while chopping vegetables blindfolded. (Don't ask, it was a very weird class.) A few weeks later, I was dining out with my mother when I saw my cooking classmate at another table with an attractive man. The kind who could fasten his necktie while carrying on a phone conversation. The kind of guy I'd go for. Prudence stopped at our table and we all chatted for a few minutes—just long enough for me to discover that her handsome dinner companion was so much more than just another clean-shaven face. Reilly O'Shaugnessay was one of New York's most highly regarded, ragingly successful international businessmen. And, thanks to Prudence's indiscretions, Reilly was brand spanking new to the singles market. The two were out discussing the terms of their divorce. I've heard of the Casserole Circuit, where ninety-year-old women in Miami show up at mourning widowers' homes claiming they were friendly with the deceased wife when in reality they'd actually just read the obituary section of the paper. So in comparison, flirting with the soon-to-be divorced Reilly seemed appropriate. Plus, Prudence seemed to be almost cheering us on, as though she had a personal stake in Reilly and me getting together. Little did I know how right I was.

Get this: Reilly's nut job of an ex-wife went off for a college reunion in Ann Arbor, Michigan, had a weekend fling with an old boyfriend; and accepted his marriage proposal—while she was still married to Reilly! Instead of coming home and letting Reilly down easily, Prudence got the harebrained idea that she would secretly find him a new wife. I know, I know, I'm planning a gender-swapped version of the same scheme, but Prudence took it too far. She hosted a singles party and gave away free mugs with Reilly's picture on them. He told me she had his face printed on white chocolates with cards beside them inviting women to "Have a Reilly—he's delicious!" That's simply not normal behavior. When I set out to find Prudence a new husband, it'll be done more tastefully. There will be no mugs. No chocolates. No wild parties. Just a simple, professional regional search for the ideal new husband for Reilly's ex-wife. Then, I can relax and we can all peacefully coexist as happily married, completely unavailable couples.

I never thought I'd find myself so wound up with thoughts of Prudence coming back to haunt my marriage. It's so incongruous with who I am, who I've always been. My parents proudly dubbed me a "cool customer" on my first day of kindergarten. My classmates shrieked with horror and wailed tears of deep mourning as their parents left them in the classroom. After my mother knelt to kiss and hug me at the door of Mrs. Ellenson's classroom, I gave a modest smile, crisply turned my maroon leather Buster Browns, and told her, "That will be all." It was a phrase I always thought sounded terribly sophisticated when my mother used it on waitstaff or our cleaning women. I'd maintained this contained demeanor throughout my life, and it's served me well. It matched my solid color sweater sets and sensible shoes. Hand wringing wasn't my style, but these days I found myself neurotically obsessing about Prudence, imagining she was plotting a hostile takeover of my marriage.

If I had to pinpoint the exact moment I started thinking about Prudence lurking in the shadows, it was Thanksgiving Day when Reilly and I were at my parents' home. As we drove through the neighborhood, there were three homes listed for sale. The yard signs were all from the same real estate brokerage—Prudential.

At Thanksgiving dinner, Reilly advised my father that investing in securities right now wouldn't be prudent.

The next day, my editor at *The Wall Street Journal* assigned a three-part series on the new direction of the Prudential Life Insurance Company.

When the kids returned to school, Hunter's first-grade teacher, Mrs. Polly Friedman, went on maternity leave and was replaced by Miss Prudence Cantor. I felt like Jan Brady in *The Brady Bunch* episode where the middle child was lamenting that she was constantly compared to her older sister. At her wits end, Jan shrieked, "Marcia, Marcia, Marcia!" That's how I felt. But the Bradys' first daughter's name was replaced by Reilly's first wife's—Prudence, Prudence, Prudence!

When Reilly and I were dating, I was the picture of poise, listening to the horror story of Prudence's affair and subsequent wife hunt without the bat of an eye. I never bad-mouthed Prudence or her actions. I simply encouraged Reilly to explore his own feelings and watched him untangle himself from the rage he justifiably felt toward her. I was so proud of how emotionally disengaged I was from the whole thing. As I mentioned, it was even my idea to invite Prudence to our wedding. My dear, often brutally honest, friend Gwen suggested that my invitation was not, in fact, an act of generous composure but, rather, unseemly gloating. "Inviting Reilly's ex-wife to your wedding is ludicrous!" she snapped when I told her. "You may think it makes you look like the Patron Saint of Second Wives, but it's transparently rubbing the woman's nose in your happiness."

Honest to God, this was not the case. Gwen was usually spot on with her observations, which was one of the things I simultaneously loved and hated most about her. This time I thought she was wrong, though. Having Prudence at the wedding was not intended to make me appear gracious. Okay, maybe a little. Far more important, it was a symbolic gesture that would mark a new era in Reilly's life, one where he was so emotionally disentangled from his first marriage that having his ex-wife attend his second wedding wouldn't have the slightest effect on him.

A colleague of mine—one of those unfortunate thirtysomethings living a protracted adolescence—said something that summed up this sense of detachment quite well. As her chandelier earring bobbed about, she said of her failed relationship, "I'm *so* over it." Looking like somewhat of a wedding cake in her three-tiered lace miniskirt, Serena said she would never give her ex-boyfriend a second thought. Having Prudence at Reilly and my wedding was a way of saying to the world, *We're so over Reilly's first marriage.*

Gwen said that if I were truly over it, I wouldn't have ever even contemplated what her presence would or wouldn't mean to others. "If you're so 'over it' why are you even thinking about her?" she asked. At the time, I dismissed Gwen's comments. I figured we didn't see eye to eye on this one. We'd been friends since she moved to New York in our freshman year of high school. In the twenty years we've known each other, we've respectfully disagreed on many issues without it ever getting ugly. I nodded as she gave me her opinion and went about my merry way, knowing Gwen was utterly mistaken about my wedding invitation list.

After I'd battled the snow and arrived home that evening, I knew I'd have about an hour to myself because Reilly had taken Hunter, my six-year-old, to Rockefeller Center to ice-skate. In less than a year, Reilly had become the ultimate hockey dad, sans the screaming fights with hairy, beer-drinking fathers. Frankly, I would have preferred that Hunter take up tennis, or even soccer, but after his and Reilly's first Rangers game, Hunter insisted we find him a peewee team. Of course, tonight my boys wouldn't chase each other around with sticks, but join a hundred or so New Yorkers and visitors as they enjoyed skating against the familiar backdrop of the enormous Christmas tree and golden statue of Prometheus.

I plugged in the light cord behind our family Christmas tree, filling our home with the perfect holiday ambiance. Through the oversized living room window of our brownstone, I watched the streetlights illuminate the snow falling through the periwinkle sky. In this quiet moment, I thought about what Gwen had said last summer and realized she may have had a point. Six months after Reilly and my wedding, I was feeling anything but "over" Prudence Malone.

Everything about our home suggested the season had changed. Our tree sparkled with tasteful white lights buried deep in the branches of our tall evergreen. I was thrilled when Reilly hung my familial hand-carved, painted, and blown glass ornaments a good four inches into the tree, instead of plunking them onto the branch ends, as my first husband did. I begged Rudy not to do this because it made the greenery look depressed. I told him repeatedly that hanging ornaments at the very tip of the branches made them sag—and showed the hook. As was the case in most of our marriage, Rudy didn't really care all that much how I felt and proceeded to do it exactly as it served him. My insistence on inset placement of tree ornaments sounds highly anal, I know, but everyone deserves a few areas in life where things are done properly. And properly means *her* way. But I digress. Not only did everything inside our home indicate that six months had passed since our summer wedding but also outside: women wore wool coats with muffs to match the fur trim. Kids wrapped raspberry-colored wool hats around their heads and ears. On every corner, Santa Claus rang a bell and shouted, "You're his wife now, Sarah!" Obviously, I stretch the truth for emphasis, but you get the point. Seasons had changed for everyone else but me. All of the Christmas decorations were just that—decoration. I wasn't filled with my usual holiday spirit.

Typically I loaded ten holiday CDs in the player and kept it going as our seasonal soundtrack. This year, I dragged myself to our music selection to find something tolerable. I dreaded going to Saks, one of my all-time favorite holiday spots. And the only party I planned to attend this season was the one I'd just been to at Hunter's school.

Though I've thought about her nearly every day this past month, I was especially preoccupied with Prudence because I just found out that one of her close friends is a mother at Hunter's school. As luck would have it, this woman's twins are in Hunter's class. Miss Cantor was leading the children in a song about the happy little snowflake, and Reilly rushed in and parked himself in the small wooden chair beside me. He pecked my cheek, then did a double take when he saw the J.Lo-sexy mother standing near the window. She seemed to recognize him as well and gave him a friendly, but not overly enthusiastic, wave. After the happy little snowflake melted, the woman approached us. Reilly immediately greeted her as Sophie.

"You must be Sarah!" Sophie said warmly. She wore a form-fitting cream cashmere top, a herringbone skirt with buttery leather boots, and a funky purse. Reaching a soft manicured hand toward me, she said she's heard so many nice things about me. I smiled as we shook hands. "From Prudence," Sophie finished.

"Sophie and Prudence are friends," Reilly filled me in. "She was a cohort in the whole, well you know," he said.

Sophie smiled her obnoxiously white teeth at us and said she hoped Reilly didn't hold a grudge. "It all worked out for the best, didn't it?" She smiled. "You know how Prudence is. Heart in the right place, head in the clouds." Reilly smiled as if to say there were no hard feelings and placed his hand on my shoulder. A normal person would have taken some comfort in this gesture. The real me would have seen how clear it was that Reilly was with me 100 percent. I silently reminded myself that Prudence had never so much as phoned our home to ask Reilly about the heating system in their loft. Instead of finding peace in this and Reilly's measured interaction with a woman who'd helped plan a find-a-new-wife theme party, I was unsettled by the way Prudence was creeping her way into my life. Now every blessed morning when I saw Sophie for school drop-off, I'd be reminded of Prudence.

Something had to be done. At home that evening, I lit the fireplace, sank into the chaise, and called Gwen. She always knew what to do. And when she didn't, she acted as if she did, which for me was deeply comforting, as it reminded me of my mother. "You need Paxil," Gwen immediately shot when I told her about seeing Sophie at Hunter's class holiday party.

Rolling my eyes with my voice, I said, "You're simply hilarious, Gwen."

"I'm quite serious. You're creating undue anxiety for yourself, Sarah. Every day, you call me and ask if I think Reilly's having an affair with his ex-wife, despite the fact that there's not a shred of evidence to suggest he is."

"It's a hunch," I snapped. "Doesn't women's intuition count for anything anymore?"

"It's paranoia, Sarah. Reilly's a model husband. I've seen the way the man is around you. He's smitten. He adores Hunter. He's a great guy. Why can't you leave it at that and be happy?"

"Don't you think it's odd that Reilly *never* mentions Prudence?" I asked.

"Um, let me think about it," she said in a tone that let me know she was not thinking about it at all but, rather, mocking my suspicions. Without missing a beat, she finished, "No." She didn't find it one bit unusual, she said. "Why would he talk about his ex-wife?! He has a new life with you. A wonderful new life, if you'd just relax and enjoy it. I'd worry if he *was* talking about her, and I have a feeling you would too."

"It just seems like he's hiding something," I said, watching the flames dance behind our velvet stockings.

"*You're* hiding something, Sarah—your good sense," Gwen said. "Listen, you're my dearest friend in the world, and I'm sticking with you through this, but I have to say, I'm a little concerned. The obsessing, the worrying, the constant fear that your sweet and adoring new husband is cheating on you, it's just not who you are. What happened to the self-assured Sarah I know?"

I also wondered what had happened to that Sarah. I was no longer a cool customer, but an adult version of the high-strung kindergartner clinging to her mommy's pant leg. "I don't know," was the hollow truth.

I heard Gwen light a cigarette and inhale. "Look, if you're really worried about her, why don't you just find her a new guy to keep her occupied?"

"Find her a new husband?" I repeated.

"Isn't that what she did to Reilly?" Gwen laughed. "Payback's a bitch, Sarah."

We laughed for a moment. It was the first time I felt truly at ease in a month. "Do you really think I should?"

"No!" Gwen returned, as though the answer was obvious.

"Really? Because this is the first laugh I've had in a while. I felt a huge weight off my shoulders just at the thought of Prudence busying herself with someone new."

"Sarah, she isn't busying herself with Reilly and even if she wanted to, he's in love with *you*! You, his wife of six months. The honeymoon isn't even over yet and you're already fast-forwarding to the jealous-wife-who-hires-a-private-investigator phase. Isn't that supposed to be another ten years off?"

"I'm not hiring a private investigator!" I defended.

"No, you're entertaining ideas of finding a new husband for your new husband's ex-wife so she'll break off their nonexistent affair. Do you realize how utterly Fox television this sounds?"

"Maybe you're right," I said.

"I always am," she teased.

* * *

I popped my favorite holiday CD in the player and smiled contently as I looked around my home. What was I so wound up about anyway? Life was good. Hunter was excelling in first grade. His show-and-tell coach said he was making excellent progress on his oral presentation skills. I was doing so well with my freelance reporting, I had to turn down assignments. And Reilly was exactly what I'd always wanted in a husband.

Some may characterize Reilly as dull, but after three years married to an alcoholic I found his steady demeanor reassuring.

What was I worried about? We had a beautiful new life and nothing threatened to take any of it away. The rug couldn't be pulled out from under me because there was too much heavy furniture resting on it. It was time for me to take a few deep breaths, let the holiday music lift my spirits, and start enjoying my first Christmas with Reilly.

With that thought, I heard the keys opening the door. Hunter burst in immediately before Reilly pulled him back out onto our front stairs and told him to shake the snow off his boots. "You know how your mother loves her wood floors," he said. I smiled.

"Hi, guys!" I said, to let them know I was in the living room.

Still in his scarf and coat, Hunter ran to me and started his frenetic report. Reilly wiped out in the ice. He beat Reilly in a race. Reilly bought him some "awesome" gizmo that sounded like it might be a computer game. Reilly is the best. Reilly and he are going to go skiing this year. Reilly once went on a snowmobile. Before I could follow up on any of these statements, Hunter was onto the next. In the midst of Hunter's account of the day, Reilly walked to me and leaned down to kiss me. "Good afternoon?" he asked. "Were you able to start your holiday shopping?" I shook my head. "Don't worry about it, sweetheart. You'll get to it when you feel like it, and if you don't, you'll take care of it online." Turning to Hunter, he shouted, "Stop right there, little man." My son was my spitting image, right down to his quizzical facial expressions. "Hat off. Coat off. Hang 'em in the closet. You know the drill."

"Sounds like you two had a good time," I said, as Reilly watched Hunter struggle to get his coat sleeves through the points of the hanger.

"Yeah, it was great. Guess who we ran into?" Reilly asked. Hunter burst into the living room and told me that Daddy's friend bought them a cup of hot chocolate at Rockefeller Center.

"What friend?" I asked. "I thought you two went alone?"

"We did," he said. "We ran into Prudence. She was doing some shopping at Saks and said she came by to watch the skaters. Boy, was she was surprised to see us there."

I'll bet she was. She just *happened* to be shopping at Saks and decided to stroll over to Rockefeller Center at the exact same time Reilly and Hunter were there. How likely is that? Okay, it's not all that suspicious. Intellectually I understood that, but my heart raced like I'd just downed Excedrin with espresso. "Oh," I said, feigning serenity. "How is Prudence?"

"Seems happy," Reilly answered.

"How did she look?"

"Pretty good," he said. "She's no Sarah Peterson, but she looked nice. Healthy. Clean."

Clean? She looked clean? What man describes a woman as clean, or healthy for that matter? What was he, her doctor? And how dare she buy hot chocolate for my son and my husband. Clearly, Prudence needed to get her own life and get out of mine. And I knew just how I'd do it.

Chapter Two

The next morning I opened the Manhattan Children's School directory and found Sophie's telephone number. I spent most of last night awake thinking about the best strategy to find Prudence a new husband. I decided I would need two things. The first was good intentions. Although it was amusing to imagine Prudence on a date with a Sumo wrestler or gold-toothed wannabe rapper, I soon realized that it wasn't in me to be unkind to her.

The second thing I'd need was a support system. That is, a little help from my friends. And hers. Of course, Reilly could know nothing of my plan. He wouldn't understand. Even Gwen didn't understand when I explained it to her that morning, but she also said that she'd try anything I thought would help me get back to my old self.

To be perfectly honest, I didn't understand what was driving me to find Prudence a new husband either. My head and my heart had parted company recently. Once a well-paved two-lane highway, logic and emotion had now split—one road darting north, the other heading south. The wiser version of my newly neurotic self scolded, *Sarah, this is absurd. If there is something wrong with you or this marriage, focus on that—not a phantom ex-wife who poses absolutely no threat to you.* That was the voice of the real me. God, I missed her. This new, lesser version of me couldn't help myself. I was losing myself to an insane person who looked exactly like me.

Years ago at an Al-Anon meeting, one of the other wives of an alcoholic said that at some point in everyone's lives they lose their minds temporarily. I remember thinking she was being overly dramatic. Now, as I recalled her comment, I thought, *My time has come.*

I started going to Al-Anon when I was pregnant with Hunter. My husband, Rudy, and I had been married for two years before it occurred to me that he had a drinking problem. I'd always imagined alcoholics as homeless guys on the Bowery who pass bottles in brown bags around a flaming city garbage can. Rudy was an attorney—a prominent one at a silk stockings firm, at that. He made an impressive salary, earned bonuses every year, and used cedar shoe trees. We had season tickets to the opera. Our names were engraved in benefactor plaques at the best charities in New York. Rudy was even once featured in *Wired* magazine for his work with emerging tech companies. This was not my image of an alcoholic. To me, Rudy was simply a charming, successful guy who enjoyed heavy drinking—daily.

It was Gwen who suggested Rudy was more than just a social drinker. At first, I thought she was just on Oprah overdrive, but more and more as I watched Rudy, I realized Gwen was right. Rudy worked all the time. I mean *all* the time. Now, I know many attorneys work long hours, but they shouldn't come home at four in the morning smelling like gin and soap. The gin could not be showered off, as thankfully everything else from his late nights at the office could. One night, Rudy would be the dynamic guy I fell in love with, erupting with ideas of all of the wonderful things we were going to do together. The next day, he practically ignored me. I wasn't being oversensitive. It wasn't as though he was just in a blue mood and needed some space. Rudy was withdrawn and hostile when I dared inquire about his state. One night we were at his firm's Christmas party, and Rudy was regaling his colleagues with a story about his interaction with the guy at the deli around the corner. He seemed to be having the time of his life at the black-tie gala. He never missed a server passing with champagne, and after probably about three too many, his voice started getting far louder than anyone else's. He wasn't upset; he'd just lost control of his volume control. I elbowed him and said, "Rudy, keep it down." Suffice it to say, this did not go over well.

In the cab ride home, Rudy proved just how loud he was able to get as he shouted that I'd embarrassed him in front of his partners. I doubt anyone even heard me, but he was convinced they were all laughing about how "whipped" he was. (I'll spare you the full verbiage.) Even the taxi driver asked if everything was "okay back there."

"Just fucking drive," was Rudy's reply.

"Don't tell me to fucking drive, mon. I don't have to take that shit from fares. You can get out and walk."

"What's your license number, you dumb fuck?" Rudy shouted at our driver.

"See it for yourself," the driver said, as he pulled over. "The lady can stay but you get out."

There was never any question in my mind that I'd get out of the taxi with Rudy and hail another for the rest of the trip back uptown, though sometimes I fantasized about what it would have been like to leave him behind that night. Of course, we all have to live in the real world, but I confess that on more than one occasion, I imagined what it would be like to leave Rudy on the curb permanently. I decided if things hadn't improved with him by our fifth anniversary, I would definitely leave. At that point, no one would be able to say I hadn't made a valiant effort to make it work.

I got pregnant with Hunter during one of Rudy and my many honeymoon periods. These were weeks filled with apologies, promises, and earnest attempts by Rudy to control his temper and spend more time at home. But Rudy didn't do moderation. We never had quiet nights with a movie rental and popcorn. It was either complete physical and emotional absence, or over-the-top gestures like expensive jewelry, five-star restaurants, and daily roses. I had only one rule with Reilly when we first started dating—no roses. Every time I see them, I quite unfairly ask of the bearer, *What's the louse done now?*

Roses are a thorny issue with me also because there were far too many of them at Rudy's funeral, a day marked with not only loss, but abject humiliation. I knew that when guests offered me their sympathy, it wasn't simply for the loss of my six-month-old baby's father; it was for the circumstances surrounding his death.

Not surprisingly, Rudy was a casualty of his own drunk driving. I'm thankful that he didn't injure any other drivers on the road, but he did take one of the firm's paralegals, Madeline, to her death as well. I met her twice at holiday parties. Young. Attractive. Blonde. I can only assume she and my husband were having an affair since they were driving to New Jersey, where Madeline lived, at eleven at night.

The police officer who came to deliver the news to me assured me that Rudy and Madeline were killed instantly. "Chances are they didn't know what hit 'em," the officer said as sympathetically as he could after having delivered this message hundreds of times. *Lucky them,* I did not say aloud. The officer went on to say that neither Rudy nor his tart mistress felt a moment of pain, so I vowed I'd do likewise. I inhaled deeply, thanked the officer for his time, and closed the door on this chapter of my life. I stayed up all night rocking Hunter, despite the fact that he slept soundly and needed no extra coddling. As I looked at his pudgy face, his gumdrop nose, and puckered lips, I promised myself I'd focus on the future and not dwell on the past. Rudy was gone, and that meant it would be especially important for me to be a strong parent, since I now had to fill the role of both mother and father. At seven the next morning, I called the firm and told Rudy's secretary that my husband had been killed in an auto accident.

"Oh my God!" she shrieked. "You're kidding!"

Yes, Kendra, I am kidding, I thought. *Isn't that hilarious? Rudy's dead and so is his paralegal. They were probably having sex while driving. Nah, just joshing. He's got the flu. Gotcha good, though, didn't I?!*

Six years later, I picked up the same telephone and dialed Sophie's number to invite her son Oscar over for a play date. More important, I needed her input on what kind of man would be best for Prudence.

"Hello. Is this Sophie?" I asked, as she answered the phone. She confirmed. "This is Sarah Peterson. Our boys go to school together."

"Oh, yeah, Reilly's new wife. How are you, Sarah?"

"Just fine, thank you," I lied. "And you?"

"Good, good. So what's up?"

"Oh," I said, a bit startled by her directness. It seemed one step above asking why I called. "I wanted to invite Oscar over to play this afternoon if you don't have other plans. I know it's short notice, but—"

"This actually works perfectly. Devie was invited to the Nutcracker so I was going to take Oscar Christmas shopping, but I'm sure he'd rather play," she said. I heard screeching in the background, which I could translate as approval from her son. "That really takes a load off me, Sarah. Thanks."

"I do hope you won't rush off too quickly. I was hoping you'd stay for tea," I offered.

"Tea?" she asked.

"Tea," I confirmed. "My friend Gwen will be here, too. I've always thought the two of you would get along nicely."

"Well, okay."

Gwen arrived a half hour before Sophie was due. "What's the plan of action?" she asked. She tossed her heavy red leather tote bag onto my floor, seemingly without any regard for its obscenely high price tag. She says they're indestructible, but frankly, when I see Gwen's stuffed purses bending her ninety-five-pound frame, it's not the bags I worry about.

"Gwen, please. I don't want it to feel so contrived."

"You want an organic setup?" she said, laughing.

"It's not a setup," I replied. "Our sons go to school together. She seems like a lovely person. Why not befriend her?"

"This is Gwenny you're talking to," she said. "You can drop the Goodie Two Shoes routine. I remember you when you were fun," she teased. "You're using this woman to pump info about Prudence. I'm fine with that. Just tell me how I can help."

The crassness of it all repelled me, including Gwen's blind acceptance. I suppose she was being loyal, but what I really needed was someone to remind me that I was not a user. I was a good person, above this sort of thing. As I picked up the phone to call Sophie and cancel, I heard a woman's and a boy's voices ascending the stairs to our front door. It was too late to cancel, but I decided to call off my plan. Either way I sliced it, I was not acting like the person I was raised to be.

The doorbell rang and I reminded myself of the holiday film *It's a Wonderful Life.* Oh sure, vowing not to execute one's twisted plan is hardly the stuff of an angel earning her wings. But it marked the moment for me. The moment I decided to go through with the boys' play date—and women's tea—with no agenda. I breathed freely for a moment, feeling like my old, sensible self again. The bell rang again.

"Wanna see my trains?!" Hunter shot at Oscar, as he ran to greet him. He didn't answer. The two of them just ran downstairs, beating the steps with the cadence of a rainstorm. It always amazed me how kids socialized without all of the niceties like, *Hello . . . come in . . . can I get you something to drink . . . are you ready for the holidays?* I suppose I'd worry about my six-year-old boy if he were to ask another if he were prepared for the holidays.

"Hello, Sophie." I held the door open and took her red coat, which was made from what could only be described as Muppet fur. And yet, she made it work. I always envied people who took risks with fashion. It was as if they were making a statement: *I can pull this off.* I might be able to, but I'd be too aware of other people's reactions to carry it off with any degree of confidence. "Come on in. Can I get you something to drink?"

"Fabu coat," Gwen said, never leaving her chair. "Where did you get it?"

Figures she'd like it. Gwen would get lost in a coat like that. Her tiny, angular brunette head would stick out from the top and her twiggy long legs would dangle out from the bottom like bamboo.

"Estate sale, if can you believe!" Sophie said, energized by the compliment.

"I can't! It's so, so—"

"So gaudy it transcends to chic?" Sophie proposed.

"Yes! I was going to say unique, but yes, it's so tacky, it's cute. Gaudy transcended to chic. I love it. I can't believe you got it at an estate sale. It looks so modern." Gwen extended her hand and introduced herself.

I excused myself from the Elmo-fur coat love fest and stepped into the kitchen to boil water and set out tea bags, sugar, cream, and spoons. I raised my voice to offer them snowball cookies, but neither could hear me amid their laughter.

I returned to the living room with my grandmother's Chinese teapot filled only with hot water, and three cups with Morning Lotus painted on them.

Sophie picked a tea bag, dropped it in her cup, then folded her hands across her lap. "So tell me, ladies," she began, "what can I do for you today?"

Gwen and I looked at each other stunned. She raised a single eyebrow as if to ask me how we should address such boldness. "Sarah thought it would be nice if we could all get acquainted, that's all."

"Oh, why's that?" Sophie asked, smiling as she blew steam from the top of her teacup.

"We have boys in the same class," I said, not really sure how to respond if she continued. In my job as a reporter, I ask tough, even impolite questions, but socially, this type of directness was unheard of. "You seem like an interesting person," I stumbled.

"Oh, because I was certain your invitation had something to do with Prudence."

"Prudence?" I said, because nothing else came to mind.

"Yes, Prudence. Reilly's first wife," Sophie said, not sharply, but not softly either. "When you called, I figured it had something to do with her."

"Whatever would give you a silly idea like that?" Gwen asked. I immediately cringed because I could guess Sophie's reply.

Sophie was not combative. She had an air of serene fortitude that let us know that neither Gwen nor I was going to rattle her. She was pleasant, but more curious to see how we would respond to her brand of candor. "Well, Sarah and I have seen each other every morning at school since September and she's never so much as said hello. Yesterday she found out that I'm friends with Prudence and now—" Sophie concluded her thought by gesturing with her arms as if to say, *Here I am.* She smirked victoriously and finished, "Tea and holiday cookies and all. I hope you'll forgive me if I'm mistaken, but the timing struck me as odd. I thought you might have invited me here in hopes that I'd leak information about Prudence."

"Information?" Gwen asked, as if the notion was absurd. "Why would Sarah want information about Prudence?!"

I know Gwen meant well, but her defensive questions only gave Sophie an opportunity to advance her case.

"Oh, why are women ever curious about other women?" Sophie asked.

It was unsettling to be so obviously transparent to strangers. Sophie immediately knew my invitation was loaded with ulterior motives. What else could she see in me? Did she know I was coming unglued? Did everyone?

Gwenny jumped in, again trying to save me. "Well, now that you've brought her up. How is Prudence?"

"Ladies, you seem nice enough, but the gig is up. Why don't you come clean and tell me what you're up to?" Sophie shot back. How I longed for the moments we shared over Elmo-fur coats.

"We were just curious, that's all," Gwen said, gently setting her teacup on the table.

"I'm sorry, Sophie," I said, silently reminding myself that I'd decided against finding Prudence a new husband. As soon as my guests left, I was going to hop in a cab and make my way to Saks for some retail therapy. It was time to focus on my own mental health instead of filling my head with diversions from my holiday blues. "It was inappropriate for me to ask about Prudence. I hope she's well, and please send her my best."

"You have a beautiful home," Sophie said. I lived with my parents in this brownstone on West Seventy-fourth Street for my entire childhood before they moved to Greenwich, Connecticut and sold it to me well below market value. My parents did things a bit backward, retiring to the suburbs, but they've always marched to the beat of their own drummer. When everyone was carrying on about Aruba, they stayed true to Barbados. When all of their friends were engaged in mortal combat to get reservations at the city's newest, trendy restaurant, they remained loyal to their favorite chef at Lutece.

"Thank you," Gwen replied. "Since Prudence got the loft in the divorce settlement, Reilly was lucky to marry a woman with a location like this."

"Back to discussing Prudence now, are we?" Sophie asked.

"Sophie, I do apologize. I think we've gotten off on the wrong foot," I said. "I know you're new to New York, but apartments are a pretty big deal here. A good one is harder to find than a good man, so we tend to prattle on a bit about our digs. All Gwen was saying is that a man in Manhattan is lucky to go from a loft in SoHo to a brownstone on the upper West Side without so much as a stint in a residence hotel." Gwen and I laughed, but Sophie did not join us.

"I had to screw three doormen to find my place," Gwen joked.

"Oh, Sophie, she's kidding. I've known Gwen since high school and she's a complete prude," I said. Gulp. "I mean she doesn't have casual sex."

"It's always a black-tie event," Gwen said uncomfortably. The tension flooded my living room.

Sophie reached for her purse and started to stand. "Clearly you two have some sort of ax to grind with Prudence, and I'm not going to be any part of it. I may be new to New York, but I can spot bitches with an agenda in any city."

I felt a lump in my throat and tears begin welling in my eyes seconds before I burst into tears. Crumbling, I sobbed, "She's right!" I bawled into my palms. My hand lotion smelled so nice, I wish I could've enjoyed it. "I am a bitch."

"No you're not, Sarah!" Gwen said, straightening upright in her chair. "Look, missy, I don't know where you come off calling us bitches or saying we're plotting a scheme against precious Prudence, but you are dead wrong!"

Sophie scrunched her mouth to one side, skeptically. "Sarah just said I was *right*. She called herself a bitch!"

"She's out of her mind!" Gwen defended, sort of.

"Look, I owe you both an apology," I interrupted. "Sophie, you were right. I did want to know about Prudence, but it's not what you think. I wasn't going to do anything malicious. I just wanted to find her a new husband." I sighed at the absurdity of it. "I don't know what's going on with me these days, but I'd feel more comfortable if she had a new man in her life. But none of that matters because as soon as you rang the doorbell, I decided I couldn't go through with it."

"Why do you care if Prudence has a husband?" Sophie asked. "Prudence dumped Reilly in case he failed to mention. I see her every week and she's never brought up his name once."

"She hasn't?" I sniffed gratefully. "Didn't he mean anything to her?"

Sophie laughed. "Look, I've been trying to fix up Prudence for months now, but she's not interested. Ever since she got back from Italy last summer, all she wants to do is work on her wire sculptures. Jennifer and I have tried to fix her up on dozens of blind dates, but she refuses. She says she did enough dating to last her a lifetime. She says if the right man is out there, he'll find her."

"Really?" Gwen asked, fascinated and appalled. "Does she know she has a better chance of getting struck by lightning?"

"I think that theory was disproved in the nineties," Sophie returned.

"What are wire sculptures?" I chimed in now that my eyes had dried.

Sophie exhaled deeply as if she was contemplating whether or not she trusted Gwen and me. "You two wanted to find Prudence a new man out of the goodness of your hearts?"

"Not just that," Gwen shot, in an attempt to establish credibility. "Sarah's lost her mind and she says this will calm her nerves."

"Have you considered Paxil?" Sophie asked.

Gwen shrieked with delight. "That's what *I* said!

Sophie, bitch's honor, I'm telling you, Sarah wouldn't harm a fly. Look how easily you made her cry. Do you honestly think she has some nefarious plan for Prudence?"

"And what about you?" Sophie asked. "What's in this for you?"

"What do you mean?"

"I mean why are you spending your time concocting plans to set up your friend's new husband's ex-wife? What's your angle?" Sophie asked.

"My angle?" Gwen repeated. "I have no *angle.* This is what friends do for each other. My friend said she'd feel better if her new husband's ex-wife had a new husband, so I said, darling, it sounds absolutely insane to me, but if it'll bring you out of your funk, count me in."

"I helped Prudence with this last time. It's a big job," Sophie said.

"It's the season of giving," Gwen explained, folding her arms.

"What do you do?" Sophie asked.

"What do you mean what do I do?"

"For work? What's your job?"

Gwen knit her brows. "I'm a philanthropist. I have lunch."

"Oh," Sophie said as if that explained everything. "And just out of curiosity, when you said bitch's honor, does that mean you're a graduate of—"

"Vilma Veeter's Bitchcraft class?" Gwen finished, as though they were two sorority sisters just discovering each other's Pi Beta Phi charm bracelets.

"Yes!" They clasped hands.

"You remember the pledge, right?" Sophie asked.

"How can I forget?"

"Excuse me," I chimed in. "Do you mind if I ask who in good God's name Vilma Veeter is and what bitch's honor means?"

"Another time, Sarah," Gwen dismissed, still clasping hands with Sophie. "Shouldn't Sarah take that class?"

"She'd never cry like that again," Sophie said, laughing. "Seriously, Gwenny," *Gwenny?!* "you remember what Vilma said about the Bitch's Code of Honor. If you're lying to me, you're saying it's okay for me to take revenge, right?"

"Of course," Gwen assured.

"You're saying that if it turns out you're lying to me, I can throw a rock through Sarah's beautiful window here, right?"

"Absolutely," Gwen said, filling with the enthusiasm of promise.

"If you are planning anything that will hurt my friend Prudence—a fellow bitch by the way—"

"No doubt," added Gwen.

"If you do anything that hurts her, I will strike back by Photoshopping Sarah's head onto Paris Hilton's sex tapes and blasting them over the Internet," Sophie said.

"Absolutely!"

"Wait a second," I said. "I don't want my face on Paris Hilton's naked body."

"Then don't screw my friend," Sophie said.

"Yeah, Sarah, it's simple. Don't screw her friend."

A moment later, I found myself locking middle fingers with my two compatriots and reciting some crazy Bitch's Pledge of Allegiance.

"Okay, so here's the deal," Sophie began. "You remember how Prudence took off the day after your wedding last June? Well, while she was in Rome, she volunteered for a mosaic restoration project, where she met this artist who taught her how to twist wire every which way. So now she's making sculptures full-time. She quit her job in accounting and everything. I don't think she's had a single date since she and Matt broke up."

"Matt?" Gwen asked.

"The guy Prudence dumped Reilly for," Sophie said.

"And you say she has no regrets?" I asked. "She never misses him?"

Sophie began, "I think she missed him more when they were married."

"What does that mean?" Gwen asked. "Do we have any sherry?"

While searching for something sweeter for Gwenny, I explained that Prudence was suggesting that Reilly was an absentee husband. Pouring, I defended him. "Well, I don't find that to be a problem."

"Oh, okay, I'll be sure to tell her that he's changed his ways," Sophie said. "Maybe she'll want him back now."

"You obviously passed the bitch class," I said, smiling.

"If you two want to help find Prudence the man of her dreams, by all means you're welcome to help. Jen and I have been trying to find her a man for months now, so consider yourselves on the committee. But I'm warning you, if you cross me and screw Prudence, it'll be the worst mistake you ever make." She walked to the doorway that led to the lower level of my home. "Oscar, time to go!"

Gwen mouthed, *I like her.* Oddly enough, I did too.

Chapter Three

That night I dreamt I was Paris Hilton, but as luck would have it, I wasn't ripping loose enjoying her party life. My wrists were bound with telephone wire and I was tied to the hand strap in the back of a Checker Cab. As I struggled to free myself, the driver turned around and asked if I needed help. The driver was six-year-old Thomas, one of Hunter's classmates. Of course, it was unusual that a child was driving a taxi, but Thomas has cerebral palsy and is confined to a wheelchair so it was that much more implausible that he was a cabbie. Because he speaks with an electronic device, I've never heard his voice before, but in my dream, Thomas had an English accent and began singing the Happy Snowflake song. Then he crawled into the backseat to help me untie my hands. "Watch the road!" I shrieked, as car lights swept into us. I bolted upright into consciousness, waking Reilly beside me.

"Another bad dream?" he asked, placing his hand on my back.

"It was nothing," I said and urged him to go back to sleep. Thomas had been on my mind a lot recently. Weeks ago, he and his family were featured on the cover of *New York Times Magazine* because his father, Richard, fought to reform the city school system to create an immersion program for kids with disabilities. More than that, the child was on my mind because I saw them on Friday at the school holiday party. I couldn't help notice how his father posed such a stark contrast to me. He bounced all over the place, amusing the children. He made silly faces and seemed as though he were genuinely filled with delight to be with his son's classmates. If anyone could feel sorry for himself, it was Richard, whose son's list of challenges dwarfs my myriad of trivial complaints. Yet he seemed thrilled, while I was weighted with the troubles of the world.

Sophie, Jen, Gwen, and I were scheduled to have lunch the following day while Hunter and Reilly saw a movie about Santa Claus as an action hero. In the animated film, the North Pole is the target of attack by a band of rogue reindeer led by Rudolf, who was tired of being laughed at and called names.

The four of us were supposed to bring a list of names of single men we thought would be a good match for Prudence. Thomas's father, Richard, came to mind as a good one for Prudence until I remembered he was already married—to an attractive doctor, no less. Only one of the fathers in

Hunter's class was single and he was so fat, he looked like Shrek with white skin. As Reilly snored beside me, I began listing all of the smart, interesting, single men I'd interviewed over the years.

At seven in the morning, I bolted upright in bed. This time, it wasn't a bad dream but, rather, an idea I was surprised I hadn't thought of earlier—Doug Phillips. Doug is an absolutely stunning-looking stock broker who would give Prudence all the attention she ever needed. He was so full of compliments that every time I saw Doug, I felt like the billion bucks he probably earned for his clients that day. I remembered Doug telling me that he got into the office no later than six every morning. When I heard Reilly's shower running and *Sesame Street* on downstairs, I realized that I could call quickly from my cell phone. I stepped out onto the bedroom balcony that overlooked the small yard, forgetting for a moment that it was winter. But only for a moment, as the terra-cotta flooring sent chills through my bare feet straight up to my arms. The crisp air filled my flannel nightgown. I let down my ponytail, so I'd at least have a scarf of hair.

"Hey, gorgeous," Doug answered.

"Hi, Doug, it's Sarah Peterson," I said, not sounding quite as confident as I'd hoped I would.

"I know who it is. Whaddya think, I answer the phone like that all the time?" It occurred to me that he just might. "Happy holidays. It's been a while. Doin' a story?"

"No, actually, I was calling for, well, not for business," I said.

"Then for pleasure? Excellent," Doug said. The fact that Doug looks quite a bit like Pierce Brosnan makes his persistent flirting bearable. Okay, enjoyable. The truth is that even though I know better, I always held the hope that Doug was sincere when he flirted with me. That maybe he did think I was gorgeous. That maybe when he looked at me as though I were the only woman in the world it wasn't a well-rehearsed routine. That maybe I was the only woman who could tame this dangerous cad. Thankfully, my head was always in charge of my heart. Doug asked me out three times before I met Reilly, and while it was always incredibly tempting, I knew it would lead to heartbreak—mine. So I declined. Unfettered, Doug always asked again. Until he didn't. But whenever I saw him, he made it clear that he found me attractive. *Gorgeous* was what he called me, as if he knew just what words would make me tick. I've been called pretty. Reilly even says I'm beautiful. But Doug was the only one who's ever characterized me as gorgeous. Gorgeous is flowing waves of platinum blond hair, not a gold bob. Gorgeous is bedroom eyes, not home-office specs. Gorgeous is Victoria's Secret, not L.L. Bean. I am pretty. I feel certain of this. I feel equally certain that I'm not gorgeous, though when Doug says it, I honestly believe he just might mean it. Rudy used to call me Hot Stuff when we were together. I miss the lies of sexy men.

"Well, I *am* calling for pleasure, Doug, but not mine," I said, reining in my desire to add a cool, smoky tone that suggested smoldering sex between us.

"Oh ye of little faith," Doug said, laughing. "Most guys don't know how to please a woman, but I promise you that's not the case with me, Gorgeous," he said. How such smarmy shit can sound charming was beyond me.

"Do you realize it's seven in the morning?" I said. "Seriously, Doug, I have a friend I want you to meet. I think you'd be perfect for each other."

"What's she look like?" he asked. I heard him begin to peck at his keyboard in the background.

"Oh," I said, taken aback. I suppose it was reasonable for him to want to know about Prudence's appearance. Maybe I was most surprised by how quickly he got over me.

Snap out of it, Sarah! a stern inner voice reprimanded. It was mine! I was back. Please, dear God, don't let this be a cameo appearance. I need my old, level-headed self back in the driver's seat. *You have a fine husband in Reilly O'Shaugnessay. Stop flirting with this womanizing freak show and get back to work.*

"Her name is Prudence and she's an accountant. She used to be, at least. Now she's an artist. Oh, right, she's got short black hair and blue eyes. She's really very pretty. Very thin, though."

"Can you send her over digitally?" Doug asked, now all business.

"Send her over digitally?"

"Her photo," he clipped. "Does she have a website or something with her photo on it?"

I heard Reilly step into the bedroom and knock on the glass door to the balcony. With his towel wrapped around his waist, he shrugged his unclothed shoulders as if to ask what I was doing outside. I held my finger up, signaling that I'd need only another minute.

"I don't think I have a photo of her, but she's very pretty," I said, hurried.

"No offense, but a woman's idea of pretty usually isn't the same as a guy's. Can you tell me someone famous she looks like?"

"Um, Parker Posey?"

"Who?"

"Hillary Swank?" I offered. "Look, why don't you go out with her and see for yourself what she looks like, and what *she's* like while you're at it?!"

"Because, Gorgeous, time is money and if I'm going out to lunch with Penelope—"

"Prudence," I corrected.

"Whatever. If I go out with a woman, it means I'm not doing something else. I want to make sure my time is well spent. I have a short list of things I like to do. Making money, playing basketball, watching the Yankees, getting laid—all high on the list. Wasting an hour with some woman I have no chemistry with—*not* on the list. Now, if it was you we were talking about, there'd be no questions other than where and when."

"Doug, I really ought to mention that I'm married now, so this little flirtation we have going is no longer appropriate," I said, feeling quite satisfied that I'd taken part ownership of a game that had been his. It was the old responsible Sarah coming back to life. As I hung the Olympic medal of moral superiority around my own neck, I realized it had been a while since Doug spoke. "Are you still there?"

"I'm here," he said.

"What's wrong?" I asked. But I knew. Poor Doug was devastated that I was married now. It hit him in a place he hadn't known existed. I was the cause of this womanizing louse realizing that he had a deep chamber within his heart reserved for true love.

"Nothing's wrong," he said. "I just thought you knew."

"Knew what?"

"I'm married too."

"Since when?!" I shouted loud enough that Reilly heard. Now fully dressed, he gestured to see if I needed his help.

"Since ninety-four," Doug said. "I guess you don't want me to go out with your friend anymore," he said, though his statement had a twinge of a question mark.

"No! I certainly do not, you, you, you adulterer!"

"Okay, then, never mind with the picture," he said.

"Never mind with the picture?! Is that all you have to say for yourself?"

"Merry Christmas?"

I slammed down the phone and returned into my warm home. "What's wrong?!" Reilly asked, surprised to see me stampede around the house, especially at this hour. "Bad interview?"

"Very bad interview," I said.

Reilly shrugged. "I assume we're doing carryout

again tonight?" I was struck by the guilty realization that I hadn't prepared a meal for my husband or child in nearly a month. Who had the energy to cook every day? Okay, no one was asking me to cook every day. Just recently I wasn't able to do much of anything *any* day.

"Meaning what?" I shot defensively.

"Meaning I've got a coupon for the new Chinese place on the corner and was wondering if you wanted to give 'em a try," Reilly returned.

I cried the tears of decompression, which can easily be mistaken for tears of joy. I wrapped my arms around my new husband's neck and sobbed into his sweater. "Do I tell you enough how wonderful you are?"

"Sarah, what's the matter?" Reilly lifted my chin and looked into my eyes. "You're not yourself these days. I've never seen you get so choked up about Chinese food."

"It's not the food, Reilly. It's how sweet you are. I guess I didn't realize how much I missed being loved this way. I guess I'm realizing that I never was loved this way before you."

"And that makes you cry?" he asked.

"Yes," I sniffled. "I know I don't make much sense these days. Believe me, crying over being loved is the least of my craziness this holiday season."

"Do you want to see someone?" Reilly asked.

"I most certainly do not!" I shot before I realized he was talking about a therapist and not another man.

"Let's not dismiss it out of hand, Sarah. Maybe

you're having the holiday blues, but if by the New Year you're still not feeling well, we need to talk about counseling for you." I nodded in agreement. "I'll pick up some Chinese on the way home, and I promised Hunter we'd watch *Freaky Friday* tonight. Y'in?"

"*Freaky Friday?* Isn't that a girl movie?"

"You said *All Santa's Deer* was too macho. I thought you'd be happy to see him get into a chick flick."

I smiled and agreed. "I'm lucky to be your wife. Hunter's hockey bag is packed by the door. I get him at three, right?" Reilly nodded his head. "Six for dinner, seven for the movie?"

"Ten for—" Reilly raised his eyebrows suggestively.

"Pencil me in," I said.

"Pencil? You expecting a better offer?"

"Reilly, there is no better offer," I said, plopping myself onto the bed and weeping again.

"What's wrong now?!" Reilly said, putting his arm around me.

"I don't know. You get going. Hunter's not dressed yet, nor has he eaten," I admitted. "His bag is packed, though!"

"Sarah, I hate to ask this, but is Hunter's bag packed with the same gear that was in it from yesterday's camp?"

"Yes. He doesn't need new skates today, does he?"

"Honey, he needs new socks and shirt. His mouthpiece needs to be cleaned. Forget it; I'll take care of it myself," Reilly said, in a tone that suggested it may be he who would cancel our ten o'clock appointment.

As my taxi was stopped at a red light, I watched a blind woman cross Twenty-third Street with her dog. The day was as gray and icy as New York could get. Not the picturesque city Christmas featured in postcards, the ones where the Flatiron Building looks like a generously iced slice of cake sitting on a plate dotted with electric gumdrops. As they fought the cold, most people held an expression of steely determination. The happiest person who crossed in front of my taxi was the blind woman, who, when reaching the sidewalk, grabbed a treat and held it out for her dog. She patted his head, laughed, and continued their walk.

Where was she going? Why was she out walking and not in a warm taxi like me? And how could she stay happy in the face of blindness? I felt like such a failure of a human being that I was reduced to tears over trivialities like Doug Phillips and Chinese food when people had real problems to deal with this holiday season.

"Ma'am?" the taxi driver asked. "You okay back there?"

"Excuse me?" I asked, realizing that I was crying again. "Oh, thank you. I'm okay," I said recomposing myself. "I always get a little sad around the holidays."

"You and my wife," the driver said.

Oh, then you certainly mustn't drive yourself and your mistress to your death and leave your wife behind with an infant or she may find this time of year especially difficult in the future.

"You know us women," I said instead. I despised myself for not being more like the blind woman who was enjoying the present instead of dwelling on whatever hardships were behind her. I had Reilly now. My son had never been happier. My family was finally complete. It seemed that if ever there was a time to be celebrant, it was now.

I paid the driver and gave him an extra ten dollars.

"Sorry it was a bumpy ride," he said, thanking me for the tip.

"No it wasn't. Your driving was perfect."

"You sure are sweet, lady. Most people woulda been bitchin' nonstop about those last three potholes."

I grabbed my purse, my umbrella and checked again to be sure I put my wallet back in my purse. "There were no potholes. Everything was as smooth as silk. Thanks again."

I walked into the restaurant to find Gwen seated and chatting with our waiter. She placed her hand on his conspiratorially and the two laughed. She saw me and popped like toast, waving her hand and smiling. "Sarah, this is David; he'll be our server today," Gwen said giddily. "He's pre-med *and* Jewish."

"She only loves me for my resume," David said. "Can I get you something to drink? Catch up with Gwenny?"

"I don't drink," I said flatly.

"Since when? We drank sherry yesterday," Gwen reminded me.

"I'll give you two a moment to decide," David said, excusing himself.

"Don't you think he's a little young for you?" I said, trying not to sound annoyed. I can't imagine why her flirtation with the twenty-year-old waiter would irritate me, but it did.

"Quite a bit too young for me, thank you for rubbing it in," Gwen said, laughing. "But my niece Jessica is transferring to NYU in three weeks, and I think David would be perfect for her."

"Why, because he's Jewish?"

"No, because he's a scuba enthusiast, loves cooking, is into jazz, and is a complete cutie pie."

"Oh," I said. She showed me.

Every night, I go to sleep early thinking that when I wake up, my spirits will naturally lift. I convince myself that I'm overtired, though honestly I've been doing less than ever before. And sleeping more.

"Why do you look like that?" Gwen asked. "Are you ill?"

"Like what?"

Gwen looked shocked by the question. "Like *that.* No makeup, messy hair. Your outfit looks like you threw it together while trying to escape a fire."

"I'm busy with the holidays. I don't have time for primping," I said. "Look, there's Sophie."

Gwen turned to wave Sophie over to our table and quickly shot, "Since when is showering primping?"

"Hey, girls," Sophie said, leaning in to kiss Gwen, then me. Decidedly warmer than yesterday, she asked if I had a cold. "Your eyes are all bloodshot. Were you crying?"

"*It's a Goddamned Wonderful Life,*" Gwen explained. "Gets her every time. I tell her not to watch that sap, but she can't help herself."

"Aw, that's sweet." Sophie tilted her head and sat. "Jen can't make it today, but she gave me her list of names and said to remind you that we're putting our trust in you two. I told her that I *know* you're doing this with Prudence's best interests at heart, and that I already made a bunch of threats that we don't need to rehash, right?"

Gwen and I nodded. David returned to our table and Sophie and Gwen ordered wine. "Let's share a bottle," Sophie suggested.

"Sarah doesn't drink anymore," Gwen said.

"Are you an alcoholic?" she asked. I raised my hand to my chest in shock.

"Do I look like an alcoholic?" I said, realizing I should have taken the time to shower and put on a decent outfit.

"Sarah, don't take offense. I didn't want to be the one to toss you off the wagon if you're a recovering alcoholic. Let's order a bottle," Sophie persisted.

"Do I strike you as an alcoholic?!" I asked again.

"I don't know. You could be. Are we going to go white or red?" Sophie looked up from her wine list.

"Let's get champagne!" Gwen suggested. "I

think I may have found my niece's future husband in our server, David."

"The one with the cute butt?" Sophie asked. Gwen concurred.

"Excuse me!" I interrupted. "I would like to know why Sophie thinks *I'm* an alcoholic. I have never had a problem moderating anything in my entire life."

"Is she always like this?" Sophie asked Gwen.

"Like what?" I demanded. Tears filled my eyes again and I would not have a holiday classic or blind woman to pin it on this time. *Breathe deeply,* I instructed myself. *Recite the Greek alphabet, then count from ninety-nine to one by threes.*

"Sarah, are you okay?" Gwen asked. "You look like you're going to pop your cork."

I slammed my hands on the table, a gesture so new to me I believe my palms were shocked. "First, you say I look sick," I pointed to Sophie. "Then you say I look depressed. Then you say I look like an alcoholic. I never knew how superficial people could be. I opt for a more natural look one day, and suddenly I'm ready for the Betty Ford Clinic!"

Gwen and Sophie eyeballed each other carefully. Gwen was the first to speak up. "Honey, no one said you're depressed. Are you?"

"Of course not!" I said. "Things have never been better. I have a new husband, a beautiful, healthy son, a thriving career. What would I have to be depressed about other than being told I look like a wreck and a drunk?!"

Sophie chimed in, "Hey, my father is a recovering alcoholic. He's more buttoned up than you, Sarah. Well, than how you usually are. And my ex-husband is a total drunk and he looks pretty together most of the time. All I meant was that if you were on the wagon, more power to you, that's all." Sophie placed her hand on mine. "Order whatever you want."

On cue, David arrived. "A bottle of Cristal," I said. After he left, I leaned in to ask Sophie if her ex was really an alcoholic.

"You don't have to whisper, Sarah," Sophie said, smiling. "He can't hear you in San Diego."

It amazed me how open people were about their lives. I'd known Sophie for less than three hours and she told me more about her life than I'd told my closest friends. No one knows Rudy was an alcoholic. Well, they don't know it from my telling them. My own parents don't know that Rudy had a passenger in his car the night he crashed. I was like a treasure chest at the bottom of the sea locked and wrapped with chains. Sophie was like a wishing well with secrets tossed about as carelessly as pennies.

That's one of the reasons I only attended two Al-Anon meetings. I hated how everyone would tell every personal detail of their lives as if there were no boundaries to their privacy. I detested how everyone would say, "Hi, Sarah!" in unison after I introduced myself. And I loathed how people said, "Thank you for sharing," when someone finished speaking. It was like being licked by strangers.

I was compelled to hear more about Sophie's husband. Specifically, how she came to leave him.

"Sophie, please tell me if I'm being too personal, but did you leave San Diego to get away from your ex?" I asked.

"That's personal?" Sophie said laughing. "Yep, I told Bob that he had until July Fourth to get sober or I was leaving. I thought that was a good date to declare his independence from alcohol or my independence from him." Gwen and I nodded. This woman was like a superheroine. Like, Super Ass-Kicking Girl with fire that shot from her boots so when she kicked your ass, it burned too.

David poured our champagne and I began to relax. I was laughing with friends. Tonight I would have Chinese food with my fabulous new husband and our wonderful son. We would watch a goofy movie on a plasma television set in a fully owned brownstone on the upper West Side of the most fabulous city on the planet at the most wonderful time of the year. I once was blind but now I see. "Waiter, another bottle please."

Chapter Four

As Sophie, Gwen, and I finished our lunch we forgot to discuss the plan to find a new man for Prudence. Okay, we were a little drunk. Sophie leaned down to grab her purse. "I've got it," I said, offering to pay. Sophie smiled and pulled a manila folder from her bag, opened it, and passed a sheet of paper each to Gwen and me.

"An agenda?" I asked. Sophie confirmed.

Gwen glanced at the items and said, "Wow, impressive. 'Objective: Find soul mate for Prudence. Deadline: January 1. Budget: Unspecified.' Do we need a budget?"

"Sarah does," Sophie said. "Prudence spent close to ten thousand dollars to find you."

"You make her sound like a mail-order bride," Gwen said. "Why do we only have two weeks to find this guy?"

"I've got to be honest with you, Sarah. We're all

going to lose steam for this after two weeks, so let's just make a strong push over the holidays and be done with it by the New Year. Besides, the holidays are the perfect time to smoke out all the single guys. We should have a Christmas Eve party. Whoever's alone that night definitely doesn't have a wife and kids."

"No parties," I said. "Reilly told me about Prudence's Wife of Reilly party and he said it was humiliating for him."

"Eh"—Sophie waved her hand dismissively—"he was caught off guard by it. It was a beautiful party."

"It sounded dreadfully tacky," I reaffirmed my position on events.

"What about a New Year's Eve party?" Gwen suggested.

"Oh, that's good!" Sophie said.

"No, it's *not* good! Parties are in very poor taste."

The two glanced at each other. "*Parties* are in bad taste?" Gwen asked. "Because you and I have been to some lovely events together, Sarah."

"Charity events, Gwen."

"Think of *this* as a charity event," said Sophie.

"No, no, no! No parties," I demanded.

"Okay," they said, in united annoyance.

"We need to think outside the box, Sarah," Gwen insisted.

Sophie rolled her eyes. "That expression is so, so cliché it's actually *in* the box," she said, before asking if I'd considered going online. "There's a new site that I think you'll like. It's supposed to be an upscale Manhattan group. Go to Singleinthe city.com and check out the men's profiles. A friend of mine tried it and said the men were terrific. Some real hotties."

Hotties?

Gwen took out a sheet of paper and suggested we share our list of single men we thought would be a good match for Prudence. "I'll start. I think the first name isn't going to be a surprise to Sarah because he's a complete hottie."

Now Gwen uses the term "hottie" too? The woman is being absorbed into Sophie's persona like a spill into a Bounty paper towel.

"He's charming, he's successful, and, as I said, extremely handsome," Gwen said, as though she expected the introduction to be followed by a drum roll.

In a deadpan wry delivery, Sophie urged Gwen to spit it out. "The suspense is killing me. I can barely stand it another moment."

"Doug Phillips," Gwen blurted, with a smile. I think she may have even blushed.

"Absolutely not," I said.

"Doug Phillips. The name sounds so familiar. Why do I know him?" Sophie said.

"Why not Doug Phillips?" Gwen said, pouting. "No parties, no Doug Phillips. I have to say, Sarah, you're not much fun these days."

"Dark hair, chiseled features?" Sophie snapped her fingers, remembering. I nodded to confirm that she was thinking of the right guy.

"I dated him last year! Right after I moved to

New York. Kind of slick but good for a few laughs," Sophie said, recalling her two dates with Doug.

"Were you aware that he is married?" I asked, knowing this was a pivotal moment in our friendship. Rudy cheated on me. Prudence cheated on Reilly. That made me the virtuous one, the one who'd never do such a thing. I couldn't very well have a friend who knowingly ran around with married men. It's simply not who I am.

"Married?!" Sophie shouted indignantly. "That fucker."

"Since when?!" Gwen gasped. "Doug's dated Kiki, Meredith, and Mimi."

"Since nineteen ninety-four," I said.

Gwen was practically in tears, as if it were she who'd been unwittingly roped into the affair. "Are you absolutely certain? You know how gossipy people can be."

"I heard it straight from the whore's mouth," I said. Or at least that's what my lunch mates claimed I said. "Gwen Weinstein, why are you sitting there agape?"

"It's just that I've never heard you use that type of language. The *whore's* mouth?"

"I said the *horse's* mouth," I claimed.

"No you didn't," Sophie chimed in. "You called that fucker a whore. And you know what, you're right. He never mentioned being married. There are a lot of women who'd go out with a married man, but at least they should have the right to give their informed consent."

"Informed consent?" I slammed my hands on the table. This season was going to be the end of my soft palms. "Sophie, we're not talking about a medical procedure. This is adultery. And lying. This guy *is* a whore. And a . . . a complete fucker."

"Well, don't get me wrong; I'm pissed as hell at the guy, but let's face it, lying and adultery, well, the two usually go hand in hand," Sophie said, with a shrug.

"So Doug's off the list," Gwen said, hoping to move us along to bachelor number two, or in this case, bachelor number one.

"I'm not done!" I said. "I think we should buy some billboards and plaster his face all over town to let people know what a fucker this guy is."

"And I think it's time to cut Sarah off," Gwen said, giggling. "It's nice to see you cut loose, but I think you're going to have a dreadful hangover from this."

"I am *not* that drunk, ladies." I shook my head like a dog drying off after a bath. It was a wonderful sensation watching the light from bulbs trail themselves, like little comets of green and red. "I'm serious, we need to buy billboards all over downtown and warn women against this jerk."

"I think the *Jesus is the Reason for the Season* people have bought up all the space for December," Gwen said. "Then they do the *every season* follow-up after that."

"We could do a Christmas theme," I slurred. "We could go religious even, like Jesus died for our sins, but one fucker is using up all of our sinning credit"—I waved my arm like a game show hostess revealing prizes—"then there's Doug big face."

"Waiter, we need some coffee please," Sophie

said. "I don't know why *you're* so upset, Sarah. It's not like you dated him or anything."

"And why aren't you *more* upset, Sophie?!"

"Because I expect nothing more from men," she said matter-of-factly. "They lie, they cheat, they gamble, they drink," she said, in a tone like she was bored reciting the list. "Expect nothing, and you'll never be disappointed."

"How about Isaac Franklin?" Gwen said, again hoping to switch gears. "He's definitely available. I was at his wife's funeral months ago."

Sophie rolled her eyes. "That's uplifting. What's he like?"

Gwen described Isaac as a "little older" than Prudence. A "young" sixty-three, she later admitted. "Don't let the age fool you. He's very active. Isaac bikes one hundred miles a week, runs in marathons, and is a squash champ."

"Gwen, have you ever met Prudence?" Sophie asked. Gwen shook her head. "She's not interested in this gray lightning of yours. She hates sports and she doesn't want another guy pressuring her to try new outdoor activities."

"That's right," I recalled, "Reilly told me about Prudence going skiing with her boyfriend and how she wound up on crutches for weeks."

Gwen perked up immediately, which seemed an odd reaction to the story. She wrote herself a note with the name "Esther Finley," a widow who lives in her building.

Sophie said Prudence was looking for someone exciting and sophisticated, "Someone who she'll have a lot of sexual chemistry with," she said.

"Oh, how 'bout Boris?!" Gwen suggested. Filling Sophie in, she explained that we knew Boris Zelkind from high school. His claim to fame was his allegedly corn-on-the-cob-sized penis. Three girls who had sex with him all swore up and down that it was the thickest thing they'd ever seen and named him "Wonder Cock," or as it was printed in the yearbook, W.C. Boris sells commercial real estate and is rumored to once have been engaged to a heroin-chic supermodel known only as Udon, like the noodle. His sense of humor was sharp and dry, but delivered with such bite, it often sent the girls in our school scurrying off to the bathroom in tears. As I was deliberating whether or not Prudence would have finally met her match with Boris, Sophie weighed in.

"Prudence doesn't want some guy with a big dick," Sophie said. "Well, that wouldn't be her sole criterion."

"He's very funny," I defended Boris. "And he likes skinny women. Udon was even thinner than Prudence."

"I think the problem here is that you two don't really know Prudence," Sophie said. "She wants somebody exciting and sexy, yes, but not a married prick or this Wonder Cock friend of yours. And she certainly doesn't need the captain of the Viagra biking team. Prudence is an artist now, and to some degree she always has been."

As Sophie continued with her characterization of Prudence, I drifted off into thought. I needed to absorb what Sophie had just said about Prudence having always been an artist, and only now starting to come into that part of herself. I wondered if there was part of me that I wasn't realizing. I was terrified to consider that perhaps I was really a musician, only I had never taken a crack at it. Maybe I was a natural athlete but had never tried sports. I took some comfort in the realization that if I truly were an artist, I would have felt drawn to it at some point in my life. Some force would have pulled me in the right direction. But I was unsettled by the feeling that, like Prudence, perhaps I too was resisting who I really was for the sake of propriety, expectation—and fear. Sure, I was making a good living writing newspaper and magazine articles. My bylines appeared in the best financial journals in the country, often the world. But I also remembered that up until college I wrote a great deal of poetry. My teachers all said I had a gift for it, but both my parents discouraged it, noting that all poets wound up depressed and poor. They tolerated it. When I was finished with my homework and assigned reading, I was allowed to write. When I was in high school my father got me a summer internship at a brokerage house, which he insisted I take instead of accepting a seat at the Young Poets Workshop at Hampshire College. The final straw was when I brought home a B- in poetry in my junior year of college. What my parents didn't realize is that this was actually a good grade in that class. We had a borderline insane visiting poet from Nicaragua who thought everything American students wrote was superficial nonsense. Ava

Pelotta's was the most intense, electrifying, and unpredictable class I'd ever taken. She would come in to class with an old worn-out shoe, throw it on the conference table, and say, "In my country, a young boy was killed wearing this one shoe. He was shot while you were complaining that you didn't want the Mayor Mac Cheese toy in your Happy Meal! Write." She'd bury her head in her hands and weep for the entire hour and a half. She'd write comments like, "Crap!" or "Utter bullshit" on our assignments, and frankly, most of the time she was right. I worked harder in that class than I ever had and, although B- was the lowest grade I'd ever received in my entire academic career, was quite proud that I hadn't ranked a D like the majority of my class.

Once I wrote a poem about two leaves in autumn. They were friends and had frolicked about together all summer. When September rolled around, one leaf fell to the ground. The friends were heartbroken to be separated. The leaf on the ground relentlessly tried to return to his familiar limb. His efforts were always fruitless. After weeks of trying to return to his branch, he saw something miraculous. His friend, along with several other leaves, fell to the ground. He never could defy gravity to return home, but if he was patient, the leaf would be with his friend once again. The teacher's comment: "Trite." All of my life, teachers told my parents what a bright student I was. Such a hard worker. So respectful of teachers. Ava hadn't received the memo that I was perfect. I worked harder than I'd ever imagined I could in her class.

Not by studying hard or memorizing the works of great poets, but by digging two layers deeper than I knew I existed within me to write poetry she wouldn't dismiss as childish nonsense. By the end of the semester, she wrote "Nice" on three of my poems and gave me the highest grade in the class.

My parents insisted that I not take any more poetry classes because it would "tank my GPA." My father said it would be impossible to get into a decent journalism program if I had a low grade in writing classes. Plus they were paying the bills so there really was no refuting their decision. "You'll thank me for this someday, Sarah," my father said. "Take it from someone who knows how the world works. You can't let some crazy lady mess up your future because she has a political agenda." To add insult to injury, my father called the dean of the English department and got her to change the B- to a "pass" on my transcript. The day I feel grateful for this has yet to arrive.

Sophie's voice returned me to the present. "So you have to think about a man who's going to be sophisticated and exciting. Well read but not academic. Fun but not an idiot who thinks tickling a woman shows how playful and cute he is. And if he has a big dick, I'm sure we won't hear any complaints." She sat upright with a spark. "Hey, why don't we do this? Prudence and I are going out tonight. Why doesn't Gwen come along and get to know her and what she likes. Sarah, you should Google her and get to know her that way. And while you're online, check out *Single in the City* and see if you can find a few good men there."

That afternoon, Hunter threw a snowball at me. We built a fortress in front of our home and tossed snowballs at passersby. They were so softly packed, they broke open like fireworks immediately after we launched them. As we watched *Freaky Friday* that evening, I wondered what it would be like to switch bodies with Prudence Malone.

After Hunter went to bed, Reilly lit a fire as I placed peppermint tea bags in mugs with candy cane handles. "When do you want to set our New Year's goals?" Reilly asked, as I returned to the couch. When we were dating, Reilly and I talked about how we were the only two people we knew of who set their New Year's resolutions in mid-December so they could hit the ground running in January. We both agreed that it was rather silly how people wrote down all of these grand ideas without an action plan to achieve them. We agreed that the holiday season was the perfect time to devise a strategy for realizing our New Year's goals. But this evening, as I enjoyed the warmth of the fire and tea, I wanted nothing to do with setting goals for the New Year. I wanted to enjoy the present with my new husband.

Reilly went to sleep at 11 P.M., as he always does, and I went online to troll for men, as I never do.

I filled out my personality profile as Prudence

Malone after scanning her photo into the Single in the City site. After answering the basics about my general interests, the site wanted me to write a series of short essays. "My idea of a perfect date," I said aloud, repeating the question on the questionnaire. I'm not even sure of my idea of the perfect date, much less Prudence's. "My ideal date would happen spontaneously," I wrote, without thinking. "Once a guy took me to an absolutely horrible play and at intermission he asked how I liked it. I knew I couldn't bear another moment of the awful play and decided I'd come clean. I knew that his reaction to my candor would determine the rest of our night. I told him I hated the play and wanted to skip the second act. He said he was relieved because he thought it was awful too. We walked through Central Park talking (though if any man ever suggested we 'take a walk and have a long chat,' I would consider him contrived, cliché, and unforgivably cheap) about whatever popped into our heads. We ended up playing a vicious couple of rounds of air hockey (again, invite me out for air hockey and I'd make you swallow the puck), then found this horrendously 'laid-back' coffee shop where it took thirty minutes to get our drinks, and we played Scrabble till 3 A.M." I sighed nostalgically recalling this date—until I realized it never happened.

"I'm an artist," I continued, when asked about my lifestyle. "I suppose I've always been one, but it wasn't until last year that I realized this was what I was meant to do. Rather, this was who I was meant to be. I was an accountant, which is a fine way to make a living if you enjoy it, but when you start wondering if you could actually slit your throat with triplicate forms, you know it's time to get out." I deleted that last sentence, fearing that my suicidal references might not come off as whimsical and artsy, as I was hoping to portray Prudence. "Life is fun," I continued. "And I like living!" I deleted that part too. If you like living, you don't really need to say it. And something about stating it on a general questionnaire seemed too weird. I revised. "I was an accountant, which is a fine way to make a living, but if you get creative on the job, it'll land you in federal prison."

"What do I do for fun?" I read aloud. I sat silently for a few moments before I was relieved to remember that the question was directed to Prudence, not me. "Biggest heartbreak?" I read aloud. "Discovering that I married a bottle of gin," I deleted as soon as I wrote. I thought of Sophie and how she walked out on her marriage, and how Prudence had recently become the person she was always meant to be, and felt a sinking sense of inadequacy. Of cowardice.

Chapter Five

I decided to finish my profile later and look at the guys' photos. There was a forty-two-year-old man kneeling with a football. He wasn't terrible looking, but I shuddered at the headline, "Strong and Silent Type." More like a lobotomized Goliath. I always hated guys who described themselves as "silent." Why not just say, "Dumb" or "Antisocial"? Or better still, "Has nothing to say."

A grainy headshot of a man tilting his head near a tabby cat read, "I like to cuddle." I rolled my eyes. At least he didn't say he likes pussy. I giggled at my departure. I'd become such a bore this last month that it was nice to shock myself with an uncharacteristically crass remark.

One balding guy with a goatee and disturbing smirk was pictured leaning in to what was probably a computer keyboard out of the photo frame. Headline: "Sexy Ladies Apply Here." In capital letters he wrote, "I am a sexy, real man." Oh, to be that delusional.

Clyde offered in his headline that he was STD-free. If this was his greatest bragging right, I'd have to pass.

There was Todd, the word butcher. "I'm a celebral kind of guy whose analization of my last relationship is that it was a catapulist for change in my life." I suppose that means his girlfriend hurled his sorry ass out the door, along with his celery sticks.

Almost as bad as the Terminator of the English language were the wannabe intellectuals—those who try so hard to sound smart that they actually seem like blathering morons. "Insofar as the dynamic of interpersonal relationships, one must always maintain a fatalistic view of the options that disclose themselves," wrote Tim. What was that even supposed to mean?

One guy featured a photo of himself holding a cardboard sign that read, "Will work for love." Sweet sentiment. I almost would have gone for it if he weren't completely naked behind the sign. Another implored, "Break glass in case of emergency." I guess he was trying to say that if you shattered your computer monitor, he'd be there behind the screen. I'm not sure. The only thing I knew with certainty was that his gimmick wasn't working.

Steve said that looks weren't very important and intelligence wasn't important at all.

Martin said in the first paragraph that he was kind to animals. Shouldn't this be a given?

Ron tried to show how quirky he was by revealing that he liked to leave the windows open when it rained. His windows, my floors. Not a good combination. Oh, yes, this was about Prudence. I can't imagine she'd have much tolerance for rain man either.

"I was separated from average children when I was younger," I read from Kyle. *You were probably a danger to them.* Kyle was pale with a tense-looking neck and stringy moustache. Like the drivers on the New Jersey Turnpike probably couldn't help craning their necks to see Rudy's mangled car, I couldn't help reading Kyle's profile. "I wrote advanced poetry and sonnets that were beyond the comprehension of even my teachers," he continued. I laughed aloud. *Poor misunderstood darling.* "I hope my special someone is out there, wherever there may be for you." *What?!* My *special someone?* Oh, yes, Kyle is such a poet. And *wherever there may be for you?* Like the average children in his school, I do believe my best course of action is to separate myself from Kyle.

"Wow me!" a headline implored.

"Fuck you," I said to the Donald Trump look-alike, posed leaning on his car. I loved the anonymity of life online. Through the two degrees of separation of our computer screens, I felt free to say exactly what I wanted to these single-digit IQ losers. Never had I been so harsh and judgmental of others. Never had I used such language. Never had I had so much fun.

"Smokin' hot firefighter looking to spark a

flame with a spatial lady," said twenty-eight-year-old Manny. The man made time to pose in his uniform (bare chested) and yet couldn't be bothered to check his spelling. And, I'm sorry, if you're looking to spark a flame, that wouldn't make you much of a firefighter. You'd be a pyromaniac. Just FYI, there are no flames in space, dip-shit.

Spewing out anger at these men was incredibly uplifting. I felt a tad guilty that in the season of comfort and joy, I was getting my jollies yelling at men who were simply looking for love. Then I got over it and went on to the next profile. Who needed Vilma Veeter? I was unleashing my inner bitch all by myself.

My favorites were the guys who came up with the catchy headlines like "Dragon Slayer Seeking Fair Maiden"; "Urban Cowboy Needs Pretty Philly"; "Sit on Santa's Lap"; or the best, "Alien Recently Landed on Earth." Exactly what type of woman would respond to him?

"If I can make one person smile, my day is complete," wrote Sam, a twenty-nine-year-old fitness instructor. Okay, Sam, it's time to raise your expectations. Your day is *complete* if you make someone smile?! I was so appalled, I had to write back. And when I was done with Sam, I'd write to the others. I'd urge The Donald wannabe to get rid of his picture with the Miata. Football Guy would need to be told to let go of his past. Sure his days on the Lafayette High School Spartans were glorious, but it was time to grow up and develop a few things to say to women instead of copping out with the "silent-type" crap.

Dear Sam,

I was intrigued by your profile on Single in the City. You seem innocuous enough, but I must say I found one of your self-characterizations quite off-putting. You say that if you make one person smile, your day is complete. Perhaps you should set higher expectations for yourself. Making one person smile really isn't all that ambitious, is it? What if I found a cure for cancer, but on that same day, the other researchers were feeling grumpy, so no one smiled at me. Would that mean my day was incomplete? Further, why do you allow other people smiling or not smiling to define what kind of day you're having? Find out who you are, Sam, and stop whoring yourself for smiles, trying to please the world and begging everyone to approve of you. Dare to be yourself, Sam. Underneath your candy-coated shell you may find someone truly worth smiling at.

Sincerely,
Prudence Malone

Suddenly my Instant Message alert sounded. It was from an e-mail address I didn't recognize. As I opened it, I realized that Prudence was getting her first online suitor.

DrJay: Up late tonight, Prudence?

It was a little obtrusive and spooky, but I was enjoying the low-stakes interactions the Internet provided. I was safely hidden behind the safety of a computer terminal and my husband's ex-wife's name.

Prudence: Who wants to know?
DrJay: I was up reading profiles and yours jumped out at me.
Prudence: It's only half finished.
DrJay: I noticed. Should that tell me something about you?

What did that mean? Was he accusing me of being half-assed about my profile? Was he trying to be clever?

Prudence: I think we're all half finished, so I wanted my profile to reflect my deep sense of incompletion.

There, that'll show this Dr. Jay fellow that he's not the only one who can be obscure.

DrJay: I like that. Why the deep sense of incompletion, though? Are you always this depressing?

I laughed.

Prudence: I don't think it's depressing to have an awareness that we're all projects in the works. If we all felt fulfilled and complete, how could the therapists of Manhattan afford to stuff their children's Christmas stockings with useless crap this season?

DrJay: You're clever, Prudence. Dark as the night, but I like you.

Internet men. You rattle off a few downers and they love you for it. Still, it was nice to chat behind the shield of my terminal.

Prudence: I'm not sleeping with you so don't get any ideas.

DrJay: Why so crabby?

Good question. Why so crabby during the most wonderful time of the year? I wouldn't even characterize it as crabby. I was downright furious at people I didn't even know. Poor Sam would wake up tomorrow morning and read my vicious invective. Why was I feeling threatened by an ex-wife who wasn't even a presence in my life? Why was I fascinated by how Sophie just walked out on her alcoholic husband? Why was I cursing like Lenny Bruce? Why was I surfing the Internet talking to strange men when I had a wonderful husband sleeping in the next room? To any observer, my life appeared to be more together than it has since Rudy died. I have a great new husband who's a wonderful father to my son. My career is thriving. I have no financial woes. Why do I feel as though I'm coming apart at the seams?

Prudence: I'm not sure.

DrJay: Tell me about yourself. I see you're thirty-two years old and living on the upper West Side. Says you're an artist, but you left out the part about your past relationships. You stopped filling out the survey when it asked if you've ever been married. Do you mind if I ask why?

I thought the Internet was swarming with perverts. I got a guy who likes to talk about my feelings and wants to know about my past relationships.

Prudence: Are you a woman?
DrJay: Why would you ask that?
Prudence: Are you?
DrJay: No, I'm as man as they come.

Okay, here it comes. He's sporting a fire hose. He regularly pleasures women with five-hour Tantralectric orgasms. He and Hef pal around on his thirty-foot yacht.

Prudence: Why the interest in my ex-husband?

DrJay: So there is an ex-husband? I thought so. Tell me about him. Any kids?

Prudence: My husband was killed in a car crash while driving drunk with his mistress. That was my son's first Christmas. They just don't have good stickers for that in the scrapbooking section at the crafts store, so my "Baby's First Christmas" album just isn't all it should be.

DrJay: Wow, that's tough. How'd you deal with it?

Prudence: What do you mean?

DrJay: That's very traumatic, Prudence. How did you deal with the loss? How did you grieve?

Shit! I forgot I was supposed to be Prudence!!!

Prudence: What kind of doctor are you anyway, a therapist?

DrJay: I am. You're avoiding the question.

Prudence: If I wanted a therapist, I would've signed on to Psychointhecity.com.

DrJay: I'm sorry if I've overstepped, Prudence. Has anyone ever told you that you're very good at avoiding difficult subjects?

Prudence: It's not a difficult subject. How did I deal with it? I thanked God he didn't injure any innocent people, buried him, cashed a life insurance check, and moved on.

DrJay: Didn't you mourn at all?

Prudence: I wouldn't give that louse the satisfaction.

DrJay: What about you?

Prudence: What about me?

DrJay: Don't you deserve the chance to process that whole ordeal?

Prudence: I'm not into that. Sorry if that offends your psychoanalytical sensibilities, but I think the best way to deal with a situation like this is to move on and spend as little time dwelling on the past as possible.

DrJay: Prudence, I'd like to meet you for coffee. Are you free sometime this week?

My heart began to pound so hard I felt the pulsating in my ears. I knew that some men would want to meet me—to meet Prudence, that is—but I hadn't yet thought out how I'd manage this. I guess if they seem like a good fit, coffee would be an acceptable first date. But this Dr. Jay guy was not a good candidate.

Too nosy.

Too pushy.

He was treating me more like a patient than a prospective girlfriend. I don't like people who presume they have a right to know intimate details of my life simply because we've met. Or in the case of Dr. Jay, simply because we've chatted online.

Prudence: Sorry, Jay, I'm not free. I'm shackled by the unprocessed grief from my past.

DrJay: I know you're being sarcastic, but I also think your assessment is right on.

Prudence: I happen to think you have a lot of nerve. You know nothing about me, and in ten minutes you act as though you've got me all figured out. There's a lot more to me than being the widow of a philandering drunk.

DrJay: Tell me more then.

Prudence: Ugggh! I can just see you there in your leather chair, smoking a pipe, thinking you are just soooooo insightful. Let me tell you something, buddy. Your analysis is pitifully shallow and way off the mark. They should take away your license, you quack!

DrJay: Prudence, when did you become so angry?

About thirty-six hours ago, I did not type. *My fantasy man turned into a nightmare. Sophie makes leaving a wretched marriage seem so easy I wondered why I hadn't done it. My best friend finds Sophie Come Lately endlessly more interesting than she ever found me. And Prudence is finally pursuing the art she's always dreamt of while I toil away at my passionless career. Put this on top of the fact that I was teetering dangerously on the edge of reason prior to my drunken luncheon, and I think I have every right to be a tad miffed Doctor Know Nothing!*

Prudence: I am not angry. I'm only sorry I wasted time chatting with a loser like you. Good night, Dr. Jay.

DrJay: Good night, Prudence. Would it be okay if I IMed you again?

Prudence: Suit yourself.

When I looked at my clock, I realized I'd spent far too long chatting with Dr. Jay. It was time to focus. I would spend no more than three minutes with candidates. If they didn't seem like a good match for Prudence, I wouldn't waste an extra second on them. I had only ten days until the New Year. It was time to be a mercenary matchmaker.

I decided to call Gwen and see how her night with Prudence and Sophie went. When I got her answering machine, I tried her cell phone. I heard background noise that sounded like a premature celebration of the New Year. It was a wall of laughter. "Oh, hi there," Gwen said, sounding secretive about talking to me. "I'm out with some friends right now. Can I call you back?"

"Are you with *her?*" I asked.

"That is correct," Gwen said, in a stilted voice. She'd make a terrible spy.

"What's she like? Does she seem fabulously happy?" I asked.

"We all are," Gwen said, giggling.

"I don't mean right this second. I mean in general."

"Oh, yes, definitely," Gwen said. "The weather is beautiful here in New York, Mom."

"You sound too obvious, Gwen! Stop talking like a robot."

"I'll call you later, Mom. Say 'hi' to Dad for me, okay?"

My head fell onto my desk. Tears absorbed into my sleeve and I fell asleep for a moment at my desk.

Soon I was screaming horror-movie cries of terror from the window of a burning building that was not my home. "Help me!" I shouted as flames lunged behind me. The heat wrapped around my body, increasing in temperature as my screams increased in volume. I was certain I was going to die. Finally a man with curly hair and a strong nose appeared on the sidewalk. He wore a tweed jacket and held a yellow legal pad and gold pen. I knew it was Dr. Jay.

"Why so angry, Prudence?" he shouted up to me.

"I'm not Prudence and I am *not* angry!" I cried. "I'm burning alive in here! Help me, Jay!" I wept.

"It's time to come to terms with who and what you really are," he answered calmly.

"Are you out of your mind, fuckwit!" I shouted, still weeping. "I'm going to die in here!"

"There never seems to be time, does there, Prudence?" He shook his head with pity and contempt.

I heard the sirens of a fire truck and felt momentary relief. Until I realized that it wasn't slowing. From the passenger side, a topless firefighter smiled and tipped his hat to me. "No one can hear your screams in space, Prudence!"

Were they all really going to just let me die up here?

My eyes shot open as I heard Reilly speak my name at the door. "Y'okay, hon?" he asked.

"Fine," I said quicker than the knee reacts to a hammer tap.

"You were crying in your sleep, hon. I'm worried about you."

"I'm tired. This is how I get when I need sleep," I explained.

"You must be awfully tired. Why don't you come to bed?"

As I heard Reilly drift into sleep, I tried to refocus on finding a new guy for Prudence. Dr. Jay was an annoying distraction. I promised myself I would quickly dismiss him.

* * *

The next morning, I was stunned to see how many responses Prudence's profile had generated. I was a bit jealous that between midnight and 8 A.M., sixty-seven men had made contact with Prudence despite her half-assed attempt at a character profile and mediocre photo. I wondered if I would've fared as well.

Sam wrote back to tell me I was a total bitch for thinking his "smile and complete me" line was weak. He was pleased to report that he was getting an overwhelming response to his ad, thank you very much. For a moment, I contemplated writing a fake profile just to see how many responses it would generate. "Breathing, warm body, not ugly, bites only when provoked."

Chiming in during vampire hours was Randy who liked taking Jell-O baths with women. "I hope this doesn't come across as perverted or anything weird like that, but I like to be real honest about my preferences, so there are no surprises when we get into things. I definitely like the tangy flavor of the citrus. Lime is my favorite, but some of my lady friends have said the lemon is better. These are merely suggestions." *Oh, no, Randy, this doesn't seem weird or perverted in the slightest.*

There was Todd who wrote that I, rather Prudence, was "quite attractive," but wanted to be sure she had no tattoos. "On someone with whom I am not considering a long-term relationship I could overlook a small, discreetly placed tattoo provided it were a flower or a heart, but would rule out anyone who wore skulls or Chinese writing. I must be up front about the fact that any tattoo on a woman would seriously jeopardize her candidacy as the potential mother of my children." *The nerve!* Who was campaigning to be the mother of his children?! And why was my tattoo status so important to this guy that it was the very first thing he wanted to discuss? Had his former girlfriend needled, "I'm with asshole!" onto her lower back—in Chinese?

Morton described himself as a "teddy bear," which invariably means a lot of stuffing.

Peter said he was incredibly masculine despite his penchant for dressing in women's underwear. His picture was unconvincing. Peter's harplike ribs protruded above a hairy curtain of stomach, and his panties were so last season.

Omar wore a short top hat and black cape, which made him look like he was either a magician or something out of turn-of-last-century New York.

Tim posed winking at his high-gloss grand piano with the opening line, "I'm a player." *At least he didn't write, "Let's make music." Scratch that, it was the fourth line.*

Frank said he wanted a chill partner, then went on to describe himself as a "blissful, contemplative psychic who enjoys moonlit walks on the beach and gentle lovemaking." Translation: Self-important, patchouli-smelling granola boy whose idea of foreplay includes hair brushing and foot massage.

The sex metaphors were endless. Mark said he wanted to navigate his ship into my port. Fred had the key to my lock. And the worst—Larry who said he sees the entire doughnut, not just the hole.

When did people become so nonchalant about sex that they discussed it in introductory e-mails? I pondered the lasciviousness of my peers, wondering if I'd ever passed one of these lonely souls on the streets. I must see the faces of at least a hundred men every day. Most of them appear relatively normal, but among this group were panty-wearing, tattoo-phobic freaks who just want to chill in a tub of lime Jell-O. But look who was talking. Here I was pretending to be my husband's ex-wife sniping at men on the Internet while trying to find her a new love.

Joey's response was bizarrely hostile considering we had no interaction. "Get to no me before you judge me, because if your not intristed and you didn't give me a chance then screw you anyhows! I'm not looking for a goddamn penpal neither so if your not willing to step it up than don't waste my time. I'm a verry bussy man and I have a lot going for me and if you're the write girl, I could be the best friggin' thing that ever happned to you, so how do you know if you don't even try?"

The phone saved me from responding to another Guido who started his reply to me with "Not for nothin'."

It was Gwen. "Sarah, she's fantastic," she launched.

"Who is?" I asked.

"Who do you think?! Whom did I spend last night with?" Gwen reminded me that she'd been to Prudence's art show at a gallery in SoHo. "She's so talented, Sarah. You should see what this woman can do with a few hundred feet of silver wire. It's exquisite. I bought one myself and one for my parents. By the way, is your editor, Zach, at the *Journal* still single?" She was bouncing from one topic to the next like a game of four-wall handball. "It's no wonder she hasn't met anyone since she and Reilly split. There were eighty women and about twenty men at her show—two of them straight. Anyway, I met this gorgeous woman, Perla, who just moved from Miami and she would be *perfect* for Zach. Can I get his number from you?"

"Slow down, Gwen. Tell me about Prudence. When you told her that you know Reilly, did she ask about him? Did she seem interested?"

"I didn't mention Reilly," Gwen said. "We were having such fun. This was her first show and I can't tell you how well her sculptures were received. She completely sold out. She took orders for several more and said she's going to have to work straight through till Christmas to fill them all. I was so lucky we got there early."

"Okay, I get it, Gwen. Prudence is a goddamned genius with a spool of wire. But didn't you even mention Reilly—or me?"

"Sarah, you said they ran into each other at Rockefeller Center just a few days ago. If she wanted to know anything about him, she would've just asked him then and there."

"In front of my son?!" I shouted. "Does this woman have no respect for my marriage?!"

Gwen laughed. "Calm down. Prudence is a doll. She's not after Reilly, but I do think we should find her a man. Such a beautiful woman going to waste like that."

"Gwen!" I gasped.

"What?!" she asked.

"A single woman isn't a waste. *You're* single! There are a million single women in this city."

"All of whom would rather be with someone, believe you me."

"Gwen, I'm sure not all of them want to be with a man," I said. "Aren't you happy being single?"

"No," she answered without pause.

"I was," I replied.

"Easy to say now that you're married to Reilly. And easy for Prudence to get all caught up in the excitement of her big art show, but I told her there's a perfect match for her, and Mr. Right is out there looking for her."

"You told her that?!" I said, panic-stricken that she'd tipped our hand. "What did she say?"

"She said she's happy on her own. I told her I had the perfect man for her, but she just laughed. Didn't even want to hear about him."

"Who?!"

"What who?" she asked.

"Who's this perfect man for her?"

"I haven't met him in person yet, but I have a crystal clear image of him in my mind."

"Does she know this? I mean, did you tell her that the soul mate you're going to introduce her to resides only in your imagination? Because she's going to think you're crazy, and frankly I do too."

"It's not crazy," Gwen defended. "Now that I've

met Prudence, I know exactly the type of man she needs. Remember Isaac Franklin?"

"No."

"The widow," Gwen reminded me. "The one you and Sophie thought was too old for Prudence?"

"Oh, right, the ninety-year-old marathon runner," I recalled.

"He's sixty-three. And it's biking. Anyway, I set him up with Esther Finley in my building and when I saw her this morning in the elevator, she was nothing but smiles and gratitude. I'm telling you, I think I have a gift for this."

"Maybe she was just smiling because she was filled with the Christmas spirit," I suggested.

"She's Jewish," Gwen returned, with satisfaction. "So how was your night? Did you meet any nice men after your husband went to sleep?"

Chapter Six

Reilly called that afternoon to tell me that he won a set of lift tickets at his office holiday party raffle. "I know you said you didn't want to ski this year, but how 'bout letting me take Hunter up for a few days and teaching him how to ski?"

"A few days?!"

"We'll be home before dark on Christmas Eve," Reilly explained. "Why not, Sarah? Hockey camp ends today. Skiing will help his game." Realizing that this argument held no appeal for me, he changed tact. "Did you know that half of all business deals are made on the golf course and on the slopes?"

"Really?" I asked.

"No, not really, Sarah. It was a joke. Hunter's six. What type of deals do you think the kid's gonna make?"

"Oh," I said.

"It'll be *fun,* Sarah," Reilly said, stressing the

word as if to remind me that there is value in recreation. He wasn't the first person this month to notice that I'd lost my ability to enjoy life.

Though I'd miss my husband and son, the reality was that I wasn't spending a lot of time with either of them as I wallowed in self-pity and anger. If Reilly thought taking Hunter off to the slopes for a few days was a good way for them to bond, who was I to argue? They'd be back by Christmas Eve and in the three days that they were off, I could screen plenty of potential husbands for Prudence.

"Okay," I said.

The next morning, I watched Reilly and Hunter's taxi pull away and checked my watch. I had less than an hour until my coffee date with Ron, thirty-eight-year-old actor. His photo was quite impressive. He had *GQ* bone structure and his brown hair was attractively cut. I'd cast him as a leading man, and with any luck, so would Prudence.

Ron was waiting at a table reading a newspaper. Or, rather, posing as if he were reading a newspaper. "Hey," he said, looking up and shaking his hair from his eyes. "You must be Prudence's friend," he said, standing and kissing my cheek.

"Yes," I said, smiling at him, though I was disappointed to find that he was about twenty pounds thinner than he looked in his photo. And the *GQ* bone structure in his head shot was actually good lighting used by the photographer. Still, Ron was above average looking and seemed nice enough during our chat online just ten hours earlier.

"Tell me," he said, in his radio announcer voice, "why is it that women always hide their underwear when they go into the gynecologist's office? I mean, do you ladies think they don't know you wear panties?"

What? Was he testing material on me? I stared blankly, hoping he'd realize I was not amused.

His facial expression was pure anticipation.

It was a standoff.

Finally, after a few moments, he spoke. "My grandfather says women are like toothpaste. As you get farther to the end, you need to squeeze harder, but there's still good stuff in there," Ron said, laughing alone. He stopped to gasp from laughing so hard, only to observe that I had "no sense of humor." Now, I'll be the first to admit that I've had a definite case of the holiday doldrums, but this was not the cause of my antipathy for Ron. Ron was.

"I have a perfectly good sense of humor," I said, as flatly as I could deliver. "I just haven't sensed any."

"Ouch!" he said, pulling his hand from the table as if he'd burnt himself. "You don't hold back, do ya? S'alright, s'okay, I like that in a woman," he said, as though he might actually be in a position to judge. It was only after that comment that I laughed.

"I'm sorry," I began. "I may not have the greatest sense of humor, but I do have a pretty good sense of people. As terrific a guy as you are, I don't think you and Prudence are going to click."

"Really? Why not?"

"Why not?" I repeated incredulously. "You just wouldn't, that's all."

"'Cause I can knock off the jokes. What's she looking for?" Ron asked desperately.

"Ron, this isn't a casting call. You and Prudence just aren't going to work, okay?"

"But how do you know for sure?"

For the first time during our coffee, I felt sorry for him. "I just know. Look, it's not you."

"Don't say that!" Ron snapped. "Of course it's me. You want your friend to find someone nice, you met me, and you decided I'm not the one. How is that *not* me?"

When did everyone in the world get so damned blunt? Didn't anyone value subtlety, gentility, or even social lying anymore?

"I'm sorry, I think you're a very nice man, but the combination of you and Prudence together is not going to work. It's neither you nor her; it's the coupling that's wrong."

"Well, this is fine. I've been dumped on the first date before." *I believe it.* "Even *during* a first date." *I believe that too.* "But never before a first date, and by the friend, no less," Ron said, shrugging. He laughed, though it was clear he didn't find his failure with women at all funny. I stood to leave, realizing that my early dismissal would give me an hour to do a little Christmas shopping before my lunch with Sophie and Gwen. "You're not leaving, are you?" Ron said, looking up from his brown eyes.

"I'm sorry, Ron. I really need to run along. I have a million things I need to do and I'm already hours behind schedule. It was really a pleasure meeting you, though, and good luck finding someone compatible." I smiled and began walking away from the table.

"Stuck-up bitch," I heard him mutter. I hadn't been called that since Rudy, who, though he was a successful attorney, was always quite cognizant of the fact that he came from far more humble a background than I. I should have had the composure to just ignore Ron's comment the way I was able to dismiss Rudy's outbursts, but I was unable to contain my rage.

"Excuse me," I said, my body snapping back to face him.

"You heard me," he said defiantly.

I glanced over at the table next to Ron and saw a preschooler coloring his place mat. I decided not to challenge Ron to repeat himself. And yet, I felt physically unable to leave the coffee shop without doing something to defend myself. I'd spent a lifetime doing the whole Katharine Hepburn thing. I knew how to deliver smart one-liners and leave a man disarmed by my coolness. But on this day, I decided to give myself the early Christmas gift of complete emotional freedom. I knew I'd maintained an ounce of sanity because I remember thinking that throwing hot coffee at Ron was definitely crossing the line. So I reached at the closest cold drink I could see; which was the child's milk; tore off the plastic lid, and drenched Ron in a tidal wave of years of repressed anger. It was so liberating that I picked up the kid's half-eaten biscotti and threw it at Ron like a dart. I was pleased with my aim.

The little boy was overjoyed with my outburst,

but no one else in the place seemed to understand the therapeutic value of splashing an imbecile with milk. Sure, my actions were extreme, but so what?! The man called me a stuck-up bitch. I had reached my limit on how much I could swallow and just walk away from.

"What's wrong with you?!" the boy's mother shrieked. A twentysomething came rushing out from behind the counter with a mop.

"He deserved it!" I told her. "He's an obnoxious jerk."

I'd hoped she'd take my side, but instead she was annoyed with me. "They're all obnoxious jerks, lady. Deal with it."

"You should call the cops," Ron said, capitalizing on his public approval rating. Instead, Ron's comment turned the tide.

"What are you going to charge her with, assault with a cookie?" she snapped.

"Biscotti," the mopping clerk chimed in.

Gwen couldn't believe what I'd done, but Sophie seemed thoroughly unimpressed with my lactose revolution. "The guy was a jerk," she said, shrugging. "He had it coming. Good for you, Sarah." Then she took out a sleek notebook with an abstract design on the cover and continued, as if she heard stories of biscotti pelting every day, "So that guy's definitely off the list. Who've we got next?"

"I met a wonderful man at the ballet last night," Gwen said.

"Straight?" Sophie asked.

"With his mother," Gwen explained. "I love this assignment. It gives me an excuse to approach all of these great guys I would've only admired from afar."

"So is he single?" I asked.

Gwen nodded. "He's going out with Rachel tomorrow night."

"Rachel?" Sophie asked.

"Rachel, your sister Rachel?" I asked. She confirmed. "What about Prudence?"

"No, no, no, this is Rachel's future ex-husband, trust me on this one."

Sophie threw her hands in the air and suggested we just host a party. "We haven't found a single good one out there. Jennifer went to this speed-dating thing last night and said it felt like she was visiting inmates in prison. They had to face off at these school desks and spend four minutes chatting while in a crowded room. The only thing missing was the glass window between them." She continued. "I screened this guy this morning who was trying to impress me with all of the deals he was making on his cell phone, until guess what happened?" We waited. "His cell phone rang."

"What? I don't understand," I said.

"He wasn't really on the phone. It rang because he wasn't really talking to anyone on the other end. Get it? Big deals were not happening." Sophie sighed. "I liked him, too. They're not the most trustworthy lot, are they?"

"Maybe we *should* have a party," Gwen conceded. "It seems an efficient way to go."

"First of all, men aren't going to show up at a party to meet their soul mate. They don't put as much effort into relationships as we do," I said. "We all knew that when Prudence said she wasn't looking for a guy, we'd need to do it for her because he wasn't going to put out the effort. The lazy bastard is probably at home right now watching some stupid college bowl game."

Sophie grimaced. "She has a point. Hey, what if we don't let them in on it? What if we simply bill it as a party with free drinks, sports on big screens, and strippers?! And we can hire dancers who all have short black hair like Prudence and put them in little cages?"

"Have you lost your mind?" I asked. "You want to put dancing naked women who look like Prudence in cages?"

"Yeah, why not?" Sophie asked.

Finally Gwen came to her senses and remembered that we are cut from a different cloth from that of Sophie. "I have to agree with Sarah on this one, Soph," she said. "Why limit ourselves with dark-haired girls? Let's mix it up and throw in some blondes and redheads."

"What?!" I gasped.

"Don't be so uptight, Sarah," Gwen chided. "Stripping is very in now. We're taking a class at the Y next month."

"We are?" I asked.

"Soph and I are. You're welcome to join."

"What type of guy are we trying to attract with strippers?" I asked, hoping to return the conversation to a rational one.

"Guys with dicks," Sophie said plainly, jotting something in her notepad. "Come on, Sarah. We want to get a lot of guys in. What better way than to promise sports, free booze, and naked women?"

"What about promising them the possibility of meeting the woman they're going to spend the rest of their lives blissfully in love with?" I asked.

Sophie and Gwen laughed before realizing I was serious. "I'm sorry to laugh," Gwen said, patting my thigh. "But you're in a state of marriage-induced delusion. No men are going to come to this party if we're honest with them. I say we go with the strippers."

"I say we nix the idea of a party entirely. Let's stick to our plan and we'll find a great guy for Prudence."

That afternoon I was stood up by Bill Tourmaline, a man who said he was really looking forward to meeting me when we spoke on the phone. I wondered if he had an accident on his way to meet me.

When I arrived home it was already dark. The stillness of the apartment was soothing, not lonely as I'd feared it would be. The answering machine light was blinking with a message from Reilly and Hunter, who had arrived safely at their cabin. Hunter said he saw reindeer on the road.

After dinner, I checked my e-mail. As I thought about my day, I laughed at the image of my sole date drenched in milk. My only regret was that

Rudy wasn't alive for me to throw drinks at. The outburst really was like hitting a reset button, one I wished I'd discovered years ago.

I heard the familiar chime of an instant message and saw that it was Dr. Jay. When will technology allow women to throw drinks at their computer screens and have it splash out at the jerk on the other end?

DrJay: Hi Prudence!
Prudence: No.
DrJay: No to what?
Prudence: Whatever it is you want.
DrJay: Why so angry at me?
Prudence: I find you irritating.

My heart raced with excitement as I typed such rudeness. It was freeing to be so unabashedly blunt. It was nice to finally tell the truth after a lifetime of making excuses, like "I'm not angry," or "I'm sorry. It's not you. I've just had a hard day."

DrJay: Why is that, Prudence?
Prudence: Because you ask too many questions. You are presumptuous and generally pesky.

I got up and walked around my desk, unable to contain my energy.

DrJay: I apologize. I'm trying to get to know you.

Prudence: Isn't anyone else out there interested in you? Why do you keep coming back to me?

DrJay: I find you interesting. I get a lot of bland responses from women on the Internet. I must say, that is not the case with you.

Prudence: Guess what I did today?

DrJay: Tell me.

Prudence: I threw milk at my date. Then I nailed him with a biscotti.

DrJay: Why did you do that?

Prudence: Because if I can throw milk at just one person, my day is complete.

DrJay: I'm not sure what you mean.

Prudence: Look, Dr. Know It All. I have spent a lifetime politely dealing with whatever crap has come my way, and you know what? I'm tired. Throwing milk at this moron today was such fun, I think I'm in danger of becoming a serial milk thrower. You're a shrink so you've got to maintain confidentiality, right? So if you hear about random guys in Manhattan being hit by milk-filled balloons, you can't turn me in.

DrJay: Well . . . you're not a patient, though the more I talk to you, the more I think you should be. I'll refrain from any bad puns about your serial milk hits.

Prudence: Very funny.

DrJay: Tell me more about the milk throwing. What led up to it?

Prudence: I simply told the guy that I didn't think we were a good fit and he called me a stuck-up bitch. My dead husband used to call me that. I wish I'd thrown milk at him!

DrJay: You did.

Prudence: No, this happened today. I threw it at some guy named Ron who came in with a string of cheesy jokes.

DrJay: Prudence, I really want to meet you. What are you doing tomorrow?

Prudence: Sorry, Doc. I have a ton of shopping to do. Would you believe I haven't done any shopping yet?

DrJay: Is that unusual for you?

Prudence: Everything that's happened this week has been unusual for me. Do you mind if I ask you a question?

DrJay: Not at all.

Prudence: Have you ever heard of a person freaking out when everything in her life is going perfectly?

DrJay: Yes. People who are extremely organized.

Prudence: What do you mean?

DrJay: Have you ever heard of mothers who get sick only after they've taken care of every other ailing member of their family? It's good planning. Their bodies finally say, "Okay, everything's taken care of; now it's time for me to break down."

Prudence: That's how I feel. Like I'm breaking down. But it makes no sense because things are better than they have been in years.

DrJay: It makes perfect sense, Prudence. I'd really like to meet you.

Prudence: Maybe, but tomorrow is out. I really have to do some shopping.

DrJay: If you change your mind, please e-mail me.

The next morning I woke up feeling like my old self again. A good night's sleep can be incredibly transformational. Plus, I had a naughty dream that I wasn't the least bit embarrassed by. Who else had to know that in the wee hours of the night, I was Paris Hilton dancing naked in a cage? When I burst out from behind the bars, everyone was cheering wildly for me. Sophie and Gwen were there. Prudence was in the back capturing the whole spectacle in silver wire. Reilly was among the cheering masses.

"Looks like you're having fun, honey!" he shouted above the roar of the club. Even Dr. Jay was there, asking how I felt.

"Free!" I shouted to him. The truth was that I felt more than just free. I felt alive. I was beaming as I looked into the mirror and saw that I had Paris Hilton's lean, youthful body. Who knew I could dance like this? Suddenly, that idiot Ron appeared and threw milk at me. But in our dreams we can be victorious even in the face of attempted humiliation. The cold milk splashed against my skin and glowed under the black light of the club. Much to the chagrin of Ron, the Borscht Belt reject, the milk made me look even hotter. I was glow-in-the-dark sexy.

It's a given that I would never do something this brazen in real life, but until last night I hadn't had the nerve to even dream about it.

After I showered, I blew out my hair and put on makeup for the first time in weeks. I was ready. Not for my next date, but for something more important.

As the doors opened, I heard a choir of angels singing. This time, I wasn't dreaming. It was a Madrigal group performing in the lobby of Saks Fifth Avenue. My husband and son would be home tomorrow evening and I hadn't purchased a single gift for either of them yet.

Five hours later that had changed. My taxi driver actually had to help me carry all of the bags from the car to my front door. I rushed in to the ringing of the phone and a blinking answering machine. I dropped a pile of holiday cards on the kitchen counter and picked up the telephone.

"I found him," Gwen said, without introduction.

"Found whom?" I asked.

"Mr. Right. The perfect guy for Prudence," she explained. "I don't know if you remember Ken Wenrich from the Snow Ball last weekend?"

"The Snow Ball?"

"Sarah, you and Reilly were there. The fund-raiser that makes it possible for underprivileged kids to go on ski trips."

"Oh, yes," I recalled. At the event I made the mistake of questioning the wisdom of an organization that takes poverty-stricken children from their freezing roach-infested tenements and sends them to Vail for the weekend. Not only did it seem like an imprudent use of funds; it seemed downright cruel. It was like saying, *Hey, kiddies, in case you hadn't noticed the depressing conditions you're currently living in, let us pose the most stark contrast to make you painfully aware. Happy holidays!* But, as Reilly said, half of all business contacts are made on the ski slopes and golf courses. So, in a way, this was an economic affirmative action program. It just seemed that the money would have been better spent on scholarship funds or the neighborhood library.

"Ken was on the committee with me," Gwen finished. "I think he'd be perfect for Prudence."

"Why?"

"I just do," Gwen said. "Anyway, Sophie brought up a good question the other day. When we find these guys, how are we supposed to get them together with Prudence? Sophie said she and Jennifer have been trying to set her up on blind dates for months, but she won't go."

"Oh," I said, pondering the question. My effort to find Prudence a new husband was so poorly planned, I had to wonder if finding her a man was ever really my real focus. Or if fretting about Prudence was simply a convenient way for me to avoid what was going on with me—a downward spiral into neurosis and rage. After all, Prudence told Reilly that she'd "dated" over eighty women before she found me. I had one "date" and I threw milk at him. Then there was Dr. Jay, a therapist with a seemingly endless tolerance for my hostility. Perhaps he would be a good match for Prudence.

If anyone had more issues than I did, it was Prudence Malone.

"Maybe we should just have a party," Gwen suggested. "How 'bout a New Year's Eve party."

"I think a party is in poor taste," I said, as the image of myself dancing in a cage flashed before my eyes. "Gwen, I've got another call. Let's talk later about Ken. Keep up the good work."

"Hey, hon," Reilly said.

"Hey," I said, extending the word to show my elation. "How are you guys doing up there?"

"Sarah, the boy's a natural," Reilly said. "He skied a black diamond today. Are you sure the kid's never been on skis before?"

"He's really doing black diamonds? How's his form?" I asked. "I'm going to come with you guys next time." Then I had a wonderful idea. My staying home while my family was off skiing was ridiculous. I belonged with Reilly and Hunter, not being Prudence's secret proxy date. "Reilly, I'm going to drive up there tonight. We can ski all day Christmas Eve and maybe even stay up for Christmas Day if there's room at the inn." I giggled with giddy anticipation. "I bought presents for you guys today. I can wrap them, pack, and be on the road in an hour, two at the most." My heart raced at the thought.

"Roads are closed, hon," Reilly said. "That's one of the reasons I'm calling. There's a chance we won't be able to get down the mountain tomorrow."

"What?! But tomorrow's Christmas Eve!"

"Yeah, well, tell that to the snow," Reilly said.

"I'm sorry, Sarah. You know how much I want us to have Christmas Eve together. They haven't said for sure that the roads will be closed, so keep the faith. Worse case, we'll be back to the city just after noon on Christmas."

I was such a fool not to have gone with them. A good ski vacation was probably all I needed to chase away my holiday blues. After hanging up the phone with Hunter, who was utterly nonplussed by the potential itinerary change, I sat down at my computer and made a list of my New Year's resolutions. This year I would have more fun with life. I would go skiing with Hunter and Reilly. I would sign up for poetry class at the New School. I would snap out of my funk once and for all. And I was on my way. Throwing milk at Rudy was a christening of my new life.

I meant Ron. Throwing milk at Ron was exhilarating.

I decided to get to sleep early. The shopping wore me out. All the pushing through crowds. The tug-of-war for sale items. The flying elbows working their way through couture. I hope I didn't hurt anyone.

But before I turned in for the evening, I wanted to check if Prudence's personal ad had generated any more response.

First, there was Dr. Jay, who wanted to get together for coffee. My hand immediately reached for the delete key. I pulled it away and thought I'd save it for later. Perhaps I would go. He was a therapist and Prudence is mighty screwed up. Maybe I should check him out as a prospective new husband for her. Who knows, he could be cute.

EddieR: Hey, baby, wanna sit on Santa's lap and tell him what you want for Christmas?
Santashelper6: I'd like to stuff your stocking full of my goodies, Prudence.
BobbyX: Won't you ride my sleigh tonight?

Was there some sort of directive from Singleinthecity.com to send out stupid holiday jokes? I'm sorry I missed Chanukah, when the Jewish guys were offering to light my fire—eight nights in a row.

Dr. Jay was starting to look pretty good.

Chapter Seven

I woke up groggy the next morning. I got eleven hours of sleep, though never for more than two hours at a time. I hadn't had so many interruptions since Hunter was a baby.

First I dreamt that I was Mrs. Claus sitting in the passenger seat of the sleigh as my jolly husband made his Christmas Eve rounds. "See how nice this is?" I said, resting my hand on his red velvet pants. "I told you it was safe for me to come along, silly." Just then Rudolf turned his head back to face us. Not only was his red nose shining through the fog, but his eyes were nuclear green with no pupils. He looked like that possessed puppet from the horror flicks. The sleigh jerked forward and wind wrapped our bodies as the sleigh sped through the air. Then suddenly the sleigh descended dangerously quickly. We were dropping until I bolted upright into consciousness.

A few hours later I was once again woken by the

feeling of my own body sitting up in terror. This time I was walking a blind dog. Not a seeing-eye dog, but a dog who was blind. We were in a blizzard and I was walking my dog in Times Square. He looked like a wet Toto from *The Wizard of Oz.* I remember feeling sorry for the dog because he couldn't see the billion bright lights of electronic billboards and Broadway marquees. I handed him a dog treat as we waited for the light to change. Somehow, the leash disappeared and Toto started walking across the busy street. He was calm, too calm. It was a creepy image—a catatonic dog miraculously crossing Broadway as taxis whizzed by him, honking and swerving. As he reached the middle of the street, I realized that this was *my* blind dog. I had to save him. I sped into the street, holding out my hand like a crossing guard. The dog turned his solid white eyes to me and raced toward the other side, leaving me in the middle of traffic. The last thing I saw was a Checker Cab screeching its brakes to avoid hitting me. It was inches away from hitting me before I was shocked awake.

The next dream was the most disturbing of all. I was back in the nightclub where I was dancing as Paris Hilton in the cage. This time, though, I did not have the benefit of Paris's hair extensions or nineteen-inch waist. It was just me with my Wellesley bob and birthing hips. Being naked was not sexy this time. I knew that the crowd was not cheering for me but, rather, anticipating some sort of public lynching or witch burning. As I huddled in the corner of the cage, in burst Ron, tossing glasses of Chivas onto my body. The crowd roared as he lit a match and threw it into my locked cage. As the burning stick crossed the bar, I sat up in my bed, coated with sweat.

Whatever happened to good old-fashioned holiday dreams led by liaison ghosts from Christmas past, present, and future?

The next day I decided to revisit a ritual from my Girl Scout days. Each summer, our troop leader took us on a four-day camping trip. We did all of the usual things like hiking, orienteering, and bingeing on S'mores, but on the last day, we had to remain completely speechless. We weren't aloud to charade, write notes, or even use sign language unless it was an emergency. This monastic exercise was supposed to help us "hear ourselves," as our troop leader said. All of the girls hated it, and I pretended to as well, but secretly I loved the opportunity to turn off the chatter of my own voice and those of my giggly girlfriends. While my friends now have far more interesting topics to discuss—like who should marry my husband's ex-wife—it would still be nice to spend a day without talking. I've lived in Manhattan my whole life and always thought it would be fun to walk from my house all the way down to Washington Square Park in Greenwich Village. God knows why I've never done this. It's only four miles. I could walk that in heels. I decided today would be the day I made my silent trek. I'd cross through Central Park, then head down Fifth Avenue all the way down to the Arc de

Washington Square. I was more excited than when I left for Europe for the summer after college graduation. But, first, I needed to speak with Reilly about when he and Hunter would be home.

"Still closed, hon," Reilly said. I looked out the window and saw thick snowflakes floating onto the white-carpeted sidewalk. I imagined children celebrating and grabbing their sleds, and tugging on the bottoms of their father's sweaters, begging to go to the park. The parents would sigh. They too had prayed for a white Christmas, but only so they could light a fire and snuggle under a down comforter as their children played video games in the next room. They'd look at each other and agree that the kids could go out and play. They'd pretend they were reluctant but both would secretly share the deliciously frustrating bond of delayed intimacy by parenthood. If only I had gone with Reilly and Hunter, we could all be snowbound together. For years, we could recall that first Christmas when we were snowed in at the cabin.

"When are they going to open the roads?!" I whined.

"When it's safe to drive on them," Reilly said. "Look, I'm as sorry as you are about this, Sarah, but we don't want to take any chances."

"Of course," I said. "You're right. I'm just disappointed, that's all."

"Me too, hon. We could still be home Christmas morning. I'm not sure, but I'll call you tonight once we get off the slopes." How I longed to be on a ski slope with my husband and son. My silent trek in the snow would probably take several hours with the inevitable stops along the way. When I ski, I can make it down four miles in minutes.

"Okay," I said stoically. I then explained to Hunter how very sorry I was that we couldn't spend Christmas Eve together. He replied that Reilly hadn't made him take a bath since they'd arrived.

"I love you," was the last thing I said. I thought that would be a good note on which to leave verbal communication. My eyes welled with tears at the thought. I did love Reilly and Hunter so much. It was so disappointing that we'd miss our first Christmas Eve together as a family, but I was more overwhelmed by a deep sense of gratitude that we had found each other, and were a family.

I wrapped myself in a full-length camel hair coat I'd just bought at Saks, put on the Timberland boots I hadn't sported in years, and headed toward the park. It began to snow just as I approached one of Central Park's small tunnels, under a walkway overhead. The blackened semicircle contrasted with the snow falling through the trees on the other side. I felt as though I were walking into a snow globe.

I watched my breath escape from my mouth and remembered summers when I pushed Hunter's stroller down this same path. Before Hunter was born, Rudy and I biked the park nearly every Saturday the weather permitted. We took Hunter to a Neil Young concert in the park and Rudy fed him his first spoonful of Mr. Softie chocolate ice cream. (No sprinkles because I was too nervous that Hunter would choke.) Hunter raised his eyebrows with the same expression of pleasant intrigue his father often wore and snatched the spoon in a way that made me rest assured that our son was extremely motivated. I told Rudy that Hunter was as determined as his father. He told me the baby was as beautiful as his mother. How had we slid from that day in the park to the night on the Jersey Turnpike in just four months?

I walked for about another hour, stopping to look at window displays and eavesdropping on conversations. Just when I felt I needed a rest, St. Patrick's Cathedral stood before me, offering respite. As I entered the gothic cathedral, I was struck by the flickering votive candles people had lit in remembrance of lost loved ones. Even though neither Rudy nor I was Catholic, I knew I would light one for him and sit for a moment to remember our brief time together, as ambivalent as I felt about it. It didn't surprise me that I cried when lighting his candle. I cry at anything these days. But I was rather caught off guard by my own impulse to light a second candle. For myself.

I watched skaters at Rockefeller Center and smiled at Prometheus in his eternal struggle. Sometimes I don't appreciate how good I really have it. After another leisurely hour of walking down Fifth Avenue, I reached the Empire State Building and realized that in my thirty-two years living in Manhattan, I'd never been to the top. I stopped in and saw a short line of people waiting for the elevator to the observation deck and drifted onto it without a moment of pause. As the sign promised, the visibility was zero at the top. The needle was surrounded in fog. We were, literally, standing in a low-hanging cloud. A boy who appeared to be about ten years old, wearing a Cardinals baseball cap, looked through the telescope around the periphery of the deck and shouted, "Awesome! This is so cool!" As I wondered if I should rummage for my quarters, his mother asked if he could see anything through the lens. He shook his head that he couldn't.

"What are you so excited about then?" his father asked, teasing.

"I'm on the top of the Empire State Building!" he said, with a child's voluminous animation. I remember last year I took Hunter to the zoo and a toddler pointed at a monkey and gleefully exclaimed, "He's my friend!" When do we lose that? I'm not sure I ever had it, even as a child.

By the time I reached Washington Square Park night had fallen. The park was empty save for a few drug dealers, confident that the holidays would bring out addicts who'd overestimated their ability to cope with their families. A couple clung to each other's arms and raced toward the southern exit of the park. I sat on a bench and wondered what it was that brought me on this silent journey to the park. It was beautiful, to be sure, but I wasn't exactly sure why I was there.

Then I realized that there was something settling about slowly walking the streets I rushed about every day. It was like untangling a knot.

I broke my silence when I got into a taxi and told the cabbie my address. Then my cell phone rang with a call from Reilly to let me know the roads were "probably" going to open at noon. "We'll have a late Christmas, hon," he promised. "What can we do?"

Reilly was so levelheaded. What could we do, really? He and Hunter would be on the road as soon as it was safe. So I decided to be sensible as well and make plans for myself for Christmas morning, then continue my search for Prudence's new husband while I still had the freedom to do so. "Oh, hi, Gwen," I said into her answering machine. "I just remembered you're at your parents' this weekend. Okay, then, just calling to say hi. Call me when you get home." Before dialing my own parents, I remembered that they were in Barbados for the holidays. I called a few friends and exchanged brief well wishes for Christmas and the New Year.

It had been only twenty-four hours since I'd checked Prudence's mailbox on Single in the City, and she'd already gotten 142 new responses. Was she really such a catch or did these men simply prescribe to what Daddy used to call the mud method? That is, throw mud in every direction and some of it will stick.

As I was deleting messages from the multitude of lovers of moonlit walks on the beach, I heard the ring of an Instant Message. Dr. Jay, I presume.

DrJay: Happy holidays, Prudence.

What was with this guy? I was so clearly not interested, and yet every time I logged on to the computer, there he was, cluelessly eager to chat with me. Or rather chat with Prudence. I'd have to go back and check out the photo of her that I posted. She is obviously much better looking than I gave her credit for. And there was more to Dr. Jay than I was giving him credit for. For some reason, I was glad to hear from him.

Prudence: Same to you, Dr. Jay. So tell me, why is a single, presumably good-looking single doctor home alone on Christmas Eve?

DrJay: Same reason you are, I guess.

Prudence: Highly doubtful.

DrJay: I'd really like to get together with you for coffee, Prudence.

Prudence: What are you doing tomorrow morning?

DrJay: Having coffee with you, I hope.

Prudence: On Christmas?!

DrJay: I told you I really want to have coffee with you.

Prudence: Wow, I'm feeling a little pressure. What exactly are you expecting that you'd be willing to meet with me on Christmas?!

DrJay: Don't take this the wrong way, Prudence. I really want to meet you, but it's not like I'm canceling any big plans for Christmas morning. I'm Jewish.

Prudence: Oh, I was flattered for a moment. What coffee place will be opened on Christmas?

As we finalized our plans, my heart raced as I realized I would have to explain to Jay that I was not, in fact, Prudence but, rather, her "friend" who's taken an unusual interest in finding her a new man. If Jay was the right guy for Prudence, how would I introduce them? And what if they really hit it off and *did* wind up in a serious relationship? Could I really expect Jay to keep hidden the fact that I'd posted a profile of Prudence on an Internet dating site? This is why I am not partial to doing things spontaneously. Having a plan and a contingency is a far better way to go. Unfortunately, I had neither.

Chapter Eight

Though I'd never seen him before, I recognized Jay the moment I walked into the diner. He had curly hair and a Jewish intellectual look just as he had in my burning-building dream, but he was a lot cuter than I'd thought he'd be. "Hi, Jay," I said, as I approached the table.

"Prudence?" he asked.

"Sort of."

"You look different from your photo," he continued.

I sat across from him on the sticky vinyl bench of the booth. A tired-looking waitress who looked as if she should be working at a truck stop in Wyoming nodded to let us know she'd be with us in a moment.

"I've got to come clean about something, Jay, and once I do, I'm not sure that you're going to want to have this coffee with me after all." He raised his eyebrows with curiosity, urging me to go on. "My name isn't Prudence." Jay laughed as though there was some irony in this disclosure. "Prudence is my friend who I want to fix up with a nice guy. Well, to be perfectly honest, she's my husband's ex-wife. I'd like to see her find a nice guy to settle down with now that Reilly and I are so happy together."

"Whoa, slow down," he said. "This isn't making sense."

"Reilly is my husband, Prudence's ex," I explained.

"No, that I get," Jay said. "It's the part about you being so happy that didn't make sense."

The waitress came to our table and asked if I wanted their special Christmas breakfast. After Jay inquired about it, Trudy explained that it was two eggs any style, hash browns, and bacon with juice, coffee, or milk. Pretty special. We ordered two and Jay leaned in to whisper, "What intrigued me about your e-mails was how utterly unhappy you seemed." I knit my brows, perplexed. "You seemed very angry, and frankly depressed about all that business with your husband being killed. Was that true?" I nodded. "Look, Prudence, I mean, what *is* your name?"

"Sarah."

"Sarah, I've got to come clean with you, too," he said. "I'm not really looking for a girlfriend on the Internet either. I'm doing research."

"Well, that's one thing we have in common. Research for what, though?"

"I'm a therapist. I thought it would be interesting to write a book about what type of people use

Internet dating services looking for a mate," he explained.

"What *type* of people?"

"Yeah, I thought I could find some sort of common thread and make an insightful observation about the drive to find love online," Jay said, as Trudy placed identical plates of 2,500 calories and 80 fat grams in front of us.

"Oh," I said, feeling disappointed. "So, I was just part of an experiment?"

"Not a very successful one, I'm afraid. Only three women would talk to me online. There was you, or Prudence. And you were so angry that I was fascinated by it. I thought I'd find that it was depressed women online."

"Depressed?" I asked. "You just said I sounded angry."

"Well, anger is only one symptom of depression. There're loss of interest in things that once excited you, inexplicable crying, trouble sleeping, to name a few." Oh my God, Jay was talking about my life for the last month. "Then there's focusing on everything else in the world so you don't have to deal with your own feelings."

"Jay!" I shouted. "You're describing me."

"Sarah, my name's not Jay."

"It's not? Are you even a doctor?"

"I am. A doctor who's also a basketball fan, hence the whole Dr. Jay thing. My real name is Jason."

"Oh," I sighed with relief. "That's no so far off. Jason, do you think I'm depressed?!"

"Do you?" he asked.

"So what other women did you meet online?" I asked.

"The usual," he said. "The kind who are totally honest, fun loving, and like to take long walks—"

"On the beach," we finished together and laughed.

I laughed again. "You know, if all of these totally honest men and women would just go down to the beach—"

"At sunset," Jason added.

I continued. "Right, if they all went down to the beach at sunset, wouldn't they be meeting each other there?"

"Yeah," he laughed. "You could never get a parking spot if all of these people were really going to the beach. It'd look more like a football game."

"Or a mall," I added. "God, why don't these people just say they like shopping and football? Clearly, that's what most people are doing on any given Sunday. Like the guy I saw on one dating website who said he had 'no time for phonies.' I saw his picture on another single's site with a different name and a whole different bio."

"Are you sure it was the same guy?"

"It was the *exact* same picture, Jason. Right down to the background of the sun setting on the ocean."

We laughed until it hit me. This guy *was* perfect for Prudence. He was genuine, funny, and just an overall nice guy. Not a plethora of great ideas for pop psych books but who cares?

"Jason, do you like art?"

"Do I like art?"

"Yes, do you like art?"

"Who doesn't like art?" he asked.

I wondered if it was because Jason was Jewish or psychoanalytical that made him answer my questions with his own. "Jason, yes or no. Do you like art? I mean enough to go to museums and galleries and the like?"

"You want to go to a museum?" he asked.

I laughed, feeling relieved with the inexplicable connection I felt with Jason. It wasn't simply that men from Internet dating sites had lowered my standards. There was something incredibly compelling about Jason. I liked him. Prudence would too. "No, I don't want to go to a museum. Nothing's open today anyway," I said. "But Prudence, my husband's ex-wife, is a real art lover and I thought if you are too, you might have something in common. Maybe you two could go to an exhibit and see if there's any chemistry."

"Oh, I don't know," Jason said.

"Are you married?" I snapped, remembering Doug Phillips.

"No, I'm not married. I'm very busy, though."

"So is she!" I said excitedly. "You want an independent woman, right?"

"I'm not sure I want a relationship right now," Jason dismissed.

My eyes popped wide with delight. "Neither does Prudence! In fact, she's pretty sure she doesn't want one. You two would be perfect for each other. You'd hardly ever have to see each other."

Now it was Jason laughing. "Sounds like my parents."

"Prudence has all kinds of issues with her parents too, Jason. The two of you could gab for hours dissecting your childhoods—at art museums! Doesn't this sound perfect?"

"It sounds like a Woody Allen movie," he said, placing his hand over mine. "To be candid with you, Sarah, the reason I'm here is because *you* fascinated me."

What was he saying? Jason was interested in me romantically?

As if he were reading my mind, Jason clarified. "Not that way. But clinically, you fascinate me. You lost your husband and never grieved, and now six years later your life is as tidy as can be, and you're falling apart. And now I find out that instead of working through this trauma, you're scurrying around trying to find a new husband for your husband's ex-wife."

"She did it first!" I said. "Prudence put an ad in the *Village Voice* and 'dated' dozens of women. She even had a party at an art gallery where she replaced the paintings with blown-up photos of Reilly."

"And this is the woman you think would be perfect for me?"

I retreated. "Oh, yeah, well, isn't that cute? I mean, at least she's not saying she's totally honest and likes to take walks on the beach. Jason, I don't see why you're being so stubborn about this. Can't you at least meet her? I can set something up very casual. It wouldn't even be a date. Who knows? It could work out."

Jason exhaled as if he was working up the courage to say something. "Okay. Tell you what. If

I agree to meet Prudence can we talk about Sarah? No more tangents? No more avoiding the subject? You'll answer all of my questions?"

"You want me to take the couch?" I asked. He nodded. "How long?"

Jason looked at his watch. "One hour."

"All I have to do is answer your questions?"

"And be totally honest," he said, winking.

"You want to talk about Rudy?" I asked, my eyes welling with tears.

"I do," he said softly. "I think it's time."

Moments later, tears were rolling down my cheeks despite the fact that we hadn't even started. This was going to be a tough hour. "I'm sorry," I said to Jason.

"For what?"

Again with the questions.

"For crying. I really thought I was over this," I explained.

Jason leaned in to place his hands over mine. "Sarah, how can you be over what you never started?"

Four hours later, I finished my session with Jason. My eyes were swollen with tears. I couldn't breathe because my nose was so stuffed from crying. And I was exhausted from the physical and emotional drain of sobbing uncontrollably for hours. He was especially interested in my nightmares and had me play the role of every character and object in each. At first, I felt incredibly self-conscious giving voice to the flames that threatened to kill me, but as I did, I realized that Jason was right. Every part of my dream was a part of me. The flames. The firefighter. Even Jason.

All in all, I felt better than I had in months, though. As we stood on the street corner, Jason told me that I was off to a "good start" and urged me to start grief counseling as soon as possible.

"I thought that was grief counseling?!" I said, laughing and crying again. Wasn't I done?

"Like I said, Sarah, you're off to a good start," he said, leaning in to hug me. Our bodies bonded to one another's, not like lovers, but like lifetime friends who'd recently reconnected after years. I didn't want to let go.

"You know you have to meet Prudence now, right, Jason?"

"I'm looking forward to it."

"Thank you," I said before turning to go. "I needed to do this."

"You needed to *start* this, Sarah."

"I'll call you soon!" I said, waving. "Keep an outfit clean and pressed. You have a mission now, and you've already chosen to accept it."

"Merry Christmas, Sarah."

I blew him a kiss. On my walk home I decided that in addition to enrolling in a poetry class, I would call one of the therapists Jason had referred. Therapy. Poetry. What was next, wearing black and smoking cigarettes?

Chapter Nine

Reilly and Hunter arrived home just as the sun was setting on Christmas night. Cold air rushed in with them and woke me from the hazy Christmas content I felt as I was cooking their favorite meal. As indifferent as Hunter seemed on the phone, when he burst through the door and hugged me, it was clear he'd missed his mommy. My arms wrapped around his down jacket, deflating it until my hands were pressed against his small frame. He smelled like pine trees and the smoke from the wood-burning stove Reilly said was in their cabin. When Hunter pulled off his wool hat, his blond hair stood with static electricity. "Want a candy?" he asked, pulling a handful of red and white swirl buttons from his pocket.

"What smells so good?" Reilly asked, leaning in to kiss me.

"I made lasagna," I said, smiling. I knew Reilly

adored my mother's recipe where the tomato sauce was left off until the moment before serving.

"What's the special occasion?" Reilly asked.

"That you're home," I answered.

"Aren't you sweet? Hunter take off your boots in the house!" Reilly shouted to our son, running downstairs. "Grab the bag too, little man."

"And I made pumpkin cheesecake," I added.

"Wow, you went all out."

I lowered my voice and gave him flirty eyes. "I will."

Reilly's head snapped up to look at me in surprise. "Sarah Peterson, what has gotten into you today?"

"I don't know," I said, with a slight giggle. "The Christmas spirit, I guess." I wondered if Reilly would misunderstand and think I was suggesting that a romantic evening with his wife was a gift, but thankfully he was not overly sensitive to my comment. I couldn't tell if he was blushing or if his ski trip had wind whipped his face.

Reilly slapped his hands together and asked if he could help set the table. "We skied a bit this morning so I think Hunter will drop off pretty easily tonight. Could we put a little something in his eggnog just in case?"

The next morning, I woke up and watched Reilly sleeping the way I did after our first night together. The bed was warm, the sky still dark and wind swept past the tree in our yard. Life was good.

I thought about my morning with Jason and wondered when I would tell Reilly about my accidental therapy session. How would I explain meeting him? Though we'd been married only a few months, Reilly knew me well enough to know I'd never seek a therapist on my own. I'd shared with him my feeling that therapy was self-indulgent dwelling on the past. I always had disdain for those who couldn't deal with their problems without the assistance of an outside consultant. Now, I was about to join the ranks of New Yorkers whose Christmas shopping lists included a little something for their analysts.

As it turned out, I had to come clean just hours later. Reilly took a phone call and spent the better part of five minutes giving short responses, like, "I see" and "Hmmm." It was tough to tell what he was talking about, but I knew it had something to do with me because Reilly darted glances at me and knit his brows. "Well, thanks for the call," he concluded. "I'll look into it."

Reilly hung up the phone and coldly asked if Hunter could go to his friend Stephen's house for the morning.

"I'd rather he stay home with us," I replied. "I missed you guys. What's up? Who was on the phone?"

"It was Bruce Piper from work," Reilly said.

"Okay," I said, inviting more. "What did Bruce have to say that requires me to send my son off for a play date?"

"Well, Sarah, it's not a conversation I want to have with Hunter in the house," he said, challenging me with his defiant tone.

"Why, what happened? Did something happen at the office? What could've gone wrong over Christmas?"

"Sarah," Reilly said, glancing toward the door that led downstairs.

"Oh, Reilly, come on. Let's sit at the kitchen table and keep our voices down."

He sighed and walked to the table, plopping himself onto a chair. Reilly lowered his voice. "Bruce said he saw you yesterday with some guy," he began. "Said you looked very chummy, hugging on Amsterdam Avenue."

"Oh," I said, obviously busted, though not for the crime for which I'd been accused. "That was Jason."

"I don't care what his name is, Sarah!" Reilly said sternly. "I've been through this already with Prudence and I thought I was pretty clear that I have no tolerance for infidelity."

"Good," I said. "Neither do I."

"So who is this guy groping you?"

"Reilly," I said, laughing. "Jason was not groping me. He's a friend. When you told me that you and Hunter weren't coming home, I called him for breakfast. He was very helpful to me in getting over my holiday blues. Don't you see how different I am today? I've been depressed for a month now, and Jason helped me get over it. Um, start getting over it," I corrected myself. I held Reilly's hands in mine. "Honey, I am not cheating on you. Jason is *just* a friend. A friend whom I want to set up with Prudence, in fact."

"How come I've never heard of him before?"

"Oh, boy," I sighed. "Look Reilly, I've got some explaining to do, but trust me, Jason is a friend, that's all." I took a deep breath and explained to him how I had embarked on this crazy scheme to find Prudence a new husband just in case she got any ideas about trying to reconcile. "I feel like an idiot, Reilly, but I felt like I was protecting our marriage by making sure Prudence was busy with another man, when all the while I was really busying myself so I wouldn't have to deal with the reality that I never grieved for my drunk of a husband, who killed himself and his mistress two nights before Hunter's first Christmas. I remember how you told me about how Prudence placed an ad to find a new wife for you, and I thought I'd try the same approach. She's doing quite well on Single in the City."

"Single in the City?" Reilly said, absorbing all of this as quickly as he could.

"Dot com," I said, though it came out as more of a question than statement.

"You put Prudence on the Internet?!"

I nodded, embarrassed, anticipating his response.

"And this guy Jason? You found him online?"

"He's a therapist," I said sheepishly. "He wasn't really looking for a date either, so I guess that makes us the two biggest frauds on the Internet, which is no easy thing to do, let me tell you. Anyway, as I said, he's a therapist and was interested in

Rudy's accident, and I've got to tell you, Reilly, I'm actually really glad I found Jason because I feel like a huge weight has been lifted after talking to him. You know me, I would have never gone to a therapist on my own, but judging from how much better I feel after one breakfast, I dare say, I needed one—and still do. Can you please say something?"

"I didn't know Rudy's accident was alcohol related," Reilly said.

"Everything with him was alcohol related, Reilly. Are you mad?"

He smiled. "No, but clearly you are. I still can't understand why you'd want to find Prudence a new husband."

"So she wouldn't come back for you," I said. "Life is so good with you, Reilly. I was afraid to lose it all, so I decided to find her a new husband." My eyes welled with tears when I saw Reilly looking so betrayed.

"So you've been dating men?" Reilly asked. "How many calls am I going to get from friends who've seen you around town with other guys?"

"Only one other," I said. "And I threw milk at him."

"How'd that go over?" Reilly asked, his tone softening.

"Not so well," I said, letting out the slightest laugh.

With that, all of the tension left our home. He got it. He got me. "How did I find the craziest women in New York?" he asked, shrugging his shoulders.

"Just lucky, I guess," I said. "Are you mad?"

"Honestly, Sarah, I'm a bit sad."

"Sad?"

"I would've liked to have been the one to help you work your way through your holiday depression. I wish you could have confided in me about all of this. We're supposed to be a team."

"We are a team, Reilly," I insisted. "But when one of the players is screwed up, sometimes things don't go exactly as planned."

"So I took one for the team?" he said, forgiving.

"Sort of."

"I guess I'm just happy that you found your way out of this funk, though I've got to admit I'm a little jealous that I couldn't be more helpful. When I asked you to marry me, I wanted to be your everything."

"Reilly, I need to be my everything."

"Okay." He shrugged. "Fair enough. So bring me up to date. You've gone on one date, threw milk at him, and met a therapist for yourself?"

"I think he and Prudence might hit it off," I said hopefully.

"Look, Sarah, you know it's you I love, don't you?" I nodded. "You have to know Prudence isn't a threat to us, right?" I nodded again. "So, how far into this are you? You haven't set up any parties where you give away mugs with her face on them, have you?"

"Sophie and Gwen want to throw a New Year's Eve party," I told him.

"Sophie's in on this?!" he asked incredulously. "I didn't know you two were friends." He sighed as if to give himself a moment to collect his thoughts.

"Well, a New Year's Eve party is out of the question 'cause Prudence always goes to Chad and Daniel's bash."

Reilly seemed to slip right into planning mode, contemplating a better night for such an event.

"Reilly, please tell me you're not mad at me for doing this."

"Oh, I'm mad all right," he said. "I'm pissed as hell that you didn't let me in on this from the beginning. Do you know what that woman put me through with her little *I Love Lucy* episode of trying to find me a new wife so she could run off with that surfer boy? I only wish I'd thought of this myself. What goes around comes around, Prudence. It's time for the ex-husband of Prudence to have a little fun."

Chapter Ten

By the next day, Reilly's zealousness had subsided a bit, but he was still fully on board. In fact, it was his idea to host a dinner for Sophie, Gwen, and the two of us so we could figure out a way to finagle ourselves an invitation to Chad and Daniel's New Year's Eve party.

Sophie accepted the invitation, quickly adding that she'd met someone at a friend's Christmas dinner whom she thought Prudence might like. Less surprising was the fact that Gwen had also met someone for Prudence. Over the last week, Gwen had transformed herself into a modern-day yenta, approaching men at parties, restaurants—anywhere she happened to be. She had set up three first dates, all of which were tremendously successful.

The following evening as the four of us sipped our wine, Gwen casually announced that she was planning to launch her own matchmaking service in the New Year. Smiling at Sophie and I, she said, "I can't tell you what fun I've had. It's like I have free license to approach men and ask them out because it's not for me. It's been positively liberating not to mention extremely rewarding because I really do have a knack for this. So far, everyone I've paired up has hit it off fabulously."

"What about your career in lunching?" Sophie asked.

"This is the perfect complement to it," she replied. "Do you have any idea how many people I meet at charity events? Now I have the perfect excuse to introduce myself to New York's hottest guys."

"And women," I added.

"Oh, they'll be introducing themselves to me," Gwen said.

Reilly chimed in. "So it sounds like everyone has met someone they like for Prudence. The question is, how do we get them—and us—to Chad and Daniel's party on New Year's Eve to meet her?"

"Reilly, you've been to their parties before," Sophie reminded him. "You know security is not a big issue. Chad and Daniel don't even know most of the people there. Last year, there were about two hundred people at their New Year's party, remember? We'll just bring them."

"Isn't that a bit presumptuous?" I asked.

"Those two queens opened their gallery to hundreds of women who came to see an exhibit of me," Reilly said, laughing at the memory. "Prudence used their place as a storage facility for my stuff so when her boyfriend came to visit, it looked like she lived there alone. I'd say Chad and Daniel owe me one."

"Better yet, why don't I just call and tell them what we're up to?" Sophie suggested.

"Oh," Reilly said, disappointed. "We could go that way if you want." I think he was enjoying the prospect of mischievousness.

New Year's Eve arrived. Reilly approached me from behind as I fastened my earrings and kissed my neck. "You know where I was last year at this time?" he asked. I shook my head. "On my way to Chad and Daniel's party with my wife who was having an affair and secretly trying to find a new wife for me. This year, I'm off to the same party with my new wife who was having a clandestine online relationship with a therapist while trying to find a new husband for my ex-wife." I laughed. "Without my wives, my life would be very boring."

The doorbell rang before I could respond, which was a good thing. As I scanned my mind for a witty retort, I came up blank. It was the babysitter, Megan, a freckle-faced teen with a mop of brown hair burying her face down to the retainer.

Chad and Daniel's apartment was a shrine to pop culture with their images morphed into well-known artwork. There was the Chad and Daniel American Gothic; Chad as "The Scream," with the background transformed into the Barneys half-yearly sale; and a Lichtensteinesque image of Daniel, with a dialogue bubble reading, "What would

Judy do?" There were the hanging and pregnant Chad mosaics made from colored card stock and a three-foot wire sculpture of a woman wielding a hanger overhead. I can only assume this was Joan Crawford as captured by Prudence. My favorite, though, was Chad and Daniel's bedroom, which was decorated like the inside of Jeannie's bottle with pink sashes fanning from the center of the ceiling to the corners of the floor. The round pink bed was too perfect, but I wasn't sure I understood how the statue of the short, fat Indian guy fit into the theme.

When I say a garage band was playing music, I don't mean a group of kids who practice in the garages of their suburban homes. These guys played car parts as instruments. A guy beat dip sticks against hub caps resting inside tires. A woman played several different car horns as a third member plucked away at fan belts. It didn't seem possible that these thick, cloth belts could be pulled so taut that they could be plucked like guitar strings, but somehow it worked. Personally, I think they had a track playing in the background and just toyed with the car parts as a gimmick.

"What do you think?" I asked Jason, as we looked around.

Before he could answer, Chad approached us with champagne and wishes for a happy new year. "Reilly, good to see you," he said. "The second wife of Reilly," he said, leaning in to kiss me. Looking at Jason, he said, "And you must be Bachelor Number Two? Sophie and Brad got here about an hour ago." Sophie saw us and waved, darting her eyes as if to ask us to check out her escort. Chad stage-whispered, "Brad is a sweetie, but I think Jason here is going to smoke him in the swimsuit competition."

With that, Gwen opened the door with a six-foot Adonis on her arm. He had a superhero jaw and dark brown hair that would cooperate with any weather. "Wow," we all said together, even Reilly.

"He's probably dumber than toast," I said, trying to make Jason feel better.

"Orthopedic surgeon," Chad corrected. "For the New York Giants. He was a wide receiver in the eighties."

On cue, Daniel approached our group and quipped, "Weren't we all?" He extended his hand to Reilly. "Good to see you again. You must be Sarah," he said to me.

"And this is Jason," I said, gesturing to him. "Our pick for Prudence."

Jason was awkward in his role. "I want to say for the record that I'm only here because I made a deal with Sarah. Normally, I wouldn't allow myself to be shopped around like this."

"Oh," Daniel said, with exaggerated disappointment. "Didn't Sarah tell you that our little Prudence has a habit of doing just that?"

"Did I hear my name?" And there she was.

Prudence Malone.

The first wife of Reilly. The one to whom I owe my marriage. The one I'd spent a month thinking about, instead of myself. I exhaled thirty days' worth of tension when I saw her. She was nothing. I don't mean to sound as though I disregarded her as a person, or that she was so unattractive as to be written off without thought. When I say she was nothing, what I mean is that in my mind she'd reached iconic levels of threat to me and my marriage. But here she was standing before me with her soft leather pants and a black, sequined button-down top, brushing her shoulder-length shag from her eyes, and she was just a woman. She smiled and said hello, flashing bright eyes and pearly teeth at me. With that small gesture I realized that Prudence Malone was a happy woman. And happy women don't tread on other women's marriages.

"Prudence, I don't think you've met Jason," I said, introducing the two. "He's a therapist."

"Really? How fascinating," Sophie chimed in immediately. "You're in the perfect city for it. Tell me, when you meet people socially, do you find yourself analyzing them?"

What was she talking about?

I told Sophie last week that Jason is a therapist. Why was she cutting in to the conversation with her silly little questions? By running off at the mouth, Sophie was siphoning precious time for Jason and Prudence to get to know each other. Just as Prudence turned to speak to Adonis the surgeon, Gwen possessively linked her arm through his. Brad walked away to get a drink, and Jason was fully immersed in conversation with Sophie. Chad shot me a look as if to agree that this wasn't going according to my plan.

Jennifer and her husband arrived just before midnight. She was wearing Harvey Fierstein's gown from *Hairspray*, which posed a stark contrast to her conservatively casual clad spouse. I watched her kiss Prudence on both cheeks and laugh about something. Jason and Sophie had disappeared. Gwen scurried me off into the bathroom to tell me she planned to keep Adonis. "If nothing else, he's fabulous advertising for my matchmaking skills," she said, referring to her new business endeavor.

"Ah, the second wife of Reilly," Jennifer said, as she approached me. "How's it going?"

"Not so well," I confided. "So far, all of our eligible bachelors have disappeared and Prudence doesn't seem to care a bit."

"Care about what?" Prudence asked, appearing from nowhere.

Jennifer kept cool, but I was visibly shaken. "About nothing," I said, my eyes darting around the room searching for Reilly to help bail me out. He was chatting with Jen's husband, Adrian. As I scanned the room, I also caught a glance of Sophie making out with Jason. It seemed as if we were not only going to fail to find Prudence a new husband by the stroke of midnight, but we were also about to get caught.

"Sarah, what's the matter with you?" Prudence asked. "You just said 'Prudence doesn't seem to care.' Care about what?"

Jennifer took control. "Sarah was just saying how lovely it is that you're not bothered by her being here."

"No, not at all, why would I?" Prudence said.

"Well, it's not every current and ex-wife who could be at the same party together," Jennifer commented.

"True," Prudence dismissed, with a smile. "So, Sarah, how is your son?"

"Hunter?" I beamed, just to say his name. Who else could she mean? "He's wonderful. And Reilly is a terrific father to him. And how are you adjusting to single life, Prudence? I heard you had a real adventure in Italy this summer. Did you meet anyone?"

"I did," she said serenely. "Myself."

Patting her on the back playfully, Jennifer added, "Prudence hasn't had so much as a collagen injection since she started with the sculptures."

"Oh, yes," I said, "Gwen said they were remarkable. I'd like to come see your next show, if that's okay."

"I'd like that," Prudence said.

"And I hope you'll come to my first poetry reading," I offered.

"Sure," they both answered together. "When is it?" Jennifer asked.

"I'm not sure. I have to write the poetry first." I giggled a bit nervously. "But some time next year, that's for sure."

"Okay, sounds good," Prudence said.

Glancing over at Reilly, I had a spectacular idea. As much as I was enjoying the party, I realized I didn't need to wait until midnight to start the new year.

"Prudence, Jennifer, it was great catching up with you both, but I think we're going to head out," I explained to my husband's ex-wife and her friend.

Jennifer urged me to stay. "Oh, no! The ball's going to drop in forty minutes. Stay till the New Year, won't you?"

"Let her go," Prudence said. "Not that we aren't enjoying your company, but I know how it goes when you're tired. Who cares where she is when the silly ball drops, Jen?"

"Thanks for understanding," I said. "Please send me an invitation to your next show. Really."

"Okay, I will," she promised. "And you let me know when that poetry reading of yours is."

And that was it. She was nothing more than a lovely woman who was once married to my husband. She wasn't a threat. And she certainly didn't need my help. But I did.

Ever the easygoing husband, Reilly agreed to leave Chad and Daniel's party, and with it, my plans to find someone new for Prudence. I looked for Jason, but someone said that he and Sophie had locked themselves in the pantry, so I figured he was in good hands. I waved at Gwen, who winked to acknowledge me, then turned back to Adonis, who was regaling a group with NFL stories.

"Chad, Daniel, we're going to get going now," I told our hosts. Chad kissed me and said he hoped I wasn't too disappointed by the way things turned out. "Not at all," I assured him. "I think Prudence is happy being single, and I'm happy being married."

"And I'm happy being gay," said Daniel, leaning in for his good-night kiss.

"So, it all worked out for the best," I said.

"I hope this isn't the last we'll see of you, Sarah," Chad said.

"It won't be," I assured them. "I can see why Prudence and Sophie are so fond of you both. We'll get together soon."

As Reilly and I stood on the sidewalk, waiting to hail a taxi, I winked at Reilly. "Good party, but I have a much better way for us to ring in the New Year," I said.

"Sarah Peterson, have I told you lately how happy I am to be married to you?"

"Reilly, have I told you how lucky I am to be married to *you?*"

He squeezed my hand three times and winked at me.

"Reilly, there's a taxi!" I shouted, excited by our good fortune.

"He's off duty," Reilly said.

My hand shot up. "Let's see if he'll take us anyway."

The driver pulled over and rolled his window down. Leaning toward us, he said he would only take a fare uptown.

"West Seventy-fourth?" I said, smiling hopefully.

"Perfect," he replied.

As we settle into the back seat of the taxi, Reilly looked at me a little longer than he usually did. "Sarah," he began, "I have a feeling this is going to be the best year of our lives."

"I do too, Reilly." At the stroke of midnight, I leaned in to kiss my husband and wished him a happy new year, then sat back and enjoyed the rest of the taxi ride home.

Please turn the page for an exciting sneak peek of
Jennifer Coburn's
THE WIFE OF REILLY,
now on sale at bookstores everywhere!

TAKE MY HUSBAND, PLEASE. . . .

Okay, here's how it happened. I went to my college reunion and hooked up with Matt, the love of my life, my soul mate, the one who got away. After the most wonderful weekend together, he said something like, "I love you; let's get married," and I could swear I heard myself say "Yes!" Maybe that would have been a good time to tell him about Reilly—my husband. . . .

Honeslty, I'm not a bad person. Just crazy in love. And temporarily insane. Or maybe permanently selfish. The truth is that Reilly's a great guy but our marriage has been over for a while. Before you ask, it just fizzled between us. So what's a girl to do? Find him a new wife, that's what.

Place an ad—wife wanted. Easy as that. Everybody gets a happy ending . . .

. . . or life becomes a dizzying train wreck of continual catastrophe. Finding the perfect replacement for myself isn't as easy as I thought it would be. Sorting through the weirdos, nymphos, gold diggers, man-haters, and just plain desperate (I thought

I had issues!) while balancing a husband in New York and a fiancé in L.A. is enough to make me go stark raving mad. I've got a forty-word personals ad running, an unstoppable American Express card, and just a few months to find my replacement and make things all right. With a little help from my friends and a bit of luck, I just might find the next wife of Reilly . . .

Finding a new wife for my husband was not going to be an easy task. Keeping Reilly a secret from my new fiancé was going to be an even greater one. This sounds just awful, I'm sure. While it's true I've gotten myself in a rather sticky situation juggling a husband and boyfriend, it doesn't automatically make me a bad person. I'll be the first to admit I handled things poorly last weekend. I plead temporary stupidity. All right, permanent selfishness. But all I have is today, and today this is the reality I'm dealing with. I could dwell in regret over my mistake, which does no one any good. Or I can do something to repair the damage I've done.

I read somewhere that forty percent of married women cheat on their husbands. Nowhere have I ever heard of a soon-to-be ex-wife finding her own replacement so her husband isn't lonely after the divorce. That's got to count for something, doesn't it?

I knew my plan was a bit unusual. The good news was that so were the three friends I would enlist in my mission. Jennifer, Sophie and Chad would surely understand why finding a new wife for Reilly was something I needed to do.

My friends in Ann Arbor had a hard time accepting that I'd fallen in love with my college boyfriend over the course of one homecoming weekend. Cindy was morally outraged by my infidelity, as if it were her I cheated on. Eve was more demure in her contempt, but she was equally disappointed by my transgression. Both were too busy judging me to bother asking how I felt about the whole thing. As the cheater, the only feeling I was apparently entitled to was guilt; of this, I had plenty. But along with my remorse, I had an intense need for a friend to ask me how I was doing. How I felt about the fact that my marriage had became a straw house. If I had any conflicted feelings over divorcing Reilly. Or marrying Matt.

As I walked in the door of the Monkey Bar, our favorite midtown lunch spot, Jennifer's cab pulled up to the curbside and I watched her long brown legs make their exit. A full minute later, Jennifer followed. Even at noon, wherever she went, it was evening. Jennifer was the kind of woman who seemed to be always accompanied by a sultry saxophone soundtrack written just for her. Jennifer gets out of cab. Jennifer walking. Prelude to

Jennifer. She would've been great as one of those femme fatales in a film noir flick if only they were casting black folks as leads in those days. She was sexy, powerful and, oddly enough at six feet tall, dainty.

Chad and Sophie were already inside exchanging stories over stubby glasses. Both elbows of Chad's powder blue suede jacket rested on the table as he whispered to Sophie, conspiratorially. Sophie threw back her head of wavy black hair as she laughed, then softly patted Chad's hand. I felt like I was missing something.

Sophie moved to New York last year after her divorce. Last year, she sold her house in the suburbs, packed up her kids and drove five days straight from San Diego. She no longer works thanks to a case she won representing eighty-four plaintiffs in a class action lawsuit against a chain of Chinese restaurants in Southern California called Lo Fats. The cooks put quite a bit more fat into the recipes than the calorie count indicated on the menu. Sophie was able to convince a jury that the misrepresentation of calories and fat grams contributed to four fatal heart attacks among cardiac patients who thought they were eating light, and eighty cases of depression among women who couldn't understand why they weren't losing weight on their strict Lo Fats diet. She won a $49 million verdict, and was able to collect half for her clients before the chain ultimately filed bankruptcy.

Jennifer raised her eyebrows as if to cue my announcement. "So what's your big news?" she asked.

She's the creative director for Ogilvy and fancies herself the queen of marketing. Over the years, she's gotten me into the annoying habit of comparing things to advertisements. She shops at Off Broadway's Back, a boutique in the theatre district that sells used costumes from shows. Usually, people shop there when they're planning to attend a masquerade party, but Jennifer actually wears these getups as her everyday attire. She's shown up at work wearing the gold-sequined top hat from *A Chorus Line.* She's attended meetings with major clients dressed as Aida. Jen is attractive enough to get away with these outrageous clothes, and her agency's clients assume that anyone who dresses this way must be some sort of mad, creative genius.

"I know this is going to sound kind of weird, but, well, as you know I went to Ann Arbor this weekend, and I ran into an old boyfriend," I began.

"And?" Jennifer coaxed.

"I'm engaged."

"You're what?" asked Chad.

"Engaged," I said, softer this time.

"Engaged in what?" he quizzed.

"Engaged, engaged. You know, getting married."

"Prudence, I'm confused. You *are* married," Sophie added.

"Good Lord," Chad said. "You're not serious, are you Prudence?"

I nodded tentatively, my eyes wide for their approval. I told them I'd fallen in love with Matt and the two of us planned to marry this summer after he sold his house in Los Angeles and found a job in New York. "This is my soul mate, you guys," I said as a preamble to recalling my weekend. "I'm completely and madly in love, so can you just be happy for me?"

"I'm not following this," Jennifer said. "What did you tell, what's his name, Mike? Mark?"

"Matt."

"Matt," Jennifer corrected herself. "Does he know about Reilly? Does he know you're married already?!"

"Not exactly." I hesitated, knowing this was the cruelest part of my weekend of lies. "I never actually said this, but Matt kind of thinks Reilly's dead."

They stared incredulously.

"Look, I know this sounds bizarre, even to me," I explained. "You know I don't ever do flaky things like this. Isn't everyone entitled to a screw-up every now and then?"

"I'd say this is more than a little screw-up," said Chad. "Pretending your husband is dead so you can fool around with an old boyfriend is a tad vile, dear."

Chad owns the gallery under the loft that Reilly and I bought when we first married. He's a good fifteen years older than us, and was one of those starving young painters who had the good sense to buy a few warehouses dirt cheap in SoHo in the 1970s. He was one of the original artists who helped transform the area into an upscale creative oasis. His partner Daniel is a sculptor who bares a remarkable resemblance to Mr. Clean with multiple earrings. Both are huge fans of pop culture, so they nearly keeled over from delight when they found a computer program that would morph art and inject them into the scene. They created a gigantic *American Gothic,* using themselves as the farm couple, which hangs over their white velvet sectional. Daniel has been transformed into *The Scream* with the background changed to the Barney's half-yearly sale. Chad did himself as a colorful Lichtensteinesque figure, gasping, "What would Judy do!" Chad and Dan's room is modeled after the inside of Jeannie's bottle, complete with six thousand pillows, sashes in every shade of pink that fan out from the center of the ceiling to the floor periphery, and a fat mannequin that the guys painted light brown and put a turban on. They hugged me when I was the only one who got that the dummy was supposed to be Cousin Hodgie.

"I know it's vile," I conceded with a mix of humility and impatience. "But this is where I am now, so I've got to work with what I've got. Telling me that the situation is screwed up helps no one. I already know I fucked up, but I'm going to fix everything. I'm getting to that. Everyone's going to end up better off in the long run, I promise. Even Reilly. Especially Reilly."

"Since when are you and Reilly unhappy, anyway?" Jennifer asked. "You never even said anything was wrong."

"Have I ever said anything at all?" I asked.

"Okay, here I can add the voice of experience," said Sophie. "There doesn't have to be anything *wrong* for there to be something wrong with a marriage, if you know what I mean."

By the expressions on Chad and Jennifer's faces, clearly they did not.

Sophie sighed through her nose and tried again. "There doesn't have to be anything terribly wrong with a marriage for it to be over. There doesn't have to be a big drama. The fact that there's no drama is probably one of the reasons that Prudence felt a need to shake things up a bit."

Chad rolled his eyes and listened to Sophie's philosophy on the erosion of the drama-free marriage. "Prudence, you know we love you, darlin', but there's a big difference between shaking things up a bit and getting engaged to an old lover who thinks your husband is dead. Dead, Prudence. That's not your garden variety self-aggrandizing fib. You didn't just lie about your weight, you told a man that Reilly is dead. You know he's not really dead, Prudence, don't you?"

"She already told you to back off, Chad," Jennifer jumped to my defense. "Prudence already knows what she did was deranged. Let's not rub her nose in it by constantly reminding her of what a bizarre and disturbing lie she's told."

Sophie turned to me. "Would you mind telling us again about how he took your panties off with his teeth?" she asked.

I gladly obliged, as it signaled, if not approval, acceptance of my choice.

"Your e-mail said you needed our input," Jennifer said. "What'd'ya need from us?"

"Well, I really need your creative minds," I began.

"Good Lord, I'm frightened already," muttered Chad.

"I need to find Reilly a new wife to replace me after I leave him."

They all stared blankly. Some creative minds, I thought. All they can do is stare at me in disbelief.

"You lost me, Prudence," said Jennifer. "Why'd'ya need to find Reilly a new wife?"

"Because," I urged them.

Sophie knit her brow with confusion. "I hate to say it, but I'm not following this either. Who said you have to find Reilly a new wife?"

"Reilly hasn't done anything wrong," I explained. "It's not right to just leave him wifeless."

"Prudence," Chad said in a soft voice like he was talking to a crazy person. "People divorce all the time without finding their replacement."

"I know, but it just seems like the right thing to do. He's *such* a decent person. He doesn't deserve to be dumped like this."

"If he's so great he'll find another woman on his own," Chad said. "Mr. Wonderful doesn't need the matchmaking services of the yenta widow over here." He gestured toward me. He looked at me again. "Besides, what makes you think he'll want anything to do with a woman *you* choose for him. Don't you think he'll be a bit miffed with you for divorcing him? Why would he want your consolation prize?"

The waiter brought our check and Chad slid it

to me. "Thank you for letting me choose my own lunch, by the way, love." He winked.

"Look, I just don't feel right about leaving Reilly alone. I want to help him get a fresh start with someone new. Why is that so hard to understand?"

" 'Cause it's ridiculous," Chad muttered audibly.

"No, it's not ridiculous," I defended. "I'm cleaning up the mess I've made. I'm evening the score. Maybe it's the accountant in me that can't stand to see Reilly lose one wife without getting another. I may be a lot of things, but I do have compassion for the man. I can't stand to think of him alone."

"You sure your motives are really so pure?" asked Jennifer.

All heads turned toward her. "Maybe you just can't stand being the bad press."

Four eyes glided to me, as Jennifer continued. "Dumping Reilly for another guy is gonna make you the bad guy in many people's eyes." She paused as if to consider whether or not she was going to say her next thought aloud. "We all know how important universal adoration is to our little Prudence."

Jennifer's tone got more serious. "Prudence, I don't want to bludgeon you with the obvious, but who else in your life walked out on his family?" she continued.

"Who?"

"Prudence," she said in exasperation. "Your father."

"This is *nothing* like him!" I shouted, disgusted by the comparison. "He should have been so considerate as to find my mother a new husband instead of leaving us high and dry. My father thought of nothing else other than his own happiness when he left us. I would have loved it if he spent the time to find me a new father—a *real* father—before he took off to Never Never Land."

"You said he lived in Larchmont," Sophie said.

"I mean he won't grow up, Sophie!"

Now I suppose I must explain Father. I guess I have a lot of explaining to do so I'll start with Trenton Malone, a selfish bastard who I see about twice a year when he's gracious enough to invite me to his holiday gatherings with his wife Carla, a young tart who gave birth to my half sister Ashley, exactly six months after my father moved out of our home. Even at twelve years old, I could do the math. Then came Whitney and Paige, pushing me even further into the margins of Father's life.

I refuse to call him "my father." He's known as either "Sperm Donor" or "Father." I like to call him Father because it is so formal it reminds him that we have no familiarity. The sound of my voice calling him Father poses such a hideously beautiful contrast to the voices of his daughters calling him "Daddy." Whenever we're at events and the older Goldilocks Sisters start in with "Daddy this" and "Daddy that," I always make a point of going up to him (preferably in front of large groups of guests) and saying with the gloom of Morticia Addams, "Father, you're running low on canapés."

Chad's unexpected apology brought me back to the restaurant. "We just care about you, love," he said. "I'm sorry to be so hard on you, but I think you're making a terrible mistake and I don't want to see you get hurt."

Sophie agreed. "This all does seem rather sudden, you must admit. Let me ask you, what is it that you love about Matt?"

"I guess I love the way he makes me feel," I answered. "He makes me feel, what's the word? Visible. Heard. He makes me feel whole. He completes me."

"Isn't that a line from *Jerry Maguire?*" asked Jennifer.

"I don't remember if it is, but it's the truth!" I protested. "Matt completes me," I said, satisfied that I'd answered their question. I signed the credit-card slip and left the copy inside the folder for our waiter to pick up.

"Complete yourself, love," said Chad. "What are you telling us, that you're incomplete? Come on. You're a hip, good-looking New Yorker with an Ivy League MBA and partnership at one of the biggest accounting firms on the planet. You're in good health, spend your free time the way you like, you've got a closet full of beautiful clothes and fabulous friends like us to hang out with. I don't know how to break it to you honey, but you are complete. Whether you know it or not Prudence Malone, you *are* complete." He smiled. "Now, tell us about the underwear ripping thing again. That *was* kind of hot."

"Do you guys think I'm a slut?" I asked.

"A *complete* slut," Jennifer laughed.

Sophie had a philosophy on sluts too. When she spoke, Sophie reminded me of honey being poured on a very grateful apple. It's as if she knows she's got something special to say and isn't afraid to make you wait for it. "Women who are branded sluts are truly independent thinkers who dare to question and indeed redefine social mores. They're frightening to the patriarchal construct because they live life on their own terms. I hate when women are called sluts. It's so typically American to be so hung up about sex." Sophie regularly defended her own lifestyle through abstract arguments that sound as though they might be taught in a cultural anthropology class taught by Hugh Hefner.

The table was silent. "Before I give you the big 'you go girl,' let me clarify one thing," began Chad. "Isn't your family from Mexico? Didn't you spend most of your life in San Diego?"

She nodded again, perplexed as we all laughed.

"What is so funny?" asked Sophie.

Chad caught his breath. "Not exactly the bastion of sexual freedom, love. 'It's so American,' " he imitated her. "It's not like you're from Brazil, honey. You're from San Diego. Didn't they host the Republican convention there? Ever heard anyone singing about not forgetting to put flowers in your hair when you go to *San Diego?*"

We all laughed.

"Honey, say it's stupid, say it's rigid, but 'it's so typically American' sounds like you're from a band of gypsy whores who traveled the back roads of Turkey giving blow jobs for gas money."

She joined in the laughter. "We *did* give blow

jobs for gas money. Shut up and stop disrespecting our family business!"

"Okay, back to Prudence," Jennifer directed. "What do you need from us to help find Reilly a new wife? Sounds like you've got some kind of *I Love Lucy* type of scheme up your sleeve, and if that's the case, let me be the first to say, count me in!"

"And let me be the first to say, count me out," said Chad. "We had drinks last week. You said you were going to Michigan to spend time with your girlfriends. You said you were going for some big football weekend. This is out of nowhere, and I, for one, think you're out of your mind. I'll have no part of this. No part. Do you understand?"

Chad was right. The highlight of my weekend was supposed to be seeing Cindy and Eve. If University of Michigan won its football game, even better. Never did I predict that the homecoming weekend would begin a chain of events that would fundamentally change my life. Chad once told me that when he painted, the canvas always ended up completely different than what he'd originally envisioned. He said his process was one where unexpected choices had to be made, and that art was about being open to change that would inevitably unfold before us. I thought it sounded a bit goofy at the time, but now I'd give anything for him to apply this philosophy to my current dilemma.

Mistletoe and Holly

Liz Ireland

Chapter One

I may be twenty-eight, but I'm a five-year-old when it comes to Christmas. The sight of a trimmed tree fills me with unrealizable expectations of holiday bliss, an affliction I blame on overexposure to those schmaltzy TV commercials and Christmas movies. Though I might gripe about all the over-the-top hoopla, I secretly look forward to it. Put it this way: I am not 100 percent certain what a sugarplum is, but for a few weeks every year I've got visions of them dancing in my head anyway.

And, then, sometime between December 26 and January 1, the festivity ends and I straggle back to my apartment feeling exhausted, broke, and somehow lonelier than before. This is when I start wondering if it might not be better for everyone if Christmas were an event staged every four years, like the Olympics.

But by the next time the holidays roll around I think, *this year will be different.*

This will be the year when I'll look like I belong in that Christmas picture my sister, Maddie, sends me every January—the one taken with her elaborate, spendy camera equipment. (Dad always brags that Maddie could have been a professional photographer if she hadn't settled on medical school.) In the picture—which is always the same, every year—everyone is smiling deliriously in front of the nine-foot Douglas fir that sags with decades of accumulated holiday gewgaws. In it, my mom and dad lock arms in a way they never do on any other of the 364 days of the year. My button-downed, razor-jawed brother, Ted, with his beautiful wife, Melinda, a former Pilates instructor, hover over their two daughters, blond cherubs who strike adorable poses without being coached. Then there is my little sister, Maddie, the star of the family, who is always with her boyfriend of the moment—always an overachieving Ivy Leaguer like herself. She's seen planting an extravagant smooch on his cheek, or jumping piggyback onto him and beaming over his shoulder. They're usually dressed in matching holiday sweaters, which Maddie says is so dorky it's cute, when really it's just dorky.

And then there is me, the one with the game but shell-shocked look on her face, a smile that says, *I've drunk way too much eggnog.* For a year I've known this moment was coming, but inevitably something on me looks askew. My hair is sticking up funny, or my cardigan is sagging off one shoulder, or static cling has caused my skirt to crawl halfway up my thigh. Typically I've just had to hop out of Maddie's way as she streaks from her tripod and leaps into the arms of her significant other, so in some of the pictures I'm little more than a blur trailing off the edge of the frame.

Every year as the holiday season bears down, I think, *This is the year I won't be on the fringes.* Through some unexplainable holiday magic, I will suddenly come into my own and no longer be the black sheep of my family. I won't feel the crushing pressure of my father's disappointment in me, always couched in terms of going to grad school. And maybe this will be the year the sibling rivalry I've always had with Maddie will evaporate, along with the inadequate feeling I get when I compare my life with my CPA brother's well-ordered, fault-free life.

Most of all, I think that maybe, just maybe, this won't be another year when I skirt uncomfortably around that ubiquitous sprig of mistletoe Mom tacks up every year, glaringly aware that I am the only adult in the family not in a position to take advantage of it.

Most of the time I'm just kidding myself. But last year *was* different. Last year, I found Jason.

What can I say about Jason? He was absolutely everything—absolutely adorable, charismatic, available. Absolutely perfect. Which is surprising, because I met him in a bar. It was just before Thanksgiving. He was there with guys from his Wall Street office, and I was there with Mary Beth, a friend who gave up teaching high school economics for a six-figure job selling mutual funds. (Go figure.) I was just getting the slightest bit bleary-eyed listening to Mary Beth's office gossip when I happened to catch the gaze of this incredible guy, this Adonis, on the other side of her. The spark in those baby blues of his was like a shot of adrenaline to my system. One look and I was in lust with the man. One conversation (Mary Beth *who?*) and I was over the moon. One date and I was sure I had found *the one.*

Christmas was galloping up on us, and on our second date the subject of what we would do came up. "I'm going home," I said. "I mean, to my parents' house."

"And where is that?"

"The DC burbs—Arlington, Virginia."

When I first moved to New York City, this was a point of conflict with my folks. They wanted me to settle nearer to them, like my brother, Ted, did—or at least somewhere *nice.* For instance, Maddie lives in Boston, which is farther away than NYC, but she has an adorable little apartment in the stuffy Back Bay. But in recent years, I've noticed that they want me to move less and less. I suspect they look upon New York City the way people in the old days viewed secluded mountain sanitariums—a good place to park those more troublesome relations.

"And Christmas is a big deal?" Jason asked eagerly. He seemed genuinely interested.

"Think MGM extravaganza." I tried to explain the madness that seemed to take hold of everyone, starting the morning of the day after Thanksgiving, when my normally sedentary father, a history professor, risks life and limb to swath our Cape Cod–style house in lights and plant a trio of wire reindeer on the flat roof over the breakfast nook. In our yard, any protuberance natural or man-made gets ringed in lights, or at least has a giant bow slapped on it. In addition, last year Dad purchased a nine-foot inflatable sledding polar bear to display next to the garage.

And that's just the outside. Inside, each room is testament to my mother's shaky grasp on mental health when it comes to collectable Christmas tchotchkes. She has two separate and almost complete snow villages—collections of miniature houses, churches, and stores that rest on cotton wool snow artfully arranged on bookshelves and side tables. One village has an alpine theme; one is a Dickens village. Each scene has miniature people one can accumulate—action figures for holiday-obsessed adults. You have to be careful around these things, though. One year I thoughtlessly used the frozen pond by the alpine village for a coaster and ended up decapitating a tiny ice skater with my coffee mug.

The snow villages are just the tip of the iceberg. There are other displays everywhere you turn. Santa and his reindeer charging across an evergreen-festooned mantel. A crystal angel votive holder choir singing in the bathroom. Monk figurines sledding down a Styrofoam hillside on top of the baby grand piano. For several years, my mother was in thrall to little people fashioned out of nuts (walnuts, primarily) and raisins, so that any flat surface in the house not occupied by other Christmas ephemera is now the domain of the walnut people. There are walnut carollers, a walnut

Santa with his walnut elves, a walnut man in lederhosen feeding two peanut squirrels and a Brazil nut raccoon. (Feeding them nuts, presumably.)

And then there are all the rituals. At my house, Christmas offers about as many surprises as a TV Yule log. The arrival and emptying of cars of their gift-wrapped loot, the drive around the neighborhood to eye competitively everyone's lighting displays, the little speech my mom makes during the big Christmas Eve dinner to say how glad she is we are all together, shivering through midnight mass at National Cathedral, the orgy of presents, and then the culminating second feast centered on a very large ham my brother prides himself on bringing each year—it all proceeds according to the same set script each year.

As I described it all to Jason, I started to feel a little self-conscious, as if I were an escapee from a Norman Rockwell painting. It all sounded so bland, so predictable, so hokey.

But Jason's eyes were glazed over in a dreamy, almost envious way, and the only times he interrupted me were to ask for more detail. *The wire reindeer have lights, too? Your nieces are how old? Presents on Christmas morning or Christmas Eve?*

"What do you do for Christmas?" I asked him when I was finally talked out.

He raised his shoulders in a shrug. "It depends. Last year I went skiing but . . ." His eyes seemed anguished, and a little muscle in his jaw hopped. "Well, you see, I don't have what you would call a real family."

I was a little taken aback. Jason DeWitt looked

like the kind of man who had been to prep schools. His appearance was so impeccable, his manners so flawless, I'd pegged him for the silver spoon type, with family lined up all the way back to the Mayflower.

"I was raised in foster homes, mostly," he confessed.

And then his life story spilled out, holding me rapt for an hour. He was an *orphan*. It was like something out of Dickens: Poor boy works his way through college waiting tables. He quickly climbs the corporate ladder and acquires all the accoutrements of success but never finds real happiness, or love . . .

It was heartbreaking.

And then he dropped a hint. *Had I ever brought anyone home for Christmas?*

No, but I was going to. This year. As soon as I came out of my swoon.

I pictured us in matching holiday sweaters under that damn mistletoe sprig, or strolling mitten in mitten down to the little park not far from my house. Most wonderful of all, I envisioned the shocked looks on my family's faces. *You mean you actually found someone normal?* those not-so-subtle glances would say.

Oh, my imagination was racing. Maddie would flirt like mad with Jason and profess jealousy of me. Dad would probably just look relieved . . . yes, I had gone to a second-tier state school, run away to New York and become a schoolteacher, but at least I wouldn't be a *spinster*. That musty old nugget of a word still resonated with my dad and my brother. Every time I had seen Ted lately, I could detect pity in his eyes, because my life would obviously never be as perfect as his wife's.

I was beginning to have doubts myself.

Then Jason had fallen into my lap. It was a Christmas miracle.

For weeks afterward I was walking on a cloud, unable to grasp my good fortune, and yet, at the same time, clinging to it for all it was worth. Jason and I did all the seasonal stuff that I had given up hoping ever to be a part of, except maybe as a spectator in a movie theater. We bundled up and ice-skated in Rockefeller Center and watched the lighting of the tree there. One Saturday we braved the department stores to do our shopping together. (Jason might have been an orphan, but he had a gift list a mile long—a million people at the office, innumerable friends, his UPS man, and the nice lady at the dry cleaners who did such a great job on his shirts. He didn't want to forget anybody.) The next night we went to see *The Nutcracker.*

It was pinch-me-I'm-dreaming time. And the most amazing thing was, Jason was a gentleman. *Really* a gentleman. I had almost forgotten what that word meant. For him, a relationship wasn't a race to get a woman into the sack. Every date was a new milestone to him, and kisses weren't just preludes to something better, but wonderful events to be savored for their own sake.

It was a revelation.

It was also so damn frustrating.

For the first time, I was the one who was in a hurry. Not that I wanted to appear too pushy . . . but, you know, I sort of wanted to have sex again before the AARP found me.

"I don't want to rush things," Jason would say as he deposited me at my stoop. Then he would bestow one last sweet, agonizingly brief kiss on my lips. Which always left me in a puddle of embarrassingly acute lust. Would I ever be able to seduce him, or would we just spend the next ten years making (chastely) merry?

Then it dawned on me: Christmas was my ace in the hole. He was so excited about going to my folks' house. I would just have to bide my time and let him be seduced by all that familial Christmas madness. Maybe Perry Como on the stereo and a few walnut people would do for my sex life what weeks of pouncing on him in taxis would not.

To that end, I started readying myself. I indulged myself in facials and manicures, treated myself to a $200 haircut, and began buying and squirreling away sexy lingerie so I would be primed for the big moment.

When it came time for our private gift swapping, I was in a stew. When you've only known someone four weeks, haven't slept with him, but are pretty sure you're in love with him anyway, what do you buy? I agonized. Did I go straight for the luxury goods—a new watch, say? Or something more modest, or meaningful?

I thought about sexy gifts. Novelty holiday boxers and the like. But in the end, I sensed Jason would have considered these in questionable taste. I wanted something personal, something understated.

Then, during our shopping expedition, Jason admired a scarf. It wasn't just a normal scarf, but an extravagantly long piece of soft wool woven in a blue and burgundy stripe. A Fifth Avenue update on the old 1920s collegiate scarf. It was outrageously expensive—more than I had ever dreamt of spending on a cold weather accessory—but I sneaked back and bought it for him after work the following Monday.

Then I agonized more. Was I insane? I had just bought the man of my dreams *a muffler.*

But he had really seemed to love it.

But it was a muffler.

I kept the receipt.

My friends, who had all suffered through my periodic heartbreaks, embraced Jason in a way that surprised me. All but one friend, that is. My best friend, Isaac. And even Isaac withheld his opinion until he began viewing Jason as an obstacle. A transportation obstacle. Isaac wanted a ride home for Christmas.

In Virginia, Isaac's family and mine were practically neighbors. My mother has known his mother for ages through the local mah-jongg circuit. But I didn't meet Isaac until I was twenty-five and already living in New York.

Three years ago my mother called me up and delivered the most chilling words that had ever rattled over a phone line into my ear. "Holly, I've just gotten you a date!"

She sounded so proud, too. As if she had achieved the impossible.

I repeat, I was twenty-five at the time. Twenty-five. Though I'm not sure I would have been happy to hear those words at fifteen, or any age. Especially when followed by her next sentence.

"I'm sure you've heard me talk about Leona Millstein . . ."

For a moment I had a vision of Mom trying to set me up with Leona Millstein. "I know I've been unlucky in love, Mom, but I haven't decided to change my sexual orientation just yet."

My mother clucked at me angrily. "Leona has a *son,* Miss Smarty Pants. And he lives in New York—Brooklyn, just like you!"

"What a coincidence."

Despite my lack of enthusiasm, Mom was full steam ahead. "And guess what?"

"What?"

"He's a high school teacher!" She giggled. "He teaches chemistry."

"What's so funny about that?"

"Nothing," Mom said, switching into that carefully exaggerated tone that always heralded a joke was on the way. "Except that I was thinking that if you're lucky, you two will go out and learn something about *chemistry* yourselves."

A cold shiver went through me. *Chemistry with Mr. Millstein.* How was I going to get out of this?

Luckily, I didn't have to. Leona Millstein's darling boy called me the very next evening and immediately put me at ease. "This is the call you've probably been dreading," he announced.

His dutiful long-suffering tone touched just the right chord. I laughed.

"My mother has the big idea that since we're both from Virginia, and you're living in Brooklyn and I'm living in Brooklyn—"

"And *you're* a teacher and *I'm* a teacher," I added.

His deep chuckle rumbled over the wire. "Yours too?"

"I tried to tell Mom that two teachers do not a great relationship make."

"Right. More like the opposite. What would two teachers talk about all the time? School. Two people griping about school wouldn't go over so swell at parties."

"A social Titanic," I said.

We discovered that Isaac lived one F train stop up from me on the yuppie corridor. And though neither of us harbored any intention of making our mothers giddy with happiness, who doesn't need another person to have coffee with?

And that's how it went for three years. A couple of times a week, we'd meet up on Court Street for coffee, or to go to the bookstore, where we both spent more of our paychecks than we should have, or to splurge on a great Italian meal in Carroll Gardens. When Isaac was so sick he couldn't drag himself out of bed, I showed up at his apartment to heat up cans of Progresso soup for him. During the last blizzard, he slid down to my place with bags of Chinese takeout.

We had a lot more than just school in common. We both loved books and movies, armchair traveling, and food. Centering a weekend around going to a place in Park Slope that deep-fried Snickers bars seemed normal to us. We could spend entire days just strolling around New York looking in shop windows, poking around Russian grocery stores in Brighton Beach, or people watching in Prospect Park.

Did we ever feel that spark of chemistry that my mom had so hoped for? For my part, I have to admit, yes. Sometimes. It would be hard not to be sort of attracted to Isaac. He's six feet tall and has big brown eyes and laughs at my jokes. And he's one of those people who can't hide anything. When he's sad, every facial feature below his beetled brows sags. When he's happy, the whole world knows it by the lift in his puppy-like demeanor. He'll start swing dancing with you on Flatbush Avenue, or anywhere else. Even if you don't know a fox-trot from a rumba. (He doesn't, either.)

Every time he was in between girlfriends, which was often, I could feel a little tug. I wouldn't have called Isaac great looking—he was too much of an inveterate waffle fan and too gym-o-phobic to have a bodybuilder physique. But he was one of those guys you might meet at a party when you're alone and think, "He'd be fun to go out with." At moments, it struck me that it would have been so easy for one of us to lean over our favorite wobbly coffee shop table and change everything.

Too easy. And what would we be trading? A fun but volatile friendship for what would have to be a doomed romance. That was the trouble with Isaac and me. We fought all the time, always over silly stuff. The fried Snickers bar episode? It actually caused an entire day of friction, because while we were eating it, Isaac happened to mention that he didn't like Charles Dickens. (Sacrilege!) Another time we didn't speak for two weeks after a particularly hard-fought game of Silver Screen Trivial Pursuit. Occasionally the only thing that kept us talking at all was the fact that we had our own apartments to withdraw to for a cooling-off period, like boxers retreating to their corners.

But no matter what, every Christmas for three years we went home together. Isaac is Jewish, but he always takes the Christmas school break to visit his folks. And I had a car, a sputtering old dented Ford that hadn't seen a hubcap since the week after I moved to Brooklyn. Mostly it existed to keep me panicked about finding parking spaces for it . . . and to take Isaac and me home.

Last year, however, when the subject of going home came up, I hedged. Isaac and I were at our favorite coffee place, the one equidistant from both our apartments. "So what day should we blast off?" he asked.

"Hm?" I lifted my teeny espresso cup to my lips. I like espresso because it gives a sort of absurd illusion of daintiness. Like grown-ups playing with children's tea sets. "You mean, for Christmas?"

"Sure, what else?"

"Oh."

His smile flatlined. "You mean you're not going home this year?"

"Of course I am."

"Well then?"

"Jason's driving me down," I admitted, guilt-ridden. But why? It wasn't as if Isaac and I had signed a holiday travel contract that said *Wither thou drivest* . . . It was nonsense.

Except, of course, that Isaac was gaping at me as if I had just plunged a dagger into his chest.

After a stunned moment, he lowered his coffee mug onto the waxy tabletop. In an instant, the hurt in those dark eyes changed to challenge. "Doesn't Jason's car have a backseat?"

"It's a fairly small car. A two-door Saab convertible." I sighed. "Anyway, you can't expect me to ask my boyfriend, my brand-spanking-new boyfriend, to take passengers . . ."

"Why not?"

I wasn't going anywhere near that question. Jason had only met Isaac in passing, and the two had not seemed that impressed with each other. Naturally. Isaac was Jason's polar opposite. Whereas Jason represented an up-by-his-bootstraps go-getter, Isaac was a coaster. Jason lived to get ahead, and it showed in everything he did—the well-reviewed restaurants he chose, the conservative suits he wore, the long hours he logged at the office. Isaac didn't give a hoot what people thought of him. He wore the same cords and baggy sweaters whether he was at work or at home. I bet he even wore them on dates (yet another reason we would never fall in love). Jason was one of those guys who try to turn every conversation into a positive gain. Isaac and I spent half our time arguing—over politics, or whether we would rather vacation in Thailand or Italy (not that either of us had money to go to either place), or the latest celebrity trial, or what should happen in the next episode of *Desperate Housewives*.

In other words, Isaac was exactly like me. Eerily like me. (Only frequently irritating, which, of course, I never was.) The catch was, I don't think Jason really realized who I was yet. I was still on my best early date behavior—always carefully made up, with my $200 haircut and clothes fresh from the cleaners. We hadn't reached the sweatshirt Saturdays stage yet. We never argued. Our relationship was still a fragile thing, to be coddled and tended like a baby chick.

I wanted to give this relationship my best shot—which entailed showing Jason off to my perfect family and seducing him with a knockout blend of holiday wholesomeness and hoarded lingerie. My best shot did not include Jason being stuck in a car with Isaac and me, bickering.

Isaac tapped his fingers against his mug with impatience.

Each tap hit me like a pinprick of guilt. "Do *I* ever make you take me along on your dates?" I asked.

"That's a false comparison. A drive home isn't a date."

"The whole weekend will be sort of an extended date," I argued. "And the drive home is key. It's the beginning. I don't want anything to spoil the mood."

"Oh, thanks," he said. "I thought I was your friend, but now I learn I'm a mood spoiler."

"That's not what I meant." Though, truthfully, I suppose it was. Isaac could be so emotional, so exasperating. He would back me into a corner like this, forcing me to say things that were better left unspoken. Then he would act wounded. "Anyway, the car will be filled with packages . . ."

His head snapped up as if he'd just discovered a fatal chink in my argument. "It doesn't have a trunk?"

"A small one. It's a Saab."

He smirked. "I believe you dropped that brand name once in this conversation already."

I was ready to bash him over the skull with the sugar dispenser. "I really want this to work out, Isaac. Really."

He looked flabbergasted. "What—you think I would stand in the way of your happiness?"

"No . . ." Not purposefully, at least. "I just was imagining something more cozy."

"You wouldn't even know I was there, I swear."

Right. "No."

"Please?"

"What is the big deal?" I asked. "There are other ways to get to Virginia. Planes, for instance. Planes are quick."

"And expensive."

I couldn't argue with that. But I still wasn't going to give in.

His body twisted into a curve and his face became an extravagant pout. "So you're sloughing me off for Little Orphan Jason."

"I'm not sloughing you off."

"Breaking with time-honored tradition at the first sign of a heartthrob."

"Well . . . wouldn't you?"

He arched a brow at me. But note that he did not contradict me. "Does Jason know you're a heartless bitch? Does he know that you're the type of woman who would leave her lonely Jewish friend stranded on Christmas? Does he?"

I suddenly had an idea. I should have thought of it before. "Look, why don't you take my car?"

Isaac recoiled, almost as if I had slapped him.

I couldn't believe it. I was offering him my own car and he looked offended. "What?" I asked.

"You must *really* not want me along."

"*Isaac . . .*"

"Listen, wouldn't you rather have someone with you, in case things don't go so great? What if you and Jason have nothing to talk about for three hours?"

"You think I'll be struck dumb?"

"You should just think of me as your personal cruise director. I'll be in the backseat, jollying you two along, making sure the ride goes smoothly."

I lifted my eyes to meet his gaze. I still wasn't convinced this was wise. And I doubted Jason would be thrilled at the idea of a backseat chaperone.

"Just ask him," Isaac said. "Didn't you say you were going to see him tomorrow?"

I bit my lip. "We're going shopping."

"You already went shopping. What is this, round two?"

"We have something specific in mind this time."

His face went slack. And pale. "Oh my god. Is there something you haven't told me? Is he buying you a ring?"

My cheeks heated up. I shouldn't have said anything. "It's not like that."

"Well then, what?"

"It's *nothing.*"

No way Isaac was letting this one go now. "How can it be nothing? It's got to be something. Jewelry . . ."

"I said, it's nothing like that."

"Tropical fruit-flavored condoms?"

If only. "For heaven's sake. We're just going to look for matching sweaters to wear at home."

Isaac nearly fell out of his chair. "After all the times I've heard you rant about that sister of yours and her boyfriends doing dorky things like that!"

"It's not dorky; it's cute."

He leveled a disbelieving look on me.

"Okay, it *is* dorky," I admitted. "But that's why I want to do it."

"To rub Maddie's face in your good fortune?"

Exactly.

"She probably won't even notice," I said. "You know how wrapped in herself and her own guys she gets."

He snorted. "Her *fiancés.*"

My sister always called these men she brought home her fiancés. I could never be certain whether this was for the sake of my parents—who might feel more comfortable with their youngest dragging strange men home if she were engaged to them—or whether men actually tended to propose to her in time for the holidays, only to be shed later like an old winter coat.

Isaac was always curious about Maddie. I half expected that he was just waiting for the day when she showed up for Christmas alone so he could sweep her off her feet himself.

"Okay," he said, circling back to topic A. "So when you're shopping, that would be the perfect time to ask Jason if he's interested in a threesome."

I crossed my arms.

He grinned. "I kid. A threesome in his car, I meant."

I didn't respond.

"*Please?*"

If you could have seen those eyes. They were like Saint Bernard eyes staring up at me. Expectant. Needy. I remembered suddenly that Isaac hadn't been having such a great time lately. He had broken up with his last girlfriend, Helen, about the same time I met Jason. Even though Helen hadn't seemed like all that great a catch to me, and I think they had only gone out for two months, tops, I didn't need any reminding how long and lonely the Thanksgiving–New Year's stretch could seem when you were dateless. And because of Jason, I hadn't been spending as much time with Isaac as I usually did.

And here I was being . . . well, selfish. He was right about that. What kind of friend was I?

In any case, I was helpless against the raw pleading in those eyes. "Okay. I'll ask."

* * *

Jason couldn't have been more thrilled. "Sure, why not?" he responded immediately to my question, which I had managed to choke out only after a belabored preamble of hemming and hawing. He didn't show a moment's hesitation. "The more the merrier!"

This is why I love you, I was tempted to say. Jason was all gung-ho eagerness. He even made *me* feel eager, now. And perhaps a little foolish. Isaac was my best bud, and such fun—when he wasn't trying my considerable patience. Having him along would just add to the festivity. And he and Jason would get to know each other better. They might even become friends!

What the heck had I been worrying about?

Chapter Two

You won't even know I'm there, he'd said. Ha.

"Where am I supposed to sit?" was the first question out of Isaac's mouth.

Heroically, I restrained myself from doing the man bodily harm. He had a lot of crust whining first thing, when he had begged me to wrangle this invitation for him.

"You've got the whole backseat," I pointed out.

Jason had double-parked the Saab on Henry Street, and the three of us were now huddled in the freezing cold on the sidewalk. Isaac, whose weekender bag sagged against his knees, looked as if he were going to refuse to get into the car.

"How can you say I have the whole backseat?" he asked. "It's full of junk."

I thought we had left it empty. I peered into the backseat through the small passenger window. No, I wasn't dreaming. All that was there were a lone

Tupperware dome and a small paper bag. "All you have to do is share the seat with a bundt cake."

"And what's in that other bag?"

"Champagne," I said.

"What are you taking champagne home for? We'll be back by New Year's."

"Just because." Even though it was a pathetic answer, I thought I was doing an admirable job of keeping my cool. Actually, I had drained what little was left of my bank account and poured it into a bottle of good vintage Dom Perignon, hoping to impress Jason if we ever had reason to engage in an intimate toast.

"But what about my suitcase?" Isaac asked.

"Put it on the seat between you and the cake," I said.

"Or set the cake cover on top of the bag," Jason put in.

Isaac and I wheeled on him as if he'd lost his mind.

"The cake might fall off!" I said.

"And get goo on my luggage," Isaac added.

Jason shrank back a little, as if to indicate that he had learned his lesson and would no longer make reasonable suggestions.

I propped my mittened hands on my hips and turned back on Isaac. "It's a pound cake. There is no goo."

"It's full of butter. It could leave a grease stain."

"No, it couldn't," I argued. "That cake cover is airtight."

He didn't look convinced. He probably didn't even know genuine Tupperware when he saw it.

Jason bravely stepped into the fray again. "I've got an idea." He reached deftly into the backseat for the cake and the champagne. "I seem to remember a little corner of the trunk we haven't used. . . ."

He was lying. But he went to the back of the car and gamely started rearranging things. Isaac smiled at me; I glared back.

"I brought music," he said.

"So did I," I said, trying to head him off at the pass.

Isaac and I didn't always agree on music. His taste was more eclectic than mine, and he leaned heavily toward world music. Even if we were just listening to the radio, he'd want to have it tuned to the Latino station. "Everything else is pop swill," he had told me once.

"This is pop swill, too," I had pointed out, "only in Spanish."

"That's okay. I don't speak Spanish."

Which is Isaac all over. He pretends to be Mr. Reasonable, Mr. I Have a Master's in Chemistry, and then he'll come out with something like that.

"I brought Christmas music," I said. "You know—Bing Crosby—to get us in the mood."

"Me, too."

I darted a skeptical look at him. "Let me see."

He pulled two CDs out of his jacket and handed them to me.

"*Oy to the World?*" I asked, my voice looping up with horror. "*The Bonanza Christmas Album?*"

"That last is a rarity," Isaac said. "I burned the CD myself especially for this trip."

Jason slammed the trunk and came around the side of the car. He laughed when he looked at one of the CD covers, a cartoon Santa dancing around with a menorah. "That's great!" he said. "Let's give them a listen."

In other words, bye-bye, Bing.

Isaac grinned at me before he tossed his bag into the backseat and then slid in after it. Then Jason and I got into the front and buckled ourselves in. "Would you mind moving your seat up?" Isaac asked me. "Not a lot of legroom back here."

"Sure thing." I fumbled under the seat for the control and then managed to slide my knees right into the glove compartment. The resulting crunch of kneecap against molded plastic made me wince in pain.

"Thanks!" Isaac chirped behind me.

The stereo blared out a Klezmer version of "Winter Wonderland."

"Hey, this is great!" Jason said, tossing an approving look into the rearview at Isaac. Isaac leaned forward, inserting his head between the bucket seats. There he remained as we hopped onto the Brooklyn Queens Expressway to head out of town.

"Okay," Isaac announced, "let's talk about the one that got away."

He was obviously taking his promise to serve as cruise director for the trip very seriously. Give him a few hours and he would probably break out the Mad Libs. Which would be preferable, frankly. I wasn't sure I wanted to hold a public airing of my romantic disappointments just now. Especially since romantic disappointment was precisely what this trip was meant to stave off.

Isaac looked into my eyes and laughed silently. "I'm talking about *presents.* What birthday or Christmas or"—he lifted a hand—"in my case, I will include Hanukkah—gift did you ever *really* want and not get?"

"Oh!" I loved games like this. "That's easy. Twice I asked for an Easy-Bake Oven. Which is basically just a toaster oven with its own little mini cake pans and boxes of cake mix."

"What happened?" Isaac asked.

"Mom said I didn't need a tiny oven because we already had a big oven in the kitchen I could use. She said if I wanted to make a cake so much, I should just ask her and she'd help me."

Jason smiled. "That's nice. She wanted to make it a shared activity."

"Yeah, but I didn't want to make a cake with my mom," I said. "I wanted to make little tiny ones with my friends, like in the commercials."

"Scarred for life!" Isaac said, approving my answer.

"I was actually okay until a few years later, when Maddie asked for an Easy-Bake Oven and got one. And she only had to ask once! That was what really left me embittered."

"And I bet she never used it," Isaac said.

I shook my head. "Oh, no, she used it all the time. She would invite her little squeaky-voiced friends over and have tea parties on Saturday afternoons. I would have to listen to them through my bedroom wall."

They laughed. "What was the one that got away for you?" Jason asked Isaac.

"When I was ten, I saw an old Edgar Bergen movie on the television one Saturday afternoon, and I just became obsessed. I *had* to get a ventriloquist dummy. I had this crush on a girl who I was too scared to talk to, but I thought that if I had a ventriloquist dummy, I would be able to wow her with my wit and skill. So I found one in the Sears catalog—it was a Charlie McCarthy replica—and I asked my parents for it for my birthday."

"And you didn't get it," I guessed, since disappointment was pretty much the name of the game.

He shook his head. "I thought maybe they just didn't understand that I *really needed* a ventriloquist dummy. So I sat them down and explained to them that I really believed my future was in show business, as a ventriloquist. I thought they understood. So when Hanukkah rolled around, I agonized every day, wondering if this was the night when I would finally receive the gift that would start me on my real life as a ventriloquist and great lover. But then the first night, I got a pair of socks. And then the next night, I got a Play-Doh Super Set, which I was entirely too old for anyway. For eight days and eight nights I suffered through the spasms of disappointment, until I realized that I was just going to have to save my allowance money and send off for the dummy and buy it myself."

"And did you?" I asked.

"No, of course not. He was forty dollars! When I had twenty, I broke down and bought a cheap magic set."

"Which you never used," Jason guessed.

"Right."

"My brother had a ventriloquist dummy," I said.

Isaac's eyes widened with envy. "He did? *Ted?*"

"He used it exclusively to terrify me. I thought it was so creepy looking—those expressionless eyes and that painted rubber hair. So Ted would open the bathroom door and lob it at me when I was in the tub, or leave it under my blankets at night to scare me to death when I unwittingly crawled into bed with it."

I braced myself for Isaac to remark on all the creepy dummies I had crawled into bed with since then. I mean, I had set myself up. But he didn't. Maybe he *was* trying to behave.

He shook his head in disgust. "What a waste of a good dummy."

"What's your gift that got away?" I asked Jason.

He squinted at the road, concentrating. He hummed thoughtfully for a moment. "I can't think of anything." He flashed one of those perfect smiles at me. "I guess I always felt lucky."

Isaac and I exchanged quick glances. *Was he kidding?*

Apparently, he wasn't.

Remembering Jason's very different history, I felt my cheeks burn, as if we had just been implicitly rebuked for pettiness, like greedy children. I suddenly wanted to repeat that it was a game—Isaac's idea, not mine—and all in fun. And that I wasn't *really* bitter about that Easy-Bake Oven. I felt lucky, too. Incredibly lucky. Really.

I hitched my throat. "My *favorite* gift ever was

this coat I got when I was nine. It was fake leopard fur. I loved it. I used to take naps in it."

"My favorite gift ever was my bike," Isaac said.

"Oh! Mine too," I said.

Isaac glowered at me. "You already said your favorite gift was a coat."

"I forgot about my bike," I said. "But I guess a bike is probably everybody's favorite gift when they're a kid."

"Did you take naps with your bike, too?" Isaac asked snarkily.

I answered him with a brief raspberry, then turned to Jason, trying to rope him back into the conversation. "What did your bike look like?"

"I've never owned a bike," he said.

Isaac and I fell silent.

"It always looked like a whole lot of fun, though," Jason added.

I felt like weeping. Forget mufflers and watches and boxer shorts. At that moment, I wished I could travel back in time and buy Jason a Huffy with a banana seat.

"So Isaac," Jason said, cutting through the funeral pall that had settled over us since his bike revelation, "Holly tells me you're a Knicks fan."

I had? I couldn't remember this, but if Jason said it, it must be true. Unlike most guys I dated, who seemed to filter out 90 percent of conversation, Jason had a fantastic memory. He paid attention, absorbing every word, every inflection. He was amazing.

"My office gets tickets sometimes," he went on. "I'll have to snag a few and we can all go."

"Holly doesn't like basketball," Isaac said.

Jason darted a surprised look at me. And no wonder. We had sat through an entire televised game just the week before. It had been numbingly long, but I had been with Jason, so I hadn't minded. We got to snuggle on the couch, at least.

"It's not that I don't like basketball—"

"She doesn't like *any* sports," Isaac interrupted. Rather gleefully, too. Like a little kid tattling.

"We've had this conversation before," I reminded Isaac. "I like sports."

He snorted. "Right. Your last-five-minutes rule."

"What's that?" Jason asked.

Isaac propelled himself farther between the bucket seats, until he had almost inserted himself into the front of the car. "Holly thinks the only interesting part of a game is the last five minutes."

"Well—isn't it?" I asked. "That's the suspenseful part if it's a close game. And if it's not close, who cares anyway?"

They glared at me as if I had committed heresy, as if I had just insulted the very word *sports*. For the next thirty minutes, they talked about the Knicks and their chances for a championship. (Zero.) Also, their failures of the past. (Innumerable.)

Half listening, I stared out the window at ditches and bare trees. I started nodding off.

Then they moved on to football.

By the time we reached the first rest stop, Jason and Isaac seemed like old buds. As Isaac trudged off to get a cup of machine coffee, I stood by the gas tank with Jason, hopping and slapping my gloved hands in a failing bid to create warmth. I longed to rush inside into the heated rest stop and inspect the aisles of unhealthy snacks as Isaac was doing, but the way things were going I was afraid this would be my only chance to talk to Jason for a while.

"I like Isaac," Jason said. "I don't know why you were so hesitant to take him along on this trip."

I bent my head forward. "Hesitant?" I repeated, all innocence.

I know what you're thinking. Hesitant was a mild way to describe how I'd felt. I flat out hadn't wanted him along. But how did *Jason* know that?

"Well, I just assumed . . . you didn't ask till the last minute," Jason said. "And let's face it. When you *did* ask, you didn't sound thrilled."

"Oh, but—"

"To tell you the truth, I wasn't over the moon about it myself."

I laughed in disbelief. "You seemed so gung ho when I brought the idea up! You acted like having a passenger would make your day."

He gave his head a rueful shake. "I don't know how you could think that. To tell you the truth, I'd always wondered about Isaac. I didn't know what was going on with you two."

I leapt on this new tidbit. Was that why he had been reticent about sleeping together?

"Nothing like you were imagining," I assured him.

He chuckled. "I can see that now. You guys argue so much it's a miracle you're still friends at all."

"We just have friendly disagreements every once in a while."

He looked at me as if I had gone mad. But I hadn't, not at all; I mean, yes, Isaac and I argued, but it was mostly in fun. I didn't want Jason to misinterpret this as genuine hostility. It was as if I had been on a month-long job interview; I didn't want him to think that I was in any way difficult to get along with.

I vowed that I would avoid arguing with Isaac for the rest of the trip. No matter what happened.

"Isaac's just been cranky lately because he broke up with his girlfriend," I said.

"Over a month ago," Jason reminded me.

I tilted my head. "How did you know?"

"You told me."

"I did?"

"Our first date, remember?" To prove it, he said, "Helen."

Good heavens. He really did have a good memory. "I can't believe I wasted part of our first date talking about Isaac's love problems."

He laughed. "Why not? We had to talk about something. A flaky songwriter is as good a subject as any."

I blinked. I had forgotten Helen was a songwriter. She had aspirations of being the next Alanis Morissette. She had made a CD of her songs (accompanied by herself on guitar) that she had titled "Inspirations."

Poor Isaac!

Just as we were finishing up, Isaac came out carrying a cup of coffee and a big bag of Funyons.

(Funyons and Bugles were our favorite road food, but no way was I eating a Funyon in front of Jason.)

"Hey, do your nieces have *Frosty the Snowman?*" Isaac asked me. "The gas station has copies for three ninety-nine when you fill up."

"Three ninety-nine? I can barely stand to watch it for free." Though of course I always did. Every year. I cry during that one, too, but of the big Christmas specials—the Grinch, Rudolph, Peanuts, Frosty—it comes in a distant fourth. "Jimmy Durante's always rubbed me the wrong way."

All the creases fell out of Isaac's face. He looked perplexed. "What's Jimmy Durante got to do with *Frosty the Snowman?*"

Was he kidding? "He's the narrator. He even sings the song."

"No he doesn't. Burl Ives does."

"No, it's Jimmy Durante," I said, remembering too late that I wasn't supposed to argue with Isaac. Anyway, there are some things you just can't let pass. "Burl Ives sings 'Rudolph the Red-Nosed Reindeer.' "

"Right. He's in *Frosty,* too. He's the snowman."

Isaac could be so wrong. So mulishly wrong. (Like he was about Charles Dickens.) "*No,* Burl Ives is a snowman in Rudolph, but he's not Frosty the Snowman. He's not in *Frosty the Snowman* at all. He has nothing to do with it."

"Well, I *know* Jimmy Durante isn't Frosty the Snowman," Isaac said.

How on earth did I get into this? "I never said he was! He just sings the song."

I sent Jason a look of exasperation and discovered to my dismay that he was staring at both of us with cool detachment. *See?* His gaze seemed to say. *You argue.*

Damn.

Isaac eyed me with playful contempt and pity. "It's just tragic when someone thinks they're right and they're not."

By now I felt like hopping up and down and screeching at him.

"Um, kids?" Jason asked. He apparently wasn't used to people coming to blows over trivia, and now he was staring at us as if we had both lost our minds. *This* was just what I had been worried about when Isaac told me he wanted to come along. "Shouldn't we get back on the road?"

"Of course," I said.

The minute Jason's back was turned, I gave Isaac a swift kick.

"*It was Burl Ives,*" he mouthed.

Back in the car, Isaac put in his *Bonanza* cast CD, and we were treated to Lorne Greene singing "Home for the Holidays."

"So what's the nocturnal setup chez Ellis while you two are there?" Isaac asked.

Jason and I shifted stiffly in our bucket seats.

"My parents have a guest room," I reminded Isaac. He knew this.

"Doesn't Maddie's fiancé always stay in that room?"

"This year he can sleep on the couch," I said.

"I thought the nieces slept on the couch."

I decided that Isaac knew an unseemly amount about my family and its sleeping arrangements.

"Maddie's fiancé?" Jason asked, confused. "How long have they been engaged?"

I bit my lip. I hadn't told him that my sister was a serial bride to be. I didn't want him to think I had compulsive engagement disorder in my genes.

"Maddie brings her boyfriends home every year. She calls them fiancés. I have no idea who will pop up this year on her arm—not that it matters. I assure you we'll never see the guy again."

"Disposable fiancés." Isaac chomped down on a Funyon. "The ultimate convenience."

"That sounds . . . quirky . . ." Jason did not seem amused.

"That's just Maddie," I said, on the defensive now. How is it that your family can drive you absolutely nuts, but the moment someone else sounds the least bit critical, blood instantly becomes thicker than water? That's how I was, especially with Maddie. I guess a person always feels protective of their next youngest sibling. Even when that sibling never had an honest trouble in her life to be protected from.

Isaac returned to the top of his script. "Still, with that many people in the house, things are bound to get mighty interesting. Especially at night."

"What do you mean?" Jason asked.

Glancing in the vanity mirror, I could see Isaac smiling impishly. "You know, little feet going pitter patter after the elder Ellises have gone to bed." And he obviously didn't mean the little feet would belong to my nieces. "I bet that house will just be rife with Christmas canoodling."

Jason laughed good-naturedly. I might have let

out a halfhearted chuckle. True, I had my lingerie stash and plenty of holiday hope. But after Jason had waited a month for the perfect moment, I also reserved a little skepticism that our magic moment would arrive in my twin bed in my old room, which still had remnants of my teenage life strewn about. Back when I was fifteen I was obsessed with the movie *The Last of the Mohicans.* My prized possession from those days was the giant movie poster, picturing Daniel Day-Lewis running toward the camera. He was such a babe—that chest, those thighs bulging against his buckskins, that flowing hair! The poster was still there, the focal point of the room. Did we really want to consummate our love with Natty Bumppo staring down at us?

Isaac poked me on the shoulder. "Don't tell me *you* haven't thought about this!"

I cleared my throat. "I . . . uh . . . no."

He laughed. "Liar."

My face was beet red. Couldn't he drop it?

"I promised Holly I would be a perfect gentleman," Jason said.

I turned in shock. He had not!

Isaac asked in amazement, "You did?"

Jason nodded, then winked at me. "As always."

I tossed a glare at the backseat. But that wink confused me. Did Jason mean he really was going to be a gentleman (drat!) or did he mean he was lying to Isaac?

Isaac looked nonplussed, and for a while there was just the sound of Lorne Greene and Isaac munching thoughtfully on his Funyons.

I was hoping that would be the end of the discussion, but I should have known better.

"You mean you two have never . . . ?" Isaac let the question dangle.

"No," we bit out in unison.

Isaac laughed. *Laughed.* "No wonder Holly's been acting so crazed!"

Jason's head snapped around to inspect me. "Crazed?"

I tossed up my hands. "I've been *happy,*" I said, turning on Isaac. He was grinning like a demon elf. "And don't go criticizing me, Mr. Wiseguy. You've got your moods. Ever since the Helen breakup you've just been moping around and snapping my head off for no reason."

Since before Thanksgiving he'd been crabby. For as long as Jason and I had been going out, I had barely been able to talk to Isaac without having an argument.

"I've had reason," Isaac said.

"Well, for God's sake," I said, rolling me eyes, "don't be so mysterious. Are you sick? Have you . . . ?"

My mouth clamped shut. Blood drained out of my face.

For as long as Jason and I had been going out.

But that couldn't be . . . could it?

Isaac held my gaze in the vanity mirror for a second longer before biting into another chip. "A psychological holiday slump," he explained.

"Ah," Jason said.

My brain reeled for a moment. Was Isaac purposefully messing with my head? Or maybe I was leaping to the wrong conclusion.

But since when did he fall prey to holiday depression?

He smiled at me in the mirror. "Haven't you ever heard of those fabled Hanukkah blues?"

He *was* messing with my head. I suddenly lost patience with both him and the cast of *Bonanza*. With a sharp jab, I ejected Isaac's CD and found an oldies radio station. It was playing "Frosty the Snowman."

And the singer was Burl Ives.

Dumbstruck, I stared at the radio knobs. This was *so wrong!*

I could feel Isaac's triumphant smile beaming from the backseat. "Told you," he said.

"It was Jimmy Durante in the television show," I insisted. *Was I going crazy?* I appealed to Jason. "You believe me, don't you?"

He appeared hesitant to venture into the argument. "Is it worth ruining a friendship over?"

"Absolutely!" Isaac and I chimed in unison.

Then we burst out laughing.

Chapter Three

"I know you're in a hurry to get to your Frank Capra Christmas," Isaac told me as he was climbing out of the backseat when we dropped him off. "So I won't ask you in."

I shivered in the cold, waiting for him to grab his bag so I could get back in the car. This was the trouble with a two-door. "You'll come by the house? Everybody will want to see you."

"Maybe tomorrow," he said, playing hard to get all of a sudden. Then he leaned in the car and thanked Jason again for the ride.

"Call me!" I jumped back in, glad to be back in the warmth.

Jason idled the motor while we watched Isaac trudge up to his front door. I wondered if Isaac felt a little melancholy to be back at his parents' house, alone again. His folks nagged him about his life as much as mine did. A strong tug of camaraderie welled up inside me, of loyalty toward Isaac and all those adults returning solo to the nest this year, even though I'd hit it lucky.

"Great guy," Jason said.

"Mm."

It suddenly occurred to me that Jason had never said anything bad about anybody in my hearing. He liked everybody . . . which was sort of puzzling. I mean, yes, he liked me. But what did it mean to be liked by someone who never met a person he *didn't* like?

And I had to wonder . . . what kind of person couldn't remember one thing he wanted and didn't get?

As we drove through my old neighborhood I got fired up again, pointing out landmarks of my illustrious past. *My high school! Bungalow Billiards! My best friend from seventh grade Stacy Sheinman's house!* But when we pulled up into the driveway of my parents' place, I felt a stab of disappointment. And bewilderment. Of course it was daylight, so the fact that there were no outside lights on was not at all surprising. But I didn't see any evidence of decoration. The house looked naked. There were no wire reindeer on the roof. The mailbox and the lampposts didn't have bows on them. And where was the giant inflatable polar bear?

Most years when I come down, Mom and Dad and whoever else is already there come pouring out the front door before I can cut off my engine. But as we sat staring up at the white Cape Cod façade, the door remained firmly shut.

"Well, let's get a move on," Jason said, rousing

me out of my inertia. "Time for me to face the inspection crew."

That thought—my folks inspecting Jason, and their inevitable fawning approval—was enough to put a spring in my step as I hurried up the walkway.

"Hey," Jason called from behind. "Shouldn't we empty the car?"

I waved him forward. "Dad and Ted and everybody will give us a hand with that in a couple of minutes."

His smile conveyed that this sounded like a good deal to him, and he hurried up to my side. The day had barely warmed up at all from the freezing temperature of the morning. The wind had died down since our stop in Jersey, but the world felt icy and still. There wasn't much traffic on the street, but it was still a day before Christmas Eve, so there were probably a lot of people who were at work.

My brother's SUV was in the driveway, though, which meant that all his gang was here.

When no one appeared in answer to the doorbell, I dropped the heavy brass acorn knocker against the door. The resulting sound seemed to echo through the neighborhood; every neighbor for blocks around would now know I had returned. But the jarring sound had no effect where we were. "That's weird," I said.

"That there's no one home?" Jason asked.

That, too. But what had me really rattled was the fact that there was no wreath on the door. Had we entered some Twilight Zone where Christmas as I knew it no longer existed?

Before I could voice this troubling theory, the door's deadbolt slid abruptly, the door swung open, and there stood Ted.

Except he didn't look like Ted. My brother's squared jaw, usually so smooth he could have been a Gillette spokesman, was unshaven; his hair was squashed on one side in a bad case of bed head; and his eyes were so bloodshot that the blue irises seemed almost to be glowing dully in their pools of red. He didn't smile when he saw me. In fact, for a moment his expressionless eyes didn't seem to recognize me. It was as if Lurch from The Addams Family had opened the door for us.

Lurch, hungover.

"*Ted?*"

"Oh, hi," he said. A few seconds later the stench of his breath reached me. It was ninety proof. I looked down at his right hand, which was clutching a bottle of Jim Beam, three quarters full. He wasn't hungover at all—he was still tanking up.

My voice wobbled as I introduced Jason. Ted was forced to switch the Jim Beam to his left hand so they could shake. "Hey," he said, completely without enthusiasm.

Jason, of course, had no way to know this was very odd behavior coming from my brother. For all he knew, Ted *always* looked like Nicolas Cage in *Leaving Las Vegas*.

"Where are those nieces of mine?" I asked, in that geeked-up way people use when they're trying to inject cheer into a morbid ambience.

Ted sagged against the doorjamb and his bloodshot eyes puddled with moisture. Apparently I had asked the wrong question. "They're not"—his shoulders convulsed—"*coming.*"

"Not coming?" I repeated, stupidly. "Where are they?"

"With . . . *Melinda!*" His wife's name came out on a sob.

"But how can that be?" Ted and Melinda were such a perfect couple. They always seemed to be in perfect mental lockstep.

Ted unscrewed the top from the Jim Beam and took a swig. "She left me, Holly. She just loaded up the girls in the Escalade and drove off."

"Oh, Ted! I'm so sorry!"

I reached out to touch his arm, but he recoiled. "She said she'd been unhappy for years. *Years.* Said I was domineering."

I shook my head. Oh, lordy. "It doesn't seem possible."

"And that I was *patronizing.* How could she say such a thing?" Before I could answer, he shouted, "And where the hell did she learn to throw around words like that? Not at that gym she used to work at, that's for damn sure!" His bleary eyes started scanning the street behind me, as if Melinda might be hiding behind a bush out there somewhere. "*Little miss aerobics instructor wasn't tossing around ten-dollar words back before I found her!*"

"*Ted.*" I grabbed his arm and tugged him inside, shutting the door behind us. Then I remembered Jason. I flung the door open again. "Sorry!" I said.

He held up a hand to indicate he understood. "Maybe I should go get the bags."

You mean you still want to stay? I didn't actually ask the question, but it must have been clear in my eyes. Jason smiled reassuringly. I could have thrown myself into his arms and kissed him.

But then I heard a crash behind me and whirled to discover that Ted had disappeared. *Where were Mom and Dad?* Did they know that their son was stumbling around their house in an alcoholic stupor?

I found him in his old room on the first floor, lying on the lower bunk, where Schuyler usually slept now. The room still had a striking sports motif, including posters of Larry Bird and Pete Sampras. "The girls probably hated staying in this room," he said, in a raw, choked voice as he looked up at Larry and Pete. "I should have given Mom money to have it redone for them. At least to get new sheets without footballs on them."

"We could still do that," I said. "It's not as if Schuyler and Amanda won't visit their grandparents anymore."

My brother emitted a low moan.

"And this is just temporary, I'm sure!" I added quickly. "All couples have problems sooner or later."

"Not like this. She just went berserk, Holly. One minute we were having this great family evening—a Kodak moment, trimming the tree. The girls were singing along with that Chipmunks song, and Melinda seemed fine, and then I just happened to mention that I didn't think she should use this tinsel she had bought that afternoon. We'd always used garlands on the tree before. Tinsel gets everywhere—makes a mess, really—and what if Amanda swallowed it?"

I frowned. "Why would Amanda eat tinsel?"

"*Because she's a child,* Holly. You just don't understand about children. You have to be careful around them."

"But Amanda's almost six."

For a moment I feared I was going to be clubbed upside the head with a Jim Beam bottle.

I held up my hands in surrender, remembering whose side I was supposed to be on. "So . . . what happened?"

"She told me that I was being alarmist, and that she was tired of garlands. Said she thought garlands were stodgy. And I told her that stodgy was better than foolish any damn day of the week."

"Wait," I said, interrupting. "You mean this entire argument was over garlands versus tinsel?"

"*On the surface* it was an argument about garlands versus tinsel, but it went deeper than that, believe you me! The things she said in anger I just can't forget."

I suspected Ted threw a few choice words back at Melinda, too. "Still . . . that doesn't sound *too* terrible," I said. "What makes you think you can't work it out?"

He looked at me, stunned. "After the things she said to me?"

"Patronizing? Well come on, Ted, you do like to have your way."

"Actually, she called me a patronizing son of a bitch."

"Oh, well . . ."

"And that was some of the nicer language."

Truly, I couldn't imagine Melinda in a screaming fight with anyone. She was the type of woman who would apologize for saying *damn.* Even if she had just suffered a third-degree burn she would say something like, "*Dang! That stove is hot!*"

"Where is she now?" I asked.

"At her parents'."

"Well, then. There's still hope."

"What makes you think that?"

"How long would *you* want to live with Melinda's mother?"

My mother-in-law joke failed to squeeze a chuckle out of him. He remained gloomy, lying on the bed and clutching his bottle of whiskey like a corpse holding lilies. "I'd do anything to get her back."

"Have you tried?"

"What?"

"To get her back."

"How?"

"Well, for instance—and this is just a suggestion, mind you—but you could, maybe, apologize."

He bolted upright. "What for?"

"For insulting her tinsel—or whatever you two were fighting about."

"Hell, no, I won't apologize! Why should I apologize for being right?"

"Ted . . ."

"Go away, Holly. I need to be alone."

"No, you don't," I said. "You're a mess. You're drunk."

"And I intend to be a lot more drunk before the day's over."

Oh, God. I didn't know what to do. I had never seen Ted less than perfectly composed. Usually he was the life of the party, making eggnog for everybody and giving the girls piggyback rides around the house. I'd never witnessed a total Ted meltdown.

"Where are Mom and Dad?" I asked, in growing desperation.

"Dunno. Out. Maybe to a faculty party or something."

I couldn't believe they would leave Ted in this shape. Of course, maybe Ted hadn't been in such bad condition when they left. Still, it was hard to fathom that they would be gone when they knew I was going to be home today, and bringing a friend. Mom was usually very conscientious about providing a welcome wagon for people.

I left Ted in the lower bunk and skulked out to find Jason . . . if he hadn't already turned around and headed back to New York.

As I padded around looking for him, I got a strange feeling. Not that there was anything too amiss in the house. It was spotless. But that was part of the trouble, I realized. There was none of the typical holiday chaos. No messy table full of Christmas cards propped up in an impromptu display. No hastily abandoned wrapping projects in evidence, or even boughs of holly or pine decorating every available surface, as there usually was. Outside of a troublingly symmetrical and smallish tree in the living room, there was no evidence that it was Christmas at all.

Mom hadn't decorated, I realized with growing hysteria as I hurried from room to room. Where were the snow villages, the angel choir, the monks? What happened to all the walnut people? I skidded underneath the archway leading to the living room and gasped.

"What's the matter?" Jason asked.

"No mistletoe!" By this time, I was almost yelling.

Jason narrowed his eyes. "What?"

"There's *always* a sprig of mistletoe *right here,*" I insisted, jabbing my finger at the spot. There was even a little hole in the plaster where it was usually nailed in.

How was Jason supposed to kiss me underneath the mistletoe if the damn mistletoe wasn't there?

What the hell was going on here?

"Are you okay?" Jason said, approaching me cautiously.

I admit I was breathing hard. And then I pivoted for another look at that tree, and I almost started hyperventilating. The reason the tree looked so fake was because it *was* fake! Mother had put up a dinky artificial tree. That's why there was no scent of pine in the house. No vexing trail of Douglas fir needles trailing across the living room carpet. That's why the house seemed so uninviting, so sterile, so *not* Norman Rockwell.

"Holly, I think you need to sit down," Jason said.

"It's not usually like this," I breathed, still not quite trusting my eyes.

"What's the matter?" he asked.

"This place is usually decorated within an inch of its life. And I promised you this big traditional Christmas. Mom didn't even put up a real tree!"

Jason whirled. "Oh, I hadn't noticed."

How could he not have noticed? The tree wasn't even a good fake. "She might as well have bought one of those aluminum things."

"I *like* those aluminum things." As I eyeballed the room in a glazed stupor, Jason put a bracing arm around my shoulders. "What about that eggnog you promised me?"

I thought about the frothy, nutmeggy concoction usually served up about this time, prepared by Ted. Then I thought about my brother all liquored up in his old bunkbed. Something told me there wasn't a bowl of homemade eggnog waiting for us in the fridge. "Ted's the eggnog maker, but in the condition he's in . . ."

"Well maybe we should go make some ourselves."

His can-do optimism got me going again. We trotted off to the kitchen and started hunting through cookbooks for a recipe. "Mostly what we need are milk and eggs," I said, after I had found one.

He laughed as he shut the refrigerator door. "That's a problem then."

"Why?"

"Because your mom's out of eggs. And milk."

This I had to see. When I opened the fridge, it seemed ominously bare. There were a butter dish, a six-pack of Heineken, a bottle of white wine, a couple of wilted-looking stalks of celery. . . .

And that was it. Amazed, I started checking cabinets. Nothing. The cupboards were bare.

I cast a doubtful look Jason's way. "We did get this right, didn't we? This *is* two days before Christmas, isn't it?"

"Is there a store nearby?"

I nodded.

"Then let's go play elf and refill the fridge and cupboards before your folks come home."

"You're too good," I said.

He shook his head, smiling ruefully. "No, I'm just too hungry."

Jason's brief turn through my mom's pantry must have alarmed him; judging from our shopping basket you would have thought we were stocking up for a month in Yak valley. We bought bread (two kinds); cheese; chips; milk; every type of carbonated drink available to mankind; and more salad fixings than a hutchful of rabbits, never mind a houseful of humans, would be able to munch their way through in three days. Then, as we passed the deli section again on the way back to the checkout, Jason tossed a rotisserie chicken onto the top of the heap.

I couldn't help looking on that shopping basket as my family's cart of shame. Obviously, he was afraid we were going to starve him. And after staring deep into the cold empty heart of my mom's fridge, I couldn't reassure him to the contrary.

I had been hoping that my parents would be home when we got back, but the house was just as it had been. When we walked in the door, I heard an odd keening moan from down the hall and discovered that Ted had now barricaded himself in his old room. The door was locked and he refused to answer. Nothing could budge him, not even the lure of rotisserie chicken and Stilton cheese.

Jason and I pulled bar stools up to the butcher block island in the kitchen and started preparing ourselves a feast. For a month I had been passing up spritz cookies and foil-wrapped chocolate everything in hopes that my tummy, in the event Jason ever saw it, would be as flat as I could make it without resorting to truly drastic measures, like sit-ups. But hell, it was Christmas, and he had done the shopping. It could be I'd followed the wrong tactic completely. Maybe the paunchy Mrs. Claus look turned him on.

I hacked off a wedge of cheese and lovingly placed it on a butter cracker.

"Maybe we should go to the Smithsonian." Now that we seemed to have fallen into a holiday black hole, I was desperately casting about for ways to entertain him. I felt like a tour guide who had promised a sunny island paradise and had instead delivered a deserted volcanic wasteland. We couldn't sit in the house and listen to my brother's muffled sobs all afternoon.

Before Jason could respond to that suggestion, the front door opened. My mother's voice, rather shrill, said, "There's nothing wrong with me. *You* were the one who sat there like a lump all through lunch, boring the Finleys with your lecture on Oliver Cromwell."

"What makes you think they were bored?" Dad asked peevishly.

Uh-oh. I winced, recognizing the tone my parents reserved for their rare squabbles. Jason cut a glance at me, and I wanted to run out into the hallway screaming, *Shut up! You're supposed to be Ozzie and Harriet!*

But I was frozen, and those voices kept coming closer.

"*Laird,* their lids were drooping, and they were weaving."

"They didn't say anything about being bored."

"They were being *polite.* Do you think people actually go to Christmas parties to be lectured on the English Civil War?"

"I thought I was interesting."

Mom was emitting a strangled cry when she rounded the kitchen door and caught sight of Jason and me sitting there on our stools, blinking at being the unintentional audience for their spat. As she took us in, my mother's face changed from annoyance to frozen confusion to hostess with the mostest, all in the space of a split second.

"Well, look who's here!" she exclaimed, beaming at us. "Laird, come in here. What a surprise!"

"Um . . . isn't this when I said I would be here?" I asked.

Mom rolled her eyes as if to say, *Silly me!* "I must have let it slip my mind."

"And your memory wasn't jarred when you saw a strange car in the driveway?" I pressed, incredulous. Most of the time it wouldn't have fazed me that my parents had forgotten me, but I had specifically told Mom the date and time because I was bringing Jason.

She put her hands on her hips and turned, laughing, to Jason. "You see what I have to put up with, Justin? It's constant criticism around here, twenty-four, seven."

I could have sunk through the floor tiles. "*Jason.*"

My mother smiled obliviously on and shook Jason's hand. "We're so glad to have you here. And good—you found yourselves something to eat!"

"We had to go to the store." It was hard to keep the reproach out of my tone.

"*Laird!*" My mother yelled, in a voice loud enough for moose calling. "Come meet Jason!"

I suppose I should have been glad that she didn't call him Justin again, but for some reason, I was finding myself shrinking back like a twelve-year-old on parents' night.

My dad wheeled in, grinning, but his smile froze when he saw me. I didn't have to ask who he'd been expecting. "Holly! For some reason, I thought your mother said Maddie was here."

I gave him a brief hug, feeling the usual sting of being second best. (Okay, third best.) "Disappointed?"

He laughed a little too jovially. "No, no—"

"Laird, this is Jason," Mom said, steering him away from me.

"Pleased to meet you," Dad said.

"Holly tells me you teach history," Jason said.

Mom and I both jumped on that statement,

which most of the time my father mistook as an invitation to deliver an impromptu lecture. "Now, no work talk!" Mom singsonged, no doubt still thinking about Oliver Cromwell and the unfortunate Finleys he'd buttonholed at the party. She opened the fridge but didn't comment on the fact that elves had restocked her dwindling supplies. "Oh, look! Eggnog!" She pulled out the carton we had bought and poured herself a glass. "I love this stuff. Ted used to make it fresh, remember?"

She acted as if this were decades ago.

"Speaking of Ted . . ."

"Have you seen him?" she asked.

"He answered the door." I couldn't help adding, "Since no one else was here. . . ."

"Oh, good! So he's okay."

Okay? My brother looked like suicide hotline material. "I'm worried. He's locked himself in his room."

Mom's brows knit together. "There's nothing too dangerous in there, except maybe his old chemistry set . . . and I imagine all the chemicals in that are expired. We gave away his BB gun when Amanda came along."

It was all I could do not to clutch my head and let out a primal howl. "Mom, your son is doing a reenactment of *The Lost Weekend*."

She shook her head at me. "Just try to have a little understanding, Holly. Ted's having a rough time."

"I know, but . . ." I didn't know what more to say, or whether I should say more while Jason was standing there. "When's Maddie coming home?" Since everyone else had completely flaked out, I suddenly craved seeing my sister. I wondered what she would make of what was going on with Ted, and my parents. And what was up with the artificial tree, and the absence of Christmas collectibles? This was my mom's first ever half-baked holiday.

And naturally, it *would* have to be the year I brought home Jason.

Jason, whom Mom didn't even seem to be appreciating. She had barely looked at him! Hadn't she noticed how good-looking he was? How perfect in every way?

Mom lifted her shoulders in answer to my question about Maddie. "I'm not sure. . . ."

"You're sure she *is* coming, right?"

Mom laughed. "Well, of course." Upon reconsidering, the smile was erased from her face as quickly and thoroughly as an Etch A Sketch screen after a good firm shake. "I think so. I talked to her before she left."

"When did she leave?"

"Oh, days ago."

I frowned. "She's not taking a plane?"

"No, she wanted to drive down on that new motorbike of hers."

"Her *bike?*" Maddie had been talking about her bike all autumn long, every time I spoke to her. But her bike wasn't a real motorcycle. It was one of those little European scooters. "She's driving from Boston to Virginia *on a Vespa?* Those things were invented for Gregory Peck and Audrey Hepburn to putter around Rome on, not for cross-country traveling with a Canadian cold front moving in!"

My father, standing in front of the open fridge,

shook his head in admiration. "You know your sister! It's always something new with her. And she never does anything halfway."

"But it's *dangerous,*" I said. "She could have an accident, or break down, or meet some nut on the road."

Mom seemed unfazed. "She said she was going to take little side roads—really get to see the country."

Dad, having rustled up a plateful of food, sidled up to Jason. "Do *you* think mentioning Oliver Cromwell in a friendly conversation is a federal offense?"

Not about to allow him to put that question to the test, I hopped between them, hooking my arm through Jason's. "No time for that now, Dad—Jason and I are going to the Smithsonian."

"What a good idea!" Mom exclaimed.

"But they just got here," Dad complained.

"No, Laird, *we* just got here," Mom shot back. "They've already done the grocery shopping."

"Okay," I interrupted. "We'll be going now."

During the car ride, I let vent all my worries. "Riding cross-country on a motor scooter? In December? How could someone who's been to med school be so idiotic?"

"It sounds adventurous . . . if a little harebrained."

"A little!" I drove a few blocks (Jason had let me at the wheel, since this was an impromptu trip and I knew the territory), then pulled out my cell phone. I tried dialing Maddie's cell phone number. Of course there was no answer. She probably wouldn't have been able to hear the ring through the icy wind in her hair.

From Maddie, I moved on to other fears—like whatever might be happening at home. Seeing Ted in his current condition still gave me a shock. He was always such a brick! The ultimate big brother. And what was going on with my parents?

How was I supposed to seduce my boyfriend with family holiday magic when everything had turned so sour?

"Not one single snow village scene has been put out," I said. "That's got to mean something."

"What would it mean?"

Unfortunately, I didn't have the slightest idea. "She *always* puts the villages out. They're her pride and joy. Especially the Alpine village. She's spent years trolling eBay to get all the right pieces for it. And you'd think she would have tried to make the place cheery for Ted's sake, at least."

"Ted looked like he was beyond the reach of miniature housing displays."

I heard the cheery "Deck the Halls" ring of my cell phone and picked it up again. Maybe this would be Maddie.

"How's it going?"

It was Isaac. I bit my lip with disappointment, yet there was something comforting about the sound of his voice. My lifeline. "Disaster. Melinda left Ted and now he's rattling around the house like Foster Brooks, and my sister is riding a Vespa home from Massachusetts, and my parents are bickering and seem to have forgotten that there's a holiday going on at all. The house is bare. *Bare.*"

Isaac seemed really disturbed by that last bit. "The house isn't treed?"

"It's treed," I allowed, "but only artificially."

He clucked in a way that was very reassuring to me. I wasn't going crazy. This was weird. "Is your Mom okay?"

"As far as I know. She and my dad are just being *really* cranky."

"I've never seen them cranky at all."

"That's because you're company."

"Exactly. And you've got company now."

"Who?"

"Jason."

Oh, right. It wasn't that I had forgotten him, but it was hard to think of someone as company after they had bought your parents groceries. You tended to start thinking of people like that as members of the family. Or social workers.

"Are you coming over tonight?" I asked Isaac.

"Are you having dinner?"

I thought for a moment. "I wouldn't count on it."

I took the ensuing silence for a no.

Then, out of the blue, he asked, "Holly, what do know about this Jason guy?"

I cut a glance at Jason, who was studiously not paying attention to my conversation. "Why?" I asked nonchalantly. "What do you mean?"

"*A month?*" he asked. "And no sex?"

"That's not that weird." Were we such a degenerate, sex-crazed society that waiting a month seemed odd now?

Though, of course it had been driving me crazy.

"Not that I mind," he said. "In fact I'm glad."

"Why should you be glad?" *Celibacy loves company?*

He sighed. "Think of it. Is this person for you? What kind of guy can't think of one thing he ever wanted and didn't get?"

Now I started to get mad, even though the very same thought had crossed my mind. Or maybe because of that. I felt disloyal even having this conversation, especially with Jason right there. "What's your point?"

"I think this guy has some kind of saint complex. He's just too perfect."

"That's a terrible thing to say!" I said.

"Don't have a cow," he said, chuckling. "I just thought I should mention it. As a friend."

As a demon. He was obviously trying to rattle me, though I had no idea why. "I've got to go." Otherwise we would have a wreck.

"Okay. Say 'hi' to Mr. Perfect for me." He signed off with a laugh.

"Pest," I muttered, gunning through a yellow light.

We drove in silence for a moment.

"Maybe we should have invited him along," Jason said.

I practically howled. "Over my dead body! Honestly, he acts as if my life is the staging ground for all his moods and antics. And I've about had it with his incessant needling."

After a few moments I flicked my gaze over and noticed Jason staring at me as if I were some kind of monster.

"What?" I asked.

"I was talking about Ted."

"Oh!" No wonder he was regarding me as if I had just grown a second head. "I thought you meant Isaac. That was Isaac on the phone."

He nodded. "Maybe it would have done Ted some good to get out of the house and be with people."

Wasn't that sweet of him? Always thinking about other people. Even people who locked themselves in their rooms when he came for a visit.

We went to the National Gallery, but we didn't really look at many paintings. It was early evening, but because of the holidays there was a rushed, closing-time atmosphere in the place. All the employees looked ready to abandon their framed charges and hit the malls to finish their shopping.

Jason and I just wandered around a few rooms, then headed for a coffee shop.

I was still in a bit of a funk. After lingering over two cups, Jason gave me a nudge. "Why is it I get the feeling that you don't want to go home? Are you trying to hide me from your family?"

"Try the other way around. I can't believe you would want to go back there!"

"What's the matter?" He shrugged. "Your brother is having problems, so it's understandable he's upset. It's an awful time of year to go through the kind of trouble he's having."

I frowned. "I know . . . but even my mom and dad . . ."

"They're great!" Jason said.

"They weren't at their best, believe me."

"But I liked it that they weren't hovering when we arrived."

They not only weren't hovering; they had forgotten we were coming.

"And the house looks great. I like old houses. So the tree is artificial. And smallish. I don't know what you're complaining about." His Kenneth Coles gave me a gentle kick beneath the table. "You're spoiled, you know that?"

Maybe I was. He seemed so glad to be in the bosom of my messed-up family, it made me a little ashamed. All I could see was that the one year I was really primed for holiday cheer, no one else was cooperating. "Maybe when we get home, things will have improved."

"That's the spirit," Jason said, coaxing me along. "Why don't we take your folks out to dinner? Your mom will probably be so busy these next few days, it would be great to give her a treat."

That was Jason all over. Looking at his handsome face, feeling all that optimism radiating from him, I felt humbled, as if someone had poured the soul of all the good men of the world into Brad Pitt's body and handed the result to undeserving me for Christmas. He was perfect.

Recalling what Isaac had said, I was perturbed. Then defiant. What was wrong with perfect?

We went home, and while Jason went up to the spare room to change for dinner, I found my mom sitting in the living room with her feet propped up on an ottoman. She had Walkman headphones clapped on her ears and hadn't heard us come in.

"Mom?"

She jumped as if I had jolted her out of a deep sleep. "Oh, hi!"

"What are you doing?" What I really meant was, *Don't you have some walnut people to attend to?*

"I'm listening to *Crime and Punishment.* They had an unabridged copy at the library."

That would explain the plastic box the size of a small suitcase sitting on the floor next to her. It even came equipped with a handle.

"Mom, what's going on? It seems really weird to be in the house and not see any of the old decorations. What happened to your snow villages, and all the other stuff?"

"Those villages are such a lot of work to arrange! I just didn't have the stamina this year."

"Well, but . . ." She obviously had some stamina, or she wouldn't be listening to a reading of Dostoevsky.

"Is this really the time to be sitting around listening to depressing Russian novels?"

"Well, you weren't here and Ted's still in his room. . . ." She shook her head. "And it's not really depressing at all! I'm surprised. It's sort of like a suspense story, really. I don't know why they gave it that dreary name—they should have called it . . . well, I don't know. . . ." She tilted her head and thought for a moment. "It's got that great murder scene. Maybe something with *fear* in the title. *Sudden Fear.* Or how about *Landlady Beware?*"

"You haven't mentioned Jason," I said, changing the subject.

She blinked at me. "What should I say about him?"

I plunked myself down on the ottoman. "Well, what do you think? Were you surprised?"

"Yes, I was." She thought for a moment. "He doesn't seem your type."

"I don't know about that," I said. "Of course he's better looking than anyone I've gone out with." To me he seemed better looking than anyone, period.

Mom smiled wistfully. "I always liked Isaac."

"Isaac?" I bit my lip. I was still miffed with him.

"Did he drive down with you, too?"

"Well, yeah, but . . ."

"That's good. Don't forget to invite him to dinner tomorrow. He's always such a lot of fun!"

I wanted to tear my hair out. I had brought home Jason—Adonis—and all she could talk about was *Isaac?*

"Speaking of dinner," I said, "Jason wanted to take you and Dad out tonight."

"Your father and I already had dinner."

"Already? It's only—" I looked at my watch. It was 7:00 P.M. I should have remembered that my parents usually ate at six on the dot.

Mom shrugged. "You were gone, and there was all that food . . ."

"We can put something together here," Jason piped up behind me.

I jumped up. How long had he been standing there? I hope not long enough to hear my mother stating her preference for Isaac!

My dad came in. "Do they want to go out again? They just got here!"

"We were thinking of taking you out to dinner," I said.

"Oh!" My dad brightened. "That sounds great."

"Laird, you just ate," Mom reminded him.

"I don't mind going along for company," my dad said. "Maybe have some coffee . . ."

"Terrific," Jason answered.

Dad gave me a fatherly nudge but directed his next comment to Jason. "Maybe you can help me convince Holly here to look beyond teaching English to seventh graders. She could go to graduate school and at least teach in a college, or go to law school."

"Dad . . ." Just because I didn't want to get a Ph.D., he acted as if I were a beach bum. I could never convince him that I *liked* teaching English to seventh graders. I was even good at it.

" 'It's never too late to become what you might have been,' " he lectured.

By the time he brought out that old saw, we were usually reduced to scolding on his part and eye rolling on mine. It had been the same since I was a teenager. I wasn't trying hard enough. I didn't apply myself to the subjects that matter, or have the right kind of ambition. *Look at Maddie,* he'd say.

"You all have fun," my mother chirped. "I think I'll stay and get a little farther along in my book."

I could see why. *Crime and Punishment* was looking like a nice alternative to family togetherness to me now, too.

At that point, Jason was practically dragging me along. We passed underneath the archway where the mistletoe usually hung. I turned. "Mom, what happened to the mistletoe?"

"Mistletoe?" She looked confused for a moment. As if she had never even heard of the stuff. "Oh! I couldn't find any. There's a shortage this year—a fungus killed it all."

I groaned as I was tugged away. Wouldn't you know it? For twenty-seven years there had been mistletoe dangling in that spot, as useless to me in my coupleless state as a screen door on a submarine. But the one year I really needed it? *Mistletoe blight!*

Chapter Four

During dinner I started to get the jitters. All the time I was sawing through a chicken breast and picking at my mashed potatoes, I kept thinking, *This could be the night.* I could barely keep my mind on the conversation—something about the New York draft riots during the Civil War—for wondering what would happen when Jason and I got back home. Should I find some way to entice him to my room, or should I change into something slinky and tiptoe over to his?

At one point, Jason had reached over to squeeze my knee under the table, causing me to sploop coffee all over my crème brûlée.

When we got home, Dad announced he was trundling off to bed right away. In the living room, Ted was sitting cross-legged on the couch with our old crocheted granny-square afghan around his shoulders. He was staring at the Quality Value Channel. I was relieved to see him out of his room, even if he did appear to have tear marks on his cheeks.

"It's Melinda's favorite channel." His voice rasped with an odd blend of nostalgia and bitterness. "She always watches it before bed. She's probably watching it now."

I crossed over and sank onto the couch next to him. "Ted, don't you think you should get some sleep?"

He burrowed deeper inside his afghan. "I'm not tired. Besides, I want to see what kind of *quality* and *value* Melinda gets off this thing."

"Uh, Ted . . ."

"She's always wasting money. She thinks I'm Donald Trump!"

I patted him on the knee and got up, returning to Jason. "I guess he needs to be alone."

I tried to think of where I could take Jason now. (Besides away from my bipolar brother.) If there had been a sprig of mistletoe around, I would have yanked him under it. But, of course, there wasn't. "Feel like a glass of wine?" I asked him.

He shook his head. "I guess I could use a glass of water to take up to my room, though."

"Oh, sure."

We went to the kitchen, and I told him again how much Dad had seemed to like him.

"He's a very interesting man," Jason said.

I nodded. "I guess he's getting a little older—maybe not feeling as spry as he was. That would explain the lack of outside holiday decor."

Jason looked thoughtful. "I understand why you

were bummed out this afternoon. When we were driving to the restaurant, all the houses with the lights . . ."

Oh, God. He *was* let down. He had been trying to hide it all afternoon, just to buoy my spirits, but now the disappointment was spilling out.

Maybe I could scrounge up some lights and string them up tonight. At least around the doorway.

"Not that it's any big deal," Jason assured me. "It's so great to be here with your family for Christmas."

I poured him a glass of water.

"Of course, it's not *exactly* how you described it. . . ."

I leapt in quickly. "I'm hoping things will be back to normal tomorrow. And maybe when Maddie gets here . . . *if* she gets here . . ."

Maddie had a true holiday steamroller personality.

He nodded. "I know. And tomorrow's Christmas Eve. We'll have fun."

I handed him his water. *Tomorrow? Couldn't we have fun tonight?*

"Well"—he smiled down at me—"good night."

"Good night," I said.

He leaned down and gave me a peck on the lips, but it felt like a perfunctory gesture. Or was I just being paranoid?

When he left, I stood for a moment in the kitchen, crushed by my own cowardice . . . or Jason's reticence. What had happened to all my seduction plans? We only had three nights. One seemed to have slipped away from me already.

But what did I expect? I had hyped this trip as a sort of family Christmas Disneyland, and the result had turned out to be something entirely different. Dismalland, maybe. If Jason's ardor was attached to some kind of Christmas barometer, between now and tomorrow I *really* needed to get some work injecting some holiday fun into this house.

I went out to the living room again. Ted was still staring at the television screen, where a doll that looked like it was dressed as Martha Washington was twirling slowly on a plastic stand.

"Ted, where do Mom and Dad keep the Christmas lights?"

He had broken out the whiskey bottle again and took a slug. "Attic," he said.

I suppressed a groan. The attic was always a wreck—things got flung up there and forgotten, and then when you went looking for them, they always seemed to be covered in plaster dust and desiccated bug carcasses. The place gave me the crawlies.

The people on the television were exclaiming about how lifelike the doll's eyes were. "She just seems to be looking at you and saying, 'I want to be your best friend!' "

I didn't see it, myself, but Ted sniffled. "I should get one for Amanda."

"I'm sure she'd love it, Ted, but maybe you shouldn't buy things just now. . . ."

He shook his head. "Why not? *I'm* not the one with the trouble managing money in my family."

I left him punching the 800 number into his cell phone and went upstairs, then up the little closet staircase to the attic. I braced myself for the worst, but when I pulled the chain on the overhead light, an entirely different attic was revealed to me from the one I had previously known. This one was swept and tidy. I didn't see a dead bug anywhere, or hear the scurrying of little critter feet. Instead of piles of junk everywhere, there were stacks of white boxes of different shapes piled neatly together, all labeled with a black marker. *Dishes. HALLOWEEN. Tax Documents.* One marked *Goodwill* wasn't closed up very well, and I went to investigate.

Poking around for a minute or so, I began to understand that "Goodwill" was a euphemism for "Holly's belongings." No wonder my room had seemed so clean when I had dropped my bag there this afternoon! My PowerPuff Girl bedspread from high school was in here, and a lot of my old books, and a nearly bald stuffed orange monkey named Mr. Fabulous that I had had since I was five. The monkey came out of the box. When I pulled him out, I let out a muffled scream. Underneath where Mr. Fabulous had been lay Ted's old ventriloquist dummy, smiling at me with those eerie eyes of his. I slammed the lid shut on the box. God, that thing was creepy.

I scanned the boxes for one marked *Lights* or *Xmas* or *Snow Village,* but I didn't find anything.

Then, from nowhere, I remembered Isaac saying, "What a waste of a good dummy."

My gaze strayed back to the Goodwill box.

Then I remembered that I was mad at Isaac.

But I relented. This was too good to pass up. It

was perfect for him! I hauled the dummy out, trying to inspect it without looking too closely at that psychotic little face. His suit was a little moth eaten, but otherwise he seemed okay. I took him down to my bathroom and tried to clean him up. I brushed his suit, scrubbed an indeterminate stain off his pant leg, and took a sponge to his rubber head. Then I carried him downstairs to show Ted; the dummy was his, after all. He might not want to part with it any more than I wanted to see Mr. Fabulous go into a Goodwill bin.

In the living room, another doll was rotating slowly on the television screen.

"I thought I'd get this one for Schuyler," he said. "It's only forty-nine, ninety-five."

"Remember this guy?" I asked, holding up the dummy.

Ted barely spared it a glance. "Yeah, it's that doll that used to scare the shit out of you."

"It's not a doll; it's a dummy. Mom was going to throw it away."

"Probably a good idea."

So much for sentimentality. "Well, would you mind if I gave it to Isaac?"

"Be my guest." He gestured at the TV with his phone. "Or do you think I should pass on this one?"

I frowned at the television. "I think you should go to bed."

He ignored me, so I returned to the attic and poked around some more. Then I ventured out to the garage and found some Christmas lights, but half the string didn't work. I went down to the basement and rooted around till I found a closet holding all the snow village stuff. No monks, no walnut people, no crystal angels. Just some snow village pieces, but by no means all of them. Unfortunately, all the pieces were stored in styrofoam inside individual cardboard boxes. Already tired, I started grabbing them at random and took them upstairs in several trips. Tomorrow morning I would get up early and try to convince Mom to do a little decorating.

Yawning, I dragged the last load upstairs, stacked them in the library, and then waved good night to Ted. "What do you think about these plates?" he asked me.

The decorative plates were part of some kind of large cats collection. A set included a lion, a tiger, a leopard, and a jaguar.

"They're hand painted," he said.

"You should go to bed."

"In a minute." It was as if a fever had overtaken him.

Exhaustion had such a hold on me that I barely managed to stumble into bed in time to fall asleep. By that time, I wasn't thinking about seduction, or cat plates, or anything else. The only thought registering in my tired brain was, *What had become of the walnut people?*

I bounded out of bed the next morning, bowed but not broken. Positive thoughts loped through my head. I still had Jason, Maddie would probably arrive today, and my parents were bound to snap into holiday mode any moment now. They just needed a little nudge from me.

Mom was already up. It did my heart good to see her puttering around the kitchen, just like her old self. Even if she did have her earphones on.

I walked up to her but she didn't see me. When I tapped her on the shoulder, she jumped, sending a spoon flying. "Holly!" she said, slipping her earphones off. "You scared me!"

"Are you listening to *Crime and Punishment* at seven A.M.?"

She shook her head. "French."

"French what?"

"French language tapes."

I frowned. "Are you and Dad taking a trip?"

She chortled as if I had involuntarily told a knee-slapper. "No—I'm starting college again next semester, and I'm trying to get a head start. I have to bone up for my placement test in January."

I stared at her, surprised. "What do you want to go to college for?"

That probably sounds like an impolitic question, especially coming from a teacher, but her news jarred me. Mom had been around college professors all her life. It seemed odd that after all these years it was just now popping into her head to partake of what they had to offer.

"I want a degree."

"What for?"

"What do you mean, what for?" she asked, getting down some shredded wheat.

I shuddered at the sight of that box. "We aren't having cereal for breakfast, are we?"

"Why not?"

"Well . . . because Jason's here." It was nice to have him as an excuse, though the truth was that I didn't relish kicking off my morning with those little fiber pellets. My parents didn't even buy the sugar-frosted kind. It was breakfast as punishment.

"What does Jason eat for breakfast?"

I bit my lip. That was the one meal we had never had together, except for one Sunday brunch. And I had never once seen my mom whip up a Greek omelet, which is what Jason had ordered that time. "What about those yummy cinnamon rolls you make?"

"Those are *yeast* rolls, Holly. They take hours."

"Oh." The things you learn. "Pancakes? Everybody likes pancakes."

"Your father has to watch his cholesterol."

"Fine. We'll make them low fat."

"*We?*" my mother asked. "I'm trying to make it through indefinite pronouns this morning."

I sighed. "*I'll* make breakfast."

As soon as they tumbled out of my mouth, the words seemed to presage doom. I inspected the banks of cookbooks lining one kitchen wall and picked a huge tome at random. What the heck. It had the word *Joy* in the title. Very Christmasy.

"I don't want to be the only one in the family without one," my mother said, as I scanned the index.

"One of what?" I asked.

"A degree."

"Oh." I had forgotten what we had been talking about. Now I was more concerned with the difference between Swedish pancakes and standard American ones. A quick glance at the ingredient lists for both showed that neither were what you would describe as heart healthy.

"It's not so rare for adults to go back now," she said.

Adults was one thing . . . but Mom was fifty-three. "Well, I suppose it would be fun to take a class or two," I said, wondering if it would be okay to just leave out all the butter, "but what do you want a degree for? That's such a pain. And what would you need it for?"

"Why does anyone need one?"

"To get work," I said, "or to go on to something else."

"And you think that I would never be able to get work?"

I looked up from the book, startled. "Huh?"

"I worked hard enough to put your father's big brain through graduate school, if you'll recall."

Uh-oh. She sounded angry. At some point while scanning *The Joy of Cooking,* I had stepped on toes. People really shouldn't multitask at seven-thirty in the morning.

"I dropped out of college," she reminded me, "so he could afford to finish his Ph.D."

"I know, I know," I said. "But that's why I was saying, what do you want to go through all the rigmarole of college and job hunting now for? You paid your dues. Now you can take it easy."

"Easy!" She sniffed. "You think taking care of this family—of your father—is *easy?*"

"Well, no, that's not what I—"

She chortled at me in challenge. "You just go ahead and make breakfast for everybody this morning, Fannie Farmer, and then report back how easy you think I've had it."

She snapped the headphones back on her ears and skulked off.

I guessed this might not be the right time to ask her to put the snow village together.

I had other things on my mind now anyway. The way to a man's heart was through his stomach, after all, not through a snow village. I decided to add holiday pizzazz to the recipe by making pumpkin spice pancakes. This would disguise the fact that I was leaving out the butter and eggs so as not to kill my father, plus it would move us a little further down the road of getting the house smelling Christmasy.

Once I had demolished the kitchen and had something that looked reasonably like batter, I felt better. In fact, I really had the feeling that I could hold this Christmas together out of sheer determination and generous amounts of cinnamon and nutmeg. Why not?

The next person I saw that morning was Jason. He came bounding into the kitchen in sweats and sneakers and kissed my forehead. "What's this?" he asked, his gaze naturally drawn to the orange glop I was obsessively stirring.

"Pumpkin pancakes."

"Cool—I thought I'd take a run around your neighborhood before breakfast. Do I have time?"

Okay, I'll admit to a tiny sag of disappointment just then. I had imagined Jason bounding down to the kitchen and helping me. Or at least diving for the breakfast table and getting ready to scarf down two short stacks. I hadn't expected him to dash out into the freezing cold and get himself all sweaty first.

I didn't even know he was a jogger.

Not that I *really* minded. Anyway, I wasn't going to let him know it. "No! Great!" I practically sing-songed.

He awarded me another peck and dashed out the door. I started making coffee and getting things ready. I turned on the griddle, I dug up a red and green tablecloth with little stick snowmen embroidered on it and threw it on the table, and I unearthed the Christmas Spode and set the table in record time. I put out a pitcher of milk for coffee, and the butter, and then started searching through the cabinets for syrup.

But there was no syrup.

Not a drop.

A wave of panic hit me. I had felt pretty cocksure while I was making those pancakes, if only because I knew that some grade A maple syrup covered a multitude of culinary sins. But without it that orange glop looked more threatening. I tried to think what to do. I could plead with my mother to unearth some syrup or run to the store, but she would probably just make another snide Fannie Farmer comment. Jason was jogging—and besides, he was the person I was trying to impress. Ted . . .

Well, Ted probably wasn't in any shape to be running errands.

After a few moments of standing frozen in front

of a wall of opened cabinets, I finally gathered my wits about me. What was syrup? Sugar and water. Mrs. Butterworth didn't bother with maple trees. Homemade in this case wasn't ideal . . . but I could get it done while the pancakes were cooking . . . and spice it up with a little cinnamon and nutmeg.

Quick like a bunny, I yanked a saucepan off a shelf and tossed in four cups of sugar and a cup of water. To my surprise, it seemed to work. That is, the sugar began to dissolve.

Someone knocked at the side door, and I dashed over to open it. I was expecting Jason, but instead, Isaac blew in. "My God, it's cold," he said, teeth chattering. He stopped, looked around the kitchen, and deposited a paper grocery bag on the kitchen table. "Where is everybody?"

"Jason's jogging, Mom's studying indefinite articles, and everyone else is asleep."

"Jason's *jogging?*" he asked. "Holidays exist so we don't have to do stuff like that."

As if he *ever* jogged.

"That's how cardiovascular slackers think. Jason's different."

"Right, a pillar among men." Isaac looked around. He took off his hat, muffler, and coat and dropped them on a chair. "What are you up to here?"

"I'm making breakfast."

Deep lines furrowed his forehead as he inspected my bowl of batter. "And it's going to be . . . ?"

"*Pancakes,*" I said.

"I like pancakes," he said, then added, "usually."

I was grudgingly about to invite him to stay, when suddenly a hissing noise got my attention. My syrup was bubbling over. I dove to turn the heat down on it. Isaac was right next to me.

"Oh, are we having glue for breakfast, too?" he asked.

My confidence, already shaky, wavered some more. It didn't look right—sort of thick and white. "Syrup."

"Holly . . ."

"Could you hand me the cinnamon, please?" I said, cutting him off. The last thing I needed right now was nay-saying. I started shoveling spices into what was beginning to look like sugar cement.

"Maybe you should add something else?" Isaac ventured.

"What?"

"Butter? That usually helps."

"I can't use fat, because of Dad."

Real alarm spread across Isaac's face and he nervously eyeballed the orange sludge in the bowl at his elbow. "What's in that batter?"

"Would you just sit down and relax? I had this all under control before you showed up." I glanced at the bag he'd left on the table. "What did you bring?"

He seemed to have forgotten it. "Oh! My mom's been making gingerbread houses this year." He pulled out a picture-perfect example of confectionary architecture. "Happy holidays from the Millsteins to the Ellises."

I have to admit, after my pancake gambit, I felt

almost jealous of it. It looked like something out of a children's picture book. "That was so nice of her!"

Dad shuffled in, dressed in his usual uniform of khakis, dress shirt, and cardigan. He peered over the counter to see what I was doing and a hint of worry crossed his face. When I shot him a warning glance, he offered, "*Smells* good."

Mom sauntered back in, inspected what I was doing, then hummed something Wagnerian and gloomy as she refilled her coffee. Then she caught sight of the gingerbread house, which she positioned in the center of the table. "Just darling!" she exclaimed. "I'll have to call Leona up this morning to thank her."

By the time Jason came bounding back from his jog, cheeks rosy with health, not even breaking a sweat, it was obvious a disaster was in the making. He looked at the pancake lumps squatting on the griddle and exclaimed, "Gosh, you shouldn't have gone to so much trouble! I could have just had cereal."

When Ted came down twenty minutes later looking like death warmed over, everyone was slumped stonily over their inedible pancakes, which sat like leaden pumpkin cowpies on everyone's plates. Let's just say that folks weren't digging in. There was nothing to be done with them, either, since the syrup I had prepared had somehow turned into a sugar brick on the way from the stove to the table. They were all too polite to suggest alternatives just yet.

Ted sank into a chair. Immediately, the rest of us

straightened and attempted to lift his spirits by sheer force of will.

"I didn't expect to see you this morning," I joked.

Ted stared bleary-eyed at me.

"You were up late, remember?" To jog his memory, I added, "QVC."

"Oh. Right." He buried his head in his hands. "Oh no!"

"What is it?" we asked.

"QVC. I thought it was a nightmare."

Having lost entire weekends zombified in front of home-shopping networks, I could sympathize. "We've all been there," I said, trying to comfort him.

"Not the way I was." His eyes seemed full of anguish. "I bought those cat plates."

"What?" Dad asked.

"Collector's plates with cats on them. They were on sale—I think I bought some for everybody. Twelve sets."

We gaped at him.

"Merry Christmas," he said.

This news only added to the general gloom. As the minutes dragged by and people only picked around the (burnt) edges of their servings, I felt myself sinking lower in my chair. Even I was longing for a bowl of shredded wheat along about that time.

I was about to utter the word of surrender—IHOP—when Dad, in desperation, reached over and snapped the chimney off Mrs. Millstein's gingerbread house.

"Laird!" my mother scolded.

"Well, it's food, isn't it?" Dad chewed quickly. "Tastes good!"

Ted suddenly yanked off a little of the roof and popped it in his mouth.

I couldn't blame them. They were hungry, and breakfast was inedible. Even Jason, who had piled pancakes on his plate out of loyalty to me, was eyeing that gingerbread house longingly. In resignation, I nudged it toward him. Avoiding my gaze, he hurriedly chipped off a shutter.

I looked over at Isaac. *He* wasn't eating the centerpiece. (Then again, he wasn't eating my pancakes, either.) "Did you hear about the mistletoe blight?"

"No."

"Apparently there's no mistletoe this year," I said.

"I'll bet I could find some," he said. "I'll poke around near my house and see."

For a moment, my spirits lifted. "You would do that for me?"

My hero! Even if his mother's gingerbread house *had* stolen the thunder from my pancakes.

Speaking of stealing thunder, at that moment, the door flew open, letting in a gust of wind. And my little sister.

Chapter Five

Maddie was dressed in one of those nylon goose down–stuffed vests that would have made me look like a marshmallow. On her it looked adorable. (Everything did.) It was minty blue and matched the helmet she was carrying jauntily under her arm.

When she blew into the house, the atmosphere shifted radically. Mount Doom turned into Munchkinland. The very floor seemed to lift beneath our feet; I wouldn't have been the least bit surprised if we had all started talking in high helium voices. Mom became more like her old self, and Dad dropped ten years in two seconds. Maddie's arrival even seemed to perk Ted up momentarily. As he looked at her, his grim countenance cracked into a dopey smile.

Dad and Mom jumped up for hugs. When I noticed Isaac queuing up for same, I gave him a playful punch. "Down boy," I whispered.

But he had been noticed. Maddie put her arms around him, shaking out her elbow-length blond hair. "Isaac, you old lunatic! How the heck have you been?"

Isaac squirmed with delight, making a sickening spectacle of himself. I had to hold myself back from miming little retching gestures, but then I was swept up in Maddie's serial helloing, too. "And Holly! Holly!" she cried, giving me a brief boa constrictor working over. "When did you get home? What did you do to yourself to make yourself look so good?" I was still trying to decide which question I should tackle first when she swatted both away. "Oh, never mind! What do you think of my outfit?" she asked, handing the helmet to me. Becoming her Jeeves, I took it obediently and then helped her struggle out of her coat. "It matches my Vespa. You've *got* to get one, Hol, they're just—"

"You color coordinated with your motorbike?" I asked.

"Very Evil Knievel of you," Isaac said.

She laughed and kept moving down the line. "Ted? How are you?" she asked, her brow wrinkling in concern. Obviously she had heard about the disaster in his life. Maddie was always in the know.

At Ted's shrug, she gave him another hug and moved down the line. She was about to throw her arms around Jason when she suddenly stopped and blurted out a laugh. "Hey—I don't know you!"

I zipped over. "This is Jason."

"Oh!" She took him in with open appreciation. I felt a wave of satisfaction. *Finally* someone was acknowledging my good fortune. "Wow. He's your Christmas present to us this year?"

Everyone chortled at her little joke.

Isaac and I looked toward the kitchen door. Weren't we missing someone?

"Uh . . . Maddie?" I asked. She blinked at me. "Are you alone?"

Her mouth dropped open and she gasped dramatically. "Omigosh! I *completely* forgot!"

She yanked open the door and pulled in a half-frozen soul carrying two large backpacks. "Folks, this is Vlad!" She added, "Vlad drives a Harley. We toodled down together."

Vlad grimaced uncomfortably at us all; he looked like one of those guys who was unused to smiling. The heavy lines in the corners of his mouth were not laugh lines. Our slack-jawed response to him probably wasn't very cheering, either. But he just wasn't what any of us could have expected.

For one thing, his clothes: a black leather jacket and ripped jeans. Something T-shirty and unwashed smelling underneath. Definitely not Brooks Brothers. When he took off his helmet, he revealed a black knit cap with a white skull knit onto it. Earrings circled from the top of one ear all the way around to the lobe. When he reached out to shake hands with one of us, the top of his hand revealed a hissing tattooed snake.

My dad recovered from his instant of shock sooner than the rest of us. "Glad to have you, Vlad."

"Thank you very much," Vlad said. His voice was so heavily accented there was a brief delay before everyone understood even that simple response and nodded.

"I met Vlad at the hospital," Maddie said. Then she let out an exaggerated shiver. "I don't suppose I could trouble anyone for a warm beverage."

Predictably, three people fell over themselves to get her a cup of coffee.

The group reassembled around the table. "Isn't this great?" Maddie asked. "I just love Christmas!"

I handed Vlad a cup of coffee. "Thank you very much," he said, winking at me.

Maddie held everyone spellbound describing her and Vlad's adventure. Apparently they had had trouble in Delaware, which is where Vlad had intended to go, but his friends weren't home.

"Their house was all boarded up," Maddie said. "So I just said, no problem, Vlad, come on home with me."

His friends' house was boarded up?

So Vlad wasn't *supposed* to be here? He wasn't a fiancé? Isaac and I exchanged bemused glances.

"I'm so glad you did, Vlad!" my mom exclaimed brightly. "We're glad to have you."

"Thank you very much," he said.

"Food!" Maddie's eyes widened when she took in the gingerbread house. She cracked off a piece of wall for herself. "I'm starved."

"Have some, Vlad," Mom said, shoving the partially demolished centerpiece toward him.

Three guesses what he said.

"Was this your family you were trying to visit in Delaware, Vlad?" I asked him.

"Friends," Maddie jumped in to answer. "Vlad's from Russia."

Oos and *ahs* greeted this news flash.

"He was trying to deliver a package to his friends, but they must be visiting family."

Right. I know I always board up windows before I leave for the weekend. I looked suspiciously at the backpack leaning against the kitchen cabinets by the door. The black one, not the minty blue one. Wonder what "package" he was trying to deliver.

Isaac looked over at me. "So I'm to go on a mistletoe hunt?"

Maddie gasped. "Mistletoe hunt? Fun!"

"Isaac volunteered for that. I was going to take Jason out. . . ."

"Where?" Maddie asked.

"Um, I'm not sure. . . ."

She let out a sputtering series of breaths, like a kid in a classroom bursting with the correct answer. "Yes, Maddie?" I asked in my best teacher voice.

"The zoo!" she said, beaming a million-watt smile at us all. "Doesn't that sound fun?"

Standing out in the freezing cold staring at displaced wildlife, fun?

"Sounds great!" Jason chimed.

"You do realize there's bad weather moving through, don't you?" I asked Maddie. "They're predicting ice. . . ."

Her blue eyes widened. "You're right. We should probably hurry before it gets worse."

"Good idea," Mom said. "You all run along."

"Wait." It was Christmas Eve, and Jason and I

needed *some* quality time. Not to mention, we had to sort out when he and I would exchange gifts. I didn't want this to happen during the present madness of Christmas morning. "Don't you need some help with dinner, Mom?"

Mom waved off my concern. "No, you kids go ahead. Have fun. It's all under control."

"*It is?*" So far I hadn't seen any evidence of a big dinner in the making. No crown pork roast, no huge ham. Nothing.

"Okay!" Maddie hopped up, ready to marshall us out the door. "Let's go!"

"Do we even know if the zoo will be open?" I asked, still dragging my heels.

"I'll call!" She bounded out of the room.

I started to trail after her; then I remembered something and turned back to Mom. "I brought up the snow village from the basement, but I didn't quite get around to putting it all together. It's in the hallway."

"That's fine," Mom said. "Your father can take it back down to the basement this morning."

"Actually, I thought you might—"

"You mean I'm not going to the zoo?" Dad interrupted, crestfallen.

Mom rolled her eyes. "Laird, you're going to Jeffrey's house for drinks!"

"Oh."

"Anyway, you hate the zoo," Mom said. "You always say it's horrible to watch those beautiful creatures all caged up, enslaved for a bunch of gawking humans."

I winced as I looked over at Isaac. "You wanna come gawk at enslaved animals?"

"I've got to go on my mistletoe hunt, remember?"

"Oh, right."

"Of course, I could come back later . . . say around dinnertime?"

Isaac always had Christmas Eve dinner with us. I'd forgotten to formally invite him this year, but Mom picked up the hint. "Do come have dinner with us!" she exclaimed. "If you aren't sick of us already."

"I'll be there with bells on."

"And mistletoe in hand," I reminded him.

"Cool car!" Maddie exclaimed from the backseat. "I just love Saabs."

Jason looked pleased. I should have been, too. My choice in boyfriend was finally garnering the approbation I craved. Unfortunately, I was a little distracted at the moment. We were still huddled shivering in the car, idling in the driveway. The heater hadn't quite kicked in yet. I swung around to ask, "Where's Vlad?"

Maddie looked surprised. "Inside. I don't think this would be his thing at all."

"What *would* his thing be?"

She laughed. "Who knows? Drive on, Jason."

Jason seemed happy enough to get us under way.

"Are you two serious?" I asked Maddie, sounding like a mother hen.

Her brow puckered at me. "Serious what?"

"You know," I said, "*serious*."

She looked dumbstruck for a moment, then started giggling.

"What's so funny?"

"Vlad and me," she said. "Serious. We just met."

"You said you knew him from the hospital," I reminded her.

"No, I said I'd *met* him at the hospital. I treated him in the ER."

"What for?" I asked.

She lifted her shoulders. "He came in for a head wound . . . but, of course, you couldn't see the scar through his cap." She allowed herself a smug smirk. "Also, I did a terrific job stitching him up, if I do say so myself."

"When was this?" I asked, still trying to piece it all together.

"Last weekend."

I freaked. "*What?* You just met this dude with a head wound and invited him home right off?" Which, now that I thought about it, was practically what I had done with Jason. Minus the head wound, of course.

"It wasn't like that. I was stitching him up, and you know, because I know a little Russian, we got to talking. And he has a motorcycle, and I have my Vespa, which had a leaky tire that he offered to fix. And then later we got to talking and decided to drive down together. I felt safer having someone with me, frankly."

I crossed my arms. So he wasn't a fiancé. Which was probably a good thing, all things considered. I hated to think of my little sister going out with some nut. I'm no reactionary, but this guy looked hard core. It wouldn't have surprised me to learn he was some kind of international drug trafficker.

"I swear, Holly, he's not some coke-snorting fiend."

I jumped. Was I that easy to read?

Jason laughed. When I looked over at him, he explained carefully, "If he *were* a coke-snorting fiend, we could call him Vlad the Inhaler."

Maddie cracked up, then noticed I was *not* laughing.

"Look at you." Maddie gave the back of the seat a poke. "Miss Uptight. After all the skeevies you've been out with!"

I flinched. "I just think you're behaving recklessly. You show up late, and with some kind of Slavic slum boy in tow. . . ."

Maddeningly, she laughed off my criticism and leaned forward to give Jason an approving pat. "You must be good for her. I've never seen her worried about things like appearances or punctuality before. And you look great, Hol! You finally took my advice and found a good stylist."

That's the trouble with family. They keep you from projecting who you want to be by reminding everyone who you actually are.

I snapped on the radio. Ella Fitzgerald was singing "Frosty the Snowman."

Jason shuddered. "Oh, not this again."

"I *love* this song!" Maddie said.

Jason grinned at her through the rearview mirror. "Your sister and Isaac spent half the trip from

New York arguing about who sang 'Frosty the Snowman' in the TV special."

"It wasn't half the trip," I said.

He laughed. "Just most of the way through Pennsylvania."

Maddie leaned forward. "That's Holly and Isaac. They're like an old married couple."

I objected violently to that characterization. "I just don't believe in letting people walk around with wrong ideas in their heads, like Burl Ives singing 'Frosty the Snowman.' "

Maddie frowned. "But he *did* sing 'Frosty the Snowman.' "

Jason groaned.

Was the world filled with people conflating their Christmas specials? "It was Jimmy Durante."

"*Who?*" Maddie asked.

I could have cried.

By the time we got to the zoo, the temperature seemed to have dipped another ten degrees. The air felt heavy, expectant. No doubt about it, soon there would be annoying people running around proclaiming how great it was to have a white Christmas.

We got out and stomped around paved trails looking for wildlife, but most of the animals that weren't huddled in their naturalized concrete enclosures and burrows looked severely pissed off at having been transported from their subtropical worlds to this frigid one. Even the polar bears pacing around their pool didn't seem very enthusiastic about their conditions, from what I could tell, as I peered out at them through the slit created from where my scarf ended and my hat brim began.

My phone rang, and I walked a few paces from Maddie and Jason to answer it. It was Isaac.

"I'm at Barcroft Park," he said. "It's cold, and I don't see mistletoe, and even if I did, I don't know what I'd do about it. I think all my fingers have frostbite."

Whiner. "Remind me not to bring you along when I summit Everest."

"Everest?" He hooted so loudly I had to hold the phone away from my ear. "You get winded summiting the three flights of stairs to my apartment."

"Yeah, but on Everest they give you an oxygen tank and chocolate bars."

"I'll try to remember that the next time you're puffing past the second floor landing. Anyway, I just thought of something. What is this mistletoe for?"

"It's for me."

"For you and Mr. Perfect," he said.

What did he think? "You have a problem with that?"

He didn't answer right away. "How are things in the animal kingdom?"

"Frigid. I'm here with Maddie and Jason."

"What about Vlad?"

"He's at home." I did another quarter turn away from Jason and Maddie, who didn't seem to be paying any attention to me anyway. "Guess what?" I hissed into the phone. "She just picked him up."

"I thought he was from her hospital."

"He was a head-wound case. Jason probably

thinks I'm nuts. I promised him Norman Rockwell, and instead he's getting drunks, quarrelsome parents, and crazy Russian dudes."

"So how are Jason and Maddie getting along?" Isaac asked.

"Why?"

"No reason. I was just looking at them together this morning. Jason looks like something she would have had made to order."

What was he trying to do, make me jealous? I felt a snit coming on, but instinctively my eyes strayed over to Maddie and Jason. They were in profile, pointing at some exotic variety of goat, laughing. They did look Dentyne-ad wholesome together.

And what about Jason's little Vlad the Inhaler joke? I had never heard him crack wise like that before. It was as if he'd been showing off a little for her.

I shut my mind to this line of thinking. Isaac was just trying to stir something up. Although why he was being such a fiend, I couldn't say. "I gotta go," I told him.

"Okay. I've just lost feeling in my right big toe."

"Are you still coming for dinner? Assuming Vlad or my brother doesn't burn the house down between now and seven o'clock?"

"In that case, I heard about a great Italian place we can go to," Isaac said helpfully.

"Comedian."

Jason, Maddie, and I tromped through a little more of the zoo, enjoying the relative warmth of the snake house before going to stare at the empty panda enclosure for a few moments. In all my years of living near DC, the most I'd ever seen of the pandas was the occasional glimpse of dirty white fur visible behind a log. Today we didn't even get that.

"We should take a picture in front of the giraffes," I suggested. For one thing, the giraffes were inside a heated building right now.

"Oh, did you bring your camera?" Maddie asked.

"No—didn't you?"

"I left all my camera equipment in Boston this year," she said. "I had to travel light."

How could she have left her camera? She was the family's unofficial photographer. "You always take pictures."

"Sorry—not this year."

My $200 haircut. The matching sweaters. My camera-ready boyfriend. *No photos?* It was heartbreaking.

Was no one going to cooperate with my one and only perfect Christmas?

I confess I was still in a stew when we got back to the car.

"I guess we could stop by a drugstore and get one of those disposable kind, if you really want pictures," Maddie said from the backseat.

It didn't help my mood any that I was so obviously transparent. I swung around. "I can't believe it, Mad."

"Can't believe what?"

"You!" I said. "Ever since you were old enough to talk you've been the Christmas drill sergeant. Now you've completely flaked out."

"Just because I didn't bring my camera?"

"That—and also Vlad. Stopping at boarded-up houses doesn't make you suspicious?"

"I can't believe *you're* being so judgmental!" Maddie crossed her arms over her chest, which was rising and falling in angry little heaves. "I thought I could count on you of all people to understand."

"Understand what? That you've decided to stage a powderpuff reenactment of *Easy Rider*?"

Maddie's thin shoulders started convulsing, and she dashed several tears off her face. "No. That I'm trying to change."

"You're changing, all right." Changing into a nitwit.

"I'm just trying to be more like you!" she howled, reaching for a Kleenex. She of course had a neat little packet of them in her jacket pocket.

I gawped at her in disbelief as she honked into a tissue. Had I heard her correctly? Had she said *like me?*

"Don't you think I know what you think of me?" she howled. "That I'm too enthusiastic, too perky, too perfect?"

My mouth opened and closed several times.

"Well, of course you think that," she said, waving away my mute protest. "It's the *truth.* I am too perfect. Even my therapist thinks so."

"Your therapist?" This was the first I'd ever heard of her seeking professional help.

"Dr. Howell said I need to learn to be more spontaneous—or to just *be.*"

I frowned. "Who is this doctor? Some sixties throwback?"

"He's a *very competent* therapist," she said, still sniffling. "I did months of exhaustive research on psychologists and psychology before I called him."

Of course.

She looked up as if she'd just been caught in a trap. "Oh, God! That sounded terrible, didn't it?"

I rolled my eyes. "Maddie, for God's sake. You can't go nuts with this. Researching a doctor for months is a lot more understandable than spending that much time researching the best way to make oatmeal." Which, honest to God, she had actually done once.

She slumped, and looking at her, I felt terrible. What had happened to bring on this crisis? "Look, I hope nothing I said—"

"No—of course not," she answered, cutting me off. "It's all me. I had realized for some time that I just had an unsustainable desire for perfection. I mean, look at you! Your life is so . . ." *Half-assed,* I believe was the word on the tip of her tongue that she was too polite to voice. ". . . and you've always been much happier than me."

Where did she get *that* crazy idea?

I glanced anxiously over at Jason, who was staring grimly ahead at the road. Poor man. He must think the entire Ellis family was composed of nothing but flakes. At some point I would have to reiterate that we were actually very normal.

"You were *so smart* not to position yourself as some insanely brilliant overachiever," Maddie went on. "I mean, Mom and Dad just don't have the same expectations for you. You don't have to feel this *pressure* all the time!"

"Well, uh . . ."

"Oh, sure, they rib you about going to graduate school," she said, sort of clucking dismissively. "I mean, that's sort of a joke."

I was feeling emotionally whiplashed as we pulled into the driveway. I wanted to reach out to Maddie, but I was beginning to suspect she thought I lacked expertise to get anywhere close to feeling her pain. And what was this BS about my not feeling pressure? Had she ever had to endure Dad telling her that it was never too late to become what she might have been?

Jason left the Saab idling in the drive for a few moments—I thought to give us the opportunity to wind down or for Maddie to fix her makeup. His jaw was still set in that anxious way I'd noticed before. After a few moments, he turned in his seat to face Maddie. "You can never be too perfect," he said gently, putting his hand on her corduroy-covered knee.

Maddie's eyes widened. Mine, too, probably. I kept staring at his hand, as if I could will it away from her leg.

I couldn't.

"If that's who you are, so be it," he said. "Some people probably tie themselves in knots trying to become more like *you*."

There was a silence, during which I could feel my face turning red. Was it just Isaac's phone call making me zany when it came to Jason and Maddie, or was this really weird?

Jason gave her a squeeze. "Don't see perfection as a curse; count it as a blessing. Embrace that trait as part of who you are, and then try to work with it."

Wow. I'd never heard him come out with any pop psychobabble like that before. It was as if the man of my dreams was suddenly morphing into Dr. Phil. "Sometimes even the best therapist can say something that sends you down a mental rabbit hole," Jason said. "Believe me, I know."

Jason had been to a therapist? That was the first time he had mentioned it. But, of course, now that I thought about it, it seemed likely that he would have. He probably had a lot of issues from his weird childhood.

When Jason finally switched off the engine, Maddie got out of the car quickly. I wondered if she felt awkward after having spilled her guts. And then having a near stranger spouting Oprahisms at her.

Still, I was grateful to Jason, despite his emphasis of the touchy in his sudden touchy-feeliness. "Thanks for jumping in. I was having a hard time thinking of anything to say."

"No problem. I've done stuff like that a lot, actually."

I narrowed my eyes at him. "You're a bond trader and part-time psychologist?"

He chuckled. "No, actually, I've been involved in Big Brothers for a long time now. I'm sort of used to hashing out family problems with people."

"You never told me about that."

He raised his brows. "Well—it never came up. I always feel uncomfortable about talking about volunteer work. It would sound too much like tooting my own horn."

"I was hoping we would be able to have a moment tonight to exchange gifts," I said, meaning a moment not in a car. "Christmas morning is sort of nuts, and public . . ."

He flashed me a high-wattage smile. "Sounds like you're hoping for *a lot* of gratitude for your gift."

Heat crept into my cheeks, but I couldn't help tossing off saucily, "I might."

He leaned over and gave me a peck on the nose, and then a slightly longer kiss on the mouth. *This is more like it,* I thought, my enthusiasm for this trip returning.

When we pried ourselves out of the car, the first flakes of snow were falling out of the sky.

"Looks like we'll have a white Christmas!" Jason proclaimed.

Chapter Six

In the house, everything was disturbingly the same. There was no "Nutcracker" music booming through the house, and no tantalizing smell of dinner getting started that would presage a holiday feast.

Ted and Vlad were on the living room couch watching ESPN through heavy-lidded eyes, and Mom was sitting in the recliner chair, listening to her book on headphones. Jason said he had something he needed to do quickly, and he disappeared upstairs. I stayed down with the others.

I waved at Mom and she slipped the headphones off.

"When's dinner?" I asked. I didn't want to be pushy, but . . .

"Don't worry about it," Mom said. "It's all taken care of."

My head was practically swiveling. "How can

that be? Everything's just the same as it was before we went to the zoo."

"Then you didn't notice the piano."

I pivoted toward the old Steinway, which *was* decorated. I had to admit that. But where were the sledding monks? In their place, there was a Christmas village (the misplacement of it offended my newfound reverence for tradition), but it was sort of an abomination of a village. Scrooge and Marley's Counting House was right smack in the middle of the little Alpine buildings. And Fezziwigg's Delivery Wagon was parked on the fake pond. Not *next* to it, mind you. Right on top of it. I glared at the display for a full minute, my indignation gaining steam, before I was finally able to pronounce this conglomeration simply not acceptable.

Mom laughed. "Just move the wagon off the pond, for heaven's sake."

"But there's hardly any room—"

"Well, don't blame me. Vlad did it."

"*Vlad?*" I twisted toward the couch. His eyes slowly dragged themselves away from the football game on television to glare at me. *You gotta problem with my snow village?* those eyes asked.

I wondered briefly whether he was packing heat in his backpack. I smiled. "Looks nice!"

He nodded cautiously, then turned back to the TV.

"Since when do you outsource the decorating?" I asked Mom. "And where are all the walnut people? And why is the attic so neat?"

Mom kicked the footrest of her chair abruptly,

bringing herself upright. "If you don't mind, Holly, I'm getting sick and tired of your nit-picking. Just because this is the one year you decided to participate—"

"I've always participated," I argued. "I'm here every Christmas."

"Yes, to snigger at everything."

"I never—"

"You *always* laughed at my walnut people," she said. "But now when you want to impress your boyfriend, you act as though you can't get enough of them. Well, news flash! We're not all here to perform on cue for you."

She jammed on her headphones, grabbed her huge box of tapes by its handle, and flounced out of the room. She looked like someone running away from home.

I stood in the middle of the room, my ears stinging. I was steamed—but it was a chastened kind of steamed. Maybe she was right. Partially. I *had* always taken all the labors everyone went through for granted.

"Nice going," Ted grunted at me.

I turned to the piano. Maybe it was the house, or being around my family, but for the first time since I was thirteen I had the urge to dig my hands in my pockets and whine that *they just didn't understand me.* But I was an adult now—nominally—and I tried to channel my frustrations to productive ends. I moved Fezziwigg's Delivery Wagon off the skating pond. But then I discovered why it had been put there in the first place. There wasn't enough cotton fluff to hold all the buildings and the wagon. So it either had to go on the pond or be stuck off by itself next to the metronome. Defeated, I rolled it back down on the pond.

I managed to laugh at myself as I made my way to my bedroom. Obviously I needed to chill out. It was natural that I was tied in knots, actually—I wasn't used to feeling responsible for someone else's Christmas vacation. I had dragged Jason down here, and so far things weren't quite what I had expected. Minimal Christmas cheer, minimal romance. *But so what?* Next year—when hopefully everyone would be acting saner and all the crystal angels and inflatable polar bears would be in place again—Jason and I would probably be laughing about all this.

I flopped back on my bed and clasped my hands together on my stomach. *God I hope Isaac found that mistletoe.* Right now it felt like my only hope.

A light tapping at my door made me sit up suddenly. Jason was standing in my doorway, looking around the room with a half smile. It was an odd mix of the old me—my student desk with a pink Princess phone on it, my *Last of the Mohicans* poster, a corkboard full of pictures and mementos—and my parents' attempt to assert their dominion over my room. Mom had put a Laura Ashley–esque coverlet on the bed, and Dad's HealthRider exercise bike stood in front of my dresser.

"Come in," I said.

He had something hidden behind his back and I felt a little surge of curiosity. He sank down on the bed next to me, pushing Mr. Fabulous away with an uncomfortable nudge of his elbow. "You said you wanted to exchange gifts in private."

Actually, I had envisioned us getting together after everyone else had gone to bed—a stroke-of-midnight moment, maybe, in front of the odorless tree.

But apparently Jason hadn't planned the present swap for optimum romance potential. He brought out his gift and handed it to me. "Well, so . . . here."

It was too large for a jewelry box. From the looks of it, I expected a small clothing item maybe. Very small and featherlight . . . lingerie, perhaps? (Just what I needed.) *What the hell was it?* I wondered, suddenly overcome with curiosity. I reached around to my bag and got out his present from me.

We sat side by side and unwrapped. Jason was faster than me. When he lifted the lid of the box he drew in a sharp breath. "Wow!" he exclaimed. "This is sooooo great!"

He jumped up and wound the huge muffler around his neck. It *did* look great, but he was sort of overreacting—like a floozy in an old movie with a new fur coat. "Where did you *find* this?"

"We saw it together," I reminded him.

"Did we?" He frowned, obviously having forgotten.

But how could he have forgotten? How? He was an elephant. He even remembered the name of Isaac's ex-girlfriend, a person I hadn't mentioned more than once, I'm sure.

He grinned as he fingered the soft wool. "That makes it even better. More personal."

I should have gotten him a watch, I thought, kicking myself.

I took the lid off the small white box in front me and found a wall of tissue paper. When I peeled away that layer, I realized he had fooled me completely. There was no slip of silk—just an envelope. My heart thumped—*some kind of love note, maybe?* Or one of those hand-printed cards that promised, *"This card good for one romantic winter getaway."* I had a friend whose boyfriend had done that for her birthday once.

I ripped open the envelope and a Barnes & Noble gift card fell out onto the carpet.

"Oh!" I bent down to retrieve the card, then bashed my head against my desk when I lifted my head. The Princess phone let out an incidental jangle as my head crunched. I winced. "Oh!"

Jason reached over. "Are you all right?" he asked, his face twisted in sympathetic pain.

I nodded mutely, waving my gift card at him. "Thank you so much."

"I knew you liked books," he said.

"Yes, I do," I assured him. "Love 'em."

I gave bookstore cards as gifts all the time. To coworkers.

He frowned as he peered at my scalp. "Did you break skin?"

I shook my head. *A gift card was a practical gift. Flexible. It shows that he really wants me to have what I want.*

It also meant that he didn't even bother to guess

what I'd want. This from a man I'd watched spend an entire day racing around Macy's trying to find just the right thing for his office's mailroom clerk. Was this his way of sending me some kind of signal?

Had he simply been dating me for a month so he wouldn't be alone on Christmas?

He stood up. "Have you seen Maddie?"

"Not since we got back." Something in his tone . . . my stomach clinched. Isaac's last phone call came back to me. I glanced up at him almost hesitantly, afraid of what I would see. That distracted gleam in the eye I had witnessed so often in men who wanted to talk to me about Maddie. "Why?"

He wore a concerned frown. "I'm a little worried about her."

Don't act jealous. "Her room is the next one down the hall, after the bathroom."

He tilted his head. "You think she'd resent it if went to talk to her? I mean . . . I think I could help her."

I held my hand to the throbbing little knot on my head and nodded. "Sure, go talk to her," I said, dismissing him with a fatalistic wave. I had discovered years ago that keeping men away from Maddie was like trying to keep lions away from wildebeests.

He turned to go, then stopped at the door. "You might want to talk to Maddie yourself," he said, "and tell her about that cut. I bet she's a fantastic doctor."

I gulped. "Yup. She's fantastic at everything."

Thank God I hadn't gotten him a watch.

When I heard his footsteps retreat down the

hall, I reached over and closed my door, then leaned back on the bed with a long, teenagerly sigh. This was so mixed up. I stared at my Daniel Day-Lewis poster and suddenly remembered again why I had fallen in love with him in that movie, as he crashed through the woods in his buckskins to find his lady love. When I was fifteen, the possibility that anyone would ever love me enough to endure knife fights and dives through waterfalls and five-minute montages of running through the forest seemed like a faraway dream.

Now, thirteen years later, the dream was still just an ever-dwindling speck on the horizon.

I must have fallen asleep, because the next thing I knew there was a hand on my shoulder shaking me. "Hey! Wake up. It's dinnertime!" My eyes popped open to see Isaac looming over me. "How long have you been asleep?"

I jolted up to sitting, feigning alertness as best as I could. "I was just resting my eyes."

"Really? You were snoring *really loudly.*"

"Where is everybody?" I asked, slipping on my shoes.

Isaac sat down and dandled Mr. Fabulous on his knee. "Down in the dining room. We've been waiting on you."

"Oh—wait." Damn! It was Christmas Eve. Picture time. Except, of course, that Maddie had forgotten her camera. But someone in the family had to have a camera. "I need to put on makeup."

I frantically ran a brush through my hair and hid behind my closet door so that I could put on my special sweater that matched Jason's, which we had agreed to wear on Christmas Eve.

"How long have you been here?" I asked.

" 'Bout an hour."

I nearly shrieked. "And you didn't come get me?"

"Jason said you looked like you needed a rest. Besides, we were all watching a movie."

"What movie?"

"*Holiday Inn.*"

"I love that movie."

"It adds a whole new dimension to it to watch it with Ted. He wept."

"Well, it is awfully sentimental at the end. . . ."

"He was crying through the tap dances," Isaac said.

Poor Ted. He was even more of a mess than I was. I slapped on some lipstick and stepped out from behind the door, modeling my sweater. It was green cotton with a big Santa head on it, with googly eyes and a fluffy beard. When I stepped back into his sight line, Isaac's face fell and he actually recoiled a few inches.

"Oh, no!" he breathed.

"It matches Jason's. We're wearing them together. As a joke."

"You are?"

I nodded. "We planned it."

Isaac looked doubtful. "Holly, can I just say one thing?"

I blinked at him. "Did you ever find mistletoe?"

He rolled his eyes. "No."

I shook my head. "It probably doesn't matter." I was so confused about Jason. I didn't know what to do, honestly. I couldn't tell anymore if he was a perfect gent or a perv with a Christmas fetish.

"We should go," I said. "Mom is probably upset that I've been slacking off all afternoon." And after she gave me a tongue-lashing for being a nonparticipator, too. I looked at my face in the mirror. It still lacked something to be desired, but there was no time now.

I raced ahead of Isaac and was halfway down the stairs before I realized that something really seemed off. When I swung into the dining room, everyone looked up from various poses of reaching out for slices of pizza from the boxes that were strewn across the dining room table.

I froze. *Pizza?*

The others seemed frozen, too. They were staring at my chest.

"What's going on?" I asked.

"I decided we should go more casual this year," Mom said, in almost a singsong. "Come have a slice."

I was still having a hard time taking it all in. I don't think I had ever seen my parents order pizza. Ever. But there they all were, my assorted loved ones, balancing giant wedges in their hands, looking ridiculously pleased with themselves. Jason had a pepperoni slice that was about to spill a waterfall of cheese onto the tablecloth. Ted was leaning back glassy-eyed, chewing a crust. Vlad had a pile, one of each kind, on his plate. It was hard to tell if he intended to eat them one by one or cut into the pile as if it were a triangular layer cake.

Jason laughed. "Oh—I forgot about the sweaters!"

No kidding. He was wearing a plain navy blue sweater—no googly-eyed Santa in sight—over a red plaid shirt.

Isaac, behind me, put his hand on my elbow and steered me to a chair. I have to say, I needed the help. I felt like an idiot.

The dining room was set up buffet style, and Mom passed us plates. At least we were using the gold-rimmed Havilland china we always brought out for nice holiday meals. I flopped a piece of pepperoni on it and bit back a sigh. "Pizza on Havilland. I guess I should be glad tradition hasn't been completely thrown out the window in this family."

"Here," Isaac said, reaching for a bottle of red wine, "let's have some traditional holiday booze."

As I was pouring a few glugs into my wineglass, Ted shot up from the table so quickly he nearly tore the tablecloth off with him. He ran down the hall, then slammed his door shut, leaving us all staring bug-eyed at each other. A few moments later, his voice carried through the shut door and down the hall.

"Damn it, Melinda!" he hollered. "Are you just going to let tradition be thrown out the window?"

I drew back guiltily, since I seemed to have set him off.

"What do you mean, *calm down?*" he yelled, as we all pretended not to listen. "*You're* the one who ran off half-cocked!"

The man definitely needed a phone coach.

"Don't you hang up on me. Don't you—"

There was a short silence.

"*Damn it!*"

I guess Melinda hung up.

The atmosphere in the dining room was tense as we all waited for Ted to come out again. He didn't. He just started muttering to himself and throwing small objects around his room.

"Well!" Mom said after a few moments. She took a long sip of wine. "I was going to wait for Ted to make my little speech, but I think maybe I should just go ahead, don't you, Laird?"

Dad sighed. "If you must."

I looked over at Jason and smiled. *This* was always priceless. Every year my mom made a little speech at dinner at how happy she was to have all her family around her. It was the one time of year my family came close to vocalizing love for each other.

"I just wanted to let you all know that having you here means more than ever before."

Maddie tapped on her wineglass with her fork, like an attendee at a Lion's Club meeting. "Here, here!"

I frowned. Why would it mean more than ever? "Is everything okay?" I asked Mom.

"Everything's just terrific," Mom said, in a tone of voice that made my hair stand on end. It was a tone that had an implied *but* built into it.

My heart began to pound double-time. For some reason, through all of this I had been looking at her failing to get the house ready as just forgetfulness, or laziness. As if she could have forgotten Christmas! Now all sorts of terrible scenarios started parading through my head, supplying possible answers for that implied *but. But she has cancer. But she's checking herself into alcohol rehab. But she's been diagnosed with bipolar disorder . . .*

I cut a worried glance at Isaac. He looked startled, too.

"The thing is," Mom went on, "next year I probably won't be here."

Maddie gasped.

"Oh, God," I moaned aloud. It *was* cancer. And here I had been running around for two days whining about the fake Christmas tree, and the lack of food in the fridge. And *walnut people,* for heaven's sake.

No wonder she had given me a tongue-lashing for taking her for granted, and for selfishly worrying about trivialities! Anguish shuddered through me. "Mom, why didn't you tell us?"

Mom frowned at me. "Well . . . for one thing, I thought it was personal and we shouldn't drag you into it."

Personal, I could understand. But not drag us into it? "But—"

"Also, I just signed the lease two weeks ago."

"But—" My mouth snapped closed. *Lease?*

"I'm moving into my own apartment after the new year," she announced.

I had to hand it to Mom—she had managed to come up with a pin-drop moment this family hadn't seen since my brother had announced he'd wrecked my dad's car back in 1989.

Maddie's face, I'm pretty sure, mirrored my own at that moment. She was wide-eyed, blinking repeatedly, and openmouthed. Flabbergasted pretty much sums it up.

"An apartment!" she exclaimed. "What are you going to do with one of those?"

My mouth twisted. "I imagine she's going to live it in it."

"But why? She lives here!"

"Um, Maddie . . ."

Her eyes flashed at me. "Don't sit there pretending you're not upset, Holly. I *know* you're upset, so don't act like you can detach yourself from this one."

"What do you mean, detach?" I shot back.

"Like it's just beneath worrying about. That's what you always do during a family crisis, isn't it?"

My head was spinning. "Why are you turning this into a referendum on *me?*"

"Oh, never mind," Maddie said, flopping against the back of her chair. "You so don't get it. You never do."

I swung my gaze back to my mom. "What are you moving out for? Are you and Dad . . . splitting up?"

I glanced over at him, but he was still leaning back impassively, staring at his pizza as if he would simply rather not be having this conversation. Mom chuckled nervously. "Well, I suppose you could say that it's *something* like that. It's completely amicable, isn't it, Laird?"

"Don't drag me into this," he said, picking at his pizza crust.

"*Dad,* she's leaving. How much more dragged into something can you be?"

He lifted his hands. "Her decision. Me, I'm staying here. All my books are here. My files. Everything."

Naturally, when my parents split up, they couldn't even do it the normal way, with a lot of screaming and broken crockery. Or maybe that was just the part we had missed. Maybe we were all actors who had bumbled onto the set of the wrong play during the third act.

And now only Maddie seemed to be behaving as was expected of her in the movie-of-the-week sense. Tears stood in her eyes, her cheeks were mottled red, and she was trembling. "How come you didn't tell me any of this?" she railed at Mom. "I always know everything!"

"Are you two *divorcing?*" I asked, speaking the dread word. "I mean, have you seen a lawyer?"

"It's like professors taking a sabbatical," my dad explained to us. "Your mom needs a sabbatical."

I couldn't tell if he was in denial, or if he really believed this. Or course, maybe it was true.

But how many couples took "sabbaticals" and then wound up together again?

Maddie snatched her napkin out of her lap and blew her nose loudly.

Mom shook her head. "Right now I just want some privacy. I'm going back to school in January . . ."

"But you said this was your last Christmas here," I pointed out.

A high-pitched squeak came from across the table—my sister, dramatically holding back a wail of despair. I tried not to look over at her. *She just wants attention,* I thought peevishly.

But of course I couldn't help myself. I had to look. And when I looked, I was appalled. There was Maddie, the twenty-six-year-old victim of a newly broken home, mewling pitifully. And there was my boyfriend's hand rubbing her shoulder. Comforting her.

Vlad, who I had forgotten about, cleared his throat and mumbled something in Russian.

"Pass him a slice of Italian sausage, Holly," Maddie translated, with a pathetic sniffle. "You're the closest."

I did as told.

"Thank you very much," Vlad said.

For the next few moments the only sound in the room was that of Vlad chewing his slice. (He had a slight jaw pop, I noticed.) Except, of course, I could imagine the sound of Jason's hand, which still hadn't moved from Maddie's shoulder. If the pressing of flesh against two layers of cashmere twinset could make a sound, it was ringing in my ears right now.

Maddie jumped up. "Excuse me!" Her voice was a tremolo of pain. "I need to be by myself for a moment."

She cupped her hands around her face, almost as if she had a nosebleed, and swept out of the room.

When Jason all but leapt out of his chair to go chasing after her, I picked a greasy piece of pepperoni off the congealing cheese on my plate and popped it into my mouth. It tasted like salty leather.

"Well!" With her big revelation out of the way, Mom was her old Florence Henderson self again. "Maybe I should go see what we've got for dessert. I forgot to fix anything."

"I brought a cake," I said dully.

"Oh, terrific!" she said, getting up. "That'll hit the spot."

I hated to tell her that no one seemed much interested. No one except my dad, who suddenly perked up. "Do we have any of that peppermint ice cream to go with it?" he yelled after her retreated back. He looked over at me. "There's this really good peppermint stick ice cream—the old-fashioned kind that's vanilla with little chunks of red and green peppermint candy in it—but you can only get it during the holidays."

"I thought you couldn't eat too much fat." He already chowed down two slices.

He shrugged. "A little bowl of ice cream, what harm can that do? They only have it during the holidays."

When Mom left him, his cholesterol was going to shoot through the ceiling.

"There was a day when peppermint stick ice cream was de rigueur," Dad said, leaning forward, his brow furrowed as if he were going to lecture us on the Peloponnesian War. "When I was a boy, it was one of those ubiquitous flavors, like vanilla, and strawberry. But now everything has *chocolate,*" he said, his nose wrinkling in distaste, as if chocolate were some kind of newfangled thing that had come along with hip hop and the Internet.

Isaac and I nodded numbly. Even Vlad was nodding—confirming my hunch that wheezy geezer-speak knew no borders.

Dad tossed his head back. "Is there any of that peppermint stick ice cream?" he bellowed at my mother.

His reply was the sound of a clattering pan.

"I'd better go myself," Dad grumbled. "She can never find anything."

Isaac and I swiveled toward each other. For a moment, neither of us said a word, but it was comforting just to look into the dark, understanding pools of his eyes. I was so glad he was here.

He poured some wine into my glass. I drank it down in one gulp.

"How are things at *your* house?" I asked.

"Fine. My little brother's going on a ski trip with his girlfriend's family tomorrow. I promised to fill in for him at work at the Valu-Rite drugstore."

That sounded weird, but I really didn't give it much thought. My mind was still trying to wrap around my parents' dilemma, and the fact that my boyfriend was now providing TLC for my sister. While *her* boyfriend, or whatever he was, was sitting here without a clue.

"I'm surprised *you* didn't try beating Jason to the punch in comforting Maddie," I told Isaac.

He cleared his throat. "Jason was quick on the draw."

"He was Annie Oakley." I picked at the tablecloth. After witnessing my parents' implosion, I supposed I shouldn't whine about my faltering relationship. And I was also better off than Ted . . . which, at that moment, seemed like setting the bar awfully low.

I shook my head. "This is just so out of the blue. My parents have argued occasionally, but it never meant anything."

"Maybe it just never meant anything to you."

I folded my arms over my chest. "But I can't believe that they can just split up this way. There has to be a catalyst. And what is this apartment she's talking about?"

Isaac looked at me. "Maybe you should ask your mom, not me."

"You're right." I got up. Then I looked back at him. "Have some more pizza. I'll be right back."

In the kitchen, Mom had stacked dessert plates and was cutting pound cake.

"Where's Dad?" I asked.

She waved a hand. "Oh, he trudged off in the direction of his office, grumbling about peppermint ice cream."

I guessed we were out.

"You want some cake?" She bit her lip. "Maybe I should just let people cut their own . . . except this cake is like a rock! I don't know what bakery you used, but I wouldn't go back there again."

I tried to take comfort in the fact that my cake at least looked like a professional failure. "I don't know if you realize this, but the party has, er, dispersed."

Her eyes widened. "Really? Did Isaac go home already?"

"No, but . . . well, Mom, you sort of dropped a bombshell in there."

She looked as if she couldn't quite comprehend. "I just thought you all should know. Would you rather I hadn't told you?"

"But, Mom, you *told* us, but not in a way that we could understand. What's going on? Did you and Dad fight? Is he cheating on you?"

She laughed. "Holly, really."

"Well? Would that be so odd?"

"Yes. Your father's been teaching at a college for thirty-two years, at a place just filled with randy academics, and I've never known him to succumb to temptation. Not once. And don't think there hasn't been any. But that's just not the way he is."

"Well, then, are *you* having an affair?"

"No!"

"But you've just rented an apartment."

"Why shouldn't I?"

"Well why *should* you? Why not just stay here? Don't you care about Dad anymore? How can you just leave like this and risk ending up your life all alone?"

She tilted a frustrated glance at me. "I hope I'm not at the end yet—I might still have a few non-senile years left, you know."

"Well, of course, but—"

"And I would think that you would be the last person to lecture me about being alone. You've always lived alone, for yourself."

But not by choice! I wanted to screech at her. "Where is this apartment?"

She seemed more comfortable with concrete

facts. "It's a little fourplex not far from here, near Shirlington, on Twenty-fifth Street South. A one bedroom on the first floor. It's adorable—though a little on the small side. *You'd* feel right at home there."

Why, if she was moving, wouldn't she be going somewhere farther away? "Do you know someone else in the building?"

She tilted a glance at me. "No. It's just a place I had . . . well, seen . . . a few times. And then a one bedroom came open."

Uh-huh. I was beginning to catch on. *Love nest.* Though I shuddered to think of the term in context of my mom, I couldn't make sense of the situation any other way. Poor Dad! His life was going to be shot to pieces . . . and why? I wondered whom my mom was seeing. Or what kind of place this was she was moving into. I imagined some swingin' singles scene from the seventies. In the real seventies, of course, my parents had been the most stuffed-shirted baby boomers in existence.

Could it be that this was Mom's way of compensating for all she had missed out on?

"I think I'll go hunt down some peppermint ice cream for Dad," I announced.

"Right now?" Mom asked, startled.

"I won't be long."

"Won't you have some cake first?"

"Thanks." I grabbed two hunks and spun back toward the dining room. "C'mon," I told Isaac, as I sped by him. He was still at the dining room table, watching Vlad eat what had to be his tenth slice. I gave the cake to Vlad, who thanked me very much.

Isaac hopped up. "Where are we going?"

"We've got a mission."

We passed through the living room, where Maddie had gotten out her old student cello and was accompanying Jason on piano to "O Holy Night." I guess music therapy was preferable to touch therapy.

Outside, the snow was coming down hard. I waited for Isaac to make the expected snide comment, but instead he observed, "Jason plays piano really well."

"I didn't even know he played at all," I said. For some reason, that fact was too depressing for words. What I didn't know about Jason could apparently fill a book. "We're taking your car, if you don't mind."

He stopped next to his parents' old Pontiac. "Where are we going?"

"Twenty-fifth Street South, near Shirlington. I just want to have a look at this place."

"*What* place?"

"Mom's apartment."

"Why?"

"Because . . ." I wasn't sure I could explain. "It's just something I have to do, okay?"

His lips twisted as he measured humoring me against the risks of driving his parents' car several miles through ice and snow. "Okay."

I slid in next to him. We didn't say much on the way there. We were both adjusting to the snow smacking against the windshield in front of us. On Twenty-fifth he turned and we began to crawl slowly down the street, looking at street numbers.

I finally spied Mom's place. "Stop!"

He braked, and we skidded halfway into someone's drive.

"This is it," I said.

The fourplex was just a plain, flat-front red brick building, the kind that the DC burbs were chockablock with. Which made me even more suspicious. Mom said she had noticed this place for a long time. But what was noticeable about it? I had imagined something in a Mediterranean style with fake stucco, or an ornate colonial with a big magnolia out front. But this! It was nondescript. Dull.

I opened my car door.

"Where are you going?" Isaac asked.

"I just want to peek inside."

He put his hand on my arm. "Don't."

"Don't what?"

"Spy on your mom. It's not right."

"I just want to check it out. Peer through a window, see if she's bought any furniture, or if there's a hot-hot-hottie installed in there. It won't take a sec, and then we can go."

There was something decidedly Ethel Mertz–like in his capitulation. "Okay. But I still think it's a bad idea."

I hopped out, and although the windows in the front were dark, I ran in stealth serpentine fashion across the tiny yard. In unit A—the first floor apartment with the real estate agent's sign in front of it—the front window was dark, but there was a small office set up in there. I was wondering why there was an agent's sign out when I noticed something else. I frowned. "That's weird."

Isaac flapped his arms for warmth and looked around anxiously lest any of the neighbors would mistake us for prowlers. "What's weird?"

"Mom's using a Mac."

"So?"

I shrugged. "I just didn't know. . . ." I squinted, trying to make out what else was in the room, but it looked like a fairly garden variety office to me. One thing was clear, though. "She didn't just sign the lease two weeks ago—or else she's faster at setting up than most people."

"Okay, let's go."

"Wait. I just want to look inside one more room." I imagined I would find some middle-aged stud sitting around amid all the holiday decorations that weren't in evidence at our house. But the rest of the house was frustrating. The yard sloped down on the side, so it was impossible to see in the windows. And the backyard had a privacy fence with a locked gate. "Give me a hand up," I said.

"*What?*"

"Just let me stand on your back and peek through this window."

"In those boots? No way."

"C'mon, your parka has two inches of padding. You won't feel a thing." He looked doubtful. "Then we'll leave. I swear."

"Okay, but if a cop drives by, *you* explain."

I nodded. He bent over and I climbed up until I was able to peek through the small window, which, wouldn't you know, turned out to be a bathroom. Neat as a pin, but dark. The only thing I could make out that seemed at all personalized was a towel hanging on a rack. But it was initialed, and what's more, the initials looked like *L* something. *L* for Laird? Surely Mom hadn't stocked her love nest bathroom with Dad's towels!

In frustration, I pushed against the glass. As if by magic, the sash sailed up halfway. It was unlocked! This felt like my first piece of luck in days.

"Um, Isaac, could you lift up a little?"

He sighed but did as I asked. Using his momentum, I pushed myself through the window . . . or at least halfway through it. I put my hands down on the floor and tried to shimmy my butt through the window. Unfortunately, from the outside, Isaac had discovered my intention and was yanking on my foot. "Would you stop that!" I whispered.

"Are you crazy?" he yelled back.

My knee felt like it might snap. And then the door in front of me opened, revealing a large man in a bathrobe. Of course, I was viewing him from a cockroach's vantage, but this guy seemed huge. Over six feet tall. His head was egg bald, making him look like a cross between Mr. Clean and Jesse Ventura. He flicked on the lights, leaving me blinking up at him. He was holding a baseball bat.

"Hold it right there!" he growled. Then, to someone in the apartment, he yelled, "Tell them it's a woman. And there's someone outside with her!"

Uh-oh. Something told me this *wasn't* my mom's love nest.

I tried to smile. I couldn't. I was too afraid I was about to be crushed like an insect. "It's okay," I said, my voice quavering. "I'm not a burglar."

He took a menacing step toward me. "Save it!"

Behind him, a little girl in a pink bathrobe appeared. She was holding a giant floppy-eared stuffed bunny in front of her as if to ward off an intruder—me—yet she scrutinized me with intense interest.

"I thought Santa was a man," she said, her voice heavy with disappointment.

"Go to your room, Rebecca!" the man barked sharply, as if I were going to pull out a gun and blow away his entire family.

"I thought Santa came down the chimney."

"*Rebecca—go!*"

Rebecca burst into tears and ran away.

"And stay in your room till the police come!" the man barked after her.

The police. My heart sank.

Isaac must have heard, too, because he abruptly let go of my foot and I fell the rest of the way through the window. We were so screwed.

Chapter Seven

The Lewises were almost nice about it, once we got it all straightened out.

I stretched some facts to make myself seem less of a breaking-and-entering wacko to them. I nervously spluttered out that my mom had just rented this place (actually, she had rented the unit on the other side . . . and that I had just driven in from New York and didn't have a key. I definitely became less threatening looking when I unbuttoned my coat, revealing the Santa sweater.

After she was assured that Isaac and I were not some creepy Christmas Eve criminal duo, Mrs. Lewis even offered us eggnog, which I was tempted to accept but refused on principle. After all, I had just spent twenty minutes professing that I was not there to take anything.

After coming all this way in a snowstorm, the police seemed a little disappointed not to be dragging Isaac and me off to the hoosegow. But in the end they seemed resigned to the fact that we had resolved the situation ourselves and that the Lewises, in the spirit of Christmas and good new-neighbor relations, were not pressing charges. The cops took down our phone numbers and addresses and sallied forth into the night to find real criminals. Or at least more competent ones.

After we had officially been released, Isaac and I wobbled over the icy walkway to the Pontiac. He was opening the passenger door for me when I skated the last two feet and smashed right into him. He grabbed me, then stumbled himself. I leaned into him and laughed, and when he started laughing, too, down we went. We collapsed into the snow in a heap, whooping like idiots.

God, what a mess. What a night. I bit my lip, trying to compose myself. I was afraid to meet Isaac's eye, afraid that if I did we would break up again and be stuck rolling around in the snow forever, laughing. But I couldn't help myself.

The strange thing was, he wasn't laughing, as I'd expected. He was just looking at me. Hard, as if his dark eyes were searching my face for evidence of something. Thoughts of laughter died, and I felt something weird. A squeezing in my chest. That leap of attraction. An adrenaline rush.

"My partner in crime," he said, musing over the words as he pushed a snow-damp lock of hair off of my cheek with his gloved hand. And then he did the strangest thing. He kissed me.

It wasn't a peck. It wasn't one of those maddeningly brief things Jason had been tormenting me with over the past month. This was a full-bore, open-mouthed kiss. I was so stunned by it—by the timing and how great a kisser Isaac was—that I sort of sank against him, hanging on to the Velcroed neck flaps of his coat. I couldn't tell what was going on, and for a moment I didn't really care. I was kissing Isaac, which was one of those things I'd tried imagining from time to time for years now. But I'd never imagined that we would progress so instantly to tongue action. Or that my insides would turn soupy. Or that I would want to rip his parka off so I could feel his warmth against me.

I did start pawing at the zipper of his coat with that sort of frantic mindless desire. And Isaac, though one hand was at my nape, made a stab at the top button of my coat. But my scarf got in his way, and my mittens made operating any mechanical apparatus a near impossibility.

And what were we doing? That thought seemed to strike us both, belatedly, at the same moment. We pulled apart, gasping for breath, then flopped back against the passenger door of the car, trying to calm down.

This was so wrong, I thought. I had always been a monogamous soul. Girls who could go out with several different guys at once, or even just pursued several different guys at once, struck me as undiscriminating. It was sort of the relationship equivalent of throwing darts at a map to decide your next travel destination. When it came to romance, I wanted to think I had a plan.

This weekend my plan had been Jason. Now everything was uncertain, upended.

I had no idea what was going on in Isaac's head.

"Do you think the Lewises were watching us?" he asked.

The front room's light was now on. I shuddered. "They must think we're demented."

"Maybe we should try to get out of their yard," Isaac suggested.

I rubbed my hand on my head, inadvertently touching the bump from earlier that evening. The bump induced by Jason's gift. This was so mixed up. What was I going to do?

"I can't go home just yet," I said.

"Then we won't."

Isaac struggled to his feet and then gave me a hand up. We successfully managed to get into the car this time, and by the time he started up the motor, I was beginning to wonder if the kiss hadn't just been some expression of relief at not having been dragged off to jail. Unfortunately, for all our history of yapping each other's ears off even about the most personal matters, we didn't have the vocabulary for communicating our feelings about each other. We were as awkward and tongue-tied as two fourteen-year-olds.

I just hoped that we hadn't made a fatal error, that this wasn't the beginning of the end.

We slid past all our favorite home haunts until we found a greasy burger joint open called Five Guys. We ordered burgers and their incredible boardwalk-style fries and sat down at a corner table.

We were both still a little punchy. And unsure. It felt like at any moment we might dissolve into giggles, and I almost wished we would. That, at least, would seem normal.

"I can't believe it's not even Christmas yet," I said after we had our food. "It feels like we've been home forever."

"Maybe things will pick up tomorrow."

Isaac's gaze caught mine. His lips twitched. I burst out laughing.

It *did* feel good to laugh with him again. Maybe we should just come out and admit that the kiss had been a mistake. Or ill timed.

Or maybe we should just let it drop.

When I was calm again, I shook my head. "I just didn't expect all these family crises. Why didn't anyone warn me? The first year I bring a guy home . . ."

He blinked at me. "*I've* been going home with you every year for three years."

I felt my neck go red as I sucked on my Coke. "Right, but you don't exactly count."

He had been angling for a French fry, but his arm stopped midreach.

"Isaac," I said, realizing I had just blurted out the wrong words. "You know what I mean."

"I think I do, unfortunately. Thanks. Thanks a lot."

I suddenly felt like crying. Maybe I was going bipolar now, too. "What's the matter with you tonight? What's happening?"

"How would you like it if I announced that you didn't matter to me?"

I barely had to think. I winced. "Okay, I wouldn't

like it. I'm sorry. That came out all wrong. I only meant . . ."

"I know. I'm not your Wall Street loverboy."

"Please don't flake out on me now, Isaac," I said. "I'm already reeling from everything happening at home. And Jason."

"Jason," he repeated.

Those eyes were doing it to me again. I swear they could tie me in all kinds of elaborate knots, but now, after the kiss, there was a new one. Damn. I took a breath. "He's still there, Isaac. I brought him home with me—as my boyfriend."

His face turned a hue of red I had never seen before. "I see. I thought tonight, after seeing him with . . ."

"He's just *nice,*" I said. "And Maddie was upset. And Vlad isn't really much of a help. . . ."

He stopped me. "Holly, listen. I'm going to tell you something that I probably shouldn't."

"What?"

"I'm going to be brutally honest."

Uh-oh.

"Nobody seeing you and Jason together would know you were a couple. And Jason's behavior isn't the only reason why. It's not all his fault."

"What's that supposed to mean?"

"It means that you don't *show* it. My God—you've been running around like a nut since this holiday began, sidetracked by Ted and mistletoe and housebreaking."

"What else could I do? Things kept happening. . . ."

He shot me a scolding look. "If you really want

Jason, why are you sitting here eating French fries with me?"

I thought about this for a few moments. I felt like weeping. Was the trouble all with *me?* Was I not self-assured enough, or demonstrative enough? *What?*

Or was Jason just not right for me?

Isaac took my hand and practically squeezed the life out of it. *"Don't let him get away."*

"*What?*" I asked, astounded.

He looked as mixed up as I felt. "Look, right now I wish to God I weren't your friend, but I am, so as a friend I feel bound to tell you that if it's Jason DeWittless you want, then don't let him get away."

Had he gone completely insane? He didn't even like Jason!

I slid down in my seat, confused. Part of me wanted him to say, *Don't let* me *get away.* But that wasn't what he was saying. This was why he was so exasperating! He'd kissed me, but he wasn't declaring undying love. Instead he was telling me to go declare undying love for someone else.

I was so confused, I needed to be alone, even if it was just for a few minutes. "I've got to hit the ladies' before we go," I said, fleeing.

In the dinky bathroom I sank against the wall, trying to gather my wits. How did everything get so confusing all of a sudden? Why couldn't I think straight? I felt like I was just blundering everywhere, saying the wrong things to people I loved, making errors of judgment right and left.

When I finally came back out, Isaac was folding

up something. "Here," he said, giving it to me. "It's my Christmas present to you."

It was a neatly folded restaurant napkin. "You shouldn't have. Really."

"It's a magic Christmas napkin," he told me. "You have to open it first thing tomorrow morning."

"Won't you be over tomorrow?" I asked.

"I'd like to, but I'm busy."

"On Christmas?"

"I told you; I'm filling in for my little brother. He got invited to go on a ski trip with the girl of his dreams, so he needed someone to fill in at his stupid temp job at the Valu-Rite drugstore. I'll be in costume, so no one will be able to tell it's not him."

I frowned. "What is it you'll be doing?"

"I'm going to be the one-hour-photo Santaland Santa."

I had to take a moment to absorb this. "On Christmas?"

"I guess if you've got one-hour photos, it's never too late."

"Then I take it back," I said.

"What?"

"You don't have to bother coming by the house—I'll come to you."

The sight of Isaac in a Santa suit was something I wouldn't have missed for the world.

It was eleven by the time Isaac dropped me back home. "Don't forget your magic napkin," he said to me as I climbed out of the car.

"I won't."

"First thing in the morning," he reminded me.

I nodded.

All the cars, snow-covered mounds in the driveway, were present and accounted for, so it appeared no one had ventured out to midnight mass. *Another sign that tradition had just gone out the window this year,* I thought dispiritedly.

Of course, I myself had been too busy dealing with cops, kissing Isaac, and eating greasy burgers to go to mass myself.

In the house, all the lights were off, except for a dim glow of the oven light coming from the direction of the kitchen. The living room was empty and dark. Ted was not watching QVC (I guess his holiday shopping was finally finished), and there was no sign of Vlad, who I had expected would be bedding down on the Hide-a-Bed tonight.

On my way upstairs, my dad popped out of his study. "Holly."

Dad pushed his bifocals down and looked at me seriously. He was holding his Cromwell biography, which he had obviously been holed up reading most of the night.

"Yes?" I asked, expecting him to give me some explanation, or at least solace, for why his son was having a nervous breakdown, his daughters were flaking out, and our family was breaking up. "Was there something you wanted to tell me?"

"Did you find the peppermint stick?"

I squinted at him. "The what?"

"The peppermint stick ice cream," he said.

"Your mother mentioned you were going out to find some. Did you?"

I had forgotten all about it. It seemed years ago since I'd told Mom that fib. "No, I didn't. Sorry, Dad."

He looked crushed, like a little kid almost. Impulsively, I went over and gave him a buss on the cheek. "Merry Christmas, Dad."

He smiled. "Is it Christmas already?"

"Almost."

"Well! This calls for celebration." I grinned expectantly. "I think I'll have another glass of eggnog while I finish my chapter," he said, scuttling off to the kitchen.

I went straight up to my room, pausing briefly in front of the spare bedroom in which I assumed Jason was snoozing. There was no light underneath the door. I was tempted to rap lightly . . . or, better yet, barge right in and throw myself into his bed.

Don't let him get away, the man had said.

Maybe it was high time that I should slink into my stash of specially purchased lingerie. Isaac was right—I needed to make a move, lay it all on the line. Setting my jaw, I marched to my room and began yanking fine washables out of my suitcase. Then I stepped out of my clothes and slipped into something more comfortable. Except the silky little sheath of a nightie wasn't exactly what I would call comfy—at least not in this energy conservation–minded house where the thermostat was always bumped down at night to the Jimmy Carter–recommended fifty-eight degrees. The house felt like the North Pole. A laggard seductress I might be, but even I knew that gooseflesh and chattering teeth were not sexy.

I squeezed past my father's exercise bike to get to the closet. On a hook hung the only robe available to me, a leftover from college. I'm surprised it hadn't landed in the Goodwill box; it was worn thin and had a coffee stain trailing down one side. I loved it. It was blue chenille with appliqués of Oreo cookies and glasses of milk all over it. *Not sexy.* What was cute for staying up late in the dorm to watch Love Connection reruns didn't particularly vamp well.

I was trying to decide between goosebumps and chunky chenille robe when laughter from outside distracted me. It was undoubtedly my sister's high, bright laughter, and I drifted over to the window seat to see what she was up to out there. To spy.

Maddie must have been feeling better. Either that or she had truly gone manic. Peering into the backyard, I saw that she was building a snowman. The first two huge balls of snow had been stacked together to form its torso. I was tempted to run out and join the fun, until I caught a glimpse of someone else out there with her.

So that's where Vlad was, I thought, grinning.

A streak of white crossed my line of vision, followed by a Maddie squeal. Then laughter. A playful snowball fight, which would probably lead to some backyard cavorting in the snow. I leaned back, wrapping the warm flannel around me more tightly.

Maddie had picked up Vlad spur of the moment

and was now frolicking in the snow with him, while I was still trying to seduce Jason after a long month's campaign.

Jason wasn't a frolic-in-the-snow type. He would never want to do something with abandon like that. He wasn't . . .

My type. That's what my mother had said.

I glanced over at myself in the mirror, in my frumpy dorm robe that I loved so much. *Who was I kidding?* I picked at the Oreo appliqué on my sleeve and was suddenly overwhelmed. I could have been a poster child for the "he's just not that into you" movement.

And the weird thing was, I suddenly didn't care.

I crawled into bed, hearing the occasional shriek of Maddie's laughter drifting up to my window. My eyes fluttered closed, and I thought about the last time I'd had a snowball fight. It had been with Isaac the winter before, during the season's first big snow. We had started a little snowball war right in the middle of Bergen Street, which had been blanketed in perfect white untouched snow . . . before we got to it.

Smiling, I fell asleep.

Christmas morning I jumped out of bed feeling oddly happy, and optimistic. Nothing had changed, of course, but it was hard to be in a negative frame of mind on Christmas morning, which I still associated with cinnamony smells and long-dreamed-of presents under the tree. And, in fact, I did smell something cinnamon-like in the air. A good omen.

I showered, dressed quickly in my jeans from last night and another more dignified sweater, and galloped down the stairs. Voices drifted to me from the kitchen, which cheered me, though I wondered that no one had bothered to plug in the Christmas tree. Maybe they didn't want to disturb Vlad . . . although a quick look at the couch revealed Vlad had not slept there. Wasn't hard to guess where he *had* slept.

That Maddie!

I skipped toward the kitchen. Maddie was at the stove, expertly twirling a spatula through her fingers. At the table sat Mom, flanked on one side by Jason. He smiled at me a little sheepishly, and no wonder. He was wearing his Santa sweater—twelve hours too late—and it looked goofier on him than I imagined it would.

Strangely, I felt like avoiding his eyes. I wasn't sure that I had reached any solid conclusions—maybe it would be better if we waited till we got back to New York to decide anything—but I did feel like something had shifted.

"Merry Christmas!" Mom said, setting off a chime among us all, finishing with exclamations about how neat it was to have a white Christmas. "I thought we would wait till Ted came out to open presents," Mom continued.

I tilted my head. "Has anyone heard him stirring yet?"

Mom sighed. "No, and I don't want to wake him, poor thing. This is bound to be a tough day for him. I was thinking maybe we should try to get his cell phone away from him."

Poor Ted.

I went over to Maddie. "What are you making?"

"Spicy pancakes," she said.

"Edible ones," my mother said, with a wink.

Remembering my failure of yesterday, I couldn't help recoiling a little. Her choice of breakfast foods felt like a repudiation. But it was Christmas, and so I ignored the chuckles in the kitchen as I poured myself a cup of coffee and scooted into the seat across from Jason. "Everybody sleep okay?"

Mom said she slept just fine, and Maddie just blinked at me as if she hadn't understood the question.

"I thought I heard a ruckus in the backyard last night," I said.

"Oh! That was me." Maddie's face turned pink.

You and who else, Miss Goody Two-Shoes, I wanted to ask. I loved it when Maddie tried to act all innocent this way. I began calculating how I could get her to reveal Vlad's whereabouts in front of Mom.

"Look at the snowman she built!" Mom said proudly, in the same voice she used to point out construction paper creations on her refrigerator when we were kids. "It's a work of art."

Naturally. Maddie would not allow herself to build just any old ordinary snowman.

I pushed my chair back and peered out the patio doors. The first shock I received was that the snowman *was* ordinary. Perfect, but perfectly traditional. Three big orbs of snow, increasing in size from the head down. Its middle had stones for buttons. An old pipe of Dad's stuck out where its mouth would be, and a fat stubby carrot stood in place of its nose. Its eyes were buttons and an old Donegal cap from the front hall closet crowned its head. About the most outstanding feature of the snowman—what really made my eyes pop—was the scarf around its neck. It was a long, flowing red-and-blue-striped wool scarf.

The scarf I had given Jason.

The one he hadn't remembered he'd wanted.

On *Maddie's* snowman. Seeing it there felt like a knife twisting in my gut. Especially since seeing it there, and remembering last night, I now realized that it wasn't Vlad she had been canoodling with.

Something hitched in my throat, and I stumbled to my feet as if to refill the coffee cup I hadn't yet taken a sip of.

Jason and Maddie. While I had been attempting—and failing—to dress for seduction, Maddie had been frolicking in the snow with him. Thank God I hadn't taken my silk-and-chenille-clad bod down the hall and insinuated myself into his empty bed.

No wonder he'd looked sheepish!

Of course, a few hours earlier I had been rolling around in the snow with Isaac, so I didn't have room to throw stones. *But still.* Right under my bedroom window! I tried to clear my throat nonchalantly. "What happened to Vlad?"

Maddie flipped a perfectly golden hotcake. "He just disappeared last night." Her nose scrunched adorably in thought. "You know, I'm inclined to think you were right about him, Holly. He *was* a little odd. My New Year's resolution is to be more discerning romantically."

Sure, let me vet them for you, sis. I downed a gulp of coffee, feeling the Christmasy urge to strangle one of my nearest and dearest. Never before had I brought a guy home, and the one time I did—the first and only time in twenty-eight years—she *stole* him. It was incredible. Stole him right out from under my nose!

I looked at Jason. Heartbreakingly handsome Jason. I looked at Maddie. Perky, perfect Maddie.

God, this was so screwed up. Yes, she had stolen him. But I had tossed her a high lob—the man of her dreams more than mine, made to order for her. People looking at them would think they were the perfect couple. They were. When she had first seen him she had asked if he was my Christmas present to the family. To *her,* she'd apparently meant. And I guess that's what he was.

I remembered something and reached into my jeans for my magic Christmas napkin. Shaking a little, I unfolded it and found Isaac's cramped science-and-math geek scrawl all over it in ballpoint pen.

Dear Holly,

Here's my Christmas wish for you, selfish soul that I am. I wish you heartbreak. I admit it. I hope you're a mess this morning, utterly wretched. In a moment of dumb gallantry I sent you off to get your dream man, but I hope you failed. God, I hope so. Because here's the deal. I'm not gallant at all. I'm terrible. I love you. There. I said (wrote) it. I was

going to tell you when I broke up with Helen, but then Jason came along. Last night I thought if I kissed you it would all be clear, but instead you started jawing on about Jason and it just got more confused and now I might have lost you forever. But I do love you, and if it's not too late . . . what're you doin' New Year's Eve?
Yours, Mr. Millstein.

I read it once. Then again.

I folded it up, half listening to everyone trying to guess how much snow we'd had. Three inches. No, maybe five. I opened my magic napkin and read it again.

"Holly?" My mom's forehead was wrinkled with worry. "What's the matter?"

I shook my head, not trusting myself to speak for a moment. You know that song, "Have Yourself a Merry Little Christmas"? There's a line that tells the listener to let your heart be light. Well, at that moment, my heart was floating. I looked at Jason and Maddie and I was suddenly happy. Thrilled.

I felt like Jimmy Stewart after he'd discovered angels exist. Or little Natalie Wood when she'd been driven by her dream house. Or the Grinch after he'd heard the Whos singing on Christmas morning. I felt like whooping. Maybe it was inadvertent, but I had done a good deed. I wanted to do more.

I thought about my parents. They were beyond my matchmaking abilities right now, I was afraid. But they had shepherded me through plenty of crises in my life. Maybe that's all I could give them now in return—a little understanding. And a lot of phone time in the months ahead.

I went to the fridge and got out the $150 champagne I was saving for Jason's and my big romantic event that wasn't. "This is for you," I told Mom. "A housewarming gift for your new apartment. Maybe you could take us over there this afternoon?"

Mom seemed almost teary as she looked at the bottle. "Of course—that would be nice."

Well, it would be if we managed to avoid your new neighbors. I decided Mom could wait to hear about last night's hijinks at her place.

I turned. There was one more thing I could do here. I marched to my brother's room and pounded on the door. It took him a few moments, but he stumbled to the door, bleary-eyed. He was looking really scruffy—serial killer lite, would probably best describe it. I took his arm and started tugging him toward the bathroom, where I turned on the shower and then proceeded to slather shaving cream on his face.

"What the hell?" Some of it got on his mouth and he came fully awake, spitting in the sink between words. "What are you doing?"

"I'm sending you on a mission," I said.

"What?"

"It's Christmas morning, and you're going to take all of our presents for Schuyler and Amanda over to your in-laws' house," I said, in a voice reserved for giving careful directions. "While you are there, you are going to be on your best behavior. And at some point, you are going to seek out a private moment with Melinda, and—get this—you're going to say that you're sorry."

He stiffened. "But I'm not sorry."

"Yes, Ted, you are. You've been sorry for days, but you're just too belligerent to admit it. Stop letting your ego get in the way of your happiness. *Don't let her get away.*"

He glowered at me.

Then, slowly, as steam billowed around us, he began to shave.

I watched him for a moment, making sure he wasn't just faking me out. "What are you going to do?"

"I'm going to take the presents over to my in-laws'," he mumbled.

"And?"

"And be nice," he recited dutifully. "And I'm going to seek out a private moment with Melinda."

"*And?*" This was the most important part.

"I'm going to say I'm sorry."

"Good for you!" I said, clapping him on the back. "Merry Christmas!"

Shutting the bathroom door, I turned and veered off to the living room and picked up the package I needed. Then I headed back to the kitchen.

"Can I borrow your car keys, Mom?" I asked as I passed through, already pulling them off the peg by the kitchen phone.

Mom, looking startled, stared at the package under my arm. "Where are you going?"

"To pay a visit to St. Nicholas."

* * *

Though there was a large banner outside proclaiming the store to be "Your Headquarters for Christmas," the inside of Valu-Rite drugstore was practically empty. I saw one shopper in the antacid aisle before catching sight of Isaac in one-hour Santaland. He was slumped in a big chair, next to a tree that looked suspiciously like Mom's, which had some obviously fake wrapped packages beneath it, and some unwrapped gift ideas, as well. There was a boom box, an off-brand Barbie named Krista, and some kind of plastic kiddie car that already had one wheel askew.

He saw me, straightened, and rang some kind of jingle-bell contraption. As I approached, he smiled uncertainly and then put on a gruff ho-ho voice. "Well Me-e-e-e-rrrie Christmas, little girlie!"

"Merry Christmas yourself, Santa." I pointed to a stool next to him. "What's that?"

"That's my elf helper chair," he said, still in character.

I looked around the store. The fluorescent lighting made everything look flat and sterile, and the Muzak rendition of "Winter Wonderland" being piped in didn't enliven the atmosphere. Still, I felt so hopped up it didn't matter. "Where's the elf?"

He shrugged and suddenly dropped the Santa act. "He called in sick."

I sank down on the stool. Isaac was looking at me anxiously. Half of me wanted to jump in his lap and throw my arms around him. The other half of me wanted to strangle him. "What if I had forgotten the napkin and sent my jeans through the laundry?" I barked at him. "Did you ever once consider that?"

His forehead tensed. "You read it, then?"

"Yes."

"And . . . ?"

"And you got your wish—halfway. My sister stole my boyfriend. But I'm not heartbroken."

His eyes widened and I could detect a hint of a smile. "You're not?"

I shook my head.

He looked like he might collapse in relief. It was hard to know what to do next. We both sat there, grinning like fools.

"I brought you a present." I handed him the package.

"For me?" he asked, delighted. He picked up the big box and shook it.

I yanked the ribbon for him.

He tore off the paper and pulled the lid off. When he caught sight of the scary dummy, he gasped. "Oh, my God! He's just what I always wanted!" He immediately yanked the doll out and sat him on his knee. In a high voice, but with his lips obviously moving, he said, "Thank you *so* much!" The dummy's mouth didn't even move along with the words. Didn't even come close.

I laughed. "You're *really* bad at that."

"This big dummy got you something, too," the little dummy told me.

Isaac handed me a package. It was way too small to be an Easy-Bake Oven. I unwrapped it and found a VHS copy of *Frosty the Snowman.*

"Starring Jimmy Durante," Isaac said, looking duly chastened.

I put my arms around him. "It's big of you to admit it. In fact, I think it's my best present so far this Christmas."

"I'm not finished yet, sweetheart."

"There's more?"

"This is the best part." He reached into a pocket of his suit and pulled out a sprig of mistletoe. I drew in a delighted gasp. "You're a miracle worker!" I exclaimed.

He waggled his fake brows at me. "Wanna give it a spin?"

I nodded, and in the next moment, he pulled me close. For a moment, I forgot that we were in a fluorescently lit drugstore, or that he was wearing a ridiculous Santa suit, or that we had ever fought over silly things like Trivial Pursuit or who sang what song in what Christmas special. I began to wonder when his shift ended, and if it would be entirely untoward if I didn't get back home as soon as I said I would.

I also felt like crying. Why hadn't we done this years ago?

He pulled away, reluctantly, and I took the mistletoe as a souvenir. As soon as it touched my fingers, however, I frowned. It was fake!

"Where did you get this?"

"Aisle four."

"You let me think we were having a magic moment under *plastic* mistletoe?" I asked, outrage building.

He might have argued over whether it made any

difference or not, but he didn't. Instead, he shut me up with a devastating smile. "Worked great, didn't it?"

I had to admit it did. "We'll have to save it for the next blight year."

His eyes searched mine. "You never answered my question, Holly."

"What question?"

"Are you free New Year's Eve?" he asked.

I had a better idea. "Are you free tonight?"

My only pictures from last Christmas came from Valu-Rite's photo booth. Isaac and I squeezed in together, along with his new dummy, which he had christened Jason. (Coincidentally, the name of my sister's current fiancé.) The strip is in black and white, and the quality is a little fuzzy, but I wouldn't part with it for the world.

In the first frame, Isaac and I have our heads together, and Jason's plastic hair is just visible in the bottom of the picture.

In the second frame, I have been pushed aside, and Jason is gaping at the camera in demonic open-mouthed glee.

In the third frame, I am strangling the dummy as Isaac looks on in horror.

In the fourth, Isaac and I have our lips locked in a smooch, and Jason is completely out of the picture.

Please turn the page for an exciting sneak peek of
Liz Ireland's
HOW I STOLE HER HUSBAND,
now on sale at bookstores everywhere!

AVAILABLE: LIVE-IN NANNY WITH SCORE TO SETTLE.
HOMEWRECKING OPTIONAL . . .

Once upon a time, Alison Bell was a Dallas debutante good girl who always followed the rules. Then her dad's business went bust, her mom ran off with a jetsetter, and her high school boyfriend, Spence, was stolen just before prom by her arch nemesis, Pepper McClintock. Ten years later, the good girl routine is so tired. In debt up to her ears, dropped by all her rich friends, Alison lives for free outdoor concerts and two-for-one hamburger coupons. What she needs is a change. And then she gets her chance: a job as a live-in nanny for a Mr. & Mrs. Smith in New York City. Good-bye to humiliation, failure, and poverty; hello to . . .

Pepper McClintock? Conniving, fake, boyfriend-stealing Pepper McClintock? With the kind of horrifying clarity usually reserved for trying on bikinis under fluorescent lighting, it comes to Alison: her new boss is no other than Mrs. Spence Smith—THAT Spence—and Alison is going to be working for the enemy and her dreamy husband. Now, caught up in the rarefied world of Park Avenue nannies, New York tabloids, Barney's bags, and delicious dish on the rich and famous, Alison is learning a few new rules of survival.

Rule #1: Sometimes, you have to take what you want . . .

I never would have guessed how many people read a sleazy tabloid called *New York Now!* until a complete stranger spat on me. There I was, minding my own business, my arm stiffly extended with fingers snapping impatiently to flag down a cab, when an arc of saliva hit my cheek with a warm, sickening splat.

"Slut!" a woman yelled. As if the warm slime on my cheek weren't insult enough.

She had obviously read the paper. Though how anyone could recognize me from the grainy picture that scurrilous rag printed, I'll never know. I might not be Paris Hilton, but I usually have one chin, not five. The *Post*'s snap was much better—me looking heavy lidded and saucy in sable—but that didn't appear till the day after the spit incident.

Don't write off my assailant as just your garden variety Manhattan lunatic, either. She was a fifty-year-old lady swathed in raw silk and a Hermès scarf and carrying a Bendel's bag. When you're labeled ***NAUGHTY NANNY!*** by a newspaper, even a crappy one, you attract high-end spitters.

That was a difficult day. Even in New York, where weirder things than this happen on the street on an hourly basis, it's hard to recover your dignity after wiping a glob of some stranger's body fluids off your cheek. I was already jittery back then for a lot of different reasons—I think it's fair to say I was going through a rough patch—but being used as a human spittoon just about nudged me over the edge.

At any rate, anyone without a jot of empathy could understand how I ended up stealing an eighteen-thousand-dollar coat after that.

Or maybe they couldn't. It's still hard for me even to understand.

Sometimes, when I sit back and take a deep breath, it's hard to figure out how any of this happened. What's easy to figure out is when.

The time: Six months ago.

The place: A dentist's office in Dallas.

Not long before, I had been laid off from my job answering phones at a local travel magazine. Prior to that, I had been let go from another company where I was proofreading real estate ads. I was not setting the world on fire. At twenty-eight, I was still hovering in the cold and rubbing two sticks together.

And wouldn't you know. Everything seems bleak, and then you get a toothache.

So there I was, installed in a dentist chair, waiting for a filling to set and fretfully flipping through the latest copy of that pointless glossy, *Definitely Dallas.* I was combing the want ads, hoping that there would be something available at the magazine itself. Though pointless, *Definitely Dallas* was a venerable city institution, available in every hotel room in town and as ubiquitous in doctors' offices as *Highlights.* Surely someone there needed phones answered or something proofread?

They didn't, apparently, but one ad that caught my eye looked even better. In fact, it looked so good that at first I thought it must be a mirage.

> Live-in nanny needed. Dallas couple seeks caring female who loves children to help look after adorable girl, 3½. Must be dedicated, responsible, creative, flexible. Opportunity for relocation to NYC or London! Generous compensation! Excellent references req'd. Bilingual a plus. Call 555-0201.

Quick like a bunny, I ripped off my bib, sprinted out of the dentist office, and called the number on my cell phone from my car. I didn't even wait for the Novocain to wear off. The crunch was on. I'd been unemployed for two months and had my credit card refused at Safeway the night before while I was attempting to buy deodorant and a week's supply of ramen noodles. Poverty had even forced me to downgrade from a porcelain filling to silver, and how I was going to afford that when the bill arrived, I had no idea.

To be frank, my life wasn't supposed to be like

this. I had not been sufficiently prepped for financial woe.

Here is my dirty little secret: I used to be rich. A daddy's girl. A pampered only child. Even when my dad lost all his money after I graduated high school, I still had assumptions of forthcoming unmerited reward. When I graduated from college, I landed an incredible job and expected to be a millionairess by the time I was thirty-five. (In other words, I was naive.com.)

Now I was twenty-eight, and the most money I'd ever made in a year was when I was twenty-three. I had netted more from my allowance when I was fourteen than I had working temp for the past three months. My income, with the exception of that one anomalously prosperous year, had been dropping precipitously from childhood forward, and now was in a total free fall. I was on the fast track of downward mobility.

With money problems came other difficulties. I started suffering from insomnia. My social life had tapered off considerably. My best friend had moved to New York, and another friend had married, promptly produced a child, and become maternal and dictatorly. A few acquaintances I suspected were just avoiding me. I could hardly blame them. "Nobody wants you when you're down and out," sounds cruel, but it does have its logic. Too much bad news (and ramen noodles) makes people uncomfortable. The week before I had seen an old work acquaintance turn ill-at-ease when I sang the praises of a new salon I'd found that featured twelve-dollar haircuts.

And of course there were acquaintances—the ones who had known me in my flush younger days—who I was careful not to put myself in the path of.

So there I was. A poor friendless insomniac with bad hair. The kind of person I certainly would have avoided myself, had I been in any position to be choosy.

What I really needed was a miraculous rescue. A new life.

That classified ad was the change I needed. I felt it in my bones.

Those two tantalizing words, *generous compensation,* lodged in my head, where they gamboled about like fat furry puppies. I wanted this job. I had to have it. It was perfect! I was so ready to be generously compensated. Creativity, of course, was a slam dunk for me. I had practically been the drama queen of my high school. (Now I pictured myself putting on festive puppet shows and throwing together prize-winning Halloween costumes.) Dedicated? Of course I was dedicated . . . or I was certain I could be, if I knew what the hell I was supposed to be dedicated to. And I was bilingual—almost trilingual, if you counted the smattering of Spanish I had learned off of *Sesame Street* when I was a kid. *¡El cielo es arriba!*

I was pumped. And frankly, it's not in my personality to stay pumped for more than a few minutes, so I had to call right away, before I could think of the million and one reasons I would probably fail at being a nanny in the unlikely event anyone was demented enough to give me the job in the first place.

"I'm calling about the nanny position," I told the woman who picked up the phone. "My name is Alison Bell."

"Oh. Just a moment." Over the line, I could hear the efficient shuffling of paper and the whir of office machines in the background. "Have you worked with children before?"

"Yes, I have," I said, not entirely lying. "I worked as a teacher for one school year."

Actually, I had only lasted a few months, having quickly learned that substitute teaching has nothing to do with teaching and everything to do with crowd control and extreme survival technique. (Attention TV moguls: Substitute teaching has major untapped reality-show potential.) Luckily, given the bureaucratic nightmare that was the Dallas Independent School District, I'm sure this woman would never be able to find out that I had been a total failure and barely escaped with my life. If she called DISD, they would probably only give her the date of the school year I worked. And who knows? I had never received a notice that my sub license had been terminated. The powers that be might even think I was still out there somewhere, standing in front of a class of hostile glassy-eyed adolescents, or running for my life down some long, long hallway.

"Oh—excellent," the woman piped in.

I was encouraged. "Since that time, I have had a few jobs in publishing, but working with children is what I find most fulfilling."

"How old are you?"

Could she ask me that? I had thought there was something about age discrimination. "Twenty-eight."

"Married?"

"No, I'm single."

"That's good. This is a live-in position, you know."

I'm *so* single, I wanted to say. *Extremely* single. Live-in position meant that, on top of generous compensation, I would have free rent. That thought alone made me dizzier than the prospect of a dream date with Mark Ruffalo.

"You have a college degree, then?"

"Yes. From North Texas State."

"And when would you be available—"

"Any time! I could start tomorrow!"

"—to meet Mrs. Smith?"

I winced. *Really should not cut off the interviewer, Al.* "Mrs. Smith?"

"The Smiths are the family you would be working for. Their little girl is named August."

"Oh. Then you're . . . ?" For some reason, I thought I had been speaking to my potential employer.

"I am Mr. Smith's secretary. I have been doing phone interviews, just to screen out entirely inappropriate candidates."

And here I was, slipping through the net!

"You wouldn't believe the number of calls we've received—and from some people with no qualifications whatsoever."

I clucked my tongue. The crust of some people—trying to get my generously compensated job.

"I would be free to meet her at her convenience any time this week." I took a breath, realizing that too much freedom just made me sound like a slacker queen. "Though mornings work best for me." Employers always seemed to like those up-and-at-'em types. "I'm a morning person."

"Mrs. Smith can meet you tomorrow at eleven at her home." She gave me the address and some basic directions, which I didn't need. The Smiths lived in Highland Park, my old stomping ground.

I practically floated the rest of the way home. This was *my job.* I knew it. In a few months I would be packing up to relocate to New York or London! My dream! It was all I could do not to pace around my dirty apartment pumping my fist in the air. I needed to high-five with someone, so I called my friend Jessica, who was living in New York.

"I've done it," I told her. "I found a way to get out of Dallas! New York, here I come!"

"Excellent! What happened?"

I told her about my nanny job. I had to go into details, because the details were so great.

But really, I should have known better. Although Jessica has many wonderful traits, loyalty being tops among the many, she also happens to be one of those cautious types. Okay, paranoid. It's not just that she sees a cloud behind every silver lining, she actually sees the puddle that cloud will create, which will freeze over outside the stoop of her apartment and that she will then have the bad fortune to step on. This, in turn, will be the cause of her spending a Saturday morning in the emergency room and stumping along on crutches for two months thereafter. She is my own personal Cassandra.

Sometimes her fears can be useful. She grew up in Dallas and could tell you how to get practically anywhere in the city without having to make a left-hand turn.

Jess, of course, had reservations about my new job. "Al, are you sure taking care of a three-and-a-half-year-old is for you?"

I hadn't really been thinking about the kid. I was too wrapped up in generous compensation. And relocating! "How hard can it be?"

"Don't you remember subbing? You hated that."

"I didn't *hate* it." *Disliked it intensely,* perhaps. *Was rendered suicidal by.*

"You spent a month afraid to crawl out of your bed," she reminded me. "And when you did finally manage to mentally tunnel out, you were a maniac. Remember jujitsu?"

It's true, during that period of my life I sort of snapped. I became obsessed with self-defense, until I read a story in the paper about a guy who was a black belt in karate, who got shot at a 7-Eleven. One of my less laudable characteristics is that I'm easily discouraged.

But talking to Jessica, I was still feeling buoyant. "This is totally different. This is a tiny girl. Prehormonal. Her motor skills haven't advanced to the point that she can handle heavy weaponry."

"Uh-huh. Did you ever babysit?"

"No."

A snort. So much for high fives. I was beginning to feel a little uneasy.

"Oprah ran a story a couple of months ago called 'Kids Who Kill,' " she said. "Did you see that?"

"They killed their nannies?"

"I don't remember anything about nannies, but I'm sure it could happen. Or think about all those grown-ups who go berserk. Mothers drowning babies in bathtubs . . ."

Oh, Lord.

"But I *like* kids," I insisted, for once in my life refusing to yield to pessimism. To answer Jess's skeptical guffaw, I added, "In theory, at least."

"This kid isn't going to be a theory. Everybody loves adorable little kids in Jell-O ads, but real kids aren't like that."

"*Hello?* I never said I was Bill Cosby." I wasn't ready to angst about nitpicky details, like how good with kids I was or wasn't. "I'll have money, and I'm going to be moving. Those are the important things."

"So you'll move with this family, and then you'll quit?"

What kind of person did she think I was? "Of course not—not until I feel like I've earned my keep."

Then I would quit.

"You'll feel stuck," she predicted, "like an indentured servant."

"No, I won't."

"We'll see."

She didn't sound convinced, so we moved on to

pleasanter topics, like stuff we would do when we were finally living in the same town again. Or at least when she visited me in London. We had attended North Texas together and had been roommates for a year. Afterward, I had gravitated back to the city I knew best, while Jess had surprised everyone by taking off for the Big Apple, where she answered phones by day to pay the bills and played cello in a small group—the Hoboken String Quintet, or some such thing. It wasn't the New York Philharmonic, but I envied her. She was happy where she was.

Maybe I would be happy soon, too. After years in Dallas, most of them bad, not to mention sleepless, I really felt I needed a new start in a new town. New York or London would do me fine. I wasn't going to be particular.

That morning I woke up at two, as usual, to wrestle with insomnia. But on this night I was full of plans, not worries.

I arrived at the Smith house ten minutes early and had to park down the street and wait in the car. I stared at the house, a hulking faux Tudor with a semidetached three-car garage and an immense front yard rolling away from it that was manicured within an inch of its life. The grass was so green and clipped so short it looked like artificial turf. (The Smiths' monthly water bill was probably higher than my rent.) An old pecan tree leaned off to the side, but it was hard to imagine it actually producing pecans or doing anything so ill mannered as shedding leaves. No doubt there was a gardener on hand to scoop up the leaves the moment they sullied the ground.

It was a gorgeous, luxurious house, but not out of place on the street, which was lined with homes in various architectural styles but all of equal size and inflated value. Highland Park was the section of Dallas where the rich rich folk traditionally lived. I had lived there back when my family still had money, when private schools and housekeepers and cars that cost enough to support a middle-class family for a year were things I took for granted. Now when I drove through places like this, I felt an unhealthy mixture of smug contempt—*the waste of money!*—and salivating envy. *Was there anything more delicious than wasting money?*

Ever since college I had been avoiding this neighborhood, but now I felt like kissing the expensively landscaped ground. I was the prodigal daughter. Sure, I had suffered some bitter travails. I hadn't been able to keep my Neiman's charge, or stick to a decent manicure/pedicure regimen. In college I had denied my roots and refused to rush. But now I was coming back to my people.

At exactly two minutes till eleven, I pulled my car up in front of the house and got out. *Home!* I practically skipped up to the doorway. I wasn't going to consider the possibility of not getting the job. This was my job, my house, my golf-course lawn.

At least until I moved to London or New York.

A stout Latina woman answered the door, gave me a disapproving shake of her head, and showed me to the living room. The house was silent as only large old houses can be, the kind of silence in which you can hear your own watch ticking. You couldn't detect the whir of the air-conditioning, though the cool, tomblike temp let you know it was on.

Even though I was used to places like this from my greener years, I couldn't help gawking. The house was laden with treasures—eighteenth-century tables and Tiffany lamps and modern art-glass vases. It was all jumbled together with studied carelessness, including a framed original Buster Keaton one-sheet print for *Sherlock, Jr.* that I coveted immediately. A sprawling Persian rug on the floor took up as much square footage as my entire apartment.

If a kid lived here, she was probably only allowed in this room on Christmas mornings, for a photo op. I wondered if I myself would be spending much time here. Probably not. But I could handle that. I was so prepared to be a mere appendage to all this wealth.

The purposeful clickety sound of size-six heels on the marble of the front hall came toward me, and I turned toward the door, shoulders straight, smile in place, ready to grovel, in a dignified way, in order to secure this job.

When Mrs. Smith wheeled into the room, however, my shock was such that I'm sure the smile melted right off my face. My stomach flipped wildly as recognition struck, and my armpits started to flood. For a moment I actually felt faint.

I knew this person. Had known her practically

all my life, but not as Mrs. Smith. She was *Pepper McClintock.*

I hadn't seen Pepper since I was eighteen, on graduation night 1993 at the Bramford Preparatory Academy for Girls. Pepper had delivered a short speech that night, which was expected of her as secretary-treasurer of our senior class. It was her duty to inform the school that the class of 1993 was leaving the school a perpetually bubbling art nouveau–style water fountain.

I remembered the speech because I was one of a smaller faction of my class who had voted to give the school a line of magnolia trees. That proposal had gone down in defeat to the powerful water-fountain faction, headed by Pepper, and it seemed to me on graduation night that she was practically gloating as they wheeled that damned water fountain in on a dolly to be presented to the headmistress.

It wasn't just about the water fountain. During our senior year, Pepper had become my nemesis. First she had won the role of Madge in the senior production of *Picnic,* relegating me to a much lesser role. Then she had the nerve to steal my boyfriend of six months, leaving me to go stag to my own senior prom. Unforgivable.

In fairness I should probably mention that during that prom, and on the night of graduation, Pepper had been wearing a neck brace, and that it was sort of my fault that she had had her little accident. It *was* an accident, although naturally there was a lot of speculation at the time whether I had actually engineered the whole mess. Especially since I came out of it with a relatively minor sprain.

As I stared at her slack-jawed face now, I thought about seeing her at that prom, neck stiff in its white foam casing, dancing with Spence . . .

Spence *Smith.*

And now she was . . . *Mrs. Smith*?

Blood started to drain out of my head, leaving me woozy. Her last name couldn't just be a coincidence, could it?

At that point, I really didn't think it was possible to be any more mortified than I already was. To be caught interviewing for a nanny job with a woman you went to high school with—whom you outscored on the SAT by two hundred and fifteen points—was bad. Very bad. BP girls just didn't become domestics.

But to realize that this airhead from high school who had snagged your boyfriend *still* had him—and was doing spectacularly well—was beyond embarrassing. I wanted the earth to swallow me up, but the sumptuous Persian rug beneath my feet refused to cooperate.

Why had I ever thought I could do this? Especially in Highland Park, where I knew people. I should have sensed danger . . .

Pepper's face contorted into a series of expressions ranging from shock to disbelief to glee. She settled on glee—who wouldn't?—and then threw out her arms. Her body bounced, causing a jangle of silver and jade jewelry, and she ran toward me with childlike enthusiasm. "Al! Al! Al!" She gave me one of those sorority hugs that required minimal body contact and continued to squeal. "Little Al from BP! I wrote your name down but it didn't click! I *can't* believe it!"

"I can't either," I mumbled, willing my pulse to come under control. It was racing now, in the way that a deer's would race when finally kicking in to flee a predator. I needed to get out of there, but I couldn't think of a way to escape gracefully.

"Sit down, for heaven's sake!" she gushed, as if I had just dropped by for a social call. I had a hard time adjusting to her volume, which seemed higher than anyone I had spoken to in years. And her enthusiasm, which was too over-the-top to be sincere, yet somehow struck a chord with me.

And then I remembered. This was the sort of geeked up excitement we all used to use with each other at school. The tonal equivalent of air kissing.

"I'm so glad to *see* you!"

I'll bet she was. I had gained twenty pounds. She, on the other hand, seemed to have diminished by even more than that. When last seen, Pepper had possessed a layer of baby fat that had melted away in the intervening years, leaving nothing but a sinewy husk, a perfect couture hanger.

I gazed desperately toward the door. "Oh, I—"

"*No,* you *have* to sit down and have a drink with me. A real drink." She dashed over to the door, still clickety-clicking excitedly in her Jimmy Choos. "Marta! Could you bring us some Bloody Marys, please? *¡Gracias!*" She hurried back to me. "Sit, sit, *sit!*" she commanded, practically pushing me onto a sofa before perching onto a chair opposite. "I haven't seen you in *forever.* Nobody has. You should have been at the tenth reunion! Everybody was all, 'What's happened to Al?' Everybody said they hadn't been able to find you—and now here you are!"

"Here I am," I repeated.

She leaned forward. "Al, I was *so sorry* to hear about your dad."

"Oh, well . . ."

She cut me off with a dismissive wave. "There's no need to be embarrassed. Believe me, with Spencer working in investment, lately it seems everyone's had it rough."

Spencer. It wasn't a coincidence. I felt like I had swallowed lead.

"Sometimes it's like *half* the people we know are in Club Fed," she said.

I couldn't figure out what she was talking about. "My dad didn't go to jail."

She drew back, surprised. "He didn't? But I heard he went bankrupt."

"No, he went broke the old-fashioned way. He paid off all his creditors and then shut down the business."

"Oh!"

My father had run Bell Office Machines, a business he had inherited from his father. The company had raked in the dough after World War II, but my father was not a good businessman and had stubbornly resisted the computer era. By 1994, the company could have changed its name to Bell Office Dinosaurs. He shut it down and sold off all his business property and the old family house in Highland Park. Now Dad lived on the small ranch he bought in East Texas during the good times. He didn't ranch anything except weeds, but he was able to live on a little interest and fancied himself a country gentleman.

"I see." Pepper's tone suggested that she had just lost all respect for my father. No doubt it was better to go to jail than actually repay people you owed money to. At least when you came out of jail you wouldn't be *poor.* "That must have been really difficult for you."

"Not too bad. I switched colleges, of course."

"Oh no!" she commiserated. "And you were so psyched about going to Stanford!"

"Reed."

"Right! I knew it was one of those left coast places."

"I got a great education at North Texas."

"*Of course* you did." She patted me on the knee even though she sounded unconvinced. "You were always such a brain."

The woman named Marta huffed into the room with the Bloody Marys. "I made them weak. It's only eleven o'clock."

Pepper shot her a look then smiled sweetly. "I'll take another one, then. You can get right on that."

Marta squinted at her resentfully, turned, and walked out.

Pepper bent toward me as she handed me my drink and whispered, "She thinks she's *my* nanny."

I sipped politely. It *was* a disappointingly weak drink. I could have used something stronger. Actually, I could have used a cyanide caplet.

Pepper downed half of hers in a sip. "I can't wait to tell Spencer I saw you!" She was bouncing in her chair; jangling again. "You remember Spence, don't you?"

I almost fell off the sofa. Did I *remember* Spence? Was she some kind of a nut? Could she have forgotten . . . ?

She laughed. "*Of course* you remember Spence. You guys went out for a while, didn't you?"

"A little while." I fumed.

Six months! I wanted to scream at her. He'd been *mine.*

I forced my lips to produce a reasonable facsimile of a smile. "Where is Spence?"

"Taiwan. He's *always* traveling. Leaves me here to do everything."

Yeah, like dealing with all the domestic support staff. Must be rough.

She chuckled. "It's a good thing I know how things were back then, or I might be jealous."

"How things were?" I asked. "How were they?"

She waved a hand. "Oh, you know. Kids hooking up right and left—total hormonal madness. It's not like anything back then actually meant anything."

I felt myself gasping, but I couldn't actually form any words. For one thing, it probably wasn't kosher to blurt out to someone that, actually, you had been in love with her husband. And for another, I had thought along similar lines at the time.

"*Anyway,*" she said, leapfrogging this uncomfortable topic, "I'm *so* glad to see you, you can't believe. Ugh! I've just been interviewing so many people for this job. Teenagers, mostly. I think you're the first adult who's walked through that door in days. Like, duh, do I really want to give my daughter over to some gum-chewing adolescent to raise?"

I blinked at her. Was she implying that I was too old?

"Oh—and one *really* ancient lady came by. The sweetest old thing, bless her heart, but she was just *a mess.* I think she was already in the early stages of Alzheimer's. She kept talking about how she would teach August to knit." Pepper doubled over, hooting with laughter. "August is three!"

Tomorrow she'll be hooting over my *interview,* I thought, paranoia ramping up to full throttle. I darted another longing glance at the door.

"At least I know I can trust you," she said. "And you're so smart. And bilingual." She tilted her head. "You are, aren't you?"

Suddenly I wasn't so sure. Not that it mattered.

She squinted. "French, right?"

I nodded.

She sagged with relief. "That's good. Spencer and I really wanted a person who could speak French, but we didn't really want to have an actual French person living in the house. You know what I mean?"

I nodded again.

"A couple of people who answered the ad have been Spanish speakers, but that's *not exactly* what I meant by bilingual. I mean, sure, Spanish can be useful, but we wanted something more European."

Spain no longer counted as Europe, apparently.

"Without having to have an actual European in the house?" I guessed.

"Exactly!" Any sarcasm that might have just happened to seep into my tone sailed cleanly over her head. "We wanted to find someone with *values,*" she explained. "That's why we wanted to find a nanny here, who could move with us. Can you imagine trying to find someone to look after a child in London?"

"I don't know . . . I've heard of English nannies before. Didn't they sort of invent them?"

She eyed me sagely. "Believe me—the days of Mary Poppins are long gone. To get somebody like that now, you'd have to unload your child's trust fund. Can you imagine? Or—oh, Lord!—New York City! I wouldn't like to have to hire someone there. You hear all sorts of stories just about people trying to get reliable dog walkers there."

"I'm sure it's difficult everywhere."

"Oh, sure—but New York City! No telling what kind of *freaks* I'd have to interview to find somebody halfway decent."

My skin was beginning to break out in the crawlies.

"But we know you're a BP girl, so now our worries are over!"

I was starting to feel sick. The moment I had recognized Pepper, I had known that there was no way I could take the job, even if it was offered to me. I had enough hang-ups without having to live in a situation that reminded me just how short of my goals I had managed to fall in life. And the longer Pepper yammered on, the more cemented became my decision. *A nanny? Had I been insane?* No way did I want to deal with this crazy woman who was convinced that I was one of her. A Dallas Brahmin.

Married to my ex-boyfriend.

She had to be nuts to think that I would even consider it. Surely she knew I was just sitting here talking to her out of politeness.

"Of course I can't commit to anything just now," I said.

"Of course not! You'll want to—Oh!" she cried, startling me. "I'm seeing Phaedra this afternoon. Remember Phaedra?"

As in an old science-fiction movie, I felt as if I were flailing against the spiraling background, trying not to be sucked back in time. Phaedra had been Pepper's best friend through school.

They were *still* friends?

"Phaedra married Skip. Skip Honeywell? I'm sure you remember *him.*" I didn't. "Anyway, they got divorced. It was very sad, because they had *three* little ones. All boys, too—what most guys *dream* about! But Skip cheated on Phaedra with about six different women, so she'd have to be a real doormat to put up with that."

I mumbled an agreement.

"And anyway, he left her." Pepper sighed. "Phaedra really went berserk for a while."

I shook my head. One hated to think of someone named Phaedra going berserk. Especially when there were children involved.

She leaned closer, relishing every word. "Joined AA *and* flirted with becoming a Christian Scientist, if you can imagine. I worried she was going to turn into a real wacko. But then she met this really nice man named Flint Avery who's, I dunno, some sort of genius at marketing or something, and now she's almost back to normal. Except that she doesn't do drinks before dinner *or* take Advil."

"My goodness." I hadn't realized AA let you opt for an after-dinner-only option now. That certainly would make the whole program more appealing.

I considered whether it would be too soon to make my escape.

"I know!" Pepper exclaimed, as if I'd just agreed with her about something. "Personally, trying to get by in this world without Paxil and a little Vicadin seems too brutal for words, but you can't argue with success. Phaedra's been living this spartan existence for almost a year and a half and she *looks* great. We went to a spa in New Mexico together last month and just had a blast."

I looked at my watch and expelled a sigh of regret. "Shoot! I have this appointment at noon . . ."

Pepper's eyes flashed open. "But you can't go yet. You have to meet August!" She jumped up, clearly expecting me to follow suit.

"Oh, but . . ."

"You *have* to," she said. "I already told her we were having a visitor, though of course I didn't know then who you were going to be. She'll be so excited when I tell her you're an old school friend."

I had my doubts, but I couldn't think of a polite way to refuse to meet Pepper's kid. So I followed her crisply bustling figure up through the hall and up a flight of stairs, down another series of hallways, until we reached, at last, August's suite. She was in her playroom, which was amazing. The walls were a pale mint green, and an artist of some skill had been brought in to copy the original Pooh illustrations. The furniture was all modern and painted in Necco wafer colors, with a few Pooh motifs scattered here and there. Tigger hopped dizzily across the front of a little wardrobe. A honey jar with bees buzzing around it was painted on the door of the television cabinet.

The television was on, and loud, and right now some commercial for processed cheese sticks was blaring at us.

Pepper swept into the room. "August?"

A small blond head peeped over the top of a miniature sofa. "Mommy!" she yelled, as if she hadn't seen her mom in weeks.

The kid was unbelievably cute. She could have been in a Jell-O commercial. White-blond hair that frizzed into a sort of punk Shirley Temple look. Big blue eyes. Black lashes. She was dressed in little Gap clothes, denim overalls and a pink T-shirt underneath. When she saw her mom, she hopped off her sofa, ran crashing into Pepper's knees, and peeked up at me with shy hostility.

"This is Alison," Pepper said. "Can you say hello? Your mommy and Alison went to school together."

August's small fist went straight to her mouth.

"She's shy!" Pepper mouthed at me.

I bent down, remembering suddenly that I had come prepared to win over my small potential employer as well as her parent. That seemed so long ago now, before I was ambushed by Pepper. "Hi,

August. I have something for you." I reached into my pocket and brought out a small lime sucker. I glanced up at Pepper. "Is it okay?"

"Just this once, sure. Say thank you, August." August's fist wrapped around the sucker, which went back directly into her mouth, plastic wrapper and all. As I stood up, a finger puppet accidentally on purpose fell out of my pocket. It was a happy frog with dangling legs.

"Oh! I forgot I had the Hopster with me!" I stuck the frog on my index finger and proceeded to do a little vaudeville routine that delighted Pepper, but frankly seemed to spook August a little. She wound herself more tightly around her mom's leg.

When we left the nursery, Pepper was all praise for my clunky kid technique. "You are *so great* with August! You wouldn't believe the people who've been through here. Some of them have obviously never even been around kids before, and yesterday some girl came here with a whole set of Disney DVDs to bribe her with! Can you imagine? Of course August *loved* her."

Damn. I didn't even know how to bribe a three-year-old. Talk about inept. *Finger puppets?* What did I think this was, 1972?

Not that I wanted this job. I absolutely didn't.

The strange thing was, Pepper was acting as if it were a given that I had it, when before, when we were going up to August's suite, she had been treating me more like a visitor than a potential employee. Maybe this was just an old-school-chum courtesy, to let me think that the decision was up to me. When we both knew what the decision would be.

As we walked back downstairs, she started giving me instructions. "Now, we always call her August. No nicknames. Spencer's parents are always calling her Augie and it just drives me insane." She flicked me a look that spoke volumes about the state of in-law relations in the Smith household. "They know I don't like it, too. You can be sure of that."

"August is such a great name," I said.

"I think so. Of course we named her that before the world and its wife started naming their kids August," she added bitterly.

"I didn't know." I tried to think of kids I'd known with the name of August and came up with . . . none.

"Puh-leez!" She rolled her eyes. "Of course, the way people are popping out kids these days, no name's safe anymore."

At the door, she gave me another of those weightless hugs of hers. "I'm so glad you showed up!"

"Well, I have to . . ."

She waved away my mumbled hesitation. "I know. *Think it over.* Of course you do! I'll give you a buzz tomorrow. How about that?"

"Sure thing."

"It was *just great* to see you Al."

"*Just great* to see you, too, Pepper."

I got out of there as fast as I could without actually running.

Romantic Suspense from **Lisa Jackson**